THE TWISTED BLADE

Also by J. FitzGerald McCurdy
The Serpent's Egg
The Burning Crown

J. FitzGerald McCurdy

THE TWISTED BLADE

SARATIME PUBLISHING INC. • OTTAWA, CANADA

A Saratime Book

Published by Saratime Publishing Inc.
363 Churchill Avenue North
Ottawa, Ontario
Canada K1Z 5C4

www.saratimepublishing.com

National Library of Canada Cataloguing in Publication Data
McCurdy, J. FitzGerald (Joan FitzGerald)
The Twisted Blade
ISBN 0-9688713-3-X
I. Title
PS8575.C87T94 2003   jC813'.6 C2003-903936-6

Manufactured in Canada

First Edition: September 2003

10 9 8 7 6 5 4 3 2 1

Dedicated to
James, Samantha, Jason, Shane, Nicholas, Hugh, Eleanor, Leigh, Claire, Kizi, Brittany, Chris, Jessica, Dylan, Nicole, Matthew, Jennifer, Greg, Isabel, and Stephanie.

Special thanks to Jacquie and Dan for our weekly reads, and to Susan for her sharp eyes.

TABLE OF CONTENTS

1 Taboo 1

2 The Dark Pool 10

3 Parent Woes! 22

4 Running Away 33

5 Dropping In 44

6 The King of the Lake 51

7 A Dark Place 57

8 Tricks and Stones 65

9 A Heating and a Quenching 76

10 Not Again! 85

11 Stubby the Stump 92

12 Hunters and Hunted 102

13 On the Run 114

14 Fur and Feathers 121

15 Birds of a Feather 133

16 Another Dark Place 142

17 Calling the Dead 149

18 Caught 154

19 Separate Ways 162

20 Leaving Vark 171

21 Attack from the Skies 178

22 Head for the Hills 185

23 Flight to the Dark Lands 196

24 The Council of Bethany. 202

25 Just in Time for Dinner 211

26 The Silver Pouch 224

27 Back to the Castle. 233

28 The March of the Dead 244

29 The Castle of Indolence. 257

30 Arabella to the Rescue 267

31 Calad-Chold 276

32 New and Old Friends 283

33 The Twisted Blade 293

34 War with the Living 299

35 The Severing 310

    Epilogue

CHAPTER ONE

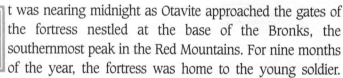

TABOO

t was nearing midnight as Otavite approached the gates of the fortress nestled at the base of the Bronks, the southernmost peak in the Red Mountains. For nine months of the year, the fortress was home to the young soldier. Tonight, he was returning to active duty in the National Mountain Patrol from his annual three months' furlough, spent with his parents and younger siblings at the family stead on the outskirts of Erog-gore, capital city of the Chiefdom of Vark, homeland of the Red Giants.

The NMP was the arm of the military that guarded the country from invaders foolish enough to attempt to slip into Vark through the back door, by way of the treacherous mountain passes that converged near the fortress. The NMP also kept watch over Taboo, a ragged fissure that led deep into the bowels of the Bronks, and the awful secret that lay within.

Shoulders hunched, Otavite climbed the familiar, twisting trail—his large boots thumping on the snow-covered ground the only sound disturbing the deep silence. He paused momentarily to adjust his heavy backpack, tilting his head to gaze at the star-studded sky. The night was as clear as polished glass. The waxing moon was only a thin sliver, a smooth cut in the gossamer fabric of earth's canopy, but the starlight on the fresh coat of white snow drove away the darkness. Otavite marveled as he always did at the dazzling brightness. He could see for miles.

The Giant took a deep breath of the invigorating mountain air, glad to be alive on such a perfect night. He felt an irresistible urge to hum which he quickly repressed for fear the sound of his deep baritone voice would disturb Eegar, who was either asleep, a rare and merciful occurrence; or dead, which was pure wishful thinking. *But there's a storm building*, he thought, focusing on the blackness growing in the sky ahead where thick clouds were roiling and banking, scraping the top of the Bronks, painting the pale red snows near the peak darker than blood, and spilling down its mighty slopes like a silent, black avalanche.

Otavite squared his broad shoulders and quickened his pace. His eyes followed the luminous, winding trail ahead, peeled for the lights of the guard tower. The Giant had lived among these mountains all of his life. He knew their moods and ways. He knew that a storm could erupt suddenly and violently. He also knew that the abrupt massing of clouds was often the only advance warning nature provided.

Ahead, the single tower forming part of the wall to the right of the fortress gates loomed against the night sky—a solid, inky shadow. Otavite slowed, suddenly uneasy. He stared at the massive block-like tower, his soldiers' instincts warning him that something was wrong. Then it hit him. *The Darkness! There should be lights! From the tower!* He should be able to see the lights clearly. But the tower windows were as black as the clouds seething overhead.

Instinctively, Otavite left the trail and slipped among the huge boulders flanking the path. For a Giant, his movements were surprisingly quick, his steps light, almost graceful. Fear made his chest hurt. He felt as if the Bronks were resting on his ribcage, slowly but surely squeezing the life out of him.

"Stay calm," he whispered harshly, fighting an overpowering urge to charge toward the fortress, calling out to his comrades as he plowed through the gates. "Just stay calm. Check things out first." Crouching behind a boulder as large as his body, he slipped his arms out of the straps on his backpack, and carefully stowed his gear in a depression under the rock. Then he straightened and peered at the dark fortress, scanning the gates and tower, his ears straining for human sounds. But he saw nothing, heard nothing.

What? What? He felt a stab of pain as Eegar pecked at his head, angered by the Giant's unexpected movements.

Otavite slapped his head hard. The Red Giantpecker that lived in the soldier's wiry hair flapped his wings furiously to escape the crushing blow. In retaliation, Eegar dug his sharp claws into the Giant's scalp, shattering the silence with a barrage of raucous squawks that, if translated into the human tongue, could not be written here.

"Shut your beak!" hissed Otavite, wondering just how bad he had been as a child to end up with the nastiest-tempered scrounger in the whole universe. "One more squawk and I'll wring your scrawny neck."

"Aaawk!" Eegar bit his ear viciously.

Otavite's shoulders tensed as the giantpecker's sharp beak tore at his flesh, but he ignored both bird and pain focusing instead on the guard tower and the black space that marked the great wooden gates. His keen soldier's eyes travelled slowly, missing nothing. As if it suddenly became aware of the Giant's change in mood, Eegar bristled in silence, blinking rapidly, alert to movement that would identify the source of his host's fear.

Despite the cold mountain air, Otavite felt sweat running down his back. He slipped a wicked-looking knife from a long casing attached to his belt and moved cautiously toward the garrison. His heart thumped like a fist against his ribs and his breath burst like giant white clouds from his throat.

He reached the gates and froze!

The colossal wooden gates stood open, their iron hinges twisted and bent, their thick planks shattered beyond repair. Dropping his knife on the ground, Otavite knelt to examine the unmoving body of a large creature lying on its side on the blood-soaked snow just outside the ruined gates. A mixture of anger and sadness washed over him as he recognized markings and old scars that told him the animal's identity. It was Ve.

Removing his thick mitts, the Giant slowly ran his hands over the dead creature's body, hoping the wounds would tell him who or what had done this terrible thing. His hands paused when they reached Ve's chest. Here, the fur edging the wound was matted—dark and crusty with dried blood. Otavite leaned closer to peer at the wound. The animal's entire chest was gone, burned to the bone as though its attacker had known where it was most vulnerable. Anger raged in the giant soldier's head as he gently stroked the soft ruff on Ve's neck. Finally, he wiped his fingers clean in the snow and pushed his frozen hands into the fleece-lined mitts.

The Carovorare was a fabulous beast, a great monster—the Giants' best friend. Standing, it was taller than an elephant. Its head was all snout and fangs—a yellow-eyed raptor in a lion's body. Under the downy white fur, the creature's sharp quills, limp now in death, could, when inflated, pierce solid stone. An enemy might evade a slash from the razor-sharp claws, or survive a bite from the jagged teeth, but no one could survive a sting from the poisonous spike at the end of the scorpion-like tail—a spike as long as a butcher's knife. Carovorari were ranked as guards in the NMP. The Giants loved and respected them.

Otavite shook his massive head. *What happened here?* Ve had been a veteran. The guard could hear a pin drop on the other side of the Bronks; its sense of smell was so acute it could detect a stranger twenty miles upwind. Nothing, absolutely nothing, could overpower a Carovorare. *What, then, had killed Ve?*

4

"Eegar . . ." The Giant's voice was a sad rumble in his throat.

The Red Giantpecker poked his head through Otavite's thick, coarse hair.

In a flash, Eegar flew into the air, flapping his wings rapidly, a series of shrill cries bursting from his throat. Out of the night came a chorus of answering cries, and a sound like a thousand hands clapping filled the air. A black cloud of hundreds and hundreds of birds shot toward the downed beast. In the wink of an eye, they were all over it, sharp beaks ripping and tearing. Then, as one giant winged creature, the birds lifted into the sky and disappeared back into the night.

Otavite bowed his head over the gleaming white bones of the Carovorare, picked clean by the flock of birds. His heart felt as heavy as lead. Speaking softly, he called on Eegar to carry out the final ritual that would enable Ve's spirit to see its way to the Great Abode. Eegar swooped down from his perch atop a tall stone outcropping and gently, at least more gently than his attack on Otavite's ear, pecked again and again at the skin about Ve's eyes. Uttering a shrill cry of triumph, the giantpecker caught one of the large, milky orbs in his beak, spread his wings, lifted into the air, and winged toward the mountaintop—a small dark speck against the sky.

The Giant remained kneeling beside the remains of the Carovorare for a moment longer. "I will find the ones who hurt you and stole your life," he vowed. "I will not stop searching until their heads are stuck on stakes outside the gates for all to see." Then he picked up his knife, stood, and moved stealthily through the ruined gates.

Expecting to find more bodies of slain beasts and comrades, Otavite was relieved after a quick search of the tower, barracks, and stables turned up nothing. The fortress was deserted and, except for the rising wind, as silent as stone. Outside, he huddled motionless in the shadows of the tower and tried to make sense of what had happened. *Where were the others—his friends?* A terrible loneliness came over him. He felt as if he were alone in an empty universe, the sole survivor of a holocaust too terrible to contemplate. He sighed heavily, forcing himself to step back into the role of soldier. He must report to Erog-gore headquarters. But before he did that, he had a duty to find out what had happened here.

Otavite stamped his heavy boots on the frozen ground in frustration. His search of the fortress had turned up nothing. Had he missed something important? Had he allowed his rage and frustration to blind him to the obvious? Slowly, methodically, he searched again, and again he found nothing. No clue, nothing to tell him what had happened. What had he missed? And then he went as still as the abandoned tower. He *had* missed something. There was one last place he hadn't searched.

The soldier's breath exploded in fierce gusts as he strode toward the black iron doors sealing the entrance to Taboo, the fissure that cut deep into the heart of the Bronks. Every Giant in Vark knew about the iron doors, but no one, not even the National Mountain Patrol, knew who had forged them or why. If he believed the elder Giants, the doors had stood there for hundreds of thousands of years, sealed for all time. Otavite wondered now whether they were meant to keep people out of the mountain. Or was their purpose more sinister? Were they there to keep something inside? It had been his job to guard the entrance into Taboo and he had done his job unquestioningly. Now, though, he couldn't believe he knew absolutely nothing about what he had been guarding for the past five years, or the reason for the strong iron doors in the first place. The Giant shivered as the black place appeared like a monster's mouth waiting to gobble him up.

A flutter of wings and sharp claws on his scalp told him Eegar had returned from his grisly chore. Otavite ignored the bird as it plucked several thick hairs from his head, and then settled down to the job of preening its soft red feathers. He reached the entrance to

Taboo and gasped in disbelief at the yawning black hole where the enormous iron doors had recently stood.

All that remained of the doors was a black puddle of molten iron, hardening on the frozen ground. Otavite whistled softly, searching his mind for the sort of creature that had the power to melt solid iron. It had to be the same monster that killed Ve, but he did not know of such a being. The young Giant gripped his knife tightly, steeled himself by taking a deep breath, and then stepped guardedly into the wide black mouth of the fissure.

The crack was large enough for Otavite to stand erect with room to spare. Inside, he paused for a second trying to peer ahead, but he couldn't see his large hand when he raised it in front of his face. The darkness was like a conscious thing, thick and suffocating. It pressed against his body and slipped into his nostrils and down his throat. He thought of turning back to fetch a light from the barracks, but in the end he decided to keep going. Whatever had come through here was strong and cunning. He didn't doubt that for a second. The liquefied iron doors were proof enough. "Forget the light," he said softly. He couldn't risk it. He'd just have to make his slow way in the dark.

Keeping near the wall on one side of the fissure, Otavite crept forward, one small step at a time. He stretched his arms up and out before him to guard against smashing his skull on unseen obstacles. Eegar shrieked when the Giant's head brushed through a thick cobweb, and Otavite felt the bird stirring frantically in his hair as it hunted the arachnid.

He walked for a long time, his ears straining for the slightest sound that did not belong. Giants were gifted with acute hearing. Dwarves maintained that a Giant could hear a mushroom growing, or the whisper of a flower straining toward the sun. But here, deep inside the mountain in utter darkness, the only sound Otavite heard was the rapid beating of his heart.

Still, he felt uneasy, as though he were being watched by something lurking in the darkness ahead. His uneasiness grew with each forward step. How far had he travelled inside the mountain? How many hours had passed? He didn't know and couldn't hazard a guess. But his legs felt as if he had walked a thousand miles while his unblinking eyes told him he had been peering into total blackness for years.

Finally, just as he began thinking that there was no end to the fissure, he came smack up against a solid wall and could go no farther. *It can't be a dead end*, he thought. It just doesn't make sense to go to so much trouble to install a set of sturdy iron doors to seal up an opening that went nowhere. *Did it?* Holding the knife between his teeth, he pulled off his mitts and ran his large hands slowly over the wall. It took a while, but he found it—a barely perceptible seam running through the rock. He traced the hairline crack with his fingers, up and across and down to the floor of the fissure.

It was a concealed door or panel. And it was huge, as if it had been built for Giants. Otavite searched for hidden locks or a device that would trigger the opening mechanism, but he found nothing. Above the top seam, his fingers traced markings that had been gouged into the rock as if an angry beast had unsheathed its claws and slashed at the wall again and again. As his fingers retraced the grooves, he realized that they were not random gouges, but carefully etched marks or letters—a message or a warning. He went over the strange letters again, laying them out in order in his mind, memorizing them for his report.

$$\text{⊥+ ᱠ+⊥ ⧣+ᴛᴛ.}$$

$$\text{ᴛ+ᴛᱡ ⟙ᱡ⊥ ⊥⊥ᱡ ⊥ᱡ+⊥ ⨟+⧊ ᱡᴛ⊥ᱡᱡᱡ ⊥ᱡᱡᱡ.}$$

Otavite couldn't read the strange marks, but he now recognized the ancient alphabet of the Druids and felt the blood in his veins turn to ice. He had never met a Druid, but he had heard stories about

* to decipher the text, see the alphabet at the back of the book.

them and their terrifying magic since he was a boy. His mother said they caught children, sucked out their brains, and then ate them. That's where they got their magic, she said. He didn't know about that, but he believed his fellow soldiers who said that to lock eyes with one of the creatures meant death. What if Druids had been sealed inside Taboo? What if they were still here, waiting beyond the hidden doorway? Otavite shook his giant-sized head, jostling Eegar who struck back by jabbing his scalp with his murderous beak until he drew blood.

In all of the Giants' history books, Druids were classified under the heading: *Magical Beings*. In one of those books, Otavite had read that Druids were habitually unpredictable and quick to anger. Their wrath could obliterate a mountain at the drop of a hat. Because Druids never appeared in daylight, there were no pictures of them in the books. But Otavite would never forget the description of the black-cloaked sinister figures with long fingers curled to unleash fire hot enough to melt solid iron. There was nothing written in the history books about Druids coming to his country. Yet, the inscription over the concealed door proved that the terrible creatures had been here, in Vark, at some forgotten time in the past. What had brought them here? And, more importantly, were they still here?

Puzzling over the Druids' involvement in Vark affairs, Otavite pressed his forehead against the cold stone and rested his large hands on the seams on either side of the concealed door. Suddenly, he felt a tremor run through the mountain. *An earthquake!* he thought, a wave of panic washing over him. To be sealed alive inside the Bronks was worse than death. The terrified Giant was just about to make a hasty retreat back through the fissure to the opening when the stone shifted inside the seam under his hands. His heart fluttered erratically. It wasn't an earthquake, or an avalanche thundering down the rocky slopes. It was the panel—sliding silently into the wall. Something was on the other side. And, it was coming out.

CHAPTER TWO

THE DARK POOL

tavite snatched his hands from the stone as if he had been electrocuted. He shrank away, backing from the sliding panel, and pushed his body against the rough wall. Closing his eyes, he forced himself to relax while he summoned Eegar's gift—camouflage. He felt the familiar tingle as cryptic and apatetic coloration emanated from the bird's body, concealing their presence and disguising his shape until he and Eegar were one with their surroundings. Then he waited, his eyes fixed on the blackness between him and the moving door.

The young soldier drew in a sharp breath when a thin line of pale light appeared abruptly along the length of the hidden door. As the stone slipped soundlessly into the wall, the light expanded, illuminating the passage where Otavite hid, his body pressed against the wall of the fissure, his chest hurting so badly he felt as if something were suffocating him. Eegar went as still as a dead rat. Giant and bird stared in horror at the black-shrouded creature that suddenly appeared in the opening, framing the doorway and soaking up the weak light like a grotesque, living blotter.

The camouflaged Giant couldn't tear his eyes away from the

black shape. It was a monster straight out of his worst nightmare. Only Otavite wasn't dreaming. The figure in the black cloak was as real as Eegar, and the overpowering reek of evil that came into the passage with it sent shivers along the Giant's spine.

A Druid! he thought. And, for the first time in his life, the soldier experienced sheer terror. It wasn't the creature's nine-foot height that caused his fear. Compared to the Giant, the black-shrouded being was small, even puny. No, Otavite wasn't intimidated by its size. It was the sharp, dagger-like claws protruding from the loose sleeves of its black cloak, and the pair of blood red eyes burning in the blackness of its cowl, that made Otavite want to drop his knife and run screaming from this place.

The Giant was right to want to run. He sensed that the creature was bad—evil, as if the specter of death had suddenly entered the fissure. But he was wrong in thinking the black-clad figure was a Druid. It was a Thug, one of thousands, and it was pure evil— a half-dead being, as cold and unfeeling as the ice-encrusted mountain overhead. Otavite didn't know that it was an assassin whose only purpose was to kill the enemies of its Mistress— a monstrous Demon called Hate. All he knew from the bottom of his soldier's heart was that he would not survive a fight with this creature. The thought of his comrades being held at the mercy of this deadly monster made the Giant sick and angry at the same time. He had to find out if they were here. And, if he found them, and if they were still alive, he was determined to free them.

The black figure glided through the doorway and paused, its obscene hooded head rotating slowly from left to right, its red eyes raking the shadows. The movement stopped abruptly when the eyes reached the spot where Otavite stood pressed against the stone wall. The Giant stopped breathing. The Thug tilted its head to one side and listened intently, its red eyes riveted to, but unable to see, the soldier. Finally, a rasping sound came from its throat, echoing eerily through the fissure. It moved past the Giant and disappeared along the passage Otavite had travelled only minutes ago.

Relieved at the Thug's departure, or angered at Otavite for some unfathomable reason, Eegar hopped up and down on the Giant's head, pecking out hairs and flicking them aside. Ignoring the perverse bird, Otavite crept from his hiding place and slipped quickly through the recessed door, careful to keep his camouflage intact. By the light from huge torches hanging in iron brackets on the walls, he saw that he was in a vast, natural cavern. He paused for a second, gazing about in wonder.

Massive stone columns rested on carved bases around the perimeter of the chamber. Like the trunks of gigantic redwoods, they soared up and up until the tops were lost in the heights. Ugly gargoyles, ferocious winged griffins, sly grotesques and gruesomes, and other strange and menacing beasts stared blankly at Otavite from niches carved into the stone walls. The Giant reached to examine one of the sculptures, a particularly savage-looking griffin, but something in the creature's blind stare warned him not to approach, and he quickly drew his hand back.

Shrugging, almost apologetically, he moved deeper into the cavern and stopped, tilting his head back and looking up. Above, suspended from huge poles set in strong brackets affixed to the tall pillars, were dozens of enormous flags. Although he guessed that they were made from silk, they were curiously preserved and hung like heavy wet canvas in the cold, still air.

Otavite tried to match each flag with its respective country. There were many he couldn't identify, but he recognized the pure white Elven banner with the golden Crown glowing like a fiery gemstone between a pair of tall oak trees whose hearts were exposed in the living bark halfway along their straight trunks. Next to it was the Dwarves' flag displaying an intricately carved architectural groin supported on six gleaming silver pillars against a deep blue background. He gazed in awe at a sharp-eyed Eagle halted in its flight across the sun, its bronze wings extended, the world spread out below. Otavite's heart ached at the sight of a flag he had only ever seen in pictures. The proud Eagle was the emblem of the Dars, a race of Giants—his Northern cousins—dead now, annihilated by the Demon in a fiercer, darker age before his time.

"Eagles made their homes in the Dars' heads," he whispered to Eegar, a hint of wistfulness in his voice.

Beside the Dars' ancient flag hung a familiar sight. Otavite gasped when he saw the white Carovorare leaping over a red-tipped mountain, its great spiked tail curled over its back. "Salient," he whispered, suddenly remembering the heraldic term for a leaping animal that he had not thought about since his school days. Otavite stared at his country's flag and felt his confusion growing. The fact that it was here meant only one thing. The Giants had used this place at one time. But why was there no mention of it in the history books? How come no one ever spoke of it? And, why were the flags of all those other countries hanging in a chamber deep inside a mountain on Vark territory? What had this chamber been used for? Otavite's brain buzzed with so many questions, he felt dizzy. Nothing made sense. The only thing he knew for certain—as the presence of so many flags attested—was that in another age, long before his memory, something momentous had happened here in this forbidden place, something that had brought the nations of the world together in secret.

As the Giant's eyes travelled about the interior of the chamber, his ears picked up the sound of voices, muffled and indistinct. He frowned, straining to pinpoint the location of the sounds, but the great oval chamber created an echoic effect making the task impossible. Keeping close to the wall, Otavite moved farther into the cavern. He discovered smaller chambers, some mere alcoves. At each, he paused in the doorway to listen. The murmuring voices were louder now. He was getting closer. What would he find when he located the voices? More Druids? Had the rest of the garrison been marched to this place? Were his comrades and the other Carovorari imprisoned in some dark chamber, to be left there to die? Or were they already dead? Otavite shook his head again. He had a very bad feeling about this.

An arched passage opened off to the right. Torchlight flickered into the tunnel from an opening at the far end. Otavite poked his head into the passage and listened. The voices were coming from a chamber at the end of the passage. Otavite turned away and looked about for an alternative escape route in case he had to get away fast. But, since he didn't want to take the time to explore the farthest reaches of the main chamber, he decided to stick to the known rather then risk the unknown. If he had to make a run for it, he'd go back through the fissure, and pray to the stars that he didn't run into the Druid.

At the end of the arched passage, he came to a low, narrow corridor that forked to the left. Because of his height, the Giant had to crouch to avoid hitting his head and squashing Eegar to pulp on the ceiling. He ran, doubled over, relieved that it was a short corridor. It opened into a large man-made chamber, not nearly as large as the main cavern, but big enough to hold the figures gathered there. What he saw made his blood boil. He opened his mouth to shout, but then closed it immediately. Shouting wasn't going to accomplish anything except draw attention to himself. On his head, Eegar trembled uncontrollably, stirring his thick hair like a stiff breeze.

His comrades, burned and beaten, stood like zombies in rows, their eyes glazed and staring. In the middle of the chamber floor was a small, dark pool. Near the pool stood a large dolmen—three upright stones supporting a thick, horizontal, black stone slab. On the weighty slab rested an iron frame holding a marble sarcophagus.

"A tomb!" whispered Otavite incredulously. Despite the fact that

Giants laid the bodies of their dead outside to feed birds and animals, the young soldier knew that many races burned their dead, or buried them in the ground, or placed them in coffins like the one on the dolmen. He also knew that *sarcophagus* was a human word that meant flesh-devouring because the marble destroyed the flesh of a corpse.

Thick chains that had been used to secure the sarcophagus had been blasted apart and were now lying in heaps on the stone floor or hanging over the sides of the dolmen, swinging sluggishly back and forth. A dozen or more small hunched-back creatures milled about the coffin, working to slide the heavy lid to one side. Otavite swallowed the bad taste in his mouth as he identified them. *Ogres!*

Two other figures watched in silence. The short, stout fellow was obviously a Dwarf. His tall, lean companion with the golden hair had to be an Elf. What were they doing here in the company of the disgusting Ogres? Abruptly, the lid of the coffin slid sideways, toppled onto the stone slab, and crashed to the floor. The startled Ogres whistled shrilly and leaped away. But one little fellow wasn't fast enough. The heavy lead lid fell on the creature, pinning it to the ground.

"Sissss!" The Ogre whistled in pain, arms and legs beating the stone floor like beached fish. The others ignored it, and went about their business as if they could neither see their companion nor hear its desperate cries. A long time passed before the ear-piercing whistles came to an end and the creature's limbs stopped flopping and went as stiff as boards.

Suddenly, the Dwarf's body convulsed long and violently. Otavite watched, horrified, as the leathery hide seemed to fold into itself before crumpling to the floor like a rubberized raincoat. The Giant's eyes, round as hubcaps, were glued to the sleek black serpent that rose from the mound of slack flesh and expanded into a writhing, coiling behemoth. The Ogres wheezed in terror and scattered across the rock floor, scampering up the walls like squirrels, and melted into nooks and crannies as if they had never been there.

As if the Dwarf's transformation were the signal it had been waiting for, the Elf moved awkwardly to the dolmen and called the Ogres out of hiding. The pathetic little creatures seemed to appear out of solid stone as they reluctantly left the safety of their hiding spots to obey the Elf's summons. Several leaped onto the black stone slab and huddled about the foot of the Sarcophagus, their feral eyes fixed on the Elf's hands as they disappeared inside. With amazing strength, the Elf raised the upper part of a large, tightly swaddled form and began lifting it out of the coffin. Following his lead, the Ogres grabbed the other end of the cloth-bound bundle. Otavite knew by the shape that it was the body of whatever had been entombed in this place. *He must have been important,* he thought, noticing the hideous crowned skull resting on top of the grisly bundle.

"Quickly! The pool!" hissed the serpent.

The Elf and his Ogre helpers grunted and groaned as they lugged the wrapped remains to the edge of the dark pool.

"Now! Do it now!" hissed the snake.

Carefully, the others lowered the bundle onto the ground and slid it into the water, backing away as the body slowly sank into the opaque liquid. Watching from the shadows, Otavite shivered as the black water sucked the bundle into itself, not a single ripple marring its smooth, glassy surface. In a second the corpse was gone. The serpent hissed excitedly, flexing and swaying as it hovered high in the air over the heads of its companions. Otavite hardly dared breathe, his eyes shifting back and forth from the pool to the Dwarf-snake. Then the hissing ceased abruptly. The vast chamber went deathly still. All eyes stared at the dark water, all except the mesmerized Giants who continued to stand in disciplined rows, their unblinking eyes fixed on something far beyond this time and place.

The serpent stared at the pool, waiting expectantly. But the water remained as thick and smooth as an ice-covered pond. In a flash the Dwarf-snake opened its terrible mouth, whipped its head toward the row of Giants and skewered one of the unfortunate soldiers in its ice-pick fangs. Then the creature spat Otavite's friend into the pool. The doomed soldier hit the water, but no splash followed. The liquid seemed to absorb him the way droplets of mercury meet and became one larger blob. The other Giants didn't even blink as their comrade disappeared. They continued to stare at nothing, their faces as blank as stone.

Otavite clamped his teeth together in rage. He couldn't watch his friends die one by one. He had to do something now. He took a step forward and felt his flesh crawl. He didn't have to look. He sensed the presence in the shadows behind him. But *it* wasn't aware of *him*. Otavite turned slowly and found himself a heartbeat away from the foul-smelling, black-clad Druid. He had been so intent on the activities inside the chamber that he hadn't heard the creature's approach. At that moment, a small red blur shot from the Giant's hair and streaked toward the ceiling.

"Ahhhhhh!" hissed the Thug, stupefied, as the Giant suddenly materialized out of thin air. Instinctively, its clawed hands shot up toward Otavite's chest, slashing like straight razors. The soldier's quick reflexes probably saved his life. He leaped back, a wave of nausea washing over him as he felt the deadly talons slice through his thick fleece vest and rake across his chest. The wounds were deep, but he hoped not life threatening.

Otavite gave a mighty roar and lunged at the Thug, his long knife raised. Startled by the Giant's sudden outburst, the monstrous Dwarf-serpent whipped about, its red eyes narrowing menacingly. For a second the creature hesitated. Surely the useless Thug could handle one witless Giant. Or were there others? Impatient to complete its great task, it hissed loudly and struck with lightning speed, snatching another Giant and spitting the mesmerized soldier into the pool. Now the dark liquid began to bubble and churn. The serpent grabbed another Giant and thrust him into the bubbling black liquid. Abruptly, the pool erupted—exploding in a violent, whirling waterspout that shot toward the roof of the chamber, higher and higher until it disappeared. The Ogres jumped up and down, clapping their hands and whistling gleefully, their small, yellow eyes darting back and forth from the terrible serpent to the churning black water.

Locked in battle with the Demon's assassin, Otavite couldn't follow what was happening inside the ghastly chamber, but he heard the clapping and whistling and knew it was bad news for his comrades. He flung his smaller foe aside again and again, but nothing seemed to slow or weaken the creature. It was incredibly strong and it seemed to grow stronger with every blow it suffered, whereas Otavite felt his strength failing. He knew he couldn't last much longer. Suddenly, a terrible voice filled the chamber, turning the Giant's blood to ice and silencing the Ogres as if death itself had descended on the Bronks.

LEAVE THIS PLACE! GO NOW!

Out of the turbulent waters rose a shadowy form that seethed and coalesced, forming itself into a black skeletal being. The serpent continued hurling Giants into the pool as if they were logs feeding a fire. Then it shot into the air until it towered above the living apparition. The deadly shadow lifted its crowned head toward the serpent.

"Who dares disturb the King of the Dead?"

The serpent coiled about the living apparition and the voice of Hate, the Demon, filled the chamber. "I dare, Calad-Chold! I have summoned you back from the darkness. Raise your dead. Amass your armies. Destroy my enemies. There will be no rest until every last Elf and Dwarf and their allies are crushed and broken, and the rivers are fouled with their blood."

For a second, the black, empty eye sockets in the skeletal head glowed angrily. Then the light went out and the King of the Dead tilted his fleshless head back and laughed—a terrible, spine-chilling sound that reverberated through the chamber and shook the mountain to its foundation.

"There is one more thing," said the voice of Hate, above the laughter. "A small thing, a mere nuisance. There's a girl, a wicked human child. Find her and snatch a small pouch from her cold, broken body and bring it to me."

Again, the King of the Dead laughed. The horrible, mind-shattering sound went on and on, a discordant clash of screeching and rumbling that smashed through the solid rock into the very heart of the Bronks. The mighty mountain trembled as its mass shifted and pushed against itself. Shaken from his perch high on the rock wall, Eegar's shrill shriek was absorbed into the grinding, scraping noise as the mountain moaned and groaned—outraged at the evil that had been awakened in this dreadful cavern. Still, laughter poured from the Dead King's mouth, filling the Ogres with madness. Most of them disappeared back into the walls, but others ran aimlessly, whistling like steam kettles, and pounding their fists on their ears and heads to shut out the awful sound. In the end, the laughter caught the wretched creatures, turned them to ice, and blasted their brittle bodies into a raging blizzard.

Instead of driving *him* mad, the King's lethal laughter made Otavite so mad, he found new strength. He grabbed the Thug by the shoulders and, with a mighty roar, flung the creature at the few remaining Giants. The dazed soldiers blinked rapidly as if they had suddenly awakened from a deep sleep, their dazed faces registering bewilderment and confusion.

"OVER HERE!" yelled Otavite, waving his arms. "RUN!"

His comrades didn't need to be told twice. One angry fellow aimed a nasty kick at the Elf, sending the creature soaring through the air and into the swirling black pool. Then, he lumbered after his companions. No one heard the Elf's high-pitched scream as the water sucked him under. In fact, it was a long time before anyone noticed that he was gone.

Relieved to find that the Druid had neglected to seal the hidden door, Otavite led his fellow soldiers along the fissure to safety amidst the confusion of falling rocks and a screaming blizzard. Outside, they paused for a moment to listen to the sound of the Bronks and they felt the ground at their feet buckle as if the earth were rebelling against the terrible atrocity that had been done to the Giants and the dead this night in Taboo, the forbidden place.

"It's a quake!" cried Otavite, breaking into a run. The others followed and they didn't stop running until they were halfway to Erog-gore.

Far away, Hate, the Demon felt a tremor rip through her black, monotonous prison. Intoxicated with pleasure, she hissed gleefully, wrapping her grotesque arms about her scaly body, her scalpel-like claws scratching and digging into her flesh, tingling as the tips of her nails mingled with her warm, black blood. This time, her servants had not failed her. They had succeeded in raising Calad-Chold, the King of the Dead. And soon, very soon, the multitudinous hordes of dead beings would erupt from the earth to march behind the revenant King, raging across the lands like an unquenchable, unstoppable fire, swelling their ranks with all who stood in their path.

Unable to curb her mounting excitement, the Demon sailed through the darkness, her long black cloak billowing behind her like smoke. The serpents writhing about her middle like a belt hissed and struck at her flesh again and again. Hate ignored them. In her upper right hand, she gripped a black iron stake with a human skull stuck near the sharp, tapered end. Red sparks exploded from the skull's eyes, cremating those creatures unfortunate enough to find themselves in her way.

Freedom was so close she could smell it. The mere thought of being free again drove her wild. She swung the heavy stake back and forth, smashing the skulls and limbs of other half-dead creatures trapped in the dark place with her. Finally, the raging fever left her and she sighed contentedly, drinking in the screams of injured and dying things that filled the darkness about her like a mournful wind.

This time, nothing could go wrong. She'd thought of everything. Hadn't she? Suddenly, an image of a young girl flashed across the Demon's mind, almost driving her into another insane frenzy. This was the wicked Elf child who had humiliated her. This was the child who had found the magic that sealed this black pit. But for the meddling of this child, Hate would not be in this bleak, empty nothingness. She would be free, ruling all the spared races from her stronghold in the Dark Lands.

Suddenly the lids closed over a pair of burning red eyes and the Demon smiled in the darkness, her gleaming white fangs the only feature visible in the blackness under her loose hood. What chance did a mere child stand against the King of the Dead—a creature that was immune to magic, a creature that no weapon could kill? The answer was simple. None! The girl was as good as dead. And so were Hate's other enemies, the Elves and the Dwarves. And, as soon as the King of the Elves and his weak subjects joined the ranks of the dead, there'd be no one left to hold the Place with No Name together. It would collapse; and when it did, Hate and the hundreds and thousands of creatures in thrall to her would be free once again. The thought of the Elven King marching with the Dead Army against his own struck the Demon as so funny she threw herself against the blackness and laughed and laughed. Others joined her, and soon millions upon millions of voices filled the emptiness with the sound of hate-filled laughter.

CHAPTER THREE
PARENT WOES!

orlds away, in Ottawa, Canada's capital, eleven-year-old Miranda D'arte Mor fumed. She wanted to kick Nicholas Hall's door in. Fighting the urge, she dropped onto the wooden steps, absentmindedly massaging the knuckles on her right hand that were red and tender from knocking on her friend's back door non-stop for at least five minutes.

Montague, Nicholas's black Labrador Retriever, nudged Miranda's arm with his blunt head, licked her neck, and dropped onto the deck, tail thumping lazily. Miranda rubbed the dog's ears. "At least *you're* still my friend," she said.

Her friend's behaviour was unacceptable. For some unfathomable reason, the boy she'd known all of her life was shunning her, and it made her see red one minute, and hurt worse than a flu shot the next. *What have I done to make him act like this?* she asked herself for the billionth time. But, no matter how often she asked herself that question, she couldn't think of a single thing she'd done that would explain Nicholas's attitude. *It's not only me*, she reminded herself. None of the boy's other friends had heard from him in over two weeks either.

Suddenly she jumped to her feet and stomped hard on the steps, her green eyes bright with determination. She knew Nicholas was home because she'd been watching his back door from her kitchen window and had seen him enter his house less than ten minutes before.

"NICHOLAS! I KNOW YOU'RE IN THERE," she shouted at the top of her voice. She glanced quickly across the backyard toward her house, noticing her curious neighbour Mrs. Smedley with her nose glued to the window. She waved at the old lady, who ducked down as abruptly as if something heavy had fallen on her.

"NICHOLAS! DO YOU HEAR ME? I KNOW YOU'RE HOME, SO YOU BETTER GET OUT HERE. I'M NOT GOING AWAY. I'M GOING TO STAY HERE, ALL NIGHT IF I HAVE TO, AND I'M GOING TO KEEP SHOUTING UNTIL YOU COME OUT AND TALK TO ME."

Without warning, the back door popped open, an arm shot out, a strong hand gripped Miranda's wrist and yanked the startled girl inside.

"Are you crazy?" hissed Nicholas, his face flushed and angry. "What are you doing? The whole neighbourhood can hear you yelling."

Nicholas's anger couldn't hide the deep worry lines on his forehead, and suddenly Miranda felt terrible for shouting. She opened her mouth to explain, and the words tumbled out as if they'd been bottled up for a long time.

"I just want to know what's going on. You've been acting so weird. Is it something I did? Are you sick? Why are you hiding in your house? Everybody's calling me to find out what's wrong with you. Anyway, if I said something or did anything to make you angry, I didn't mean it, and I'm sorry . . ."

"Mir, relax," said Nicholas, shaking his head and looking miserable. "It's not you." He started to say something else, but stopped. "I've just been really busy."

"Doing what?" asked Miranda suspiciously, her eyes locked on the boy's face.

"Stuff," said Nicholas, turning away to avoid meeting her green eyes.

"You're lying," said Miranda. "I'd rather you were mad at me than lie. At least then I'd know what to do."

Nicholas's face turned redder than a ripe tomato. He was clearly uncomfortable and Miranda felt sorry for him. "Nick, I'm your friend. If you're in trouble, I want to help you."

Nicholas bowed his head and stared at a spot on the floor. Miranda watched him, not knowing what else to say. The boy sighed heavily, his shoulders slumping forward. Then he lifted his head slowly, ran a hand through his dark brown hair, and faced Miranda. "It's not me," he said, his voice a sad whisper. "It's my Dad."

Miranda felt her heart jump wildly. *Oh no!* she cried silently. Something bad has happened to Nick's father. Either he's sick with cancer or a brain tumor, or he was in an accident. "What's wrong with him?" she asked, not wanting to hear the answer.

But instead of telling her, Nicholas took her arm and led her through the kitchen, along the hall, and up the stairs. Miranda walked softly, almost tip-toeing, because it seemed the right thing to do in a house where someone was sick or even dying. When they reached his parent's bedroom, Nicholas opened the door and ushered her inside. Expecting to find Mr. Hall wasting away in bed with lots of tubes sticking out of him, and other medical paraphernalia cluttering the room, Miranda was dumbfounded to discover the room was empty.

"Where . . .?" She started to ask, but Nicholas strode to the bed, knelt on the floor, lifted up a pale blue bedskirt, and pointed.

Miranda joined him on the floor, peered under the bed, and before she could stop herself, a loud *whoop* of laughter burst from her throat. It was the funniest thing she had ever seen. There was Mr. Hall lying on his back on the carpet under the bed, unblinking eyes staring at the box springs an inch above his nose.

"Shut up!" hissed Nicholas angrily. "It's not funny."

"I know," giggled Miranda, trying desperately to trade her grin for a worried expression but failing miserably. Finally, she turned away, her shoulders shaking with silent laughter. The more she tried to stop, the harder she laughed. Then, just when she thought she could peer under the bed again without having hysterics, Nicholas stuck his head under the bedskirt.

"Hi Dad, can I get you anything?"

Miranda ran from the room, laughing and holding her splitting sides.

"I thought you wanted to help," snapped Nicholas, closing the bedroom door and joining her in the hall.

Miranda couldn't reply at once without dissolving in another laughing fit. Nicholas brushed past her and stomped angrily down the stairs. Miranda followed, desperately trying to stop giggling. By the time she reached the kitchen, she had succeeded in gaining control over her emotions. She touched her friend's arm.

"I'm sorry. I know it's not funny. I didn't mean to laugh. Seeing your father like that . . . well, it was the last thing I expected . . ." She was angry with herself for laughing when Nicholas was obviously upset and deeply worried. She wondered if her mother had any patients like Mr. Hall and how she handled situations like this.

"How long has your dad been . . . er . . . under the bed?" she asked, daring herself to laugh.

"Long enough," said Nicholas miserably. "Three weeks, anyway."

"What happened?"

The boy sighed. "One night after dinner, he got up from the table, looked at Mom and me, and said, *'Arrivederci!'*" Then he went upstairs, and he's been under the bed ever since."

"It's odd that he said *'Arrivederci!'* Why didn't he just say *'goodbye'*?"

"How do I know?"

"Does he ever come out?"

"No."

"He must," said Miranda, incredulously. "What about . . . you know . . . going to the bathroom and stuff?"

"Maybe he sneaks out in the middle of the night. I don't know," said Nicholas.

"What does he eat?"

"Mir, I keep telling you I don't know. I bring him food, but it's always right where I left it."

"Why do you thing he went under the bed in the first place?"

"Stop with the questions! If I knew, don't you think I'd do something?" Nicholas dropped wearily onto a chair. "The thing is, I don't know what to do."

The two friends sat in silence at the Hall's kitchen table. Miranda glanced at Nicholas, noticing that his lean face was more drawn than usual. The dark circles around his eyes told her that he hadn't been getting enough sleep.

"Nick, what about his doctor? Surely a doctor could help him."

Nicholas shook his head. "Forget it. Mom won't call."

"But . . ." Miranda couldn't believe her ears.

"Look," explained Nicholas. "Ottawa's pretty small. It's even smaller if you're in Dad's business. A lot of people were upset when he got the contract for the repairs to Parliament Hill. There's a clause in the contract that says if the contractor is declared incapable of completing the work, the contract can be terminated. If Dad is going crazy, word will get around somehow, and he'll lose the contract. I'm not saying I agree with her, but Mom thinks he's been working too hard and just needs a little rest. After that, she thinks he'll be as right as rain."

"That's craz—" Miranda stopped. She thought Mrs. Hall was wrong. Nicholas's father needed help. He needed a doctor and he needed one now, but she couldn't argue with Nicholas. Not now. He was too emotionally involved. Then she had an idea. "I know a way to get help for your dad and keep it a secret."

Nicholas leaned forward, interest showing on his face. "How?"

"If you want, I'll talk to Mom," offered Miranda. "She can see your father and try to get him to come out from under the bed. Nick, you know she'd never tell anyone." When Nicholas remained silent, Miranda continued. "I know she'll say *yes*. And if she can't help him, at least she'll know what to do."

Nicholas nodded slowly, relaxing slightly as a sudden grin appeared on his face. "That's a good idea, Mir. And you know what? I think Mom will go for it."

"Good!" said Miranda, returning the boy's grin.

As she crossed Nicholas's backyard and climbed the white picket fence that separated her property from the Halls', she couldn't help feeling that she was to blame for Mr. Hall's strange behaviour. It was a warm summer evening, but she felt a chill creep over her body as she relived the events of the terrible night half-dead, nightmare creatures invaded her world.

In March of the previous year, a Demon calling herself Hate escaped from a Netherworld prison where she had been confined for a thousand years. Together with her assassins, the cold-blooded Thugs, and the Hellhags, creatures that had given themselves to evil, the Demon found Miranda in Ottawa. Miranda fled her home in the middle of the night with a mysterious stranger, a Druid, who claimed that he alone might be able to keep her alive through the night. The Demon caught up to them in the Halls of Parliament Hill, seat of Canada's government and, in the ensuing battle, the creature vented her rage by destroying the interior of the Centre Block with its soaring Peace Tower, and the beautiful Library of Parliament.

Before she knew it, Miranda found herself in a parallel world in a desperate race against time to find the Serpent's Egg, the magic needed by the peoples of that world to seal the Demon's prison. Hot on her trail came Hate and her crazed minions intent on destroying Miranda before she found the magic Egg. To show their appreciation for her help in helping to save their world from the Demon, the King of the Dwarves sent a dozen stout stoneworkers to repair the damage Hate had caused to Canada's Parliament Buildings. The Dwarves made their temporary homes in the tunnels under Parliament Hill, sleeping by day and working secretly by night.

Miranda recalled Nicholas telling her that his father was having a lot of trouble with the workers he had hired to do the repairs. Once he found them drunk, babbling that they couldn't do their work because their stone had disappeared. When Mr. Hall examined the work site, he discovered that the work had been done, and it was the finest stonework he had ever seen. He couldn't figure out how drunken stoneworkers could have done such fine work, so he posted security guards, who reported to him that the stonemasons slept all day. Yet, mysteriously, the work was always done. And now, Mr. Hall was losing his mind.

"That's it!" said Miranda, thinking out loud. "It's not because he's been working too hard. It's the Dwarves. We forgot to tell him about the Dwarves."

She was just about to retrace her steps to share her discovery with Nicholas when she noticed the light in her mother's bedroom. No, she decided, she wanted to talk with her mother first. Then she'd tell Nicholas. She ran lightly up the steps to the terrace and tapped on the French doors to her mother's room.

The woman who opened the door was a mirror image of her daughter. She had the same short, blonde hair, and the same sparkling green eyes that seemed to see more than other people saw. Both were tall and slim, their figures almost boyish.

"Hi," said Miranda's mother. "What have you been up to?" She sat at the antique dressing table, eyes fixed on her image as she began applying lipstick.

Instead of answering, Miranda stared at her mother. She looked different. Miranda had never seen her wear clothes like that before, or fuss with make-up. "Are you going out?" she asked.

"Just for a little while," said her mother. "I won't be late."

"Where are you going?"

"To dinner," said her mother. "I made something for you. You just have to heat it up."

"Who are you going with?" asked Miranda, feeling knots tightening in her stomach.

Dr. D'arte turned from the mirror toward her daughter. "What's with the third degree?"

"Nothing." Miranda was suddenly frightened. Her mother didn't have to say a word—she knew that she was going out on a date. The thought that such a thing could happen had never once entered her mind. Until now. She wanted to tell her mother what she thought. She wanted to say it wasn't right, but she didn't trust herself to speak without bursting into tears. So she remained silent.

Her mother smiled at her. Even her smile was different—as if it hid a secret. "A friend at work has been asking me to dinner every week for the past two years, and I've always said *no*. Yesterday when he asked again, you should have seen his face when I said *yes*."

The hurt was so intense, Miranda thought she'd die. She turned and ran from the room, catching her mother's startled expression out of the corner of her eye.

Dr. D'arte stared at the closed door for a long time. Then she turned back to the mirror, scolding her image silently. *You handled that nicely!* She opened one of the small drawers of her dressing table and removed a package wrapped in soft cloth. It was a silver frame, unmarred by the slightest hint of tarnish, as if it were polished lovingly and often. Inside the frame was a picture of a young man. His long hair was the colour of the morning sun, and his strong, noble face alive with mischief as he grinned at the person on the other side of the camera.

"Oh, my dearest," she whispered. "How I wish she had known

you." She held the picture against her chest for a moment before wrapping it carefully in the soft fabric and replacing it in the drawer. *Poor Miranda!* she thought. Life is so very, very complicated for the young.

Upstairs, alone in her room, Miranda heard the doorbell ring and knew that her mother's date had arrived. She forced herself to stay on her bed and not go racing to the window in one of the front bedrooms to get a look at the only person she had seen her mother get dressed up for in her memory. She felt sick, worse than when she'd had the flu in the spring. She felt betrayed. Her mother had betrayed her. How could she go out to dinner with another man? *How could she do that to Dad!*

The problem was her mother thought Garrett D'arte Mor was dead, but Miranda knew in some secret place in her heart that he was alive.

She had never known her father. Her mother and others had told her that he had been murdered by Bog Trolls in another world—the world Miranda ended up in last March, the world of Demons and Dragons and other strange creatures—the world that had been her mother's home until she ran away.

Heartsick, Miranda wiped her eyes on her arm and flopped onto the bed, not bothering to undress. The next thing she knew, she was sitting up in pitch darkness and the house was shaking like an airplane caught in turbulent air.

"Mom . . .?" she called, disoriented and afraid. And suddenly the door flew open and her mother rushed into the room.

"Hurry, Miranda." Dr. D'arte's voice was clipped and urgent. "It feels like an earthquake, a bad one."

Miranda was still in the clothes she had worn all day. She hopped out of bed, grabbed her running shoes, and followed close on her mother's heels as the older woman raced down the stairs.

"I didn't know Ottawa was in an earthquake zone," she breathed.

"Me neither," said her mother.

Dr. D'arte's mind raced desperately. She knew there were certain procedures to follow in an earthquake. *Weren't you supposed to stand under a doorway?* Or was that the worst thing to do? She didn't stop to think about it. She grabbed Miranda's hand and half-dragged the girl through the back door and into the yard, well away from the house.

Miranda's eyes travelled about the neighbourhood. People were huddled together in their backyards—children crying, dogs barking. The ground beneath their feet buckled like a wild bronco.

"Mom, where's Mrs. Smedley?" said Miranda, grabbing her mother's arm and pointing toward their next-door neighbour's house.

"I don't see her," cried her mother, gripping Miranda's shoulders. "Wait here. I'll go and bring her back here. She's probably scared out of her mind."

"I'm coming with you," said Miranda.

"No!" It was an order. "Stay here. Don't leave this spot. I'll be right back." Then she was gone, sprinting along the side of the house toward the front yard.

Miranda was scared, but curiously excited at the same time. She saw lights flash on in Nicholas's house. Then, the back door opened and Nicholas appeared. Montague bounded down the steps, barking fiercely and sniffing at the ground. After every few barks the dog turned toward its master as if to assure itself that Nicholas was still there. Nicholas backed down the steps, staggering under the heavy weight in his arms. His mother followed, holding onto Mr. Hall's ankles for dear life. Safely away from the house, they laid their burden on his back on the grass. Nicholas stood and spotted Miranda. They exchanged waves and the boy ran up the steps and back into the house.

At the exact moment the King of the Dead rose up out of the dark pool in a secret chamber deep inside a mountain in the land of Vark, the earth split apart in Miranda's world, spreading like a crack on a frozen lake and widening into a deep chasm. Then, events happened with such clarity that, for as long as she lived, Miranda only had to close her eyes to see it all again. She saw the earth heaving and cracking. She saw Nicholas reappear at his back door. For one long, vivid moment, they locked eyes. And then, it seemed to Miranda as if something came out of the darkness of the chasm and reached for the boy. She blinked, and Nicholas and his house were gone.

CHAPTER FOUR

RUNNING AWAY

"ick!" screamed Miranda, scaling the picket fence with no other thought in her head but to help her friend. She landed on the lip of the deep rift, teetering as the ground beneath her feet crumbled and cascaded into the blackness below. Desperately, her arms flailed the air for something to grab onto, but she couldn't reach the fence. As she felt herself sliding into the black hole, she automatically reached for the small metallic pouch she wore on a thin silver chain around her neck. Suddenly, her feet slipped and, for one heart-stopping moment, she was falling. Then she felt the jolt as something caught the neck of her clothing and held on tightly, pulling her up and out of the fractured earth, dragging her to safety.

Miranda brushed aside the hands of her rescuers, pushed herself up on her hands and knees, and breathed great gulps of fresh air. She knew that she had been seconds away from death and she was grateful to her rescuers, but she had to get away from the people and the noise. She desperately needed to think. Because, as she had hung suspended over the edge of the precipice, the stench that rose out of the abyss and came at her with sudden, vicious force left her numb and sick with terror. She would never, in a million years, forget that odour. It was the smell of the Demon and the Thugs—the same bad, sweet smell that had come from a dead raccoon she and Nicholas had found under the shed in the boy's backyard a few summers ago.

Miranda's mind whirled like leaves tossed in a hurricane. She pushed herself to her feet and turned to find her mother staring at the rift in horror, her face as white as flour, the hand on Mrs. Smedley's arm trembling violently.

"What did you see?" asked Dr. D'arte, her narrowed green eyes telling Miranda that she was afraid of the answer, perhaps afraid of her own daughter.

Miranda looked from her mother to her elderly neighbour.

"Not now," she said, meaningfully.

"Come with me, then," said her mother. "I want you and Mrs. Smedley with me where I know you're safe. I've got to help with the injured."

"No, Mom," said Miranda, her eyes pleading for understanding. "I have to find Nick."

Dr. D'arte's eyes filled with tears. She reached and pulled Miranda close. "Oh, Mir. I'm so sorry. Nicholas is gone."

"No!" cried Miranda. "You don't understand. He's not dead." She stopped abruptly. How could she explain what had happened in those few, long seconds as she dangled over the black mouth of the chasm? What could she say to make her mother believe her when she scarcely believed herself?

"I have to tell you something," she said, catching her mother's arm and squeezing gently. "Please. It's really important."

Dr. D'arte patted Mrs. Smedley's arm and then moved toward the terrace. She turned to her daughter, questioningly.

"It's the Bloodstones," said Miranda, surprised that the words poured from her mouth as if someone else were speaking them. "I was holding them when I was falling into the crack. They worked, Mom."

"That's not possible," said her mother, incredulously.

"I know," replied Miranda. "Don't ask me how. They've never worked in Ottawa before, but they work now. Mom, this isn't a natural earthquake. There's something down there . . ."

"Miranda—"

"Wait, please," said Miranda, gripping her mother's arm. "Let me finish. There's not much time." Then she told her mother about the terrible smell. "But that's not all. Nick's down there, too. I heard him . . . through the Stones . . . and I heard others . . . not their voices . . . I heard their thoughts." Her grip on Dr. D'arte's arm tightened. "Mom, I don't know what they are, but there are billions of them. And they're coming here."

"My God, Miranda! What are you saying?"

"They're just waiting for something to happen before they come here. But, they are coming, Mom. Believe me, they're coming as surely as the sun will rise tomorrow morning. And nothing can stop them. I heard their thoughts. They're coming here to kill everyone. That's what they do. That's all they do." Miranda stopped. There was nothing more to say. Either her mother believed her or she didn't.

"This can't be happening," said Dr. D'arte. She ran her hands nervously through her short hair. "I can't take this in."

"Listen," said Miranda, keeping her voice low. "You have to let me find Naim. He's the only one who might be able to help us."

Her mother shook her head frantically. She wouldn't admit it, but she still harboured resentment against the Druid for recruiting her daughter in his war against Hate, the Demon.

"No, I won't let you go. You're staying right here with me."

Miranda looked at her mother sadly. "You don't understand," she said. "We're going to die if we stay here."

"How do I know you know these things? How can anyone know anything . . .?"

"You have to trust me," said Miranda. "What I've said is true, Mom."

Her mother's chin quivered and tears rolled down her cheeks. "I trust you more than you know," she said. "But you're just a child and I'm afraid for you."

"Mom," pressed Miranda. "I have to go *now*."

Mother and daughter clung tightly to each other for a second. Then Dr. D'arte released her child and tried to smile. "I'll probably die worrying about you before any monsters crawl out of that hole. But go. Just promise you won't go alone."

Miranda didn't promise, because she was already racing up the path toward the street. As she drew near the intersection of Beechwood Avenue and Crichton Street, she heard someone call her name, but she didn't recognize the low, scratchy voice. She skidded to a stop and peered about. Across Beechwood Avenue, she made out a small, dim form in the darkness. As it crossed the street and drew nearer, she gave a sigh of relief. It was her best friend, Bell. Dumbfounded, she waited for the girl to reach her. She and Arabella Winn had known each other since junior kindergarten.

"What happened to you?" she asked, noticing Arabella's torn clothing and the dirt streaking her face. Even the small thatch of white hair over her friend's right eye was as black as the rest of the hair on her head. Then, her heart lurched as she noted the state of her own clothes and realized the terrible truth. "The earthquake!"

Arabella nodded vigorously, and a sob escaped from her lips. "Penelope's dead! And Muffy, too!"

"Tell me," urged Miranda, wrapping her arms about the stricken girl's shoulders.

"We were walking Muffy," cried Arabella. "And the ground opened right at our feet. Mir, there was no warning. One minute everything was normal, then it just swallowed Muffy." Arabella was sobbing uncontrollably now. "B-before I c-could s-stop her, Penelope jumped into the hole after the dog. It happened so fast, they were gone before I could do anything to save them. B-but I tried, Mir. I really tried."

Penelope St. John was a liar and a major pain in the butt, but she had saved Miranda's and Arabella's lives once and had become a friend despite her obvious failings. Muffy was another matter. Most of the time, Miranda felt like stepping on the evil little poodle. But, Penelope was devoted to Muffy and when Miranda heard that they were gone, sadness threatened to overwhelm her. She wanted to cry too, but she knew if she let the tears flow she wouldn't be able to stop them. Instead, she thought about the earthquake and found that she was barely able to take in the extent of the damage. How far did the rift extend? What if it went all the way from Ottawa to the end of the United States—to Miami, for instance? And what if those creatures were lurking down there all along the length of the crack? The hair on her neck bristled.

"It doesn't change anything," she reasoned, unaware that she was thinking out loud. "If it's a mile or a thousand miles long, those things are still there. I've got to reach Naim."

"What are you talking about?" sniffed Arabella, her shoulders suddenly tensing. "What are we going to do about Penelope and Muffy?" And then as if she suddenly understood Miranda's words, her eyes widened. "You said *things*. What *things*?"

Miranda grabbed her friend's hand. "Come on Bell. I'll tell you on the way."

"Tell me *what?* Where are we going?"

"To find the Dwarves," answered Miranda, breaking into a trot and heading across St. Patrick Bridge, which spanned the narrow Rideau River.

They ran through the dark streets, the wail of sirens drowning out the usual night-time sounds of traffic. On the way, Miranda told Arabella what had happened to Nicholas, and what the Bloodstones had revealed to her as she dangled over the chasm. Arabella listened in silence, her breathing harsh as she struggled to keep pace with the faster runner.

It took them a long time to scale the limestone cliff from a path behind Parliament Hill. They felt drained when they finally reached the narrow ledge near the top and removed a loose iron bar from one of the arched vents. They squeezed through the gap and into a large tunnel that formed part of a vast underground system of tunnels under the Parliament Buildings. To their dismay, they discovered that they didn't have a flashlight.

"Forget it," said Miranda. The thought of having to go all the way back home to fetch a light was just too depressing. They pushed on, feeling their way silently along the damp, musty passage.

Here, deep within the limestone mass, Miranda felt that she had entered another world. No outside sounds penetrated the heavy, oppressive silence. She strained to hear the wailing sounds of the sirens as fire trucks, police cruisers, and ambulances sped to and from the earthquake site, but she heard nothing except the eerie grinding sounds as the cliff shifted under the weight of the stone buildings overhead.

"WHO'S THERE?"

Miranda was so startled by the gruff voice she almost jumped out of her skin. Arabella's quick intake of breath told her she was having a similar reaction.

"Is that you, Emmet?"

"None of your business," snapped the voice. "Who are you?"

"It's Emmet," whispered Arabella. "No one else could be that obnoxious."

"It's Miranda," said Miranda.

"And Bell," said Arabella.

There was a long moment of silence as if the owner of the unfriendly voice were making up his mind whether to believe them or not.

"Emmet," said Miranda. "We ran all the way here and . . ."

"What do you want?" interrupted Emmet rudely, lighting a

lantern and raising it toward the girls. "What are you doing here? Should be home in bed?"

And you should have your mouth glued shut, thought Arabella. "Do you think we're enjoying this?" she snapped, glaring daggers at the short, stocky figure behind the light. "Do you seriously think we came all this way in the middle of the night just to be insulted by you? So, if you're not going to help us, get out of our way!"

"Please, Emmet," said Miranda, squeezing Arabella's arm to quiet her angry companion. "Something's happened. We've got to talk to Anvil and the others."

"Well?" demanded Arabella.

Grumbling something that sounded suspiciously like, *'Never liked that girl,'* Emmet turned and silently led them along a side tunnel.

"I never liked that Dwarf," whispered Arabella in Miranda's ear. "He's so mean. I don't understand how Nicholas puts up with him."

"I think it's a male thing," answered Miranda. "Remember when you guys were captured by the Bogs? You were separated from Nick and Emmet, and they only had each other to rely on. Nick said he wouldn't have made it out alive if it hadn't been for Emmet."

"Maybe," said Arabella doubtfully. "But he'd better shed the attitude or I'm going to get really mad."

Soon, they saw the glow from a small fire at the far end of another passage. The smell of sausages sizzling in a cast iron pan over the flames made their mouths water, and almost made them forget the reason for their visit.

"YO!" shouted the six sturdy Dwarves, jumping up from chairs that were grouped about the fire.

"It's Miranda," barked Emmet.

One of the Dwarves came forward and slapped Miranda on her back. The blow knocked her off balance and she would have fallen in the fire if another Dwarf hadn't caught her.

"Miranda, eh! Good, good," said Anvil, grinning sheepishly. At least *he's* happy to see us, thought Miranda. The Dwarf motioned to one of the empty chairs. "What brings you here?"

Miranda noticed that the chairs were made of stone and beautifully carved, more like stubby stools with short backs. The Dwarves had been busy since she had last been here. Then, they had sat on crude stumps. She took the offered seat and turned to the others. Arabella refused to sit, preferring to crouch as close to the fire as she could get.

"I must find Naim," said Miranda, waving away a pan of sausages and a slab of crusty black bread that smelled like molasses. "Something terrible happened tonight . . . and Naim's . . ."

"Aha!" snorted Emmet, looking at his companions as if to say, 'I told you so.' He pointed a pudgy finger at Miranda. "Admit it. You're behind it."

"Behind what?" said Miranda, feeling her hostility toward Emmet suddenly spike.

"The quake," said Anvil. "Thought the cliff was coming down."

Miranda sighed impatiently. "That's why we're here," she explained. "And no, Emmet, I didn't cause the earthquake. It happened along the river near my house. But it's not just an earthquake. It's the Demon. That's why I need to find Naim."

"Demon's shut away," said Anvil, exchanging quick glances with his fellow Dwarves.

"I know that," agreed Miranda. "But, she's involved. I just know it." Then she took a deep breath and told them about the disappearance of Nicholas and Penelope, at which point Emmet gave a loud roar of rage and stomped his boots repeatedly on the stone floor. Miranda knew that Nicholas and Emmet had become lasting friends, but she hadn't known how protective of Nicholas the Dwarf was. Some of the things he threatened to do to those responsible for his friend's disappearance made Miranda's hair stand on end. It took about ten minutes for his companions to get him to calm down.

When they were all seated around the fire once more, Miranda continued with an account of how the Bloodstones had let her hear the thoughts of the creatures in the rift. "I know it sounds crazy," she said, "but they're going to attack Canada and the whole world. They're just waiting for something to happen, or for someone to tell them what to do, and then they're going to come out of the rift." She turned her pale face toward Anvil, praying that he'd take her seriously. "So, you see. That's why I need to find Naim."

Anvil nodded, but remained silent. Miranda glanced at Arabella anxiously. Her friend shook her head and shrugged. She didn't know what the Dwarves were going to do anymore than Miranda did. Had they believed her? Would they take her through the magic Portal to Bethany? They were her only hope, because she could only pass through the Portal in the company of someone from the other world. Miranda sighed and stared into the fire, waiting for Anvil and the others to make a decision. Finally Anvil turned to the Dwarf seated next to him.

"Check her story. Report back."

Without a word, the Dwarf scuffed his boots on the stone floor and stood. He nodded curtly at Miranda and Arabella and stomped off down the passage. Anvil watched until he disappeared into the main tunnel and then turned to Miranda.

"No offence, girl," he said. "I believe you. But, need a Dwarf report."

Miranda smiled weakly. She realized she was so hungry she was close to passing out. She reached for a sausage and rolled it in a thick slab of bread. It was scrumptious, absolutely the best thing she'd ever eaten. She wolfed it down, licked her fingers, and reached for more.

And then she felt a strong hand on her shoulder. Her eyes flew open and she jumped to her feet. She had fallen asleep. The Dwarf scout had returned and was huddled about the fire, deep in conversation with Anvil and the others, their gruff voices lowered until they sounded like far away base drums. Miranda nudged Arabella awake with the toe of her running shoe.

Anvil saw the movement out of the corner of he eye. He heaved his squat form off the stone stool and turned toward the girl. "Come," he said, motioning with his arm. "Portal's this way."

Miranda and Arabella found themselves running flat out to keep up with the swiftly marching Dwarves. Miranda tried to memorize the route they were taking, but after counting eleven different passages, she gave up. They finally stopped at a dead end and could go no further.

"Where's the horn?" asked Miranda, gazing at the walls on the side of the tunnel near the end wall.

Emmet and the other Dwarves stared at her curiously, until she felt her face burning. "When we went through the portal with Naim, he blew into a long horn that was hanging from the wall. He used it to call these big bubbles that took us down to the lake."

The Dwarfs exchanged amused glances and one or two of them chuckled gruffly.

"A Druid trick," said Emmet, removing a rock pick from his belt and tapping the end wall.

Even though she was expecting it, the sight of the solid stone wall melting like ice under hot water startled Miranda. Her heart leaped into her throat as she peered out through the opening into the night. She stepped closer to the edge and looked down, down thousands and thousands of feet to where she knew Ellesmere Island, land of the Elves, nestled like a brilliant emerald in the sapphire blue lake. But it was also dead of night in that other world and all she saw that told her she wasn't gazing out at Ottawa was the absence of city lights and a sky glittering with stars that appeared bigger and brighter than the stars in the night sky over Canada's capital.

She was relieved that they didn't have to descend to Lake

Leanora in the giant bubbles. That had been a nightmare. "How are we getting there?" she asked, eyes straining at the darkness.

"Like this," said one of the Dwarves.

Miranda and Arabella felt the hard whack on their backs that pitched them over the edge of the cliff and then, to their horror, they were dropping through the freezing air, their ears ringing with harsh Dwarf laughter.

CHAPTER FIVE

DROPPING IN

A s Miranda and Arabella plunged like lead balloons through the night sky to certain death, below in Bethany, capital of Ellesmere Island, the King of the Elves could not sleep. He lay on his back on top of the covers, arms locked behind his head, a feeling of dread eating away at him as he stared into the darkness.

He had been working late in his study when he heard the unusual rattling sounds. Looking up from a raft of papers, he noticed that the ancient brass handles on the drawers of a high, dark wooden chest were vibrating rapidly, tapping against the wood as if the contents of the drawers had suddenly come alive and were trying to get out. At first King Elester thought his eyes were playing tricks on him. But then, the floor beneath his feet rippled, and a shudder spread from the palace foundations and ran up the walls until the structure trembled like an aged and fragile being. The tremor lasted for less than a minute before Elester's world went still again. One look about the room told him he hadn't imagined it.

The wrought-iron wall sconces and colourful paintings hung askew, as if a mischievous sprite had purposely set everything crooked. Priceless bowls and vases had been jiggled from where they rested and now lay shattered on the floor, or balanced precariously on the edge of small tables and delicate chests. Books had wiggled free from ordered rows on the bookshelves and leaped to the floor, where they lay in confused piles.

Earth tremors were not unknown on Ellesmere Island, but they were rare. This latest tremor wasn't the reason for the growing sense of foreboding that was keeping the Elven king awake. No! What filled him with dread and made his blood flow cold was something he had heard at the peak of the tremor—an alien sound like a faint rustling or susurration. It was an odd sensation, as though millions of voices were whispering secrets in his ears simultaneously. Elester strained to identify sentences or individual words, but he couldn't isolate the sounds. And then, for one microsecond, the unintelligible whisperings of the multitude had separated and become distinct, and he heard each voice singly and clearly. What he heard made his flesh crawl.

The voices ranted against his people. They shrieked with laughter as they whispered of a plan to purge the lands of the races of Elves and Dwarves, gentle River Trolls, the Red Giants of Vark, and many others. The voices rose to a frenzied pitch at the prospect of killing humans and slaughtering animals—destroying all traces of their existence, wiping out entire civilizations. The excitement in their voices at the expectation of unrestrained and bloody carnage made Elester sick. Then, they spoke of a King who would call them forth and lead them, a King who could not die. And they whispered a name—*Calad-Chold!*

Elester sat upright and swung his legs over the side of the bed. Leaving the room in darkness, he opened the top drawer of a small, oak chest beside his bed and removed a rectangular-shaped box. He lifted the top of the box and took out a medallion. On a heavy chain, amidst a circlet of curling gold oak leaves nestled a large, green stone—his father's Wisdom Stone, now his. He held the emerald in the palm of his hand and peered into its depths.

Nothing happened. The clear green gem was as cold as ice against his skin.

Elester thought about the evil voices. Where had they come from? To whom did they belong? In his mind, he searched to the farthest reaches of his world, identifying each of the races by name, but none fit the sounds he had heard. Not Bog Trolls. Their language was crude: the words crass and cacophonous. No, the whisperers hadn't been Bog Trolls.

For a second, he wondered about the Simurghs, a race of wicked, roly-poly creatures with sharp, pointed teeth that would sell their own children for a handful of dirt. They were certainly articulate, and cunning enough. Finally, the King shook his head, dismissing the Simurghs. *No*, he thought, *if it had been the Simurghs, I would have heard them fighting and arguing among themselves.*

Were the voices a result of the earth tremor? Or was it sheer coincidence that they happened together? Again, Elester shook his head. He was convinced the evil voices came with, or were made audible by, the tremor. But what did that mean? Had the tremor opened a rift between Ellesmere Island and some dark place that did not exist in his broad knowledge? The King sighed in frustration. Each question he asked only gave rise to a dozen others.

He stared at the Wisdom Stone. "I do not feel wise," he said, grinning sardonically. He was just about to replace the Stone in its box and put it back in the drawer when a pale light flickered within its green depths. Elester's hand tightened about the Stone. It felt warm in his hand. This had never happened before! Suddenly, a name and an image filled his mind. The name was *Miranda*, and the accompanying image was of a slim Elven child with large, green eyes and hair of gold—an impish expression painted on her freckled face.

Elester waited for more, afraid to breathe for fear of jinxing the magic Stone. But, the light faded and the jewel went cold. Elester placed the Wisdom Stone in its box and put it back in the drawer. "Miranda," he said, wondering now if thoughts of the child had come to him unbidden, or had the Wisdom Stone planted them in his head? He said the girl's name again, thoughtfully this time. Was she part of the puzzle? Could she provide the answers to his questions?

"It's the Bloodstones!" he said, wishing that he could speak with the Druid. He hadn't seen his oldest friend since his Crowning almost a year ago, and he missed him, especially now.

Knowing that sleep would elude him, Elester decided to check with the Watchers and Wardens, just to put his mind at ease. The Watchers were specially trained Elven men and women who, as the name of their unit implied, kept watch over the Portals that Elves and others used for travel between worlds. The Wardens monitored the magic that held the Place with No Name, the Demon's prison, together. A little more than a year ago, the monstrous Hate sensed an eroding of the warding spells that had sustained her prison for a thousand years. Quick to take advantage of the disintegrating Elven magic, the poisonous creature hacked away at the invisible wall, creating a hole big enough to slip through to freedom.

For as long as he lived, the young King would never forget what happened after the Demon and scores upon scores of her bloodthirsty minions escaped from the nameless place. The terribly sad images of the twisted and broken bodies of Elves and Dwarves at the Battle of Dundurum were burned into his mind. The screams of the wounded and dying haunted him still, invading his dreams night after night. Elester lost his King and father when the Demon had shot a lethal, living missile at Ruthar, beloved King of the Elves, the man she considered her bitterest enemy. As he thought about the Monster that had murdered his father, Elester felt the temperature of the room drop sharply until he was actually shivering.

He dressed hurriedly and left the palace through a concealed door from his private apartments. Outside, he followed a white stone path toward the rear of the building. Suddenly, a chilling thought formed in his mind. Were both the voices and the earth tremor the work of the Demon? Had she somehow reached out from her lightless prison and unleashed a new menace that was about to fall upon the Island Kingdom of Ellesmere like an iron fist? Who or what was Calad-Chold? He did not know the name and his lack of knowledge worried him. He must get word to the Druid. If anyone knew this name and the history attached to it, it would be the old man. Elester quickened his pace, anxious to reach the small domed structure where recently-formed units of Watchers and Wardens vigilantly monitored the magic that the first Elves brought with them when they came to this world from Empyrean untold millions of years ago.

Ahead, the building loomed before him like a ghost in the night, its smooth white stone gleaming like polished bone. Elester loved the building. He had designed it and had it constructed after the death of his father. But tonight he barely glanced at it. Instead, he wracked his brain for something that would tell him the source of the voices.

"It does not make sense," he said. "If they have never met us, why do they hate us so much?" He spoke the question aloud, but no reply broke the deep silence of the palace grounds.

For a second, his thoughts turned again to the green-eyed child who had risked her life to help defeat Hate and drive her back into her prison. *Miranda has to be the answer!* he thought, his mind racing to find a thread to link the courageous girl to the strange voices and the earth tremor. He did not like to think that she might be in danger.

Elester's keen Elven sight picked out the Guards concealed in the shadows on both sides of the small building. In their black uniforms, they were extensions of the night—living shadows. No one but an Elf could have detected them. They didn't acknowledge their King's presence, but Elester knew that they had been aware of him from the instant he set foot outside the palace. Just as he stepped under the arched entry to the domed structure, a figure barreled through the opening, colliding with him and knocking the wind out of him. Elester laughed out loud at the sight of his junior aide sailing backwards and landing on his rump on the rock-hard floor.

"S-sorry Sire," stammered Andrew Furth, sheepishly. "Are you all right?"

"Fine," grinned the King, extending his hand and pulling the red-faced young man to his feet. "Where were you going in such a hurry?"

Andrew groaned, self-consciously rubbing his smarting backside. "I was on my way to the palace to see you, Sire."

"What is it?" asked Elester. The uneasy feeling was back, flooding over him like scalding water.

"The Bethany Portal, Sire. Someone is coming through."

For a second Elester stared at the younger man, not sure that he understood the reason for his aide's obvious apprehension. Then he shrugged and clapped Andrew on the shoulder. "It must be one of the Dwarves coming back for supplies." Or could it be Miranda? he wondered, dismissing the thought even as it formed in his mind.

"That is not the problem, Sire."

"What *is* the problem?" said Elester.

"The tremor," answered Andrew. "The sea is too rough. Our patrols can not pick up the traveler." He looked at the silent King, his face a picture of helplessness. "If they do not drown, Sire, the creature will get them."

"Then, for their sakes," replied Elester grimly. "Let us hope they drown."

He turned and hurried back to the palace, his aide close on his heels. It was going to be a very long night.

CHAPTER SIX

THE KING
OF THE LAKE

iranda looked about wildly, calling Bell's name over and over until she was hoarse. She was plummeting through the air so swiftly the wind blinded her and snatched words and breath from her throat. At first, the freezing air had stung like sharp knives, but after awhile, she was so cold that all sensation fled from her body, leaving her numb. The only thing speeding faster than her fall was her heart.

She dropped for a long, long time, expecting at any moment to feel the blood-chilling waters of Lake Leanora smash her body to bits, as if she were an ice sculpture crashing onto concrete. Thinking of how she'd survive the impact made her laugh harshly. Slamming into the dark waters was the least of her problems. There were worse things than being dashed to pieces or drowning. *Don't go there!* she thought, refusing to turn her mind to the dangerous creature that lurked beneath the Lake's surface—the creature she and Bell had encountered the first time they had journeyed to the land of the Elves. If she let her mind wander there, she was afraid the terror would stop her heart long before she hit the water.

Abruptly, Miranda felt her momentum slowing. The air, while

still chilly, was definitely warmer. But she was still falling way too fast. Although she had been bracing herself for thousands of feet, the shock that coursed through her body as she slammed against the solid water was a hundred times worse than anything she could have imagined. The force drove the air from her lungs and sent pain shooting through her limbs. As she sank into the black Lake, her waterlogged clothes dragged her deeper, fighting her efforts to reach the surface. Frantically, she kicked and pumped her arms, finding strength she didn't know she possessed.

Please don't let me drown. She cried the words in her mind.

Once, she almost panicked, thinking that she was swimming away from the surface in the pitch-black water. Another time, she was certain the Lake creature was just below her, its hideous mouth open as wide as the gaping mouth of a cave. When she finally broke the surface, coughing up water and choking for air at the same time, she found herself in the middle of a sea raging with mountain-sized waves that swept her up and tossed her about as if she were a sodden rag doll.

Instinctively, Miranda reached for the Bloodstones. Afraid of losing them in the violent sea, she clutched the small silver pouch tightly. To her surprise, the metal felt as warm as the summer sun on her bare arms.

"BELL-LLL!" In the howling wind, her shout was a mere whisper.

Danger! screamed the Bloodstones in her mind. *Danger!*

Miranda tried to focus on the surface of the lake, but the dark night and the high waves blocked her view.

Below! screamed the Bloodstones. *Danger below!*

Reluctantly, scared to death of what might be homing in on her kicking feet from beneath the surface, Miranda took a deep breath and plunged her head under the water. At first, everything was black and confining—close, as if a thick black hood had been pulled over her face. She felt sudden panic erupt like a waterspout inside her. *Get away! Swim!* Her mind screamed. She wanted to obey, wanted to flail her arms and swim away as fast as she could. It took every ounce of will power to stay where she was, to peer into the darkness and concentrate on what was hiding there.

Slowly the blackness began to dissipate and she could make out vague forms weaving purposefully through the nocturnal waters. And then, the forms materialized into living creatures. She saw them as clearly as if she were looking in a fishbowl in broad daylight. And still the images magnified until even the haze of miniscule bubbles rising from a guppy's waving tail and contracting gills were sharp and clear. Everywhere she looked things appeared with startling clarity.

Except for the great blackness rising rapidly like a hideous, throbbing blob from the depths and coming at her. Her eyes fastened on the network of pulsing veins in the monster's oily flesh and she felt her stomach churn. She knew the creature instantly, but it was so much more terrifying than she remembered.

The sharp spikes protruding from its spine were as long as lances. The wicked claws snapping like wolves' fangs on either side of its swollen body could sever a limb as effortlessly as biting into soft butter. But, it was the ghastly, white, unseeing eyes that made Miranda feel weak with terror.

Please don't let me die, she begged. Then, something scraped against the back of her legs and her heart stopped.

For a second, she almost forgot about the giant creature Naim, the Druid, had dubbed 'Dilemma.' Whatever had brushed against her had to be faced now. Keeping her head submerged, Miranda turned to confront the unknown terror behind her. She remembered watching a television show about sharks and how they brushed against or nudged the diver before attacking. Were there sharks in Lake Leanora? She didn't think sharks lived in fresh water. But this Lake was huge, bigger than the combined waters of the Great Lakes in her world. And besides, the rules were different here. In this world, dragons flew in the skies, and dinosaurs still roamed the ancient forests. Who was to say that sharks didn't live in lakes?

Miranda's fear turned to relief when she saw two human legs kicking the water as if they were climbing an invisible stairs. *Bell!* She suddenly realized that she had been holding her breath for ages but, surprisingly, her lungs weren't bursting. *It's the Stones!* she thought. She knew there wasn't time to deal with her friend before Dilemma reached them, so she grabbed her companion's pant leg and peered down.

The Lake Monster was as ancient as the planet. It had survived untold ages, changing and evolving from a land behemoth to a water-breathing creature. It lived on the bottom of the vast lake, miles below the surface, where deep-water prey lurked in waters as black as the space in the Demon's hood. Lake Leanora was its domain—and Dilemma was King. It prowled and hunted, ruling with ripping teeth and sharp spike. It was the largest predator in the Lake and, like a bloated, bejeweled despot, feasted on its lesser subjects. But over the centuries, the creature had developed a taste for human flesh.

Dilemma's eyes were useless from centuries spent in the dark waters of Lake Leanora down where sunlight could not penetrate, but its sonar was so acute it could feel the vibrations from a minnow darting through shallow water. The vibrations that sent a thrill along its spine as it shot toward the surface weren't coming from a minnow, or even a thousand, thousand minnows. Only humans, afraid and out of their element in the deep water, made erratic, agitated movements like these. There were two humans near the surface. Their fear teased its brain, filling it like the coppery smell of fresh blood. Opening its cavernous mouth and extending its double row of sharp, jagged teeth, Dilemma surged upward.

Fear paralyzed Miranda. There was nothing she could do to stop this creature, and no way she could out-swim it. She knew she was crying, but her tears dissolved and mingled with the Lake. *Please, please help us*, she begged the Bloodstones, silently. *Don't let us die like this!* Then her eyes widened as she suddenly thought of something that might stop the creature, if only she wasn't too late.

Frantically, she formed an image of the scariest thing she knew in the oceans—a great white shark. She kept her mind locked onto the image as she moulded it into a mammoth predator, making it bigger and bigger until it dwarfed the giant Dilemma. Recalling that the creature intent on devouring her was blind, she wrapped the image about her and Arabella, centering them at the heart of the illusory shark monster. Then she focused on her heartbeat and synchronized it with Bell's, merging the dual beats into one sound and then turning up the volume until the thumping was like a thousand drums rolled into one in her ears. Her mind worked feverishly to push the vibrations from their flailing arms and kicking legs as they treaded water out and away to the great fins and gills of her creation. She knew she had only seconds to stop Dilemma before the Lake Monster swallowed them alive, or worse.

Quickly, she sent the image to the Bloodstones, amazed when she actually felt the pictures flow from her mind into the Stones. Would it work? She waited, watching the creature zeroing in for the kill.

Dilemma's brain seethed with images of the two humans—surrealistic montages of white bone and red flesh. Abruptly, the fragile human heartbeats were gone, as if the creatures had been snatched from the water, or swallowed by another predator. And then, wave upon wave of vibrations slammed into the monster. Dilemma braked and stopped as suddenly as if the creature had run smack into a solid wall. The lovely red and white images vanished from its brain like mist and in their place came an image of a menace so horrific, so deadly, the Lake Creature cringed and backed away—confused and frightened by the sheer immensity of the predacious shark-like thing. In the blink of an eye, the wily survivor jack-knifed and shot toward the bottom of the Lake.

On the surface, Miranda saw Dilemma's hideous jaws slam shut as the creature flipped about and streaked downward. She watched, holding onto the image, until Dilemma disappeared into the blackness below. Still she held the image, only releasing it when she felt the Bloodstones go cold in her hand.

It was Arabella who pulled her face out of the water, flipped her onto her back, hooked an arm about her neck in an attempt to keep her face out of the water, and tried to swim through the rough waves.

Miranda struggled and fought free of the stranglehold.

"Let me go!" she yelled.

Arabella grabbed her arm. "You're alive!" she gasped through chattering teeth.

"Of course I'm alive," shouted Miranda.

"Ten minutes!" yelled her friend. "Mir, you were underwater for ten whole minutes. You weren't breathing." Arabella's eyes were as wide as if she were staring at a ghost.

"Not now," said Miranda, suddenly feeling the strain and the cold working on her body. Her mind was foggy and her limbs felt as heavy as lead. She knew that her little remaining strength was fading fast. "We've got to get to shore," she shouted. "I can't last much longer."

"Just wait till I get my hands on those Dwarves!" shouted Arabella, choking on a mouthful of water and struggling to stay afloat in the tumultuous waves.

CHAPTER SEVEN

A DARK PLACE

t first, Nicholas thought he was dead. Then, a wave of nausea washed over him and he almost sobbed with relief.

"Ohhh," he groaned, opening his eyes and immediately snapping them shut. It was darker with his eyes open. *Where am I?* he wondered, his thoughts slow and fragmented. *What happened?* He opened his eyes again and tried to sit up, but something large and heavy was pinning him to the floor, driving the air from his lungs. For a moment, he remained still, his ears straining for sounds. But he heard nothing. The darkness was as silent as a graveyard.

Nicholas ran his hands over the heavy object and realized it was a door. Suddenly, he remembered everything. The Earthquake! And then, the sickening sensation that had gripped his stomach, as if he were falling off a cliff! He realized he must have fallen down the stairs and bumped his head when he had gone back into the house to fetch his most prized possession—his Elven short sword. He stretched his arms out to either side and felt about on the ground. It had to be here. The last thing he remembered was holding it in his hand as he started down the stairs. The thought of losing it made him sick.

Laury, Captain of the King's Riders, had presented him with the sword in a special ceremony in Bethany a year ago. Forged by the Elves, and tempered in ice water from a brook in the mountains north of the Elven capital, the sword was the most beautiful thing the boy had ever seen. Because it had come from Laury made it even more special. The Captain was gone now, killed in his own barracks by a band of Bog Trolls. Nicholas felt his friend's loss like an open wound that would never completely heal. He considered the sword a link between him and Laury.

The boy groaned. He couldn't lie here forever. He had to get up and make sure his parents were OK. His eyes blinked open. It was still blacker than midnight and he wondered if the quake had caused a power outage. Using his arms as jacks, he pushed against the door and at the same time eased his lower body to the side. Finally, he managed to slide free, letting the door drop. The sound of solid wood thudding against the slate tiles on the kitchen floor echoed eerily in the silence. Nicholas blinked again. It was brighter now. He looked about for the source of the light, amazed when he spotted several flaming torches set in brackets on stone walls. He knew it was impossible, but for a moment he thought he was in a huge cavern. *Where am I?* he wondered, not for the first time. Wincing from pain in his legs and back, he slowly pushed himself to his feet and staggered back in shock.

The house he had lived in all of his life lay in shambles, leveled like a cardboard box. As he stared in disbelief at the devastation, Nicholas realized he was lucky to be alive. Nothing had been spared. His house and every scrap of furniture in it lay smashed and broken.

"Mom! Dad!" he called, looking frantically about for his parents. Fearing that they were trapped beneath the collapsed building, he tore through the rubble, heaving large boards aside, heedless of the danger from sharp spikes protruding from broken bits of wood. He had to make sure his parents were OK. He called again, but only the echo of his own voice resounded in his ears. For a second, he wondered if he were the only person left alive in the aftermath of the earthquake.

Nicholas worked for a long time, both relieved and worried when he found no signs of his parents. Wearily, he gazed about at his surroundings. He had been right the first time. It was a vast cavern. The boy frowned, confused and puzzled. How had his house ended up here?

Without warning, a series of shrill barks shattered the silence. Nicholas turned toward the sound, his eyes widening in astonishment as a small dog bounded toward him, barking excitedly. It sounded like Muffy, Penelope's miniature poodle, but it couldn't be. Besides, this poodle was as yellow as a buttercup, and the last time he'd seen Muffy she looked like a fresh lime, with legs.

"Muffrat?" said Nicholas, wondering if Penelope dyed her in order to be able to tell her apart from other poodles. In Nicholas's eyes, all poodles looked alike, whereas Labrador Retrievers, like his own Montague, were easily distinguishable from one another.

"Yap! Yap!" barked the yellow dog, whizzing past Nicholas and sniffing through the ruins near where the refrigerator lay on its side, the open door hanging crookedly. Suddenly, the dog's tail wagged furiously. The poodle pounced upon a pound of butter and began attacking the foil wrapper.

"Hey! Drop that!" shouted Nicholas, taking several quick steps toward the animal.

At the threatening tone, The dog turned toward Nicholas. She bared her tiny fangs and snarled ferociously. Nicholas froze. "OK," he said, slowly backing away. "Go ahead. Eat the butter for all I care. I hope you choke."

Satisfied that she had driven the boy away, the yellow poodle sank her teeth into the butter and streaked into the shadows where, to Nicholas's disgust, she wolfed it down foil and all. Suddenly, the boy stiffened, the hair on the back of his neck rising. Someone was watching him.

"Hey! Get away from my dog, you . . ." snapped an angry voice from somewhere behind him.

Nicholas spun around. "Oh, no!" he groaned, watching Penelope St. John march toward him. Then, he realized he was glad to see a familiar face, even Penelope's.

"Penelope! It's me, Nick," he said. "Are you OK? Is anyone with you?"

"Oh! Thank goodness!" cried Penelope. "Nick, is it really you? Where are we? How did you get here?" She looked around. "By the way, where's Muffy? What have you done to her?"

"What do you mean, what have I done to her?" retorted Nicholas. Then he lifted one foot at a time and examined the soles of his running shoes. "She's not there," he said, laughing uproariously.

"You're so childish," hissed Penelope. "MUFFY!"

Nicholas pointed toward one of the giant columns. "She's over there somewhere," he said. "Eating something."

Penelope tried to catch Muffy but, finally, sighing in exasperation, she gave up the chase and rejoined Nicholas among the ruins of his house. "Where are we?"

Nicholas shook his head unable to shrug off the feeling that something was watching them, something nearby. The two friends sat on the edge of the collapsed roof and told each other what they remembered of the earthquake. When they finished, Penelope stood and peered about at the vast stone cavern. "How did we get here? Where is this place?"

Nicholas also stood and looked up. High over his head, hanging from strong poles fixed on massive columns, were dozens of giant flags.

"Look!" he cried, pointing to a flag depicting two sturdy oak trees under a Golden Crown. "Don't ask me how it happened, but I think we're somewhere in Bethany."

Penelope grabbed his arm. "Nick, what's going on?" she asked, her voice low and urgent. "I don't understand how we got here. Do you think something brought us?"

"I don't know," said Nicholas. "Come on, help me find my sword. Then we'll explore and search for a way out of here." He moved purposefully toward the spot where he had been lying when he regained consciousness. "And Penelope," he added, turning back to the girl, "if you find any of my stuff, don't touch it."

"Oh, shut up," said Penelope. "As if I'd want to."

"And don't go wandering off. I don't want to have to look for you."

"Who made you my minder?" snapped Penelope.

The youngsters rooted through the debris that had once been the only home Nicholas had ever known, but they couldn't find the sword. Disappointed, Nicholas looked about, wondering where it could be. His heart jumped when he saw the creature crouching in the shadows. He stopped and waited, hissing at Penelope to be quiet. The creature slipped from the shadows and sidled away, as if it intended to circle them.

Nicholas stared at the thing, the hair on his neck bristling. It was the ugliest creature he had ever seen. *Not human!* he thought, noting the small head and the pair of glassy yellow eyes that returned his stare unwaveringly. It was about his height, with long, sinewy arms that brushed the ground by its sides. Its hands were large; the fingers long and curled. Jagged nails extended from the tips of its fingers and the toes on its bare feet. Nicholas shuddered, suddenly afraid.

If it's by itself, maybe Penelope and I can fight it, he thought, casting about for a weapon.

The creature continued to circle Nicholas and Penelope, moving in the same curious sideways scuttle, its yellow eyes fixed on the boy. Every now and then, it came to a stop and tilted its head as if it were listening for something. Nicholas shot his friend a quick glance. Then the creature whistled and, to his horror, Nicholas heard answering whistles coming from behind and to either side. His hopes of overcoming the creature scattered like ashes in the wind. There were others, lots of them judging from their sounds. He and Penelope were trapped.

Then, some sixth sense made Nicholas look up just as one of the creatures released its hold on the nearest column and dropped. Nicholas leaped aside, his heart ticking louder than a bomb. His attacker landed hard on the section of roof where the boy had been standing a second ago, its weight carrying it clean through the weakened timber. The sickening sound of bones snapping echoed loudly through the cavern. But that didn't stop the creature. It clambered out from among the cracked and splintered beams, wheezing and spitting in rage, and launched itself at the boy.

Nicholas heard Penelope scream, but he couldn't help her now. He grabbed a piece of the wooden banister that had broken away in the earthquake and swung it with all his might at his ugly attacker. The blow caught the thing on the shoulder and knocked it sideways, sending it rolling through the debris. But it was back on its feet in a flash. It crouched on all fours, swaying from side to side as it sized up the boy, sharp, jagged teeth gleaming from behind its hideous smile.

Nicholas was terrified out of his mind. The piece of wood in his sweating hand, already cracked from the collapse of his house, had broken in two when it had collided with the horrible creature. Out of the corner of his eye he saw several figures advancing on Penelope.

"Get away!" screamed the girl, waving a metal refrigerator shelf threateningly, the fear in her voice as palpable as if it were alive. The whistling sounds grew sharper in pitch.

Desperately, Nicholas's eyes sifted through the rubble for another weapon. *Please, let me find the sword*, he begged. He thought he caught a glint of silver near the door that had almost crushed him, but it was too late. The creature was already lunging at him.

Nicholas barely had time to react. He dodged to one side, losing his balance and falling on a loose shingle. Before he could scramble to his feet, the thing was on him, crouching on his chest, sharp toenails tearing through his shirt and into his flesh. Then, he felt strong, moist hands tighten about his throat and begin to squeeze. He kicked and struggled, but he knew the fight was over, and he had lost. As the creature's foul breath filled his nostrils, he looked into the other's face and read his death in the twisted features and cold yellow eyes. The clammy hands about his throat tightened.

"Stop!" hissed a voice that pierced Nicholas's heart like a knife.

Instantly, the hands about his neck went slack. The shrill whistling sounds stopped and a deadly quiet came over the chamber.

"The boy is to be kept alive, for now," hissed the voice.

Several of the creatures appeared out of their hiding places and pulled Nicholas roughly to his feet. Their grips on his arms felt like iron and their jagged nails resumed their attack on his skin. The boy swallowed the bitter taste of failure and looked at Penelope sadly. His friend's head lolled forward as if she were unconscious, as the creatures dragged her across the floor. Almost as if they were acting against his wishes, Nicholas's eyes were drawn to the speaker. Slowly, he turned his head and felt coldness creep into his chest as he recognized the short, stout figure.

It was the Dwarf, Malcolm!

Wrong, he thought. It might look like Malcolm, but he knew that Malcolm was dead. The evil weasel wearing his body was one of the Demon's minions, and its heart was as black as the obsidian egg that it had slithered from. Nicholas had seen that particular creature before. It had filled him with terror then, and it petrified him now.

On a previous adventure, he, Arabella, and Emmet, the Dwarf, had been captured by Bog Trolls and taken to one of their populous cities in the vast Swampgrass. Late one night, Nicholas escaped from his captors and made his slow way toward an isolated shack that was heavily guarded. He managed to elude the Troll guards and enter the building undetected. Inside the one-room structure, he saw a figure asleep on a cot by the far wall. Believing that he had found Miranda's missing father, he crept toward the still form. But, when he touched the captive on the shoulder, he was horrified to discover that it was a Dwarf, and a dead one at that. When the Dwarf's eyes popped open and a black serpent began to emerge from the poor creature's mouth, Nicholas tore out of the shack as if the Demon herself were after him.

Now, as he stared at the body that had once belonged to Malcolm, something within him suddenly snapped, and his heart almost exploded from rage. He despised the creature for its callousness—for the way it stole life from the living and used the remains of human beings for the Demon's obscene purpose. What was wrong with these creatures? Were their hearts made of stone? Didn't they have even the tiniest speck of remorse? Or were they really as emotionally dead as they acted? *Maybe they're the ones we should pity*, he thought, wondering if the creature animating Malcolm's body had ever been given a choice.

Someone's got to stop this monster, he said silently. *And maybe I'm that someone.* He didn't have a plan. He just knew that the Demon's servant had to be destroyed before more people died.

"MURDERER!" he shouted, breaking away from his captors and diving into the rubble where he had glimpsed a shiny object buried under part of the stairs. Grabbing the hilt of his Elven sword and waving it menacingly, Nicholas advanced on the Dwarf that had taken Malcolm's life and his body.

CHAPTER EIGHT

TRICKS AND STONES

iranda let herself drift. Curiously, she wasn't afraid anymore. The cold was gone. Now the water was like a bath on her skin. It cradled her in a warm embrace— urging her to let go, to let it take her where it would.

"Miranda . . ."

She hated that voice. The sound raked along her nerves and set her teeth on edge. *Go away!* Why were people always bothering her? All she needed was a little sleep. Was it too much to ask?

"Miranda . . ." There it was again.

"I SAID GO AWAY!" she snapped angrily, opening her eyes. "What . . .?"

She was astonished to discover that she was sitting bolt upright in a giant canopied bed in a chamber that was larger than her entire house back in Canada. In fact, even the bed was bigger than her room. Her eyes swept the room, taking in everything at once. The walls and ceiling were painted a warm hawthorn yellow. The moulding and baseboards were a rich golden caramel colour. Dozens of paintings of all shapes, sizes, and subjects, hung from thin chains on the yellow walls. Black iron sconces with tall emerald green candles adorned the wall on either side of a white marble fireplace that was decorated with round, glazed, green tiles depicting mythological Elven women. Crystal vases filled with white, pink and gold flowers sparkled on highly polished chests and tables. The wooden floor was covered with thick rugs with brightly coloured designs of fabulous creatures and strange birds. Over eight long windows hung white drapes embroidered with gold birds. It was the most beautiful room Miranda had ever seen. Her eyes finally settled on the figure leaning forward in a deep chair beside the bed. She stared at the figure, blinking in confusion.

"Naim! What are you doing here? Where is here? I'm sorry I yelled at you. Where's Bell? How did we . . .?"

Chuckling softly, Naim, one of the five Druids, reached and took Miranda's hand, sandwiching it between his large hands as gently as if he had trapped a butterfly and feared he might inadvertently crush it.

"I had forgotten your unquenchable appetite for questions," he said in the same brusque voice the girl remembered so well. "But one at a time, if you please."

"First, where am I?" asked Miranda, staring at the Druid, afraid he'd disappear if she blinked or looked away for even a second. She noticed the large gold ring on the middle finger of his right hand. The stone was an oval, the rich, flaming orange colour of lava. Miranda couldn't see it now, but she knew that inside the stone was a tiny Fire Serpent, all black with a blood-red line running along its back. Over the Serpent's head was a ruby-studded crown. It was called the Druid's Stone, the symbol of the Druids.

Switching her glance to the man's face, she thought that there was more white streaking his long black hair now than when she had seen him last. He still wore it tied back against his neck in the Elven manner. Miranda had never thought of Naim as old. But he was old. She saw that now. The deep lines on his face looked as if someone had taken a whittling tool and carved them into his skin. But, beneath a pair of white eyebrows the man's blue-black eyes were clear and intelligent. Miranda tried to imagine what he would look like if she could take away the years. *He has never been young*, she decided, liking his hard, chiseled face just the way it was.

Naim released the girl's hand. "You are a guest in the King's palace," he said, meeting her gaze, studying her as she had studied or memorized his features. Miranda felt that he was peering deep into her mind, reading every thought she'd ever harboured there.

"The King . . .?"

"In Bethany, girl," said Naim, becoming impatient.

"You mean, Elester . . .?"

"It is *King* Elester, now," snapped the Druid, reaching for the long wooden staff. "And to answer your next question—"

"I haven't asked it yet," laughed Miranda.

Naim ignored the interruption. "You and Arabella were fished out of the lake early yesterday morning by none other than *King* Elester." He waved the staff at Miranda for emphasis. "Who, I might add, spent the entire night combing the seas for you at great peril to him and those who joined in the search." Then the old man suddenly smiled. "But I am happy to see you child. You were half-drowned, barely alive, when they found you."

Miranda went as white as a sheet as images of Dilemma's huge, gaping mouth filled her mind. Instinctively, her hand flew to her neck to clutch the small silver pouch. It wasn't there.

"The Bloodstones!" she cried. "They're gone!" She must have lost them in the lake.

Naim reached inside his cloak and rooted through the pockets. Finally, he uttered a gruff, "Aha!" stretched out his arm and opened his large fist. There, nestled in his palm was the precious silver pouch. "The Ministers found it clenched in your hand. The chain was broken but it has been repaired."

Miranda sighed with relief as she unclasped the chain and fastened it about her neck, unaware that the Druid was watching, his expression unreadable. The thought of losing the Bloodstones made Miranda want to throw up. How would she ever survive without them?

"Thank you," she breathed, suddenly remembering the reason she had come to Bethany in the first place. "I'm sorry if I caused a lot of trouble for King Elester and everybody. But, Naim, I had to find you. There isn't anyone else. Nicholas and Penelope are gone . . . and something bad is going to happen in Ottawa . . . and . . ." She felt a lump form in her throat, making it harder for the words to escape.

"Not now," said Naim gently. "Get up and dress yourself. I will instruct the guard outside your door to escort you to the King's apartments when you are ready."

Miranda nodded, afraid that if she spoke now, she'd burst into tears.

Naim used the long wooden staff to push himself to his feet. Miranda's green eyes followed his every move. Standing over seven feet, he was the tallest man she had ever seen. Without a backward glance, he moved toward the door and left the room.

When the door clicked shut behind the Druid, Miranda stacked the four downy pillows behind her and leaned back into their softness. She suddenly noticed that she was wearing a long white night shirt that definitely didn't belong to her. She glanced about for her clothing, but her backpack and the rest of her gear were nowhere in sight. Suddenly, she felt an irresistible urge to get out of bed and do something.

She threw back the covers and peered over the edge of the bed. It was a long drop to the floor. She crawled to the other side and saw a block of wooden steps resting against the bed. She used the steps to reach the floor and then she wandered about the room, looking at the rare prints and paintings, and examining small silver and enamel boxes on tables and chests.

"Wow!" she whispered, opening a pair of doors into another chamber. This was a sitting room. Miranda wanted to spend more time wandering about and running her fingers over the delicate wood furniture, but she moved toward another pair of doors and pulled them open. They led into a wide hall. She grinned sheepishly at the young Elven guard waiting there patiently, and quickly closed the doors. On the opposite wall she saw more doors. These opened onto a small private terrace. She stepped through the doors, tensing as her bare feet met the cold marble floor. Walking to the stone railing, she looked about for a familiar landmark that would help pinpoint her location, but she didn't recognize anything. She wondered where the palace was in relation to the park and the Council Hall that she knew so well.

A mouth-watering aroma drew her to a table, set for one, under a green silk awning. She lifted a silver dome covering a platter on the table and almost fainted from hunger. On the platter was the fluffiest omelet she had ever seen. She lifted up the edge and stuck her finger into the filling. It was sweet and made from fresh sliced strawberries. She perched on one of the comfortable wicker chairs placed about the table and slid the omelet onto her plate, embarrassed that she was drooling, but relieved that she was alone. When had she eaten last? It was so long ago, she couldn't remember. It must have been the bread and sausages with the Dwarves. But it seemed like years ago now. She wondered how long she'd been sleeping. She wolfed down her breakfast in practically one bite, following it with a light frothy beverage in a silver pitcher.

"Ahh!" she sighed, feeling like a princess. She poured a cup of tea, noticing the other cups on the tea tray, and suddenly she thought of Nicholas and Penelope and felt ashamed for enjoying herself.

"You are such a sloth," observed Arabella from the open terrace doors.

Miranda jumped to her feet and spoke with a stuffy accent. "How nice of you to drop by, Arabella. Would you join me in a cup of tea?"

Arabella peered into one of the cups. "I would, but I don't think we'd both fit."

Miranda crossed her arms and frowned at the other girl. "Has anyone ever told you you need to work on your manners?"

"All the time." Arabella sank into a chair and stared at Miranda. "Look at you. You're not even dressed yet."

"Do stop fussing, dear, and tell me what you take in your tea."

"Just milk," said Arabella. "Hurry up and get dressed, Mir. After almost drowning, I don't want to waste a second of the rest of my life. Let's go and look for Nick and Penelope."

"Do you know where we are?" asked Miranda mischievously, carefully pouring milk into the bottom of a cup and then adding hot tea. She set the cup and saucer in front of her friend.

"Some old fleabag castle," laughed Arabella, raising the cup to her lips.

Miranda's hand closed about the Bloodstones. She watched, wearing her most angelic expression, as her friend attempted to take a sip of the warm, steaming brew.

Arabella tilted her head back and back until the cup was practically upside down, but the liquid stayed in the cup. As soon as she started to take the cup away from her lips, the liquid escaped, and trickled down her chin. She tried again with the same result. Then she discovered that in addition to the tea being stuck in the cup, the cup was stuck to her lips. Talking was also extremely difficult. The noise that finally made it out of her throat sounded like "Wah-id-ou-oo? Ake-it-op!"

Miranda struggled to keep a straight face. "I didn't do anything to your tea," she finally giggled, releasing the liquid in Arabella's cup. "It was the Bloodstones, all by themselves. They thought you'd look cute with a cup stuck to your lip. Big improvement."

"That was so not funny," snapped Arabella, grabbing a napkin and wiping her chin and neck. "Look at my shirt. It's ruined."

"Well, you just can't go around calling people sloths, Bell," quipped Miranda, picking up her cup and saucer. "That's not funny either." She started to go inside and then turned back. "We're in King Elester's palace. He's the one who rescued us. Oh, and guess who I saw this morning?"

Arabella shrugged.

"Naim. He was there when I woke up. He's the one who told me about Elester. Naim said we almost drowned. Oh Bell, if it hadn't been for Elester, I don't think I'd be standing here talking to you now."

Arabella exhaled slowly and Miranda saw her shiver despite the warm sunshine. "No kidding," she said. "I get so scared thinking that so far we've been lucky, but one of these times . . ."

For a moment the girls were silent, thinking of how close they had come to drowning, or being eaten by monsters, or killed by the Demon. Miranda knew they'd been lucky so far, but she, too, worried that the odds were now against them. Arabella finally broke the silence.

"Mir, I'm really worried about Nick and Penelope. More than a day has gone by since they disappeared. We've got to do something."

"OK," said Miranda. "I'm going to get dressed."

Miranda left her friend on the terrace and went in search of the bathroom. When she finally found it at the end of a huge walk-in closet, she couldn't believe her eyes. The copper tub stood on brass legs in the middle of the floor before a small sandstone fireplace. Huge, fluffy towels hung from racks beside the fireplace. For a moment, Miranda was tempted to light the logs and luxuriate in a warm bath, but then she remembered that Naim was probably waiting for her in the King's apartments and she turned toward the shower instead.

She couldn't find her own clothes, but in the walk-in closet, she found pants and shirts in her size, and a pair of boots. When she was ready, she fetched Arabella and followed the silent Elven guard down a long passageway lined on both sides with portraits of Elven kings and queens. *It's not really like a palace*, she thought. *The rooms are big, but warm and friendly*. After five or six turns into different hallways, the guard finally stopped before a heavy oak door, knocked once, and pushed it open. Then he stepped aside and directed Miranda and Arabella into the room.

And suddenly the King of the Elves was before them, his strong arms open wide and a big grin plastered on his grim Elven face. For a second, Miranda thought she saw a halo about his head and then she realized it was his golden hair glowing in the sunlight streaming through a window. Arabella hung back, but Miranda ran to him, and burst into tears.

"You are safe now," said Elester gently, releasing Miranda's stranglehold on his neck, and holding her at arm's length. "I swear you have grown two full inches since last we met."

Miranda wiped her eyes. *Why do I always have to cry and ruin everything?* she thought, wanting to run and hide when she noticed a wet spot on the King's shirt where she had pressed her face against his chest. But Elester didn't notice, or if he did, he didn't seem to mind. "I can only imagine how frightened you must have been, having encountered the lake creature once before." Then he stood, clasped Arabella's hand warmly, and motioned the girls to a small sofa at the side of the fireplace where Naim, the Druid, was slumped forward on a small bench, dozing, his long legs stretched out before him.

"We didn't see the creature, Your Majesty," said Arabella. "And anyway, I was more afraid of drowning."

Miranda smiled at Elester. She hadn't wanted to send Bell into hysterics, so she had kept the details of their close shave with

Dilemma to herself. "He didn't bother us this time," she lied, squirming under Elester's hard stare. She knew he didn't believe her.

"I don't understand, though," continued Arabella, "why you don't do something about that horrible creature." She turned to the Druid. "What good is it? Everybody thinks it's nothing but a menace. Surely you could use some magic or something to get rid of it, or turn it into something harmless."

Naim opened one eye and regarded the girl. Then he shook his head, the corners of his mouth lifting in amusement. "Who am I to decide Dilemma's fate—or another's, for that matter? The creature's life is dictated by its nature. Should it cease to exist because its nature conflicts with yours and mine?"

"In this case, I'd say *yes*," said Arabella.

"Arabella," said Elester. "You are right when you say Dilemma is a menace. But the creature may be the very last of its species. I do not know what good it does, or what would happen to the Lake if it were not there. Perhaps its presence in our waters benefits us in some way that we may never know until Dilemma is no longer there."

"You are typical of your race, girl," snapped the Druid. "If you do not like something, or do not understand it, or fear it, your first impulse is to get rid of it."

"Like the Tasmanian Tiger," said Miranda.

The others looked at her questioningly.

"I read this in a book at the public library. This man, I forget his name, lived in Australia. One day he shot this animal without even thinking about it. It was the last female of its species. And there was only one male left. It died in a zoo in Australia in 1936. And now there are no more Tasmanian Tigers. They're extinct."

"That's horrible," said Arabella. "But sometimes it really bugs me that we worry more about animals than humans. Everybody says it's wrong to kill animals, but look at all the people who get killed in wars." She glared at the Druid. "I suppose you think that war makes it OK to kill people?"

"It might surprise you to learn that people are the one thing this poor battered earth can do without, young lady," snapped Naim. "But no, war does not make killing OK, as you put it. Nothing makes it OK."

Elester sighed and, for a second, Miranda thought he looked sad. "Arabella, Naim is right. It is never OK to kill, not even in war, because it changes you. Once you take a life, you cannot give it back. An evil seed sprouts inside you. But, as long as there are people on this earth, they will fight, they will die. My nation goes to war when the evil threatening its very existence cannot be stopped or turned aside by non-violent means. Do not misunderstand me. It is still wrong to kill. But I will order men and women to kill if that is the only way to avoid annihilation." He ran his long fingers through his hair, and looked at Arabella. "It is wrong to kill," he whispered finally.

"Enough!" said Naim. "We can discuss this issue for a thousand years and another thousand after that. But now," and he pointed the staff at Miranda. "Tell us what brought you here."

Miranda leaned forward, sitting on the edge of the sofa. She glanced quickly at Elester. His clear green eyes were focused on the small table in front of the fireplace but Miranda guessed that he was seeing something else far away. She switched her glance to Naim. The old Druid was leaning back, his eyes closed, but she knew he was waiting for her to speak. She took a breath, then slowly, methodically, she told the two men what had happened in Ottawa. She left nothing out. She saw the Druid tense when she got to the part about the voices she heard as she hung over the abyss.

"They're waiting for someone or for something to happen, and then they're going to attack Ottawa," she finished, her eyes seeking the Druid's. "That's why I had to find you."

For a second, the only sound in the room was the faint ticking of a small clock mounted on a finished hardwood block on the wall.

Miranda felt Arabella's eyes on her as she looked from Naim to Elester, waiting for their reactions to her story. Finally the King rose and walked to the window.

"I also heard the voices," he said, without turning his head, his back to the room. "I do not know what they mean, but I heard something more. The voices spoke a name—the name of one who would lead them." He turned to the Druid. "The name they spoke was Calad-Chold."

Naim reacted instantly. He suddenly sat forward on the bench. His eyes shot open in disbelief as his head whipped toward the young Elven King.

"Do you know that name?" asked Elester.

Miranda shook her head, but realized the question had been directed at the Druid.

For a moment, Naim didn't reply. He seemed confused. Finally he inhaled deeply and his dark eyes met the King's.

"Yes," he answered softly, his face as white as chalk. "Yes, I know that name."

CHAPTER NINE

A HEATING
AND A QUENCHING

he room was deathly still. Three pairs of eyes were fastened on the old man sitting on the fire bench. Naim bowed his head and stared at his long, narrow hands resting on his knees. He remained that way for such a long time, Arabella started to fidget, and Miranda wondered if he had forgotten about them. When he finally raised his head and spoke, his voice was so low that the others had to strain to catch the words.

"The name Calad-Chold has not been spoken for thousands of years," he began. "But when the man who bore that name walked the earth, the mere thought of his name created terror in the hearts of seasoned soldiers, compelling them to drop their weapons and flee to hide in the nearest dark corners, like frightened children. Calad-Chold was King of Rhan, a land that is no more."

"What happened to it?" asked Miranda.

"Patience," said Elester. "Let him finish."

"In the early years of his reign, Calad-Chold was a good and fair leader. He ruled the Rhans with reason and compassion. Theirs was already a very advanced civilization when the Dwarves were just beginning to make fire. Education was free and mandatory. Schools and universities flourished. Laws were fair and just. The Rhan legal codes remained models for other civilizations for thousands of years after the fall of the Rhan Empire."

The Druid glanced at Elester and nodded. "Except for Ellesmere, Rhan was the most liberal society in the world—a shining star for other emerging civilizations to gaze upon and emulate—"

"What does emulate mean?" interrupted Miranda without thinking.

"Copy!" barked the Druid, his voice daring her to interrupt again.

"Sorry," whispered Miranda, trying to make herself sink into the sofa.

"Rhan was a rich nation. The source of the country's wealth was in minerals, particularly gold. The histories tell about an Evil that sprang up like thistles, but the nature of the Evil remains unknown. Some historians believed that it was rooted in the yellow gold that sustained the country's economy. They say it created a hunger that nothing could satisfy. And, they compared the hunger to a starving man who eats and eats but grows thinner and thinner, and finally dies of starvation while in the very act of gorging.

"Whatever the source of the Evil, it transformed the country. The outward looking government became closed and self-sealed—and it became incapable of self-criticism and self-correction. In this new closed system, it was easy for Calad-Chold to debauch human values and break down laws that had taken his civilized forebears thousands of years to frame in order to protect themselves against their own destructive fantasies.

"But still the hunger raged. Then, Calad-Chold looked outside his country's borders for the power he craved. He made war against his neighbours, and he brought prisoners back to Rhan and made slaves of them." Naim paused, staring off into space for a second.

"Then the King of the Rhans claimed that he had a vision of a process that would make his army invincible." He paused and looked at Miranda and Arabella. Miranda knew he didn't want to tell them the rest.

"Please," she said. "We're old enough to hear things. I'd rather know everything."

"What he did was so vile that I can barely speak the words," said Naim. "Do you know what makes a sword blade strong?"

Miranda and Arabella exchanged looks and shook their heads. "Nicholas has told us a billion times," laughed Miranda. "But we only pretend we're listening when he talks about his sword."

"Doesn't it have something to do with the way the heated metal is shaped?" asked Arabella.

"Yes, Arabella," said the Druid. "It is called tempering, but it is the process of heating and quenching the metal that strengthens the blade of a sword." He glanced at the young King. "The Elves, whose swords are undoubtedly the finest and strongest anywhere, use water to quench the hot metal."

"Ice water, to be precise," corrected the King. "From a brook in the mountains."

Naim nodded. "Well, ice water would not do for Calad-Chold. Oh no! He quenched the heated metal by driving it into the hearts of living slaves."

"That's sick," cried Miranda, turning as pale as death.

"It is not only sick, child. It is evil," said Naim. "It is what happens when a civilization cuts itself off from others and becomes corrupted. I said before that the Rhans were a wealthy people. In their hunger, they built bigger houses for smaller families, they built more centers of learning but lost judgment. Individually and collectively, they multiplied their possessions while reducing their values. They did larger things, but not better things. And in cleaning their air and water, they polluted their souls." He paused for a moment, shaking his head as if to clear it. "Forgive me. I get carried away when I read about things that should not have happened. Where was I?"

"You said Calad-Chold quenched the swords by killing slaves

so their blood could be used to make the blades stronger." That from Arabella.

"Ah, yes. There was another reason Calad-Chold tempered Rhan steel weapons in the blood of human slaves. He convinced himself, and remember, there was no one to question or criticize him, that a weapon quenched in fluids from the River of Life—human blood, would not only make the blade stronger, it would bridge the incalculable distance between life and death, by absorbing into itself the life force of the slave."

"What does that mean?" asked Miranda.

"I do not know," answered the Druid. "It could mean that Calad-Chold believed that a person killed by one of his weapons could be brought back from the dead."

But, how?" asked Miranda, truly puzzled. "When you die, you die. Even if your spirit comes back . . . I mean what's the point?"

"I think the point has something to do with the voices we heard," said Elester, before shifting his attention back on the Druid.

"When the Rhan army had been outfitted with the new blood-quenched weapons, Calad-Chold looked beyond his borders for an enemy upon whom to test these unstoppable swords. He sought a worthy adversary, a powerful neighbour that he had never been able to conquer. He turned his army toward the Red Mountains and the Giants of Vark."

"Yikes!" cried Arabella. "I've got a bad feeling about this. Nobody said anything about Giants."

Elester laughed. "There are Giants in our world. And a great many other species that did not thrive in your world."

"There are no Giants in our world," said Arabella.

The Druid and the King exchanged knowing looks, but it was Naim whose harsh voice provided the answer. "Your early writings contain untold accounts of Giants. In the book you call a Bible, the Anakim and Rephaim were tribes of Giants. And what about Goliath of Gath? Even your legends are filled with Giants, such as Atlas, Gog and Magog, and Alifanfaron. Children's nursery tales include Jack the Giant Killer. And in your libraries you will discover more recent Giants, such as Eleazer, Gabara, Chang, and your Charlemagne, to name a few."

Arabella bit her lip. How come the Druid knew so much about everything? It bothered her that he should know more about her world than she could know in a zillion years. "I just thought they were stories," she mumbled, feeling very young.

"So did I," said Miranda.

Naim thumped the wooden staff on the floor. "Pay attention now, I have almost reached the end of my tragic tale. The Red Giants were bigger and stronger than the Rhans. When word of Calad-Chold's invasion reached the ears of the Giant Chieftain, the man was mildly irritated, no more. He sent a small contingent of soldiers to deal with the nuisance and send the Rhans fleeing back to their own country with their tails between their legs. But then a messenger arrived with the disturbing news that the soldiers the Chief had sent to frighten the Rhans were dead, slain by magic weapons. The Chieftain scoffed at the notion of magic weapons, but he began to take the Rhan invasion seriously. He made marks on a map and ordered the country's massive army to defend those strategic areas."

Naim raised his head and looked at the two wide-eyed children huddled together on the small sofa. "The Giants couldn't hold against Calad-Chold's weapons. When it became as plain as the big nose on his face that no mode of passive or non-violent resistance could halt Calad-Chold's accelerating program of enslavement and extermination, the Chieftain sent a messenger to the other races begging their help to stop the Rhan menace before the entire race of Giants was eradicated. In his message, he mentioned a powerful weapon."

"When did this war take place?" asked Elester, shaking his head in wonder.

"Long ago," answered the Druid. "Before the Demon began to build her army." He paused for a moment as if he suddenly remembered something important. "But I have always suspected the Demon's hand in the corruption of Rhan."

"Were you there?" asked Miranda.

Naim threw back his head and laughed. "My dear child. The events of which I speak happened tens of thousands of years ago. I am mortal, or did you think I have been around since the dawn of time?"

"No," said Miranda, aware that her face was as red as the inside of a watermelon. "I know that people here live longer than in Ottawa, but I don't know how much longer."

"Well," said Naim shortly. "Rest assured it is not tens of thousands of years longer."

"How old are you, anyway?" asked Arabella, suddenly.

"Oh, oh!" muttered Miranda, gulping and jabbing her elbow into the other girl's ribs. "You shouldn't have asked that."

But the Druid only looked at Arabella and smiled gently. "I am old, child." Then he took a deep breath and exhaled slowly, his shoulders sagging as if they bore the burden of too many years. "Very old," he added, almost in a whisper.

For a moment no one spoke. Miranda stared at the man she had come to think of as a friend. No, she thought. Naim's more than a friend. Not friendly, like a grandfather for example, but safe and true. She would trust him with her life—as indeed she had. The thought that he might die, that she might lose him, filled her with terror a thousand times worse than her fear of losing the Bloodstones.

"How do you know about Calad-Chold?" asked Arabella.

"I read about it," answered Naim shortly. "In a book."

"I read LOTS of books," claimed Arabella. "I've never heard of Calad-Chold."

"Humph!" snorted the Druid, looking as if he'd like to shake the girl until her teeth rattled. "I read about this matter in a journal I discovered in the libraries at The Druid's Close. The journal was written by a slave and is an excellent account of his life in Rhan." Naim's sapphire-blue eyes twinkled. "I doubt that you would have come across this book in your reading, Arabella."

Miranda giggled and kicked her friend.

Arabella took the rebuke in good form. "Well, I do read a lot," she said."

"The other races responded swiftly." Naim continued, turning to the King. "Your people sent a great fighting force and others who might counter the magic mentioned in the Giant Chief's message. All of the races, except Ogres who remained hidden, allied for the first time in history to stop the menace. The Dwarves fought alongside their old enemy, the Simurghs. Trolls stood with Elves. The Dars, northern ancestors of the Red Giants, fought alongside Dragons. Even the Druids went to war. For the first time in our history, all five Druids were away from The Druid's Close at the same time.

"It took three years to defeat the magic and stop the Rhans. Thousands died on both sides. And then, an Elven arrow pierced Calad-Chold's heart and the evil man fell from his horse. His army faltered and began to fall back. But, when the dead man pulled the arrow from his chest and stood, his army went mad. Their King had come back from the dead. He raised his arms for all to see and then he reached for a knife with a twisted blade that he had dropped as he fell from his horse. Before he could grasp it, an Elven soldier snatched it and, without hesitating, plunged it into the wound left by the arrow. This time, when Calad-Chold went down, he did not get up."

"That proves that he was wrong," said Miranda. "He was killed with his own knife and he stayed dead."

Naim shot her a fierce glance. "The blood-quenched weapons were gathered in a great pile and destroyed with Druid Fire. The

King's remains were sealed inside a marble sarcophagus, bound with thick chains, and taken deep inside a natural fissure in the Red Mountains. There, Calad-Chold's body was imprisoned. The Dwarves fashioned great iron doors to seal the fissure and the Red Giants swore an oath to guard the opening into Taboo until their race had vanished from the face of the earth." The Druid stopped, his story told.

It was Miranda who finally broke the heavy silence. "I don't understand why all of those voices I heard are waiting for Calad-Chold. You said yourself that he was killed with his own knife. How can he lead them? Even if what he believed is true. . . that he will come alive again, how is he connected to the voices? I'm sorry, but I just don't understand."

Naim nodded. "Your questions are well thought out," he said. "But there is another part to the story that I have always put aside as pure fantasy, until now." He thought for a minute. "As the knife entered his heart, Calad-Chold was heard to say, 'I only go to rest— to await the summons. When I return, I shall call upon the dead and they will follow where I lead.' Calad-Chold is called the King of the Dead, and I fear that the earthquake and the voices are indications that the King has been summoned."

"Then the voices . . . Do you mean . . .?" Miranda couldn't make herself utter the words.

"Yes, Miranda. What you and Elester heard were voices of the dead, called back by their King and awaiting his orders."

"What if they're already in Canada? What if Calad-Chold told them to attack?" Miranda slid off the sofa and rushed to Naim. "Please! My Mom's there. Tell me what to do. I've got to save the people in Ottawa. They don't know anything about the dead. We've got to go home and help them."

"Forget it Miranda," said Arabella angrily. "From what I've just heard, nothing can stop Calad-Chold. Isn't that right?" She glared at

Naim as if he were responsible for calling the King back from the dead.

"You are still quick to anger," said Naim, dryly. "But, I suspect you are wrong. I believe there *is* something that will stop Calad-Chold."

Elester leaned forward. "Tell us," he said, his voice hard.

"Think," said Naim. "What destroyed him the first time?"

"The knife!" cried Miranda and Arabella with one voice, looking at each other and grinning proudly.

"Not *the* knife," said Naim. *"His* knife—the Twisted Blade he chose for his own, the blade he took in his own hands and drove into the beating heart of a slave, quenching the hot metal in human blood."

"Do you know where we will find this knife?" asked Elester, getting up and pacing back and forth in front of the window.

Naim shook his head, gripping the wooden staff in frustration and getting to his feet. "No," he answered. "Confound it!"

"What are we going to do?" cried Miranda.

Naim rose to his full height. "I may not know its location, but if you will use the Bloodstones to help us see our way, we are going to find the Twisted Blade of Calad-Chold."

CHAPTER TEN

NOT AGAIN!

aving his sword, Nicholas closed the distance separating him from the thing that was Malcolm. He twisted and dodged to escape the hordes of Ogres coming at him from all sides. Some dropped from perches in the walls and hurled themselves at him recklessly. Others kept their eyes on the gleaming Elven blade and shrank away in terror.

"RUN PENELOPE!" he shouted. "RUN!"

Nicholas didn't dare look behind, but from the sudden shouts of surprise he knew that Penelope had heard the warning, and had no intention of going meekly into the great unknown. He was almost on top of Malcolm when an ominous hiss erupted from the Dwarf's throat and fire streaked from its eyes—a bolt of deadly red lightning. The fire struck the sword, wrenching it out of the boy's grasp, and sent it spinning through the air. The force of the blast jolted Nicholas off his feet and launched him backwards where he landed in a heap among the loose timbers of his ruined house.

Pain like a burning light blinded him for a second as he forced himself to his feet. But, he was young and strong, and moving, even as his eyes darted about for the sword. The Ogres were ready for him. They lunged at him and knocked him sprawling again. Others pressed about their companions, forming a tight circle from which there was no escape. Nicholas fought like a wild tiger, punching and kicking until the last of his strength gave out. But, in the end, there were just too many of them and only one of him. It was no contest. When the Ogres hauled him roughly to his feet, he was pleased to see that he had given worse than he had received. Many of the creatures were injured, their ugly faces twisted in pain as they limped, or held gnarled hands over bloodied noses.

But Nicholas's satisfied smile faded abruptly when he took one look at the evil Dwarf waiting for him beyond the circle of Ogres. The monster's face, frozen in a mask of rage, told Nicholas that he was as good as dead.

"Bring him to me," hissed Malcolm, his cold, burning eyes riveted on the boy.

The Ogres dragged Nicholas across the rough stone floor of the cavern and dropped him at the Dwarf's feet. True to their nature, the nasty creatures kicked him in the ribs and on his legs before scuttling back into the shadows.

"GET – UP!" ordered the Dwarf.

Nicholas groaned silently as he struggled to push himself into an upright position. He felt as if every bone in his body was pulverized— run over by a steamroller. He didn't feel at all brave now. In fact, he was terrified half to death. *Don't show fear,* he cautioned. *Don't do anything to provoke him.*

Suddenly, Nicholas was jolted to his feet, as if he were a puppet and an unseen hand had pulled invisible strings attached to his back and shoulders. He looked about wildly, but saw nothing tangible. *Magic!* he thought, gritting his teeth to keep from crying out in pain. He desperately tried to avert his eyes from the horrible, leering Dwarf, but he seemed to have lost control over his movements and he found himself staring into the creature's dead, red eyes.

The malice reflected in their burning depths entered his body and froze him to the bone.

"How does a human boy come to have a filthy Elven sword?"

Nicholas wracked his brain for an answer that wouldn't result in his immediate death. "Elven sword?" he asked, hoping his expression matched the incredulity in his voice. "You mean the sword I found over there?" He moved his arm in a vague arc.

Abruptly, the Dwarf leaned toward the boy, his body swaying back and forth as if it were balanced precariously on stilts. Nicholas flinched, squeezing his eyes shut and raising his arms to protect his face from the red fire that was about to erupt from the creature's eyes. *This is it!* he thought, feeling sweat freeze on his back. He wanted to scream out his rage and helplessness at the thought of dying without being able to lift a finger to save himself. The utter silence told him that the nasty Ogres were holding their breaths, waiting for him to die.

When nothing happened, Nicholas dared open his eyes. At that moment, the Dwarf's clenched fist shot towards the boy's face, stopping an inch from his nose. Then, the creature opened his fist and Nicholas saw the round black object lying in his palm like a deadly black hole, and his heart stopped.

He had already imagined every conceivable way this creature might kill him, but never in his wildest dreams had he considered that his fate would mimic Malcolm's, that he'd end up like the Dwarf—a lifeless shell—a casing for one of the Demon's serpents.

He couldn't take his eyes off the black object in Malcolm's lifeless hand. He had never seen it before, but he knew what it was, and he shuddered at what was waiting inside. It was the last of the eggs Hate's serpent had left behind to do the Demon's evil work. Inside its black obsidian shell was the fifth lethal sibling of the monster wearing Malcolm's body. *I can't let that happen to me*, thought Nicholas. *I won't let it happen.* But he knew he couldn't run even if the Ogres suddenly moved aside and opened a path through their midst. The stark fear that overwhelmed him had already paralyzed his legs.

The Dwarf hissed, pleased at his power to render the boy senseless with terror. For a second, he was tempted to fling the egg at the boy and watch his sibling crack through the hard black shell and strike the pathetic human—claiming both his life and his body. But he chased temptation away. His Mistress had another purpose for the egg and she would not be amused to learn that it had been wasted on a boy who was nothing to her. There was no fun to be had with this creature. The game had become tedious.

"Get this snivelling whelp out of my sight!" hissed Malcolm, dismissing the boy.

Several Ogres grabbed Nicholas and dragged him toward an opening in the cavern wall. Just as they were about to disappear into the dark fissure, Malcolm's voice stopped them in their tracks. The Dwarf's parting words echoed in Nicholas's ears for many years.

"Fool! Little nothing! The egg is for your friend. But you will be kept alive long enough to watch her die—watch as my brother sinks his poisoned fangs into her neck. Her screams will drive you mad. I know, because I killed the Dwarf and took his body. He was still screaming when he died." The serpent hissed and turned to the Ogres. "Keep the little simp alive until we have the girl. Then . . . eat him."

"Oh, no!" sighed Nicholas. "I've got to warn Miranda." And then, as the Ogres whistled gleefully over the prospect of serving him up for dinner, Nicholas suddenly burst out laughing. "Just my luck," he muttered. "Cannibals!"

When she heard Nicholas shout, *Run!* Penelope reacted instantly. She aimed a wicked kick at the knee of the Ogre on her left and sank her teeth into the wrist of the one on her right. Caught off guard, her captors released their hold on her arms and the girl took off like a gazelle, her eyes searching for a way out of the cavern. Ahead, a small yellow blob waited, barking furiously. "Muffs!" she called, picking up speed and racing toward the poodle. As she drew near, Muffy barked again and darted through a narrow passageway in the wall of the cavern. Penelope didn't dare look behind. She ducked into the passage, running full tilt with her eyes glued to the tiny dot streaking through the darkness ahead.

She followed Muffy for an eternity. Just when she thought her lungs would burst, she saw the poodle disappear into brightness in the distance. And then she was outside, bent double, breathing deeply of the biting mid-morning air. Penelope looked about, turning in a slow circle, and almost broke down. Where on earth had they ended up? As far as she could see in every direction were mountains as high as Heaven—their snow-capped peaks painted as red as blood. Muffy, a mere dust mote against the vast soaring heights, barked savagely at the towering rocky monsters.

"We're lost, Muffs," she cried, teeth chattering. "And we're going to freeze to death."

Penelope knew she had to keep moving. The nasty creatures that had captured them were probably getting closer by the second. "We've got to find a place to hide," she said, gazing about.

They were in what appeared to be a giant fortress. Studying her surroundings, Penelope saw an opening where the massive gates has been ripped apart and now hung ruined and broken. "Come on, Muffers," she called, running toward the gates and the huge, square blockhouse that formed part of the wall of the fortress. Just outside the gates she came to an abrupt stop before the bones of a monstrous creature lying on its side on the packed snow. She crept closer, staring in wonder at the gleaming white skeleton.

"It must be a dinosaur," she said, directing the comment at her furry companion, as if the little dog understood every word. Then Muffy caught sight of the carcass and bounced toward the creature.

"NO!" shouted Penelope, forgetting to keep her voice down. "COME HERE."

As usual, the poodle neither listened nor obeyed. She wrapped her jaws about one of the creature's large toe bones and tugged furiously, trying to break it free.

"BAD MUFFY! Drop that!" Penelope stomped toward the bristling animal. "I said STOP!"

Then she scooped up the snarling yellow ball and stuffed her down the front of her thin cotton jacket. For a second, she stared at the white bones and at the blood-soaked snow, trying to assimilate what she was seeing. These weren't the bones of some pre-historic beast. This creature had been alive until very recently.

"What are we going to do?" she cried. Until now, she had thought that once she escaped from the clutches of the fierce, ape-like things in the cavern, and got help to rescue Nicholas, the worst would be over. But the sight of the grisly, giant skeleton made her want to run as fast as her legs would carry her back into the arms of her captors.

"What are we going to do?" she repeated, pulling a tissue from her pocket and wiping her sniffling nose. One thing she knew. She couldn't stay here. Somehow, she had to get help for Nicholas. But where? Where on earth was she going to find help out here in the middle of nowhere? At that moment, she saw movement out of the corner of her eye, a mere shifting of blackness in the shadows along the fortress wall. Dropping abruptly to her knees beside the bones of the slain Carovorare, Penelope squeezed Muffy, squinted to block the glare of sun on snow, and peered into the shadows. She saw the creature. It was one of those from the cavern. Terrified that the thing would spot her through the gaps in the skeleton's ribcage, she looked about for a better hiding place. The only thing she saw that might work was an old rotting wooden barrel, lying on its side in the snow about ten yards behind her.

She glanced back at the shadows, but she couldn't make out the creature's shape in the darkness. Then, slowly and cautiously, she began to crawl backwards toward the overturned barrel. When the sole of her boot bumped against wood, she slithered along the side of the container, praying that it was empty. It was. Quickly, she crawled into the barrel and held her breath, listening for the crunch of the Ogre's feet as they broke through the crusty snow.

She could hear the thing coming closer. *Don't let it look in the barrel!* she pleaded silently. *Don't let it find us!* Now, Muffy picked up the creature's scent and squirmed like an eel inside her jacket. Penelope could barely control the poodle, but she desperately clamped one hand around its muzzle to prevent it from barking. Then the barrel creaked ominously, and shifted position as the Ogre perched on the side of the container. Penelope was frantic with fear, her mind filled with only one thought: *He's going to find us!*

It seemed like forever before the wooden barrel creaked again and slid as the Ogre left its perch. Penelope listened intently. *Go away! Please, go away!* Then, to her horror, the Ogre kicked the barrel and it began to roll, slowly at first and then faster, and faster. Before the girl could react, the container was careening out of control down the steep mountainside.

CHAPTER ELEVEN

STUBBY THE STUMP

aying that he and King Elester had important matters to discuss, the Druid opened the study door and waved Miranda and Arabella out of the room. "Do not stray too far," he cautioned. "We leave for the Druid's Close before this day is out. Be ready and waiting at the stables in one hour." Then he closed the door in their faces.

"I hate when he treats us like little kids," said Arabella, sticking out her tongue at the closed door.

Miranda laughed, her green eyes sparkling with mischief.

"What are you up to?" asked Arabella suspiciously.

"Come on, Bell," urged Miranda, grabbing her friend's arm and tugging. "We've got just enough time to pay a little visit to Stubby."

Now it was Arabella's turn to laugh. "OK," she said. "I'd like to see for myself that the little creep is still where we left him."

The unfortunate Stubby, or Mr. Little, had been the girls' homeroom teacher when they were in grade four at Hopewell Elementary School back home in Ottawa, and the bane of their existence. On a previous adventure, the mean-spirited teacher became obsessed with Miranda's Bloodstones and stole them from her locker. When he lost the Stones, he followed Miranda through a portal into the old world, determined to get them back. It didn't take him long to team up with the wicked Wizard Indolent, and a nation of Trolls in league with the Demon. When the ex-teacher attacked Miranda outside the Council Hall, in order to protect the girl, the Druid turned the nasty fellow into a tree stump, and left him in that condition until they could decide what to do about him.

The girls followed a different Elven guard through the palace until they saw the main entrance in the distance. Then, giggling excitedly, they raced ahead and burst through the doors onto the wide front steps. Pausing on the top step, Miranda peered about at her surroundings.

"Do you know where we're going?" asked Arabella, who didn't recognize a single landmark.

"I think so. The Council Hall should be on the other side of that hill." Miranda pointed to a low hill in the distance off to their left. "If I'm right, we should come in to the park near the side of the Hall."

"Ha!" scoffed her friend. "This I've got to see. You know you get lost in a movie theatre."

"I bet you I'm right," said Miranda.

"No way!"

They set off, jogging across the grass toward the hill. Miranda marveled at the colour of the grass. It was a dark blue-green. But she didn't see any signs of water hoses, or fertilizer, or those little signs warning about chemicals that appeared like miniature grave markers on lawns in her world. She wondered how the Elves managed to make their lawns so perfect. She made a mental note to remind herself to find out before she went home. *Maybe it's something we can do in Canada,* she thought.

As they reached the crest of the hill, Miranda picked up her pace and raced ahead, her eyes searching through gaps in the trees for the Council Hall. Then she stopped and turned to wait for the slower runner. Arabella took one look at her friend's defeated expression and broke out in a wide grin. "Ha!" she shouted. "You lose."

Miranda remained silent until Arabella reached her side and then she pointed through the trees. "Oh, no," groaned Arabella, spotting the familiar building. "It's not fair. You're supposed to be wrong. You're always wrong."

"Not always," grinned Miranda.

"You cheated," accused Arabella, slapping Miranda's hand away, and stomping down the hill toward the park.

Miranda smirked but didn't bother to reply. Her heart beat faster as they approached the Council Hall. Her head was filled with memories of this place—good memories that would sustain her for the rest of her life, and sad memories that still brought an ache to her heart. The Hall, as the Elves called it, was a low, white building with sturdy oak doors. Inside, the King and his chief advisers, the Erudicia, met to discuss matters concerning national security.

Suddenly both girls walked faster, their eyes fixed on the ground to the right of the thick oak doors. They stopped at the spot occupied, until recently, by a large tree stump. Their mouths dropped open and they gaped at each other speechlessly. Miranda found her voice first.

"He's gone!" she cried, anger and disbelief flooding through her.

"Tell me something I don't know," groaned Arabella. "We'd better warn King Elester and the Druid."

Miranda couldn't believe that Stubby was on the loose. She suspected that her former teacher was not only crazy, but dangerous. How had he managed to break Naim's spell? She touched her friend's arm. "We don't know that he's really escaped," she reasoned. "Maybe the Elves locked him up somewhere, or dug him up and moved him. It's been over a year."

Arabella shivered, remembering how Stubby had treated her, slapping her face and yanking her hair practically out by the roots when she and Nicholas had been captured by a band of Trolls and taken to the Swampgrass. "If that's so, why didn't someone tell *us?* Why didn't the Druid say something?"

Miranda squeezed her friend's shoulder. "We'll ask him," she said. "Don't worry, Bell. Stubby won't hurt you ever again."

Arabella grinned weakly. "He doesn't scare me."

Instead of going directly back to the palace, the two friends wandered through the park, uttering loud exclamations of delight when they recognized the solitary wooden bench near a small pond where Miranda had gone whenever she had wanted to be alone.

"And look," cried Bell. "The Portal trees!"

Miranda gazed at the twin oak trees and, for a fraction of a second, was tempted to step through into her own world to satisfy herself that the creatures hidden in the rift were still there. But the thought of the Dwarves pushing her off the cliff, and her body rocketing through the air and plunging into Lake Leanora, only to confront Dilemma again, was too terrifying to contemplate. She turned away from the trees.

They circled the small villa that had been their home-away-from-home on previous visits to the Elven Capital, pressing their noses against the windows and peering into the downstairs rooms. Then, Miranda led Arabella up the steep steps cut into the face of the cliff behind the villa, her heart swelling with pleasure at her friend's reaction to the sight of Bethany spread out below. From where they stood, the city was a vast, green sea of leafy trees, swaying in the breeze, and the blinding white roofs looked like unmoving islands amidst the green.

"I wonder why all the roofs are white?" asked Arabella.

"For water," said Miranda. "They're made from limestone. And see all those grooves. When it rains, the rainwater runs down the grooves into holding tanks under each building, and don't ask me why, but there's a fish in each tank."

"I guess," said Arabella. "But wouldn't it be simpler to dig wells?"

"We don't think . . . I mean the Elves don't think like people in our world, Bell. They think we're wasteful. They can't understand how we've managed to poison most of our water and air and soil in the short time we've lived there. The worst crime here is injuring the planet."

"We are pretty self-destructive," agreed Arabella. "And remember what Naim said about Rhan? I couldn't help but feel that he was really talking about us."

"I know. I felt the same."

"Yikes!" cried Arabella, noticing that the sun was no longer overhead but creeping into the west. "We're late. The Druid's going to kill us."

Twenty minutes later they arrived at the stable, out of breath, their faces flushed and shiny. The doors stood ajar, latched back against the outer wall. Calling "Marigold!" Arabella disappeared inside. Miranda paused in the open doorway, letting her eyes adjust to the soft lighting inside the stable. Her heart warmed when she spotted the Druid's horse. She watched the young male groom patiently combing the stallion's long tail. She looked about and grinned when she recognized Noble, Elester's gray stallion, up to his old trick—nudging the pockets of a young Elven girl for treats. Watching the activity curiously while chomping lazily on clumps of hay was a pair of pale brown horses. Miranda smiled, happy that Thunder and Lightning were contented in their new land. The Druid had *borrowed* the Belgian browns from a stable in Ottawa over a year ago, and brought them on the adventure of their lives. Near the back of the stables, Arabella was perched on a stall door chatting happily to Marigold, a small gray mare. Miranda felt as if she'd burst with happiness as she gazed upon the horses she knew and loved. It was like a party—a meeting among old friends.

Miranda stepped into the stable and walked up to the Druid's great red roan stallion. "Hello Avatar," she said softly, reaching out to stroke the animal's soft nose.

Without warning, the stallion screamed and reared into the air, his forelimbs striking out threateningly. Miranda jumped back, startled and frightened.

"It's OK, Avatar. It's me," she managed in a shaky voice. But the stallion stomped and reared, advancing toward Miranda, his eyes white with fear, or hatred. Suddenly, to her horror, Miranda realized that she had backed into a corner from which there was no escape. The flustered groom pulled on Avatar's reins, trying desperately to protect the girl without injuring the mighty stallion, but he couldn't control the crazed animal.

Within seconds, the entire stable was in an uproar. Alarmed by Avatar's screams, the other horses went berserk, screaming and rearing, striking their forelimbs against the stall gates, and kicking out with their hind limbs. Out of the corner of her eye Miranda saw Arabella disappear into Marigold's stall. The groom's face was as red as a beet as he struggled to settle the Druid's horse down, but he was swept aside as if he were a flea.

And then, miraculously, the Druid was there. Slowly, he came alongside the red stallion, speaking softly to the horse in a language Miranda had never heard before. Avatar's ears twitched in recognition of his Master's voice, but that didn't stop him from rearing and striking out at Miranda again and again. Naim moved in front of the screaming horse, one hand reaching to stroke the animal's neck.

"Walk slowly out of here," he ordered, without changing the tone of his voice. "Go now!"

Miranda was half-paralyzed with fear, but she forced herself to take slow, measured steps out of the corner. She realized that she was screaming as hysterically as the horses, while tears streamed down her face. But she was heartbroken too. What had she done to provoke the huge stallion? She loved the Druid's horse. Avatar had risked his life for her before. Now, he acted as if he were afraid of her, or hated her enough to try to stomp the life out of her. Why?

Miranda moved slowly along the stalls, crouching to hide from the other screaming horses. She caught a glimpse of Elester, one hand gripping Noble's reins, the other gently stroking the terrified animal. The place was in utter chaos and for some strange reason it was all her fault. Gasping and choking on her tears, she ran outside and around the side of the building, wanting only to put as much distance between her and the screaming horses as she could.

"Mir, what happened? Are you OK?" It was Bell, her wiry body as tense as the strings on a violin, her face pinched with worry.

"I-I d-don't k-know," sobbed Miranda. "B-Bell, h-he t-tried t-to k-kill me."

Arabella put her arm about Miranda and pulled her close. "No, no," she said soothingly. "Something scared him. The whole stable went mad. One minute they were OK, and the next minute everything went crazy."

"Yeah," said Miranda, sniffing loudly. "Everything was OK until I walked in." She noticed that the screams had died down. The stable was quiet again. For a second, she almost believed that she had imagined the whole nightmarish scene. Then she realized that Bell was speaking to her.

"I don't know why they'd be scared of you," mused Arabella. "Did you do anything to weird them out?"

"No," said Miranda. "What do you think?"

"Mir, I'm not accusing you of anything. I know you'd never scare the horses on purpose, but maybe you did something without meaning to."

"I did nothing," insisted Miranda, feeling anger rise up like a wall inside her. "Nothing."

"Tell me exactly what happened," said the Druid, dropping onto one knee and gently placing his hands on Miranda's trembling shoulders.

Miranda was in such a state she almost giggled, thinking how the Druid was calming her in much the same way he had calmed Avatar.

"Nothing happened," she said. "Bell went in the stable, but I stopped in the doorway. I didn't do anything. Honest! I could never do anything to the horses. I just wanted to watch Avatar getting his tail combed and I was wondering if he'd remember me after all this time. Then I walked over to him, and he . . . and he . . ." She couldn't finish.

"It is all right," said Naim gently. "I know you would never harm or frighten Avatar." He gave her shoulders a gentle squeeze and stood up. "But something happened—something that I do not understand. And I am worried. So we must talk about it, and try to understand what happened. But, first, I want you to come back inside with me."

Miranda backed away, her eyes frightened, the blood draining from her face. "No," she said, shaking her head furiously. "I can't. Don't ask. I can't."

"You must, child," pressed Naim.

"Come on, Mir," said Arabella. "He's right. You've got to go back in the stable, or you'll always be scared. Come. I'll go with you."

"No, Arabella," said Naim. "I will take care of this." He patted the tough little girl's shoulder. "You are indeed brave, but no match for a stable of frightened horses." Seeing that the girl was about to argue, he held up one hand. "I promise you that I will keep her safe. I have ways of controlling the horses that you do not."

Arabella nodded. *He's right*, she thought. *He's got magic.*

Reluctantly, Miranda allowed herself to be led back to the open stable doors. Naim whistled softly. Avatar's ears twitched as his head pivoted toward the sound. Then the proud animal trotted toward his Master. Miranda, half hidden behind the Druid's long cloak, stared at the powerful creature, her eyes dark with fear. How could she ever have thought that horses were tame, gentle beings?

Had she really believed such a thing? Avatar was neither tame nor gentle. He wasn't human. He did not think or rationalize like a human. He reacted according to instincts developed over millennia.

"You do not have to be afraid now," said the Druid.

Breathing rapidly, Miranda stretched out her hand and touched the horse's warm, silky head. For a second, Avatar stared at the girl as if he were seeing her for the first time. Then he whickered softly and pushed his head against her small hand. Miranda looked into the animal's black eyes and, suddenly, her head was filled with words in the same strange language Naim had used earlier. Without knowing how, she knew the words were real and they were meant for her. Surprisingly, she understood the language as if she had always known it. And, as she gazed into Avatar's dark eyes, she knew the words were coming from the horse. Avatar was speaking in her mind, and what he said brought tears to her eyes. *It was not you,* he said. *It was never you. There was another standing in your place, blocking you.*

Miranda blinked back her tears and pressed her forehead against Avatar's nose. "Thank you," she whispered. Then she turned to Naim, her eyes round with wonder. "He spoke to me," she said. "He told me what happened."

The Druid chuckled. "Hmmm! Well! Now that you have recovered from your fright, perhaps we can set out." He started to turn away but Miranda clutched his sleeve.

"Naim, I'm not making a joke or lying. Avatar really spoke to me."

"Miranda . . ." The big man sighed. "Very well. What did my horse say to you?"

"He said 'It was not you. It was never you. There was another standing in your place, blocking you.'"

For a moment, the Druid was speechless. He looked at the horse as if he expected the creature to confirm what the girl had said, but Avatar merely swished his tail and stomped his hooves on the hard earthen floor, anxious to be away.

"You don't believe me," said Miranda. "But it's the truth."

"I believe you," said Naim, his voice soft but his face hard. "There is magic here," he said. "I do not know what it means. But I recognize magic. It is not the Demon's magic. No, this is a different rendering—almost as if something, some presence left here or was taken away." He shook he head. "Confound it! I do not understand what is going on."

Miranda felt goose-bumps form on her arms. "How could something leave and I didn't see it. Naim, I didn't see anyone. Even the Bloodstones were still." Miranda shivered as she reached out and touched the Druid's hand. "Naim, I'm scared. What's going to happen to me next?"

CHAPTER TWELVE

HUNTERS
AND HUNTED

"re we there yet?" asked Miranda, leaning sideways and peering around the Druid.

Naim chuckled. "I will repeat what I said five minutes ago. You will know when we are there."

Three nights ago, two ships slipped silently out of Bethany Harbour like ghosts in the night. The first to lift anchor carried messengers sent by the King of the Elves to warn the Dwarves, the River Trolls, the Giants of Vark and other races of the awakening of the King of the Dead. Another group had orders to scour the mainland for the human boy, Nicholas, and the girl, Penelope. The second boat carried the small group accompanying the Druid on his quest to find the Twisted Blade of Calad-Chold, and included the two Ottawa girls, Elester and his chief aide, Andrew Furth, and a dozen dour Elven Riders. The small company debarked on the mainland north of Ellesmere Island an hour before dawn. They set out on horseback almost immediately and travelled until nightfall with only brief stops to rest and water the horses. This morning the company broke camp in the darkness and had already covered many miles by early afternoon.

Miranda wanted to ride with Arabella on Marigold, but she was too tired to argue when the Druid vetoed that suggestion, insisting that he could protect her better if she rode behind him on Avatar. She was unusually quiet, her thoughts jumbled. Much as she wanted to see the Druid's Close, where Naim lived with the other Druids and Pledges, she was sick with worry over Nicholas and Penelope, anxious about the voices of the dead in the rift in Ottawa, and scared to death by the thought of the hateful magic that had enraged the horses. Miranda was also feeling young and unimportant, partly because she was the only member of the company who wasn't an accomplished rider, and partly because she was afraid that she wouldn't be able to help Naim find the Twisted Blade.

As the day wore on, she couldn't shake the feeling that they weren't alone. She sensed that they were being tracked, hunted by something moving in the shadows of the tall evergreens that flanked the dirt road. Her eyes kept darting from one side of the trail to the other, but she saw nothing. Still the feeling stayed with her, curling around her and cutting her off from her companions like an impenetrable wall.

"Naim?" she asked after a while. "How come the Bloodstones worked in Ottawa when I couldn't get them to work before."

"I do not know," answered Naim. "I cannot imagine why they did not work before, unless *you* are different in your own world. Remember, it is easier to believe in magic here, because it is more evident. But in your world, people do not believe, and perhaps that belief inhibits *your* use of the Stones."

"Hmm," mumbled Miranda, digesting the Druid's words. "I don't think so. When it happened, I thought it must be the rift that made them work."

"If it opened into this world," said Naim. "You may be right."

"I know the Demon's magic works in my world. Does yours?"

"I have no reason to believe it would not," answered the Druid. "My magic, as you call it, is nothing more than the measure of my self-confidence."

Miranda sighed. She had no idea what he was talking about. How could you make fire explode out of a wooden staff just by being confident? As usual, the Druid made it sound easy, but she knew it wasn't.

"What did Avatar mean when he said that someone was standing in my place?"

"I do not know," answered the Druid. "But, since you are the only one who claims to be able to talk with my horse, ask him what he meant. Perhaps he will tell you."

"Perhaps I will," snapped Miranda, sarcastically.

"Listen, Miranda," said the Druid after a while. "I know you are afraid. I wish I could tell you what happened back in the stable, but I cannot. As I said before, I sensed magic, but whose I do not know.

"The Demon!" breathed Miranda, her voice barely above a whisper.

"I told you it was not the Demon," said Naim. "At first, I thought it might be Indolent—"

Miranda felt knots form in her stomach. She knew the Wizard Indolent. He had once been a Druid Pledge but was booted out for breaking the Druid Code by carrying out forbidden experiments. Naim had once said that Indolent used magic to gain power and, like Calad-Chold, the nasty Wizard craved power.

"What does Indolent want with me?" she asked.

"What he has always wanted," answered the Druid dryly. "The Bloodstones."

"But why? You said yourself they're useless to him."

"That is true, but no one knows what the Bloodstones can do and that makes them afraid. But they know beyond a doubt that they are useless if you are dead."

"Do you mean that if I were to die, the Bloodstones would die too?"

The Druid thought for a second before answering. "Yes," he said finally.

How can stones be alive? wondered Miranda, reaching for the silver pouch about her neck and pouring the Bloodstones into her hand. She stared at them for a long time, almost as if she were waiting for a sign, an infinitesimal pulse beat, anything to show that the six green ovals were living organisms. She held them for several miles before pouring them back in their pouch.

"I guess bad people and other creatures are always going to try to get the Bloodstones," she said.

"As long as you possess them, Child, there will be those who want to take them from you or stop you from using them."

"I could give them to you," said Miranda, but she knew she could never part with the Bloodstones.

"You could," agree Naim, chuckling softly. "For whatever good it would do. The Bloodstones belong to you. Sooner or later, they would find their way to you."

Miranda fell silent again, lost in her own dark thoughts. Arabella guided Marigold alongside and tried to break through the wall her friend had built about herself. But when Miranda didn't respond, the other girl shrugged sadly and rode beside Avatar in silence.

It was still an hour before sunset when Elester pointed to an opening in the trees and steered Noble in that direction. The King had noticed Miranda's dark mood and decided that what they all needed were a good long rest, a warm meal, and for the girls, some friendly horse therapy. A short distance through the forest, the track opened into a glade beside a small stream. Elester dismounted and directed the Riders to make camp for the night. Then, leading Noble, he strode to the Druid's horse and caught Miranda as she slid to the ground. Arabella was already standing beside the small gray mare, holding the reins loosely in her hand.

"Come with me, Miranda. You, too, Arabella," said Elester, taking

Avatar's reins from the Druid. "We have work to do."

The girls followed him eagerly, knowing what was coming. All about, Riders were busy setting up tents for the King, the Druid, and the two girls. Miranda wondered why they bothered with tents for Elester and Naim. From long habit, the men preferred to sleep under the stars. Miranda thought they felt safer in the open than in the confines of the tents. A short distance from the tents, another Rider had dug a fire pit and was holding a torch to a log pyramid. Nearby, his companions were setting out supplies for the evening meal.

They tethered the horses to stakes driven into the ground and removed the tack. Then, they gathered around Andrew Furth as he dug into a saddlebag and tossed thick, cotton cloths to them. Miranda gently rubbed Avatar's sides until the horse's damp hair was dry and his coat shone like satin. Then she brushed him slowly, chatting softly. As she worked, the darkness she had wrapped about her like a fortress lightened and, for the first time in days, she felt calm and relaxed. She kept clear of the stallion's powerful limbs though—the events in the stable still too fresh in her mind. *Talk to me, Avatar,* she thought, but when the big horse merely whickered contentedly, she began to believe that she had imagined the terrifying sight of Avatar looming over her, his powerful forelimbs poised to strike her dead. Chasing the image away, she gave the horse a gentle pat and moved toward Arabella.

Her friend looked up, questioningly, when she felt Miranda's hand on her arm.

"Bell, I'm sorry about today."

"Sorry about what?"

"I guess for being distant. I couldn't stop thinking about everything that's happened."

"You don't have to be sorry," said Bell. "I felt like that too."

"OK" said Miranda, grinning. "Come on. Let's ask Elester about Stubby."

Miranda rolled her eyes skyward. "I totally forgot."

The two girls went to King Elester and announced in unison. "Stubby's gone!"

"Enlighten me," laughed Elester, who obviously had no idea what the children were talking about. "Who or what is Stubby?"

"You know," said the Druid, from behind the girls. "The little stump fellow." Then he was before them, looming like a great black vulture. "Of course he is gone," he snorted. "Or did you think I would turn the man into a stump and leave him in that state forever?"

"Why not?" said Arabella. And, "Sort of," mumbled Miranda, realizing even as she spoke that she had known in her heart that Naim would let him go. When the man didn't respond, she asked. "Where is he now?"

"How do I know? The Elves offered him a place to stay, and work if he wanted it. He chose neither to stay nor to work, opting instead to take the first boat off the Island."

Miranda and Arabella exchanged quick glances but remained silent. They didn't like the idea of Stubby running around free one bit.

After a hearty meal, the girls helped rinse the tin bowls and mugs in the stream. Then they settled cross-legged in the grass by the fire, burning the ends of long sticks and whispering about Stubby. Elester and the Druid were seated on a thick log a short distance away, locked in conversation.

When Miranda looked up and caught the Druid staring at her, she couldn't help giggling. Arabella finally said *goodnight* and disappeared inside the tent she shared with Miranda.

Naim shook his head, amazed that the youngsters could lose themselves in laughter after all that they had been through. He had noticed the wall of silence Miranda had built brick by brick around herself since the incident in the stable with the horses. *She is afraid*, he thought, wondering what he could have done differently to shield her from knowing so much about evil. But how do you protect a person from knowledge? Was that not a worse evil? What if he had never gone to her world to find her? The answer to that was easy. The child would now be dead. And the Demon would be free—ravaging the lands and slaughtering all living things that defied her. Had he told Miranda more than she needed to know, burdening her small shoulders with cares that were beyond her understanding?

The old Druid sighed heavily. In his long battle against the forces of Evil, he believed that it was lack of knowledge—ignorance and half-truths—that often led one down the path toward darkness. He still believed that. *But she is just a child*, he thought sadly. *And I do not wish to be the one responsible for making her cynical beyond her years and old before her time.*

Miranda felt the Druid's eyes on her. She smiled, thinking that he looked sadder than usual. She wondered why. *He's probably thinking I'm going to freak out or something,* she thought. She wasn't a bit tired. Sometimes she wished she were more like Bell, who was usually asleep before her head hit the pillow. But, except on rare occasions, sleep never came easily to Miranda. She remained by the fire, poking the stick into the sizzling, hissing logs, sending sparks flying into the air—tiny flaming beings that burst into bright life for an instant and then faded into ashes.

She was far away, wandering among her own thoughts when she felt the touch on her shoulder. "Come sit with us," invited Elester, reaching for her hand.

Miranda threw her stick in the fire and walked beside the tall Elf to where the Druid sat on the dead log, his back against a tree, his long legs stretched out before him. Elester released her hand as she dropped lightly to the ground at Naim's feet. She glanced from the old man to the King.

"We are discussing the Bloodstones," said Elester. "Since they belong to you, you should be privy to our conversation."

108

Miranda nodded and looked at him questioningly. *Privy?*

"The Druid thinks the Bloodstones may be able to help us locate the Twisted Blade," he said.

"I know he said that in Bethany," said Miranda. "But how?"

Naim leaned toward the girl. "The Bloodstones are older than time in this world," he explained. "Elester tells me they were brought by the first Elves who journeyed to earth from Empyrean. They were here when Calad-Chold forged the evil swords of Rhan and made war on the Giants." He paused, his piercing blue-black eyes looking at Miranda as if to satisfy himself that she was paying attention.

"I'm listening." She hoped he noticed the sarcasm in her voice. Then, to show him that she really was listening, she added. "What does their age have to do with finding the Twisted Blade? I mean, why is that important."

The Druid made an impatient gesture with his hand. "I have not finished," he snapped. "From things you have said, the Bloodstones retain memories of those who possessed them." He glared at her. "Is that not what you said?"

"I don't remember that," answered Miranda.

"Listen then. I am hoping that your ancestor, the one who possessed the Stones during the siege of Vark, was among the Elves sent to stand with the Giants against Calad-Chold."

Miranda stared at the old man, both shocked and intrigued by his words. "You mean . . . are you saying that the Bloodstones might have been there and seen what happened?"

"Yes, Miranda," answered Naim softly. "That is exactly what I am saying."

Concealed in the shadows of the thick evergreens, the creature that tracked the company honed its long claws on the rough bark of the nearest tree. The razor-sharp nails sliced through the hard bark as smoothly as a knife slicing through whipped cream. The Thug glared at the Elven girl sitting on the grass near the evil Druid and the despised King of the Elves. In the blackness of its loose hood, the creature's red eyes burned with hatred. The girl was so small he could wrap one hand about her slender frame and crush every bone in her body. How could something so fragile be the major source of his Mistress's pain and suffering?

The wicked child should have died the night he found her in that dreary other world. She should have died a dozen times since then. He wanted to kill her now, but Hate the Demon wanted the girl alive.

Bring her to the Dwarf, she had commanded. *Alive!*

The heartless creature didn't know why his Mistress had changed her mind, and he didn't care. If she wanted the girl alive now, he'd let her live. Later, when she wanted her dead, he'd kill her. It wasn't his job to question the Demon's orders. He was Her servant, Her favourite, despite what the stupid Dwarf might think. He was the one Hate sent to do the unspeakable when the lesser, witless ones failed.

The Thug tilted his head and focused on the night sky. It was almost time to carry out the Demon's orders. In a few minutes he would snatch the girl and the precious Bloodstones.

The fire had died. Elester spread his cloak on the damp ground and settled down to sleep. The Druid, his back resting against the trunk of a large tree, pulled his hood over his head and was soon snoring loudly. But Miranda didn't want to turn in. Ever since Naim had suggested that the Bloodstones might retain the memories of those who had possessed them, she had felt restless and excited at the same time. Could it be true? Were the memories of all the Elves who had ever owned the Bloodstones stored somewhere inside them? The idea was so incredible she could hardly grasp it. Because, if she could read the memories of the Elf who had fought at the siege of Vark and find the Twisted Blade, then she could also read the thoughts of her father and find out what had happened to him. With trembling fingers, she poured the six oval Stones into her hand. Then, she closed her eyes and waited for the familiar tugging sensation to reach her. When nothing happened, she shifted them into her other hand and waited, but the Stones remained cold and unresponsive.

Neither Miranda nor the Riders patrolling the perimeter of the camp had any warning when the attack came. As if a thick, black blanket had suddenly been thrown across the sky, the stars disappeared, and a sound like that made by a tall building falling shattered the heavy silence. The horrible crashing sound brought Miranda to her feet. Certain that the entire sky was about to land on her head, she looked up and saw thousands of pairs of flaming dots growing bigger by the second—like hot red sparks from an enormous fire.

"NAIM!" she screamed, as a host of Werecurs dropped into the clearing, landing awkwardly and struggling to stand upright.

The Druid and the King were already on their feet, moving swiftly toward the attackers. Elester's sword gleamed like frozen crystal and his face was hard as stone. Naim's hand was wrapped so tightly about the long wooden staff his knuckles were as white as marble. "Get behind me!" he shouted at Miranda without missing a stride. Then he came to an abrupt stop and glared at the Demon's Hunters, his dark eyes travelling from one to another.

"GO BACK!" he roared, his face twisted in revulsion at the creatures that had once been human. But that was before the Demon found them, not that they were hard to find, and claimed them, and drained away the last vestiges of their humanity.

The Werecurs screeched with rage and flapped their wings aggressively. Those in the front ranks closest to the Druid bared their sharp fangs and ran at him, snarling like maddened dogs, stopping a few feet from the man, snapping and slashing, and then streaking back to join their own ranks. Naim didn't move a muscle.

He remained as still as a rock as the terrible deformed creatures came at him again and again, the pale wooden staff gripped firmly in his steady, outstretched hand.

The malformed creatures terrified Miranda and sickened her. But they also made her sad. Even knowing that they had given themselves to Hate, had willingly chosen evil over good, she couldn't help feeling sorry for them. *Why is it so much harder to be good?* she wondered, wishing that she could go to Naim now and put the question to him. But, one look at the Druid standing like a strong black door against the winged monsters told her that many days would pass before she and he had a chance to talk again. Out of the corner of her eye, Miranda saw Arabella peer out of the tent and then quickly duck back inside.

The Riders, except for two who ran to saddle the horses, gathered about their King, their sharp Elven swords unsheathed, their cold green eyes locked on the demonic red-eyed killers.

"Move back slowly," said Naim. "They cannot outrun the horses in the forest." Then he took a step toward the winged attackers. "I SAID GO NOW, OR YOU WILL DIE IN THIS PLACE!"

The Druid waited, giving the creatures a chance to flee. But the scent of the humans, the scent they once possessed and lost, stuck in their throats and drove them mad. Shrieking with rage they surged toward the man in the black cloak and the small group of Elves. White sparks exploded from the tip of the wooden staff. Like a display of fireworks, the sparks shot up and out bursting into thousands of smaller sparks that flared brilliantly before splattering on the attackers as molten silver rain. The winged aberrations screeched in pain as the burning drops ate into their flesh, their twisted limbs turned on themselves, clawing at the source of the pain and tearing out bits of their own bodies.

Elester, with the riders less than a step behind, took advantage of the confusion caused by the Druid's magic and charged the front line of the Werecur advance, swords slashing with deadly accuracy. Creatures fell, and instantly disappeared—trampled under the feet of fellow Werecurs pushing from behind. In a flash, the King and his guards retreated farther into the trees before turning to face the enemy again.

Naim glanced toward the King. "When I give the signal, ride from here as fast as you can. Head north. I will meet you at Fand, the old wall."

Miranda frantically scoured the ground for a weapon, finally snatching a heavy branch that had fallen from one of trees. She staggered under its weight and then dropped it, knowing it was no use, knowing that she was powerless against the red-eyed Hunters.

The Druid pounded the staff on the ground, and moved his arm from left to right across the wall of Werecurs. Abruptly, white fire surged from the staff, slamming into the creatures and incinerating them to small mounds of black ashes in seconds. Again, Elester and the Riders struck, downing three creatures before retreating still farther into the forest.

"TO THE HORSES!" shouted Naim, creating a wall of fire to halt the rabid Werecurs. "RUN!" he repeated, whistling for Avatar as he turned and streaked through the trees. Ahead, he saw the small shape of Arabella leap onto Marigold's back and disappear into the darkness. "WHERE IS MIRANDA?" he shouted, grabbing Avatar's reins and looking about wildly. Urging the others to flee, he and Elester searched for the girl, calling her name repeatedly, until the wall of fire weakened and the Werecurs streamed through the dying flames and entered the forest. Then the Druid and the King wheeled their mounts away from their attackers and rode like the wind through the night, their hearts heavy, their thoughts identical. *What happened to Miranda?*

CHAPTER THIRTEEN

ON THE RUN

iranda watched the wave of Werecurs surge toward the Druid and the small group of Riders flanking their King—swords gleaming in their steady hands. *There are too many of them*, she thought, fear squeezing her heart. She picked up a heavy branch, but dropped it almost immediately. Then she looked about for a place to hide. Behind, in the forest, away from the nightmare creatures, she could just make out a small rise and the shape of a tree whose growth had been stunted by a large boulder. She made her way up the rise and crouched between the tree and the rock.

From her elevated hiding place, Miranda could see the red dots of the enemy's eyes. The creatures filled the clearing and circled in the air above the camp. *They are too many*, she thought again. *We're all alone. We can't fight so many.* Rising from deep within like a waterspout gushing to the surface came a certainty that left her cold.

We are going to die here. The realization left her numb with terror. That she would die tonight in a place whose name she didn't even know was too much to bear. They wouldn't get a chance to find the Twisted Blade. Calad-Chold's dead army would destroy the Elves, and then the magic sealing the Place with No Name would vanish like fog in the sun. Hate the Demon and her evil followers would storm across the earth leaving in their wake blackened lands where nothing would grow for a thousand years, and the ruined and broken bodies of those who challenged them. In Ottawa, the millions of dead beings waiting in the abyss would teem from the hole, their ranks swelling as they ravaged Miranda's home, and her world. Her mother and the hundreds and thousands of people who lived there didn't stand a chance against creatures that couldn't be stopped.

But the worst thing of all was the thought of her mother, and Naim, and Elester joining the dead and turning on others. No! No! She mustn't think of that.

Naim had been right when he said that as long as she possessed the Bloodstones, evil people and other beings would hunt her to the ends of the earth to stop her from using them.

What were the Bloodstones? Could they think? Or feel? Were they alive in a way that was beyond her understanding? What could they do? Miranda searched her mind for a clue to their awesome powers. She had used the Bloodstones to alter another's sight—to create illusion, like the time she made Penelope appear in the guise of a monstrous dragon to scare the vicious Simurghs. Another time she had changed herself, so that when the Demon looked at her she saw her worst nightmare—a mirror image of herself, only much, much worse. She had used them to bring herself back from the brink of death, cleansing her body of lethal toxins after a gigantic Fire Serpent had driven its poisoned fangs deep into her shoulder. Once, she had even used them to travel outside her body, and create imaginary creatures to save Nicholas and a company of Dwarves from the Werecurs. Was it possible that the creatures she created weren't illusory at all, but real? And, if so, what else were the

Bloodstones capable of? Could they unleash fire like the Druid's staff? Could she turn the Bloodstones against the monsters out there and really hurt them? Maybe even make them die?

The thought that she might possess something so powerful that nothing could stand against it filled Miranda with horror. *It can't be true*, she thought. *It's not true!* The Bloodstones were Elven magic. They couldn't be powerful enough to kill. That would make the Elves no better than Calad-Chold.

"Stop!" she scolded. "You don't know anything about the Bloodstones. So just stop!"

Miranda turned her mind back to the scene unfolding in the clearing. The Druid raised his staff, forming a wall of white fire to stop the attackers. But the sight of the humans drove the Werecurs mad. They launched themselves at the flames, setting their combustible, oily hides on fire. They disappeared in a heartbeat. But others broke through the fiery wall behind their burning companions. The creatures' screams filled the night and the smell of burning flesh filled Miranda's throat, making her gag involuntarily. She watched as more and more creatures broke through the Druid's wall. She cried out as one of the Riders disappeared in a cloud of sharp claws and pointed fangs.

"I have to help," she whispered, her hand reaching for the Bloodstones.

Abandoning her hiding place, Miranda started down the hill, moving swiftly toward the battle, her eyes fixed on the black shape of the Druid. She had taken only a few steps when she felt a blast of cold air on her face. Then, she heard a sound nearby, a sound so faint that she almost ignored it. Pausing, she strained to pinpoint the sound, her eyes peering into the darker shadows between her and her companions. Exhaling slowly, she was just about to move on when something huge detached itself from the blackness and came toward her purposefully, its red eyes burning like torches. *A Thug!*

Miranda opened her mouth to call out for help, but closed it abruptly. Even if Naim and the others managed to hear her over the shrieking and screaming, what could they do? They had enough to worry about. No, she wouldn't call. She had to deal with the Demon's assassin on her own. She hadn't realized that she had been clutching the silver pouch so tightly until the chain snapped and the pouch came free in her hand. "Help me!" she said, staring at the trees hovering like giants over the Thug. She saw their strong branches reach for the half-dead creature. But, when she blinked, the Thug was less than a dozen feet away; the trees as unmoving as a painted forest.

With growing panic, Miranda begged the magic Stones to do something before it was too late. But the six oval gems felt cold through the fine silver threads of the little Elven pouch. The sensation of being drawn into the smooth pebbles was absent. Despair washed over Miranda, only to be replaced by anger as hot as the Druid's fire. Something was wrong. The Bloodstones had abandoned her. They were going to let her die. *Why? Why?* She formed a tight fist over the pouch and raised her arm at the Thug. "Is this what you want?" she screamed, taking several steps deeper into the forest as the monster hesitated. "You want the Bloodstones? Take them!" And she threw the shiny pouch at the creature and backed away.

"Miranda! Run!" Marigold burst from the trees ahead, thundering toward Miranda. "Quick! Get on!" Arabella slowed. Pressing her knees into the mare's side for balance, she reached for Miranda's arms, dragging her friend along beside the horse until she managed to scramble onto Marigold's back. "I don't know where the others went," cried Arabella. "But Naim said to ride north until we come to an old wall. They'll meet up with us there." Then, she flicked the reins and Marigold shot forward, leaving the Thug and the Bloodstones behind.

The gray mare was small, but she had a big heart. Sensing the girls' fear, she streaked through the forest like a brisk wind, dodging trees and leaping over half-buried roots effortlessly. The mare's nostrils flared as the reek of the winged creatures dissipated and was replaced by the familiar, non-threatening scents of pine and forest moss.

Arabella kept her head down to avoid being knocked off the horse by overhanging branches. She instinctively tried to lean forward and press her body flat against the horse's neck, but her movements were restricted by Miranda's presence behind her. And besides, her friend's thin arms were wrapped about her like a belt that was buckled too tightly.

Eyes squeezed shut, Miranda pressed her face into Arabella's back. So far, she hadn't spoken a single word. Her failure to evoke the power of the Bloodstones preyed on her mind. What had she done to alienate the Bloodstones, to make them turn away from her? As they fled through the night, the same question repeated itself over and over in her mind. Why had the Stones betrayed her? But the darkness brought no answer.

"We've got to stop. Marigold needs a rest," shouted Arabella, easing the mare to a halt.

The gray's breathing was laboured and her coat was wet and glistening with sweat. The girls walked ahead, leading the exhausted animal. They stumbled over the uneven ground, tripped on hidden stumps, and twisted their ankles in deep holes. Miranda marvelled at the mare's ability to navigate the perilous forest floor in the darkness without faltering.

Suddenly she tensed and peered back over her shoulder.

"What?" hissed Arabella, pinching the other girl's arm until Miranda winced.

"Shhh!" she cautioned, prying Arabella's fingers loose. "There's something back there."

"What?" pressed Arabella.

"Be quiet! Listen!"

The girls waited, motionless, watching and listening.

"Let's get out of here," whispered Arabella.

"Bell!" Miranda's voice broke with terror as she saw the Thug moving swiftly toward them like a black stain on her eyes. How had the creature caught up to them so quickly?

She turned to Arabella. "Listen to me. Take Marigold and go now."

Arabella looked at the huge black shape coming steadily closer, and planted her hands on her hips, her face wearing the stubborn expression her friends knew only too well. "I'm not leaving you." Her words were brave, but her voice was high and weak with fear.

It was too late anyway. The Werecurs dropped through the trees, screeching, and reaching out for the girls with long, misshapen claws. Arabella dropped Marigold's reins and grabbed Miranda's arm. "Run!" she hissed.

Miranda was running even before the warning left Arabella's throat, sprinting beside the gray mare whose eyes were wide and frightened. The winged Hunters furled their fleshy wings loosely against their bodies and tore after the fleeing girls. But they couldn't move as swiftly through the thick trees. Their wings, fashioned by the Demon from their own flesh, torn and stretched, and then grafted onto their arms and sides and legs, caught on branches, slowing the creatures and driving them into an enraged frenzy.

The Thug hissed at the inept Hunters, wearing his scorn for the stupid, screeching creatures like a badge. How he hated them and their ugly, discordant voices. The Demon should have silenced them—ripped their tongues out of their throats and shredded their vocal chords with her long sharp talons. He'd gladly do it for her if they failed again.

Thoughts of his Mistress tugged at the brute's black heart. It had been over a year since he had basked in her presence. But that was about to change. Calad-Chold, the King of the Dead, was on the move, amassing his Black Army of all the dead since the beginning of time. The pitiful Elves couldn't begin to comprehend what the ignoble Dwarf had unleashed against them. By the time they figured it out, it would be too late. They'd all be dead, joined with Calad-Chold against the filthy Dwarves and the bumbling Giants.

The Thug absentmindedly massaged a tattoo on his forearm—a hideous skull. The Demon had sliced pockets under his skin and fashioned the skull from slivers of pure gold that she slid into the pockets. The golden skull was the Demon's mark, and her means of communicating with her servants. The monster froze. From her dark, empty prison, Hate spoke to him now. Her voice in his head sent him reeling as if he were intoxicated.

Soon! she hissed. *I am coming to you soon. Get the girl. Do not fail me, my own creation.*

The creature's chest swelled with pleasure. His red eyes swept the trees for the Elven girl. He didn't expect to find her here. But that didn't worry him. She and the other one were running for their lives. Well, they could run, but they couldn't hide—not from him. Before this night was over, they'd wish they'd never been born.

CHAPTER FOURTEEN

FUR AND FEATHERS

egar sharpened his beak with a vengeance on Otavite's scalp.

"Quit that!" hissed the giant, reaching up and grabbing the bird in his huge fist. It would take only a second to squeeze the life out of the miserable, blood-sucking barnacle, he thought. But the giantpecker must have read the soldier's mind because it opened its beak and emitted a barrage of pathetic squawks, telling anyone within earshot that it was being murdered. The cacophonous outburst prompted soldiers nearby to turn and stare at the comical pair. To Otavite's chagrin, his companions chuckled and nudged one another.

"That Eegar," they said, meaningfully.

"Got another headache?" they said, laughing hysterically at the joke.

Otavite grinned sheepishly and slowly released the bird, who immediately went back to using his head as a whetstone. *Headache is right*, he thought. *More like a constant migraine.* Determined to ignore his tormentor, the young Giant squared his massive shoulders and continued the long march up the steep trail.

Armed with long knives and sharp swords, Otavite was leading a company of two hundred Giants in an assault on the Bronks. His orders were clear: *Secure the fortress.* Behind the soldiers, their great lion paws making no sound as they padded over the snow-packed trail, came six white Carovorari, tails curled proudly over their backs, the deadly spike poised like an arrow in a strung bow.

A day and a half had passed since Otavite and his surviving comrades escaped from the evil Dwarf-serpent and the Ogres inside the hidden chamber deep within the Bronks. Halfway down the mountain, they had come upon the Carovorari that had fled when the deadly magic fire struck down the veteran, Ve. Otavite knew that it wasn't fear that had caused the guards to flee. Carovorari were not afraid of anything, living or dead. In fact, the notion of fear was unknown to them. What the Giant had read in their silent, expressive faces told him that they understood that they would have died if they had stayed and defended the Fortress against such potent magic. They ran away in order to stay alive to perform their jobs when the evil creatures were gone.

When the survivors had finally reached Erog-gore, Otavite assigned several of his fellows to accompany the special furry guards to the stables while he and the others reported to headquarters. The Sou-Chief, commander of the National Mountain Patrol, had ordered the soldiers to stand easy while he turned his attention on Otavite.

Silently vowing to pluck every last feather from Eegar's body if the bird so much as twitched, Otavite took a slow, deep breath and gave his report in a strong, clear voice. He left out nothing and his voice only broke when he described what had happened to Ve and the mesmerized soldiers who had been fed to the dark pool in the secret chamber. As if it were aware of the dire nature of Otavite's report, Eegar behaved like a real soldier, perched at attention on the Giant's head like a wooden sculpture.

When the young Giant had finished, the commander looked to

the others to confirm Otavite's report, but they could only shake their heads, their memories as blank as a clean blackboard. They did not know how they had ended up in the chamber where the black pool glistened like oil. They knew nothing of the rising of the King of the Dead. They only remembered two things: Otavite shouting at them, and running.

Before the day was out, Otavite had delivered his gruesome report at least a dozen times to the various Sou-Chiefs of different branches of the military. And then he was summoned before the Haut-Chieftain, elected ruler of Vark. The Chieftain had listened, without interrupting, to the young soldier's story but, when Otavite mentioned the name Calad-Chold, the old Giant's gray flesh had gone as white as the fleece on a young lamb and the coarse red hairs on his chest and arms stood straight out like the stiff bristles on a brush. Then, like a parent who has just learned of the death of a beloved child, the Vark leader had stumbled, dazed, from the room, his face as grim as death.

Otavite had thought, or hoped, that once he reached Vark, he would get answers to the countless questions that whirled about in his head like Eegar stirring in his hair. But, instead of answers, he had been ordered to report to his unit. He and the others had left the Chieftain's lodge in the early evening, their shoulders sagging in disappointment and frustration.

"This stinks," he muttered. His companions growled their agreement, but otherwise said nothing.

As they had made their way through the familiar streets of Erog-gore in the direction of the NMP barracks, Otavite realized that while he still had a billion unanswered questions buzzing in his head, he was relieved to know that his superiors had believed his story unquestioningly and responded immediately. The city was teeming with soldiers. It appeared that the country's entire military had been put on alert.

Now, as Otavite and the others climbed the steep mountain trail, he saw, again, the tall, ghastly form of Calad-Chold rise from the opaque pool like a fell commander, and an icy wind, that wasn't coming from the mountain, curled about him. Who was this King of the Dead? he wondered. And what had the Dwarf-snake meant when he said 'Amass your armies'? What armies?

Suddenly a loud roar erupted from behind, drowning out the sound of giant boots crunching on the hard snow and scattering Otavite's thoughts to the wind. The Carovorari's fur bristled into sharp spikes, turning the gigantic beasts into creatures twice their size. Otavite was just in the act of spinning around when something slammed into his chest, forcing the air from his lungs. It smashed apart on impact and lifted him clean off his feet. Stunned, the Giant toppled over backwards like a human bowling pin.

Eegar let out a loud squawk and shot like a bullet toward the nearest safe perch—a towering rock pile, the only evidence left of an ancient rockslide. Confusion swept through the ranks as the soldiers bolted to either side of the trail and crouched among boulders, or dropped onto their stomachs in the snow. Otavite felt as if the missile had gone clean through him and immediately thought of the blast that had torn a hole through Ve's chest. "I'm either dead, or dying," he mumbled, feeling sad that he had to break his promise to avenge Ve's death. He tried to lift his arms but a small voice coming from the general vicinity of his chest stopped him cold.

"We made it! We're alive . . . I think."

Otavite sat bolt upright, forgetting about his bruised breastbone and the fact that he was in the act of dying. He noticed broken bits of wood lying on the snow beside him.

"Yikes!" cried the voice as the Giant's sudden movement sent it tumbling into the snow.

The soldier's mouth dropped open in wonder at the sight of the creature staring at him as if he were some sort of monster. His comrades crept from cover and shambled closer to take a look at the strange being. When he first glimpsed the curly red hair, he thought it was a Giant runt.

"Who are you?" asked Otavite. When a small, yellow, furry head poked through the little creature's jacket, he changed it to, "What are you?"

"It's got two heads!" whispered another Giant in disbelief.

"Don't be stupid," snapped the voice. "Haven't you ever seen a dog before?"

The Giants shrugged and exchanged puzzled glances. Penelope stood up, brushing the snow off her clothes as she glared at the huge monsters. "If you dare come any closer, I'll turn her loose on you. And," she added, "don't even think of eating us or you'll be sorry. You'll die, because where I come from, people are poisonous."

The sound of rumbling laughter told her these gigantic beings weren't afraid of her or Muffy.

"Where do you come from?" asked Otavite, unable to tear his eyes off the amazing creature. It was so small he wondered how it had survived hurtling into him.

For a second, Penelope almost blurted out the truth, but then she wondered if that would be wise considering she didn't know anything about these daunting strangers.

"Where are you from?" repeated the Giant.

"Ellesmere Island," said Penelope, her brain working furiously to create a plausible story.

"You're an Elf?" Otavite was astounded. He had never been to their land but he knew about Elves. In fact, he had met one once and had never forgotten the tall, golden-haired creature. The girl before him looked nothing like that Elf, or the one in the cavern, or like the pictures of Elves in books he had read. For one thing, her hair was as orange as carrots. This must be a child Elf, he thought.

"Well, duh!" said Penelope. "Correct."

"What are you doing here?" asked Otavite, realizing that the child's rude behaviour was a cover for her fear. This Elf girl was terrified out of her mind.

"First, tell me what you're going to do to us."

Otavite pretended to think for a second. "You don't have to be afraid," he said, and then grinned. "We've already eaten."

Some of the Giants laughed, but not unkindly.

A sound from above, a whirr of feathered wings, made Penelope look up. A red blur hurtled toward her. She screamed, throwing one hand up protectively while shielding Muffy's head with the other.

"EEGAR!" Otavite's yell rang in Penelope's ears.

At that moment, Muffy wriggled out of the girl's jacket, sprang to the ground, and sped in a circle under the approaching menace, snarling savagely. Then, bird and poodle collided in a crash of yellow fur and red feathers. Penelope and the forest of Giants were too stupefied to react. They watched as Muffy and Eegar tumbled over and over on the snow-covered ground like a lumpy red and yellow snowball, snarls and squawks filling the air.

"Muffy!" To the dismay of the Giants, the tiny human burst into tears and raced toward the rolling ball of fur and feathers. But, Otavite reached down and, after sustaining several bites on one hand and a dozen pecks on the other, managed to separate the kill-crazy pair.

Penelope scooped Muffy out of the Giant's huge grasp and cradled the snarling poodle in her arms. "Poor little Muffers," she sobbed. "Did that bad bird hurt you?"

"It's Eegar," said Otavite, shaking his finger free of Eegar's beak and running his large hand gently over the squawking bird's wings. Then, to Penelope's surprise, he set the bird on his head where it punished him for ruining its sport by jabbing his scalp viciously.

"Keep the dog in your jacket," cautioned the Giant, pointing at something on the trail behind the soldiers.

Penelope hadn't noticed the Carovorari until now. She took one look at the monstrous, bristling beasts and almost fainted. "Help! Murder! Do something!" She hastily stuffed Muffy inside her jacket and pulled up the zipper.

"They will not hurt you if we vouch for you," said Otavite. "But they eat small animals and they might accidentally eat your dog." Then he sat on his heels before the girl. "Now tell me what you're doing here?"

Penelope sighed, her eyes pinned on the mammoth white things who returned her stare from cold, shark-like eyes. *What have I gotten myself into this time?* she wondered silently. She didn't know what to make of the giant creatures and their strange, horrifying beasts. So far, they hadn't eaten her or tried to harm her. They were alarming, but it didn't follow that they were evil. Perhaps she should tell them everything—how she ended up here, wherever here was? Would they believe her? Probably not. *Even I wouldn't believe me*, she thought. She imagined the looks of disbelief on their faces when she told them she came from another world. Finally she blew air through her cheeks and began.

"My cousin, Elester, the King of Ellesmere, sent me on a secret mission to Dunmorrow, the land of the Dwarves. I can't tell you about the mission, but on the way, we were attacked by a band of vicious creatures that looked like . . . toads." She paused for a second to test the reaction to her story. *So far, so good!*

"Anyway, these ugly toad things killed all my guards . . . about a hundred of them . . . but they took me and my frien . . . uh . . . servant with them. They knocked us out and tied us up and when we came to, we were inside that mountain." She pointed toward the Bronks. "Nicholas . . . uh . . . that's my servant, and I escaped. But then this horrible Dwarf appeared and the toads caught Nick and me. But I fought them, actually I barely escaped with my life there were so many of them, but I got away. Then I hid in a barrel but one of the toads kicked the barrel down the mountain." She shrugged.

"That's it. But those slimy little toads captured Nick and I need you to please help me rescue him."

"Ogres," corrected Otavite. "Not toads."

"Whatever!" snapped Penelope. Then, "Really? Real Ogres? Eeuw! They're disgusting! I hate them. Well, are you going to help me or not?"

"You say that you are related to the King of the Elves?" asked Otavite, his face a study in disbelief.

"It's true!" cried Penelope, eyes flashing defiantly. "I'm not lying. King Elester is my first cousin. That makes me a Princess. And, if you don't believe me, just ask me anything. His father's name was Ruthar. King Ruthar died last year at the Battle of Dundurum. I was there."

Otavite shook his massive head. The story this child told was so incredible, he had to take a moment to swallow it. He absentmindedly ran his fingers through his coarse hair, jostling Eegar, who poked his head up and tried to lop off the tips of the Giant's fingers in his sharp beak. Otavite snatched his hands out of his hair as if he'd been burned, cursing the giantpecker until the air turned blue. Penelope stuck her fingers in her ears to drown out the words. When the other Giants smothered their laughter and things finally settled down, Otavite turned back to Penelope.

"Princess, if the Dwarf-snake has got hold of your servant, he will feed him to the black pool."

"What black pool?"

"The pool that took my friends," answered the giant.

"I didn't see any pool," said Penelope. "Just this huge chamber with giant pillars and huge flags. Oh, and by the way, it's not a Dwarf-snake. Its name is Malcolm."

Otavite breathed through his teeth and exchanged quick glances with some of his comrades. Penelope fidgeted nervously as the Giants turned suspicion-filled eyes on her. "How do you know its name?" asked Otavite. His voice wasn't as friendly as before.

"I know because I've seen it before."

"Where?"

"On Ellesmere Island . . . I mean, at home."

"What was the Dwarf Malcolm doing in your country?" asked Otavite. "And how do you know so much about it? Is it a friend to the Elves, Princess?"

"Of course not," snapped Penelope impatiently, glaring at the Giant as if he were dim-witted. "My cousin told me that Malcolm the Dwarf was doing some stonework in . . . Bethany. But the snake belongs to the Demon. It came to Bethany and killed Malcolm and took over his body."

More looks were exchanged among the Giants. Then Otavite turned back to Penelope. "Princess, what do you know about the other creature, the one calling itself the King of the Dead?" he asked.

"You can call me Penelope. And to answer your question, I know nothing about any King of the Dead. I told you I only saw Malcolm and the Ogres."

"Wait here," said the Giant. He walked over to his comrades, singling out one of the soldiers who had survived the evil Dwarf. "The Elf child's story changes everything. I don't know whether I believe *everything* she said, but she was definitely inside Taboo. She knew about the Dwarf-snake. If the Demon is involved in what happened at the Bronks, we must notify headquarters immediately. Take one of the men and return to Vark. Tell them Hate is responsible for what happened in Taboo." Then he turned to his men. "Let us go and drive the evil from our mountains and free the Princess's servant."

"If he's still alive," said one of the Giants, his expression showing that he believed Nicholas was dead.

"Ahem!" coughed Penelope from behind. "Can we go now?"

They set out at once. Penelope found herself running flat out to keep up with the Giants' long strides. Even then, she fell farther and farther behind. Finally, Otavite backtracked and, with one mighty hand, picked her up and gently deposited her on his shoulder as if she weighed no more than a bubble.

"What are you?" she asked, keeping a sharp eye on Eegar's wicked beak pointed in her direction.

"My name is Otavite," he said. "I'm a Giant."

"Oh." *Gulp.* "What country is this?"

"Vark," answered the Giant. "The most beautiful country in the world."

Penelope didn't agree, but she wasn't about to argue with the Giant. He seemed nice enough, but she decided she'd be wise to keep her mouth shut. Who knows what he'd do if she made him angry. For all she knew, he might seem nice and then suddenly turn demented if you looked at him the wrong way.

By the time they spotted the watchtower, it was late afternoon. The company of Giants fanned out in a half-circle and approached the fortress cautiously, tightening their ranks as they advanced. They kept a sharp lookout for signs of Ogres and worse. Otavite's blood ran cold at the thought of coming up against the Dwarf-snake the human girl called Malcolm, or the black-clad Druid and his killing claws. Converging just outside the fortress walls, the soldiers stared in shock at the broken timbers and twisted iron fastenings—all that remained of the massive gates.

"Wait until I get my hands on the enemy that did this," muttered one of the Giants, and from the expression on his face, Penelope wouldn't want to be in Malcolm's boots when they caught up with him. Then, a shout nearby drove the evil Dwarf from her mind. The company had spotted the gleaming white skeleton lying on its side on the bloody snow. As one, the soldiers bowed their heads in sorrow. Penelope felt tears come to her eyes as the huge, rough soldiers towered over their dead comrade, their lips moving silently as they bade farewell to the veteran Ve.

Inside the Fortress, there were no signs of occupation. But this was Otavite's first command and he wasn't going to take any chances. He dispatched a large number of soldiers to scour the fortress and eliminate the enemy. "But don't hurt the Elf boy," he cautioned. Then he marched toward the gaping black hole where a pair of iron doors had once sealed the entrance to Taboo. So far, the only evidence that something evil had passed this way were the iron puddle, the smashed gates, and the sad white skeleton. Posting guards outside the opening, Otavite picked up a long length of iron and led the company along the fissure, deep into the Bronks. This time, he made sure that they had torches to light their way.

To the Giant's relief, the concealed door was open. Taking no chances, he jammed the iron bar into the space between the sliding panel and the stone wall, effectively disabling the concealed panel. Then, he and the others passed through the opening into the huge oval chamber. Pausing just inside the doorway, he set Penelope on the ground, and tilted his head, listening with his giant ears, but he heard nothing. At his signal, the company spread out and began to search the side passageways and smaller chambers.

Oh, oh! thought Penelope, catching sight of the ruined building toward the other end of the oval chamber. *How am I going to explain that?*

"What's that?" said Otavite, moving swiftly toward the pile of bricks and timber. "Where did that come from?" He turned and looked down at Penelope. "Do you know how that got here?"

Penelope shrugged. "How would I know? I certainly didn't notice it when I was here."

When they reached the ruins, Otavite stared at the wreckage, dumbfounded. His brain told him that what he was looking at couldn't have happened. The placement of the bricks and timbers told him that this shattered house hadn't been carried here. It had fallen and collapsed. But from where had it fallen? The Giant stared up, but the roof of the cavern wasn't visible. It couldn't have come through the mountain, because the only entrance into the Bronks was through Taboo. Otavite shook his head, puzzling over the mystery. Nothing was as it should be, he thought, unsure whether that was good or bad. "I don't understand," he whispered.

"You're not the only one," said Penelope.

They searched everywhere. And then they searched again. But, the evil ones were gone, vanished as mysteriously as they had appeared. And they had taken the girl's servant boy with them.

CHAPTER FIFTEEN

BIRDS OF A FEATHER

icholas stumbled, falling to his knees on the rough track. His limbs were bruised and sore and he was physically and emotionally exhausted. If his friends could see him now, they would have been shocked at his appearance. He was almost unrecognizable. His eyes, sunk behind black circles in his thin face, had the wild feral look seen in pictures of prisoners of war. His clothes were torn and hung loosely on his lean frame, and he probably would have traded his precious Elven sword for a crust of mouldy bread. As soon as he retrieved it from the belt of the mean-tempered, foul-smelling Ogre, he called Ka-Ka, holding one end of the rough cord that bound his wrists.

They had been on the move for close to a week with only brief stops. It seemed to Nicholas that whenever he collapsed on the ground and closed his eyes for a minute, a vicious kick jolted him back to his feet and he was moving like a zombie again. He still had no idea where he was or where he was being taken. His eyes scanned the countryside for a familiar landmark, anything, that would help him identify his location, but he saw nothing that struck a chord in his memory. One look at his strange captors told him with absolute certainty that he was no longer in his world.

As the days passed, the boy began to dread the moment the Ogres arrived at their destination. Malcolm's parting words still echoed in his mind. *Eat him!* "They're going to have to get me in the pot first," he muttered. And then a horrible thought struck him. What if they ate their food raw? What if they ate him alive? He knew nothing about these creatures. Whenever they stopped to rest and relieve their thirst, they fed him something that tasted like cold oatmeal that they squeezed into his mouth from a leather pouch. But what was it? He hadn't seen his captors eating anything, but he noticed several of the creatures always slipped away from camp and all the others formed a circle about them when they returned. Had they been hunting? Had they consumed their fresh game gathered in the tight circle? Nicholas didn't know. *I don't want to know,* he thought, chasing images of dining Ogres from his mind.

The curious red-tipped mountains were behind them now. The track they had been following wound in a westerly direction among the rocky outcrops dotting the foothills. Ahead, the stark landscape faded, giving way to rolling grassy hills. The sky was clear, except for a dark thundercloud in the distance. The hairless, ape-like Ogres used their gangly arms to propel their bodies into a loping gait over the track. They set a grueling pace, communicating with one another by strange whistling/wheezing sounds, and kept their eyes peeled on the land about.

The nasty Ka-ka yanked on the rope, knocking Nicholas off his knees. The boy collapsed on his face on the ground. Ogres on either side grabbed his arms and pulled him roughly to his feet. Nicholas could hardly stand. His wrists were chaffed and bleeding, but he felt an almost uncontrollable rage growing inside him. Fighting down his anger, he gritted his teeth and forced his legs to move one step at a time.

He was young and strong, and he managed to keep going. Often, his thoughts wandered far away and he forgot about being captured for a few minutes. He wondered if his friends thought he was dead, or if his parents were OK. And he hoped that Miranda and others were looking for him. He knew that if he had seen her disappear into the black chasm, he would move heaven and earth to find her and bring her home. At times like these, he trailed behind, but a sharp tug on the rope about his wrists scattered his thoughts like clouds on a windy day and jolted him back to reality.

One evening, several hours before sunset, Nicholas's captors suddenly slowed and turned off the track onto a worn footpath that dropped steeply downhill. Shortly, they entered a narrow defile between and below the hills. The dark thunderhead was closer now, almost overhead. They were heading straight into a coming storm, but the creatures didn't appear to notice, or if they did, they weren't worried. On either side, along the hilltops, Nicholas saw more of the strange creatures—guards—clenching long poles with sharp blades affixed to one end, like makeshift spears. Abruptly the defile widened into a small circular valley. Probably a crater, Nicholas thought, caused by an asteroid impacting with the earth at some time in the past.

He scanned the area, his face registering first shock and then disgust at what had been done to the land. It resembled a battlefield; the sight of thousands of gigantic trees lying on the ground told him that the forest that had occupied this valley until very recently had lost the battle. Not one single tree had been spared. Like ants teeming over sugar cubes, countless hundreds of Ogres crawled over the felled trees, hacking off limbs with sharp axes, or carrying the huge trunks to stack on piles in cradles formed by thick poles driven into the ground. As he watched the creatures scaling the log pile with a massive tree trunk balanced on their shoulders, one of the poles securing the pile snapped, starting a chain reaction. In less than a heartbeat, it seemed to Nicholas that the logs leaped at the Ogres, and then they were tumbling and rolling over the doomed creatures as if they were avenging the slaughter of their own.

In seconds, dozens of the creatures disappeared into and under the thundering avalanche. Ogres approaching the log piles saw the giant trees pounding toward them and panicked. Whistling shrilly, they dropped their heavy burdens and scattered. Others scampered onto adjacent log piles and stared at the spot where their companions had been standing a moment before. Then they went about their business as if nothing had happened.

Nicholas turned away, pale and sick. Meeting the glance of one of his captors who had witnessed the deaths of so many of his fellows, he shook his head to express sympathy over the fate of the lost Ogres, but the creature only bared its sharp teeth and snarled viciously.

Looking up, Nicholas noticed that the black cloud was directly overhead, obscuring the terrible valley from the rest of the world. It reminded him of the Demon's billowing cloak, and something else that he couldn't quite put his finger on. The once tranquil valley was a desolate abomination—a sinkhole clogged with foul matter, over which no birds flew.

Ka-ka led him around the perimeter of the valley toward a huge building under construction. Like a living assembly line, Ogres, their backs bent almost double under the weight of heavy stone blocks, appeared out of a gigantic quarry, trudged toward the building site, deposited their burdens, straightened their backs, and disappeared back into the gaping, smoking pit. Nicholas stopped breathing and turned as white as a ghost when he recognized the huge, pasty creatures posted here and there along the Ogres' route, long eelskin whips clutched in their lumpy hands. *Bog Trolls!*

Run! Hide! Get away! The warning filled his head. Nicholas reacted instantly, digging his feet into the dirt and jerking the rope out of Ka-ka's hands. Then he turned and ran back toward the path through the narrow defile. Before he had covered a dozen feet, he heard a sharp crack followed by a stinging sensation on his back near his left shoulder. He knew, without looking around, that one of the Trolls had taken a slice out of his flesh with his whip. Still he ran. But the loping Ogres were faster. The loose rope suddenly went taut, jolting Nicholas onto his side on the ground as several creatures tackled him, knocking the air from his lungs, and kicking and punching his body until he almost passed out.

"I'm starting to get upset," mumbled Nicholas through gritted teeth, as the creatures grabbed his arms and dragged him toward a dilapidated shelter set up near the partially constructed building. He struggled to his feet and roughly pushed the nasty creatures away. Wrapping his arms about his sides, he limped slowly after Ka-ka and the others. He could feel his shirt sticking to the blood from the whip slash on his shoulder, but he couldn't think about that now. He had to find out more about this place before he was locked away to rot in a dark dungeon somewhere.

Perhaps it was the sight of the garbage littering the cleared space outside the shelter, or the sour smell that filled his throat. But whatever it was, a strong feeling of *deja vu* washed over him; something about the place triggered the feeling that he had been here before.

"That's impossible," he said, unaware that he had spoken aloud. Feeling increasingly uneasy, he slowed and peered about, spotting more Bog Trolls wielding long nasty whips. What were Trolls doing here, away from the Swamp? It didn't take a genius to see that they controlled the Ogres. But what was their purpose? What evil mischief were Malcolm and the Trolls planning in the name of the Demon?

Ka-ka yanked on the rope, almost knocking the boy off his feet again. Nicholas winced and limped faster. It was dark inside the shelter, but he could just make out the shape of a man hunched over a black box on a desk or table in the middle of the room. The uneasy feeling grew stronger as the distance between him and the shelter lessened. When they reached the opening, Ka-ka shoved Nicholas inside and went over to the hunched figure, waiting patiently for the man to acknowledge his presence. He removed Nicholas's sword and laid it on the crude makeshift worktable, a flat door-sized length of wood balanced on two square blocks of stone.

When the Wizard Indolent raised his head and glared at the boy, Nicholas wasn't really surprised. Deep inside, he had known all along, even before he was struck by the acute feeling of having been here in the past. But it wasn't the place he recognized. It was the deplorable state, the filth and litter, that spoke of Indolent.

"Well, well! What have we here?" The wicked Wizard's mouth twisted into a hideous smile as his eyes travelled over the boy.

Nicholas's eyes were glued to the table and the contents of the black box. He was fascinated and repulsed at the same time. Crawling out of the box were dozens of giant, hairy, bluish-black spiders. They looked suspiciously like tarantulas. Some had gemstones or cut crystals embedded in their backs. Then, he noticed the pile of gems on the table and beside it the miniature blood-encrusted surgical scalpel. With a shock, he suddenly realized what the Wizard had been working on so intently as he sat hunched over the table. Nicholas couldn't believe his eyes. What sort of person would cut away the flesh of insects and set jewels into the cavities? *Only a depraved, insane monster*, he thought, anger turning his pale blue eyes dark cobalt as he shifted his glance from the spiders to the Wizard.

Determined not to look into Indolent's jaundiced eyes, Nicholas stared at his nose, his mouth turning down at the unsightly blackheads clustered about the man's hairy nostrils like tar freckles. Without warning, the wizard's hand whipped out and struck the boy a resounding blow on the side of his head that sent him reeling. Eyes stinging from the pain, Nicholas fought an impulse to spit in the repulsive creature's face. He wiped all expression from his face, cautioning himself to watch his step around this unpredictable man.

At this moment, he was free and the only chance he had of getting out of here alive was to remain that way. But, to do that, he must be extremely careful not to incur the Wizard's wrath, or he'd end up hopping about in a toad's skin or with gems surgically implanted in *his* flesh.

Nicholas would never forget how he had suffered when the treacherous Muffy had led him into Indolent's trap. It seemed like a lifetime ago, but in reality the incident had happened just over a year ago. Then, the Wizard had beaten him with magic and broken his arm. If it hadn't been for Miranda and his other friends, he'd probably still be shut away in the cockroach-infested Castle of Indolence, or dead. No, this time he had to be smart. Like a light bulb going on in his head, he suddenly knew what he had to do. He must swallow his anger and hide his disgust and do everything in his power to win the Wizard's trust.

His eyes were drawn to a tattoo on the Wizard's forearm as the man rolled up the sleeves of his filthy robe. It was shaped like a skull. Nicholas recognized the Demon's mark and, for a second, he suddenly felt small and powerless. Who was he to think that he could outwit Indolent? The man was wicked, the mark was enough to tell him that, but he wasn't stupid. What had he been thinking? What did he have that the other might want? Nothing. That's what. Angrily, he chased the doubts away. He had to try, because if he didn't, Malcolm would find Miranda and she'd suffer a fate worse than death. The thought of what the Dwarf planned for her was too horrible to contemplate.

The Wizard Indolent stood and picked up the Elven sword, flinching as his hand first met the cold metal almost as if its touch caused him pain. "What is your name?" he asked, his gaze fixed on the blade.

"Nicholas," answered the boy promptly, and almost choked as he added, "Sir."

"How did you come by this sword, little boy?" The Wizard's yellowed eyes shifted to Nicholas, burning into him as he tested the balance of the sword. *Swit!* He slashed the air, knocking over the black box and scattering the deadly bejeweled spiders onto the floor. Without taking his eyes off Nicholas, Indolent tossed the sword over his shoulder where it landed with a clang on the hard ground. Then he snapped his fingers.

Nicholas couldn't suppress the gasp that escaped from his throat at the sight of the short figure that emerged from the shadows in a corner of the shelter in answer to the Wizard's summons. He stared in shocked disbelief at the man who was supposed to be living out his life as a tree stump in Bethany. It was Mr. Little, Miranda's former teacher. How on earth had Stubby broken the Druid's enchantment and managed to get away from the Elves?

"Don't let my little treasures escape," snapped the Wizard. "And Little," he added. "Don't harm them."

Beating his leg with a thin, supple switch, Stubby snapped his fingers toward the opening and one of the Ogres scuttled into the shelter and bowed before the former teacher. Nicholas almost laughed out loud at the smug grin that appeared on Stubby's face at the Ogre's servile manner.

"Catch the spiders. Harm one and you'll be sorry." Mr. Little pointed at the huge spiders and slapped the slave on the back with his stinging switch. But Nicholas noticed that he kept a safe distance between him and the poisonous insects.

Trembling uncontrollably, the Ogre reached for the black box and began scooping up the tarantulas and depositing them inside. He worked quickly, but his terror and his trembling turned his fingers into thumbs and made him fumble. A particularly large spider squeezed out of his grasp, crawled along his hand and bit the soft flesh on his inner wrist. The Ogre stared in horror at the black spider. Then he dropped the box, shook his hand furiously to dislodge the large tarantula, clutched his wrist, and whistled shrilly. In seconds, the poor creature crumpled to the ground, writhing and kicking spasmodically. Then, the Ogre uttered a long, screaming whistle and went as stiff as a board, its round, staring eyes protruding from their sockets like golf balls.

For a second no one spoke. Then, making *Tsk! Tsk!* sounds, Indolent snapped his fingers again. Stubby reacted instantly. He snapped his fingers and more Ogres rushed into the shelter, grabbed their dead companion's arms and legs and hurried away. Another fellow bent and began boxing the spiders.

Nicholas was outraged. An Ogre, a living being, had just died a horrible, painful death right in front of him, and all he had done was watch helplessly. His face burned with shame and anger. He had to get away from here.

The Wizard Indolent waved the teacher out of the shelter. Stubby hesitated for a second, cracking the knuckles on one hand as his beady eyes shifted between Nicholas and the Wizard. Then he shrugged and hurried outside.

"Now where was I?" said the Wizard.

"You asked me my name, and I told you it was Nicholas." *Maybe he doesn't recognize me,* thought Nicholas, grasping at the thin thread of hope like a drowning man grasping for a lifeline. But his faint hopes were dashed to pieces by the Wizard's next words.

"I believe we've met before," said Indolent, coldly. "I didn't like you then, and I don't like you now."

"And I don't like you either, you disgusting, smelly little lizard," retorted Nicholas, unable to stop himself.

Indolent's eyebrows narrowed and his face twisted in rage. He waved his arm and suddenly Nicholas was flying backwards through the air. "And Little! Don't let me see his ugly face around here again."

"So much for winning his trust," groaned Nicholas, a second before he landed on his back on the ground.

CHAPTER SIXTEEN

ANOTHER DARK PLACE

he damp, sticky hands on his throat woke Nicholas with a start.

"Ahhh!" he cried out, sitting up and lashing out simultaneously. His flailing arms impacted against tough, leathery hide. Then he closed his fist and punched at his assailant as hard as he could from a sitting position, knocking whatever it was backwards. The attacker scuttled away, the scraping of metal along the floor masking the sound of its sharp claws on the stone.

It was blacker than the Demon's heart inside the small underground cell where Nicholas had been dumped like a bag of garbage after being flung out of the scabby Wizard's crude shelter. *Where's the Druid's staff when I need it?* he thought ruefully. He peered into the darkness trying to fix his attacker's location.

Unable to see his enemy, and feeling terribly exposed and vulnerable, Nicholas quickly slid backwards until his back met solid stone. He felt better immediately, knowing that his attacker couldn't sneak up behind him. He winced as the front of his shirt stuck to his flesh as he had moved across the floor. He took a second to feel the cloth at his chest, snatching his hand back as if he'd been stung as his fingers touched something thick and gooey. The front of his shirt was drenched with the stuff. Tentatively, he raised his fingers to his nose and sniffed. The smell, along with the feel of the sticky substance, instantly told him what it was. *Blood!*

Then a horrible thought hit him like a hammer blow. Malcolm's parting words to the Ogres rang in his head, paralyzing him. *Eat him! Oh, no!* he groaned inwardly. *Not that!* But, he knew with a certainty that made him weak with terror that the creature crouching over him had taken a bite out of his chest or stomach and, any moment now, the pain would start and he'd be screaming. Dreading what he would find, he frantically ran his hands over his body, expecting at any moment to touch the spot where a bite-sized piece of flesh was missing. When his fingers brushed against something slimy, his heart stopped. His worst fears were true!

Forcing down his panic, he examined the sticky object, thinking that if he pressed it back against the wound, it might regenerate or something? He knew that that was what you were supposed to do with a severed limb? He wasn't so sure it would work with flesh.

"Ha!" Nicholas couldn't believe the amazing feeling of relief that washed over him as he suddenly realized that it wasn't a bloody chunk of his own flesh, but a small animal, a rat or something. And it was dead. That's where the blood had come from. "Ha!" he said again, flinging the dead rodent away. He shuddered in disgust as it went *splat* against the wall and then plopped onto the stone floor.

The boy wiped his sticky hands on the legs of his pants and stared into the darkness. Where was his attacker now? Could it see in the darkness? Was it watching him? Nicholas froze as he heard a faint whistling sound coming from off to his right. The whistling identified his attacker as an Ogre. He should have guessed. But what had it been doing with the dead rodent, and its hands on his throat? Nicholas shook his head to drive away the incredible thought that was swiftly growing in his mind. But, the thought stuck in his brain, forcing him to examine it. He could hardly believe what he was thinking. But he had to admit it made sense in a sick sort of way. Was it possible that the creature hadn't been trying to throttle him? Had the creature been trying to share its meal with him? Exactly what it had been trying to force into his mouth made his stomach lurch.

"Who are you?" he asked, his eyes fixed on the darkness between him and the spot where the creature lurked, whistling softly, almost mournfully.

The whistling stopped and a heavy silence fell on the cell. The only sound Nicholas heard was the sound of his own breathing. He waited until the silence became unbearable. He opened his mouth to shout, but a barely perceptible scuffing came from the darkness and with it, a harsh sound of heavy metal dragging on the stones. Then the Ogre uttered a soft, short whistle as it moved stealthily across the floor toward the boy.

"Stop!" said Nicholas, sharply. "Don't come any closer."

The scuffing stopped abruptly.

"Can you understand what I'm saying?" asked Nicholas. There was something so pathetic about the whistles that his heart went out to the creature. He tried again. "I don't know if you can understand me, but I'm sorry I punched you. I thought you were . . . oh never mind. Just don't sneak up on me or try feeding me again. OK?"

The creature whistled, two quick bursts.

"What are you doing in here? Did that weasel Indolent lock you in here to keep an eye on me?"

One short whistle.

"That sounded like a *no,*" said Nicholas. "What are you doing here then?"

In answer, the creature clanged the metal on the floor.

Groaning as he moved his stiff, bruised body, Nicholas pushed himself onto his hands and knees and crawled across the floor, stopping when his hands touched cold metal. Then he traced the links of the heavy chain until he came to a thick leg iron fastened tightly about the creature's ankle.

"You're a prisoner," he whispered.

Nicholas sensed the Ogre's presence, felt the heat from its body. His nose wrinkled as the strong smell of Ogre drifted his way, making him want to barf. *He probably can't stomach the smell of me,* he thought. "I've been in worse places," he said, thinking of the time he had been captured by the Bog Trolls. "So don't worry, I'll get us out of here." Then he crawled into a corner, rolled onto his side, and tried to sleep, but he found himself staring into the darkness for a long time before his eyes finally closed.

When he woke up hours or days later, he knew by the awful smell that his fellow prisoner was curled up on the floor near his feet. He wished he had a light. Every second of his imprisonment in the Swampgrass had been spent in total darkness. After days of never seeing the sun, he had withdrawn deep inside himself and for the first time in his life, he seriously thought that he might die in the blackness far from everyone and everything he knew.

"I'm getting out of here," he said, standing and pacing out the floor. He figured it was roughly eight feet by eight feet. The floor was made of stone as were the walls and, he guessed, the ceiling. Sinking onto the floor, he wondered just how he intended to escape from a windowless, stone cell. Did Indolent ever send anyone to check on them? So far he hadn't seen a soul. What if nobody came, ever? What if Indolent had left them here to die? "No way am I going to eat rats!" he muttered, jumping up and going over the cell again.

From the corner behind he heard the Ogre stirring, coming awake. Then the chain dragged on stone as the creature scuffled about along the far wall. An excited, high-pitched whistle came from the darkness, as if the Ogre had suddenly found something precious. Nicholas fought down the sour taste that filled his throat as he listened to the smacking sounds his cellmate made devouring the remains of the dead rodent he had thrown away.

A day, or days, dragged by. Nicholas lost all sense of time. When he was awake, he exercised and paced the small cell. Or, he talked to his cellmate, interpreting the creature's whistles into what he wanted the other to say. The rest of the time, he slept. But food and water were becoming a problem. He couldn't last much longer without both. Whenever he lifted his head quickly, he became so lightheaded he almost passed out. What made him sick was the way he had reached out almost eagerly for a share of the latest rodent the Ogre had caught, barely able to snatch his hand back at the last moment.

"I wish you could talk to me," he said. "I can't take one more day of this. What did you do to end up in the dungeon? Were you one of the workers? If so, you must know something that would help us get away." He squeezed his eyes shut and pressed his head back against the wall, waiting for the faint, questioning whistle. But to his surprise, it didn't come. Instead, he felt the Ogre's hand tugging on his arm.

"You want to show me something?" he said and felt the hand on his arm tighten.

Barely able to contain his excitement, Nicholas let the Ogre lead him to a corner. Then the creature took the boy's hand and placed it on one of the stone blocks about a foot up from the floor. Nicholas ran his hands over the stone and along the space separating it from adjoining blocks. The mortar was gone. The block was loose.

"You did this?" Nicholas was amazed. It must have taken the creature months to scrape away the mortar. "How long have you been in here?"

The creature blew two short whistles, and a long wheezing sound.

"OK," said Nicholas. "So it *was* you and I guess the long sound means you've been here a long time. But what did you use, your nails, or what?"

The Ogre pressed something hard and sharp into his hand. "What is it?" Nicholas asked and then he knew. It was a small bone, probably all that remained from something his companion had caught and eaten. "Good thinking," he said, reaching out and patting the creature on the arm. When the Ogre whistled, he could have sworn it was a sound of happiness.

Working together, the two prisoners jostled the block back and forth, slowly easing it toward them. It was hard, tedious work. They kept at it for what seemed like hours, but when they finally stopped to rest, Nicholas was disappointed that the stone block had moved less than an inch. His fingers were raw and blistered as if they'd been rubbed with coarse sandpaper. But he wasn't about to let that stop him. The loose stone block was like a brilliantly lit doorway in the blackness and Nicholas knew it was the only thing that kept him going.

"It's no good," he said, a day later. "We'll be dead, or at least I'll be dead of starvation at the rate we're going." Then he had a brilliant idea. "Where's that piece of bone?" he asked.

It took forever, but it was worth the effort when Nicholas heard the click as the lock on the Ogre's ankle iron opened. "If someone comes," he cautioned, "don't forget to put it back on. Understand?" He handed the bone key back to his companion.

The chain was long enough to wrap about the exposed stone block, but first, Nicholas scraped the chain back and forth over the edges of the block trying to gouge notches in the stone to anchor the chain. When the Ogre realized the boy's purpose, it took the ankle iron and smashed it against the stone until it dislodged small chips from the edges.

"Excellent!" said Nicholas, fitting the chain into the notches and wrapping it twice about the stone block. "Let's hope this works."

It worked. Using all of their strength, they pulled on the chain, shouting and whistling, as the huge stone block slid inch by inch out from the wall. Hours later, the block crashed to the floor. For a second the prisoners stood together in silence, almost as if they were afraid to approach the cavity and make their escape. "There's no turning back now," whispered Nicholas, wiping sweat from his face and neck. "We'd never get that block back in place."

He moved cautiously toward the wall cavity, and leaned inside, his arms stretched ahead to feel the earth that was all that separated them from the outside world, and freedom. Tears of bitterness stung his eyes as his hands touched stone. Indolent hadn't taken any chances in creating his dungeon. Escape was impossible. All that work for nothing! Nicholas wanted so badly to turn around and tell the Ogre that everything was going to turn out OK, but he couldn't.

He sank onto the floor and lowered his head into his hands. "I'm sorry," he said, wondering if the soft wheezing sounds meant that his companion was crying.

Abruptly, a dull thud came from outside the solid stone door, followed by the sound of a heavy bar sliding back. "What are we going to do?" hissed Nicholas, knowing they might be able to block the cavity with their bodies, but there was no way they could hide the huge stone block. He felt the Ogre's touch on his arm as they crouched together, peering into the darkness, the only barrier between them and the door.

CHAPTER SEVENTEEN

CALLING THE DEAD

n the darkness of the Demon's black tower, within the swirling Cataclysm that protected the Dark Lands, Calad-Chold's eye sockets blazed as he raised a battered, tarnished bugle to his lipless face and summoned his armies, ordering them forth from the Realms of the Dead to return to quarters. The soundless blast was not heard by living beings, who went about their business unaware that a battle, the like of which had never been fought, was taking shape beyond their borders and their understanding. Only the wolves, hunting in packs in the darkest forests, paused for a second as a draught ruffled their fur and was gone. Howling plaintively, they sniffed the air, momentarily confused but, by then, even the memory of something passing had vanished.

The silent horn blast tore through earth and stone, wood and iron, sounding a tattoo in the minds of the dead who slept in earthen barrows and undisturbed coffins. The dead stirred, then awakened with a jolt, tearing their way out of the things and places that confined them. White bones gleamed from beneath the faded cloaks of those that had been dead for centuries, while decaying black flesh hung in strings from the skeletons of others and spoke of more recent deaths.

They came silently in twos and threes, spectral shapes drifting purposefully across the lands. They came in the scores like cloud-enshrouded hosts of grim reapers, filling the air about them with a sound like a long, drawn-out exhalation. And they came in great, uncountable masses upon fleshless horses, bones shifting and grinding under black shredded cloaks. And where they passed smoke rose from the scorched and blacken earth.

They came from every country and age since the dawn of time: Kings and Queens, paupers and nobles. Unrecognizable, long-headed Cro-Magnon men, tall Neanderthals and squat Dwarves, grave Elves, slain in long ago battles, and towering Giants, ghostly Hellhags and terrible Thugs, and other beings that had not walked the earth for millions of years, now hastened toward the Dark Lands to swell the ranks of Calad-Chold's army. They came without debate or argument. They couldn't have resisted had they wanted. The call of the King of the Dead was an imperative.

There were no children, Druids, Dragons, or dogs among them. Calad-Chold's call could not penetrate the deep silence where these souls rested.

The cruel commander lowered the bugle, a sigh escaping from the space beneath the dented iron crown. His skeletal chest expanded and he seemed to soar higher, dwarfing the cowering Werecurs and frightened, whistling Ogres that had come to serve him. He turned to one of the long, narrow windows that circled the top chamber of the tower and gazed out into the darkness, his empty eye sockets seeing beyond the Cataclysm that cut off and shielded the Demon's lands from her enemies to the lands far beyond.

It was done! The dead were stirring in their grisly enclosures. Soon, the first recruits would arrive, passing unmolested between the frozen black Dar sentinels, that guarded the entrance to the Dark Lands, and spilling through the narrow cut to stand before him like an ocean of death. Then, he would take his rightful place—at the head of this deadly, fanged viper—and lead it out from this place.

Abruptly, Calad-Chold turned away from the window, a growing, all-consuming hunger blunting his satisfaction. More! He wanted, no, he ached for more! He was the King of the Dead. He had awakened his followers and ordered them to come to him. Now he would lead them against the Elves. It was as clear as glass. What, then, was the source of the sharp pang that tugged at his faded memory like cold air stabbing at the exposed nerve in a living tooth? Repressing the hunger that raged in his empty head, and sent daggers of pain along his limbs, as if he were still a thing of living flesh, he strode about the chamber, his dark thoughts puzzling over the nagging feeling that danger lurked outside the windows, beyond the Demon's impenetrable, swarming barrier.

What was it? What could possibly pose a threat to him now? Nothing could kill him because he was already dead—the living dead, awakened and set free from the chained, iron coffin in which he had been confined for thousands of centuries. Calad-Chold stopped his impatient striding and froze, grasping at a thin thread of memory that came to him as suddenly as a star shooting across the night sky. He saw a young Elven soldier lunging at him, one arm raised. What was the man grasping so tightly that his knuckles were as white as snow? Calad-Chold leaned forward, his head tilted to the side as if he were peering into the memory.

With a shock that sent a shudder rippling through his tall frame, the dead King recognized *his* dagger in the young man's hand. He staggered, one bony hand reaching for the wall to keep from pitching forward. *His own knife!* He could scarcely believe it. So that's what had brought him down on that ancient battlefield in Vark, and drained the life from his body. Calad-Chold shook his head, dry bones *whirring* like the loose horny segments on a rattlesnake's tail. Where was the blade now? If, indeed, it still existed, it must be found.

The Twisted Blade was a very special knife. Fashioned from the finest blend of metals, it had been quenched with blood and imbued with the life force of a slave. It was the only weapon that could sever the link that bound Calad-Chold to the one who called him back from the land of the Dead. And, once that link was broken, death's long arms would reach out and reclaim him.

The King of the Dead pointed at a dark shadow blotting out the window on the far wall of the round chamber. A tall figure glided forward, halting when it reached the middle of the room. From the black cavity beneath its dark hood, nothing was visible except a long strand of straggly pale hair that had defied death and continued to grow and, infrequently, the flash of white skeletal teeth, magnified by the figure's lipless death mask. Under the rotting cloth cloak, Calad-Chold noticed the fine silver mail and the haft of a long sword resting in a scabbard at the soldier's side. The King of the Dead nodded, and placed his fleshless hand on his First Officer's bony shoulder.

I leave tonight to take from the body of a thief something that belongs to me. It is a small thing, but it must not fall into the hands of the enemy. The troops are coming. I will be back in time to lead them from this place. In the meantime, I place my armies under your command. Do not fail me.

The tall creature raised its bony hand and gripped the King's arm. *No, I need you here. I will take care of this other matter.*

The First Officer nodded once, turned, and disappeared into the darkness beyond the chamber door. Calad-Chold stared after him for a long time, but he was not seeing his subordinate, his sight was fixed on the past, following the convoluted trail of the Twisted Blade as it made its way from the bloody battlefield to where it rested now on a wooden block far away from the Dark Lands.

The King of the Dead strode across the room and glided through the doorway and down the narrow spiral stairs. Where his boots touched, the stone sizzled and a thin stream of black smoke rose from the imprints. Outside, he tilted his head back and called into the night, his long, tattered cloak billowing about him like the tentacles of a huge, black sea creature in the sudden wind. Lightning forked across the sky and stabbed deep into the earth. Almost instantly, an eerie whinny came on the wind. A great, black-boned warhorse seemed to materialize out of the darkness, its ebony armor creaking as it clattered over the cobbled courtyard. The ghastly thing pawed the ground impatiently as Calad-Chold gripped the reins and swung himself into the ancient saddle. Then, he jabbed his spurs into the bones on the horse's sides and, with a mighty lunge, horse and rider disappeared into the storm.

From a window high in the black tower, Calad-Chold's First Officer stood motionless at a window, watching until the night swallowed the King of the Dead, and he was lost to sight.

CHAPTER EIGHTEEN

CAUGHT

"Wait up," gasped Arabella. "I've got to stop."

They had been running for what seemed like years. But, unlike her friend, Miranda felt euphoric, as if she had reached another plane where she could run forever. "No," she said, grabbing Arabella's arm and pulling her along. "Don't stop! Come on! You can do it."

"I can't run any farther. Let's find a place to hide."

"Bell, if we stop, they'll find us."

"Use the Bloodstones," said Arabella.

The Bloodstones! Miranda didn't want to be reminded of the Bloodstones. "They're gone," she whispered.

"What do you mean, they're gone?" Arabella stopped and grabbed Miranda's arm. "Where are they?"

Miranda shook her head, her limbs rebelling at the sudden halt. "I threw them away. Now come on!"

Arabella was frantic now. "Why?"

Miranda stopped the angry shout before it escaped from her lips. "Bell, I can't use them. I tried and they didn't work." She felt tears sting her eyes as she thought of the Stone's betrayal. *They almost let me die.*

"You threw them away because they didn't work? I don't believe you." Arabella felt like slapping her best friend's face. "Then, let's go back and get them."

"Forget it!" said Miranda, her face burning as if the slap in Arabella's thoughts had left a stinging welt on her cheek. "It won't do any good. They're gone. The Thug took them."

"Aw, Mir," Arabella cried. "What were you thinking?"

"Look, people are dying because of me, because I had the Bloodstones. I thought those things would go away and leave us alone if I gave them what they wanted."

"You thought wrong," snapped Arabella, pointing into the trees behind, where they heard the sound of twigs snapping under the Thug's clawed feet. "Hear that? Maybe that sounds like they're going away to you. But not to my ears it doesn't."

"It's no good getting mad, Bell. The Bloodstones are mine, not yours. I can do what I like with them, and I don't need your permission." Miranda snatched her arm out of her friend's grasp. "I suggest we get going, or would you rather stay here?"

Arabella was so boiling she could barely think. Part of her wanted to storm off into the woods and never set eyes on Miranda again. She broke into a run. "Then, let's go," said the other part of her, but the words were as cold as ice.

Miranda's anger died as abruptly as it had flared up. She stared at Arabella's small dark shape streaking among the trees, her heart sinking like a stone thrown into a deep well. *You are so mean!* she scolded herself silently. *Bell was just trying to help.* Sighing sadly, she took off in pursuit of her companion.

Without warning, the Werecur dropped from above and landed awkwardly on the ground in front of Miranda, cutting off her route and separating her from Arabella. It opened its hideous mouth and screeched, thrusting its head at her and flapping its wings threateningly. Heart in her mouth, Miranda skidded to a stop and darted to one side only to find the way blocked as more creatures fell through the trees and came toward her. Spinning about, green eyes seeking a miracle, she saw that she was totally surrounded by a wall of Werecurs. There was no escape. Despair washed through her at the realization that her luck had finally run out.

"Run Bell!" she screamed, knowing that her words were lost, absorbed into the ear-rending shrieks and snarls as the circle tightened and the terrifying creatures drew nearer.

Then, a hush fell over the forest. Miranda looked about wildly for the source of this new terror. Behind, back the way she and Arabella had come, the Werecurs moved aside, creating an opening in the living wall. Miranda's heart hammered against her chest. Rage as wild and untamable as a tornado erupted inside her only to be consumed by sheer terror that rose up like a wall of ice, freezing her heart and mind and limbs. Unfelt tears spilled from her eyes as the huge, black-cloaked Thug brushed the Werecurs aside and stepped into the circle, a delicate silver pouch dangling from his long, razor-sharp claws.

Red eyes glowing like embers in the black hood, the Demon's assassin hissed with pleasure at his victory over the wicked human child. He still couldn't believe that this piddling creature, trembling like a rabbit frightened by its own shadow, was the source of such unspeakable anguish, the cause of his Mistress's pain. How had something so small and insignificant managed to escape from him time after time? She should have died that night he went to her house. She should have died a dozen deaths since then. She should die *now!*

He took a giant step toward the girl, a thing of pure rage now. Miranda felt the creature's hatred burning into her as if the emotion were alive, and she knew she was only seconds away from death. She took a step back, but there was nowhere to go, nowhere left to run. The earth seemed to split at her feet and she felt as if she were teetering on the brink of a black, bottomless pit hearing the screaming voices urging her to leap to her death.

You're losing it! she thought. It took all of her strength to drive the panic from her mind. Then, a flash of silver caught her eye. *The Bloodstones!* She kept her eyes focused on the silver pouch swinging like a pendulum from the Thug's terrible claws. If the monster got close enough, and she were fast enough, maybe she could wrench the pouch from his grasp. It was a long shot, but she had to try. As long as she remained alive, she had to keep trying. But, what if she managed to snatch the Bloodstones, what then? Would they act on her thoughts? Could she make them work? She didn't have an answer, but they were her only hope. Breathing harshly, she waited for the creature to reach her.

NO! The Demon's sharp command froze the Thug in his tracks. *DO NOT LAY A FINGER ON THE GIRL! I WANT HER ALIVE!* The voice purred in his mind. *Be patient, my own. She is nothing to me. When I have finished with her, you can kill her. And when I am free, I will give you her world and everyone in it.*

The Thug remained motionless, massaging the gold skull pocketed beneath the flesh in his forearm for long moments after the voice of his Mistress had gone. Then, as if he had suddenly awakened from a dream, he raised his head and stared at the girl. The killing rage was gone, and what he saw cringing before him now was only a stupid, terror-crazed child. The sight of her made him laugh. He raised his clawed hand, signaling to something in the sky above.

Fueled by anger, Arabella ran swiftly over the uneven ground. Right! She thought. The Bloodstones were Miranda's, not hers. She knew that. She didn't want the Stones the way the Demon and the others wanted them. "And if that's what she thinks, then she doesn't know me." It was Miranda's attitude that galled her, throwing the Stones away without saying a word, and then acting like it was no big deal. Right! Arabella sniffed.

The shrieking of the Werecurs as they hurtled from the sky made her teeth chatter. Arabella spun about, her anger dissolving like smoke in the wind. Fear for her friend drove everything else from her mind, and propelled her into action. Miranda was in trouble and she had to help her. Ignoring her stiff and aching limbs, she retraced her steps, plowing through the trees, following the Hunter's strident cries. Ducking behind an evergreen, she peered ahead at the circle of warped creatures. She couldn't see Miranda, but she knew she was somewhere in the midst of the monsters. "What am I going to do?" she hissed. "Come on. Think of something!"

Arabella hated doing nothing. She wanted to charge at the Werecurs, but the impulse made her laugh. "Ha! I'd last about a second," she whispered. *What if I shouted Fire! Would that scare them? Would they panic?* Not likely! All they had to do was look around, no flames, no smoke. They'd see her and that'd be the end of her. She shook her head in frustration. There must be something she could do to help Miranda, without getting herself killed. What? What?

Suddenly a hand clamped over her mouth and a strong arm dragged her back from the tree and into the deeper brush. "Be quiet!" hissed a harsh voice in her ear.

Arabella twisted free and found herself staring into the grave face of Andrew Furth.

"I am sorry," whispered the aide, hastily removing his hand. "I did not know if you would cry out, and I could not risk it."

Arabella looked about for the Druid and the others. "Miranda's trapped," she said.

"Shhh! Stay here." Andrew moved swiftly toward his horse. "There is nothing you can do here."

"I'm not leaving her," cried Arabella, clutching the young Elf's sleeve. "Please, do something!"

And then, as if Arabella's plea had been heard, Avatar surged from the trees, powerful muscles rippling along his shiny, red coat. In the saddle, like a wild, jungle predator about to spring upon its prey, crouched the black, shadowy form of the Druid, the deadly staff glowing like a living firebrand in his raised hand. Following close in the great stallion's wake came the King of the Elves, one hand gripping Noble's reins, the other holding his gleaming sword. Eleven Riders flanked their King, their pale faces hard and cruel in the weak light. They fanned out to either side to come at the Werecurs from behind. But the Druid's courageous stallion galloped straight at the wall of winged Hunters, shattering the night with screams of hatred for the Demon and the evil that had come unbidden into the forest.

"Stay here," repeated Andrew, turning to Arabella. "I will be back for you."

"Please don't leave me," pleaded Arabella.

"Do not argue," said the Elf gently. "You will be safer here." He leaped into the saddle. "Do not leave this spot," he warned, urging the horse forward. "If they drive us from this place, I must be able to find you quickly, or you will be left behind." Then he was gone.

Arabella felt the heat of rebellion rise up inside, but she doused the flames and forced herself to obey the young Elf's orders. She knew he was right, but the knowledge didn't make her feel better. Miranda was her friend and she wanted to be there when they rescued her. Sighing in resignation, she huddled in the bushes and watched the battle unfold.

A blast of white light shot from the Druid's staff and exploded into the Werecurs forming the tight circle around Miranda directly in his path. Arabella gasped at the awesome power as the creatures disintegrated into bits of burning coals before her eyes. She dropped onto the ground, wrapped her arms about her knees, and rocked back and forth, waiting for someone to come for her.

Miranda whipped about in time to see scores of Werecurs burst into flames and fly apart like fireworks before they knew what hit them. Horrified, she stared at the spot where the creatures had stood huddled together, scarcely able to believe that, seconds ago, they had actually existed. Then, Avatar stormed through the gap in the living wall and lunged toward her, his powerful hooves digging into the ground and kicking up bits of earth. She saw Naim lean to the side to snatch her from harm's way. But, before he could reach her, something black descended from above. Sharp claws reached from within the blackness, wrapping about her, crushing her. She cried out in pain, but the pressure on her ribs and chest was so severe that no sound came from her open mouth. *It's over!* she thought, feeling a sharp twinge of regret that she didn't get a chance to tell Bell she was sorry. And what about Nicholas? Now, she'd never find him. Her mother's dear face flashed in her mind. *Oh Mom! You're going to be so sad. I'm sorry, I'm sorry.* She was crying openly now, shoulders heaving as great gulping sobs wracked her body.

The Werecur screeched, its claws tightening about the slender girl. Its wings flapped desperately as it sought to distance itself from the evil Druid and his magic fire stick. Slowly, gracelessly, like a grotesque bat, the creature lifted into the sky. Out of the corner of her eye, Miranda saw Naim aiming the staff, but then his arm dropped abruptly and a loud roar burst from his throat.

Naim burned with anger. To have come so close only to fail was almost too much to bear. He couldn't unleash the staff's fire for fear it would destroy Miranda as well as her evil captor. He threw the staff on the ground in frustration. But then he seemed to realize that Elester and the small company of Riders were doing their best to fight off several hundred Werecurs that had remained in the clearing. He leaped from Avatar's back, picked up the pale wooden staff, and ran to aid the Elves.

Miranda stopped crying. So far, the Demon's Hunter hadn't

crushed her to death. She couldn't believe that she was still alive. *You just made a big mistake,* she silently warned her captors. *As long as I'm alive, I'll find a way to escape.*

Below, she saw Naim raise the staff but, to her surprise, there was no blast of vaporizing white fire this time. Instead, the Druid went as still as a statue, both arms upraised, and it seemed to Miranda that the Werecurs on the ground suddenly changed and became distorted, like characters in a movie playing out a scene in slow motion. The rapid flapping of their loose, fleshy wings flagged, their quick-as-lightning claws slashed lazily at the Elves, who dodged the enemy effortlessly. It was the strangest sight. Somewhere in the air nearby, she heard the harsh rasping hiss of rage as the Demon's assassin watched the enemy cut down the Werecurs like trees.

When she could no longer make out the small shapes of her companions, Miranda gritted her teeth and faced her own predicament. The only thing she knew for certain was that Naim would never give up on her. He'd follow her and he wouldn't stop until he found her. Where were the Hunters going? Why had they kept her alive when it would have been so easy to get rid of her once and for all? As the black cloud of Werecurs winged toward the Dark Lands, Miranda drifted into and out of consciousness. During her lucid moments, one question loomed large in her thoughts. *They've got the Bloodstones, what do they want with me?*

CHAPTER NINETEEN

SEPARATE WAYS

"They've got Miranda! You didn't stop them!" Arabella had to scream, even though she knew it wasn't fair to blame the Druid for her friend's abduction.

Naim's eyes flashed dangerously, but he knelt on one knee and placed his hands on the distraught girl's shoulders. "I am sorry, child. I could not reach her in time."

"What are they going to do to her?" cried Arabella, wringing her hands.

"I do not look into the future," replied the Druid. "But I do not believe they will harm her, yet." He used the staff to push himself to his feet. "No," he said. "Someone wants her alive. For what purpose, I do not know." He turned to Elester. "Things have changed, my friend. The Hunters are hunting. This is where we part. I must go after the child."

Elester nodded. "You know where they are taking her?"

"Yes," replied the Druid, his voice mirroring the weariness he felt throughout his body.

"You know that I would accompany you to the Dark Lands if I could," said the King softly. "But our journey was to the Druid's Close to find a clue to the location of the Twisted Blade. And now the Hunters are loose. That, alone, tells me that a great Evil is brewing, and I am afraid it is about to fall on Ellesmere like a hammer. I will make for Dunmorrow and consult with our allies, the Dwarves, and then return to Bethany to prepare a defense against an enemy that cannot be killed." He gripped the old man's arm, his expression reflecting his despair. "For thousands of years we have kept the world free from Hate. If we fall, you know what will happen."

"Yes," repeated Naim, his dark eyes locking with Elester's. "We may not find the Twisted Blade in time, but I give you my word that I will get the girl and I will move heaven and earth to be with you when the time comes." He placed his hand over the King's and smiled weakly. "But, if I do not make it, I will send others to stand with you. Now! Make speed, my friend. The clouds are building. The storm is coming."

"What about me?" asked Arabella. "I want to go after Miranda."

"You will travel to Bethany with the King," said the Druid firmly.

"I don't want to," cried Arabella, stamping her foot angrily and then sitting on the ground. "Either you take me with you or I'm staying right here."

For a second Druid and King exchanged helpless glances and then, to the girl's dismay, she realized that her display of temper had caught the attention of the Riders. Her face flushed red as she felt their eyes settle on her like a sticky film coating her skin. She read contempt in their stares, and knew that she was acting like a spoiled brat.

"Come now, Arabella," laughed Andrew, trying to ease the tension that charged the air like an electric current. "The Druid has his magic, but we would be honoured to have a tough warrior like you in our company."

They weren't contemptuous after all, just concerned. Arabella felt so ashamed, she wanted to cry. Instead, she grinned shyly. "It's not fair. I just want to help Miranda."

"No, little friend, life is not fair. Come. Marigold is out there, afraid and probably lost. She will come to you."

"OK," sighed Arabella loudly, sounding as if she were granting a big favour. "I'll come with you and find Marigold." She stood and turned to the Druid, her fists planted firmly on her hips. "Tell Mir I wanted to help, but you wouldn't let me."

Naim chuckled. "I will do that."

"Humph!" snorted Arabella, stomping toward the horses. She didn't hear the sound of Avatar's hooves, but when she looked around the Druid was gone. For a second she stared into the darkness, feeling that a small slice of her heart left with him.

Despite the fact that the Riders were close to exhaustion after battling the Werecurs twice in one night, Elester ordered them to mount up. He knew they were also grieving over their slain comrade because their glances kept returning to the sad gray horse standing motionless under a tree, staring into the shadows, watching and waiting for a Rider who would never appear.

Arabella rode one of the spares, but she, too, kept glancing at the riderless horse and she imagined that the other Riders were looking her way and wishing that their fallen comrade were riding with them instead of her, but they said nothing throughout the long ride to Dunmorrow, mountain home of the Dwarves. The only sound was the thunder of hooves and Arabella's voice calling Marigold's name over and over.

The White Mountains, known locally as the Mountains of the Moon, were dazzling in the early morning light. Arabella squinted as she gazed at the lofty, silver peaks, remembering with a pang of sorrow what the Demon had done to the Dwarves.

A little over a year ago, Arabella and her friends had watched in horror as Dundurum, the former kingdom of the Dwarves, was sucked into the blackness of the Place with No Name along with the Demon and her demented, half-dead minions. Gregor XV, King of the Dwarves, had taken his people to Mount Oranono, the tallest peak in the White Mountains, habitat of the Black Dragons. Within the spiralling vastness of Mount Oranono, the Dwarves had begun carving out their new country, Dunmorrow, after successfully negotiating a ninety-nine year lease with Typhon, chief Dragon, and guardian of the treasure.

As the White Mountains loomed ever closer, Arabella felt a growing sense of excitement. Despite her tiredness, she couldn't wait to see what the Dwarves had accomplished in carving out their new country since her last visit. Early the next morning, the company guided their horses under a massive archway into the great courtyard at Dunmorrow. Arabella looked behind hoping to see Marigold *clip-clopping* along in their wake, but there was no sign of the gray mare.

In the courtyard just inside a pair of enormous iron gates, Dwarf guards, armed with short swords and sharp axes, issued from the guardhouse and surrounded the companions. Their stony faces cracked into grins when they recognized the King of the Elves. Grooms came scurrying and led the weary horses to the stables to be fed, watered, and brushed. After a hearty bout of boot stomping and backslapping, Cyril, Captain of the Guard, led the company to the King's work chambers.

"Well met, Elf friend," said King Gregor gruffly, dispensing with formalities as he bear-hugged Elester warmly, and clapped him on the back until the Elven King staggered. Then he spotted Arabella and stomped over to the girl, whacking her heartily on the back. "Miranda's friend, eh? Where's the girl then?"

"The Werecurs took her," sniffed Arabella, embarrassed by the tears that suddenly trickled from her eyes.

"WHAT?" Gregor's blunt face turned as red as a sweet pepper. He stomped the ground hard.

"And Nick and Penelope are also missing. Mir and I think they're somewhere in this world. We came here to find them."

"Demon's loose? Young ones gone?"

"Listen, my friend," said Elester. "I will tell you what I know."

They perched on uncomfortable stone benches before the King's desk as Elester repeated all that had happened since the earth tremor shook Bethany. Gregor listened impatiently, but he didn't interrupt except to smash his thick fist on the desk and stomp his heavy boots on the stone floor when he heard how the Werecurs had flown off with Miranda. When Elester finished, the Dwarf King stood up and paced back and forth behind his desk. "Demon's work," he muttered, his voice as hard as the soles of his sturdy boots. "This Dead King will go for Ellesmere's throat first?"

Elester leaned forward and gripped the edge of the desk. "It is the only thing that makes sense. If the Demon is behind this, as the sudden appearance of her Hunters from their holes in the Dark Lands would indicate, then they are hatching a plan to free her from the nameless place. The warding spells sealing her prison will fail if my race is destroyed."

"Yup," said Gregor, nodding vigorously. "Kill Elves, free Hate. This Dead King. What else do you know?"

"Nothing," said Elester simply. "I have told you what the Druid said."

"The Twisted Blade must be found," said Gregor.

"This is a vast world, my friend," said the Elven King, smiling sadly. "Where do you suggest we look?"

"Hrumph!" muttered Gregor, pulling his wiry hair, absentmindedly. "Vark? Last seen there."

"No, the Druid believes that the blade was taken by the Elven soldier who dispatched Calad-Chold."

"Look in Bethany, man!" sputtered Gregor.

"The Twisted Blade is not on Ellesmere Island," said Elester. "I know this because I, or others, would have sensed its presence, and we have not."

"It's magic, this blade?"

"Not magic so much as force," explained Elester. "As I understand it, the Twisted Blade was quenched in the flowing blood of a living slave. The Dead King believed it absorbed into itself the life force of that unfortunate creature."

"I've got an idea," cried Arabella, who had been listening intently to the discussion going on around her.

Gregor's bushy eyebrows rose questioningly as his sharp eyes shifted to the little human girl. "Speak, then!" he commanded.

"It would take years to search every country for the Twisted Blade, but couldn't you send messages to all the leaders of the world and get them to ask their people to look for the knife. It might take a while, but not as long as if we had to search."

For a moment, everyone looked at Arabella. *Oh, oh!* she thought, suddenly feeling young and foolish. *Dumb idea!* But to her surprise, the King of the Dwarves banged his fist on the desk and let out a loud bark of laughter.

"Might work," he said. "Send messengers."

Andrew Furth nudged Arabella and grinned. "See, I told you we needed you."

Arabella was so proud, she felt ten feet tall. Imagine if the knife turned up because of her idea. She couldn't wait to tell her friends that she had suggested a way that might solve all of their problems, and maybe stop the King of the Dead before he started killing people. But, thinking of her friends made her sad, stripping away her elation and filling her with an empty feeling that wouldn't go away. She thought of Miranda all alone in the clutches of the Werecurs. Was she terribly frightened? Was she still alive? What if she never saw Mir, or Nick, or Penelope again? What would she do without them?

"Seen this blade?" asked King Gregor.

Elester shook his head. "We hoped the Druids would be able to provide a description, or that we would find answers in their library, but now that the girl's gone, I must return to Bethany."

"Send them a message," said King Gregor, grinning widely at Arabella. "Druids can read."

Elester turned to Arabella, chuckling softly. "It seems you may be helping Miranda more than you think," he said. Then, noticing that Arabella's head was nodding and her eyes were half-closed, he motioned to his aide. "Show the child to her quarters. She is dead on her feet."

King Gregor and Elester continued their talks in the Lodge over pints of Boot, the strong beer brewed by the Dwarves and blackened, or so the Druid claimed, by the addition of boot polish.

"Why take the girl?" asked Gregor, who was genuinely fond of Miranda, and thought of her as a Dwarf daughter.

"The Demon fears the Bloodstones. You would be surprised, perhaps alarmed, at what Miranda can do with them, old friend. I remember when my father gave them to her. She could not use them at all. Since then, I have seen her travel outside her body to save the boy, Nicholas. She takes risks that would turn your hair white. The Demon does not understand the power of the Bloodstones. Elven power. But she knows that if she gets her hands on them, there is nothing left to fear."

"You. She fears your magic."

"Yes," said Elester. "I have great magic, but it is different from the Bloodstones. They work through the senses. With the hearing stone Miranda can make you hear what she imagines, like the roar of a wild beast in her mind. But it also allows her to hear a whispered conversation through a stone wall. She is just beginning to experiment with the powers of the Bloodstones. I am afraid for her. And, I am afraid of what others will do to prevent her from using them."

"Doesn't answer my question," said Gregor. "Why take the girl? Why not kill her and snatch Stones?"

Elester thought for a minute. The Dwarf's question was both puzzling and worrying. Why *had* the Hunters taken Miranda? No logical answer came to him, but he knew that whatever the reason it had something to do with the Bloodstones. Did the Demon think that she could wield the power of the Stones through the girl? Was that her purpose? *Yes!* He knew with every fiber of his being that he was right. But that meant Hate had to control Miranda. How was she planning to gain that control? And what if she succeeded? Could she unleash Evil through the Bloodstones? Elester ran his hand through his golden hair, suddenly aware that he could do with a long, cleansing shower.

"I can only guess at the reason they did not destroy Miranda when they had the chance," he said. "I was wrong before when I said that Hate wanted the Bloodstones so they could not be used against her. Her plan is much more devious than that. She does not simply want to eliminate the Bloodstones as a threat, she intends to grab the power of the Stones for herself."

"Impossible!" rasped Gregor, bouncing to his feet and pounding the long refectory table until the tankards jumped, spilling black, foamy Boot over the rims. "Girl owns them. Power's hers."

"That is what we always believed," agreed Elester. "But what if Hate controls Miranda? Does that mean she also controls the Bloodstones?"

King Gregor opened his mouth to protest, but the thought of the Demon using the Bloodstones for evil was so horrific, so unspeakable, that he could not find words to express his denial. He dropped back into his seat, slumping forward as if someone had punched him in the stomach and left him gasping for air. Finally he raised his head. "It's the end," he said, his habitually gruff voice a faint murmur. And, for the first time in the course of their long friendship, Elester read utter hopelessness in the other man's eyes.

Early the next morning, as the first pale streaks lightened the eastern sky, heralding the rise of the sun, hundreds of trained messenger pigeons were released from a narrow slot high on the mountain. For a minute they flew as one unit, filling the early morning silence with the sound of wings beating the air like sheets flapping in the wind. Then they separated, veering off in different directions, and flying swiftly toward their destinations. In cylinders attached to their legs, they carried messages to the heads of state of all the known nations in the old world, requesting their help in finding an old battered knife with a tarnished, twisted blade. One messenger winged northwest where, far beyond its keen sight, white stone pillars and gleaming towers marked the Druid's Close.

They had already merged with the far horizion when, shortly after dawn, the King of the Dwarves and a massive company of soldiers streamed from the mountain to accompany the Elven King to ships waiting to transport them to Bethany, where black clouds, foreshadowing the coming storm, were already roiling in the sky. When they came to sections of ground that smoked and reeked of decay, even the brave Elven grays balked and refused to tread on the scorched and blackened earth where remnants of Calad-Chold's army had passed. Elester pulled his cloak tight across his chest to melt the ice in his veins and he noticed the child, Arabella, shivering uncontrollably.

CHAPTER TWENTY

LEAVING VARK

tavite raised his large hand to scratch his head, but thought better of it and dropped his arm to his side. Eegar didn't stir a feather. The bird was still pretending to be dead, lying on its back in the Giant's coarse red hair, legs as stiff as twigs. It had been that way since Otavite had settled Penelope on his shoulder—almost a full day now.

Penelope hated the stupid bird, but she knew that Otavite was growing increasingly worried about Eegar. "He has never done anything like this before," he said, throwing up his hands in frustration.

"I know why he's acting like that," said Penelope. "He's j-e-a-l-o-u-s." She spelled the word in case Eegar was listening.

"No," said Otavite. "E-e-g-a-r is not j-e-a-l-o-u-s. He is just being E-e-g-a-r."

"I'm telling you, he's j-e-a-l-o-u-s of me and Muffy."

Otavite shook his head, dismissing the girl's suggestion. It was ridiculous. Or was it? Surely what the Princess said couldn't be true. He and Eegar had been together since the Giant was a boy, and they would remain together until he died. That was the way of things. Sighing heavily, he decided to have a talk with the stubborn giantpecker later when the little Elf girl was sleeping.

Penelope had stuck to Otavite like a second shadow since they arrived at the fortress, asking a zillion questions about life as a Giant and relentlessly hounding him about rescuing Nicholas.

"You must care very much for this servant," said Otavite.

"Well, you know how it is with servants," quipped Penelope. "When you find good ones, you'll do anything to keep them. After all, good help is hard to find these days."

Otavite had no idea what it was like with servants since he didn't have one. In fact, most of the time, being in the National Mountain Patrol, he felt exactly like a servant.

Sitting on a tall stool that looked more like a round table than a seat in the soldiers' mess after dinner, Penelope tried the guilt approach. "If you heard Malcolm tell the King of the Dead to destroy the Elves, don't you think you should warn my cousin?"

"You are right," mused the giant. "I put all that in my report. The King of the Elves will be warned."

"But," persisted Penelope, making the young soldier's head spin. "You should be the one to go to Bethany."

"My duty is here," said the Giant.

Penelope changed tacks. "I know someone who might know about Taboo and Calad-Chold." She stopped for a second to make sure she had his full attention. She had. The Giant was staring at her as if she were the most amazing person in the world.

"Who is this important friend?" Otavite's brain told him not to believe everything that came out of this girl's mouth. But, because of her knowledge of the Elves, he believed she was whom she claimed and he wanted to believe that she really had a friend who could clear up the mystery of Taboo.

"Oh no," said Penelope, shaking her head smugly. "If you help me get my servant back, I'll take you to meet him. He knows everything."

"I would like to know about Taboo and the things that happened there so long ago that no one remembers. I would write it in our histories and then it would not be a dark secret anymore. Every Giant in Vark would know about it."

"Well?" pressed Penelope. "All you have to do is agree to rescue Nicholas."

Finally, to Penelope's relief, Otavite sent a message to headquarters requesting leave to accompany the lost Princess to her home on Ellesmere Island, land of the Elves.

"My cousin, King Elester, will be so happy to see me that you can bet he'll give you a big reward."

Otavite grinned. He found the Elven girl fascinating, and he felt that since her small yellow companion had only bit him a dozen times, he must be making progress with the dog. Later that night, as he walked from post to post checking that all was well within the fortress and along its broad walls, he searched for words to comfort the stiff, motionless bird on his head.

"Listen—er—Eegar," he began. "The Princess and her little companion are far from their home, and they need our help for a little while longer. Are you upset because you think I like them better than you?" He waited for the familiar stirrings in his hair. When nothing happened, he continued. "I like them, but they are not you. Nothing could ever replace you." He thought he felt a feather brush gently against his scalp, but then he decided it had been his imagination. With a heavy heart, he made his way to the barracks, but sleep eluded him.

Two days later word came from Vark granting Otavite's request, and giving new, secret orders.

"When are we leaving?" asked Penelope, burning with impatience. She couldn't wait to get away from the fortress. The structure and everything in it were so gigantic, she felt terribly small and about as important as a drop of water on a duck's back. When she ate her meals in the company of two hundred huge creatures who could knock her over with a look, she ached to be with friends her own size. Although the rough Giants treated her kindly, laughing a lot when she was around, and suffering Muffy's bites good-naturedly, she knew they would also be relieved when she was no longer there. For one thing, when they weren't sitting together, they were jumpy and nervous because they were terrified of stepping on her or the little poodle.

"We'll go tonight," said Otavite. "I like to walk through the snow in the moonlight."

That evening, the mess hall was unusually quiet. The soldiers ate their dinners in silence, heads bent over their plates. By the end of the meal, Penelope found to her surprise that she was crying. At last, Otavite pushed his plate away and rose to his feet. Penelope caught Muffy and stuffed the poodle in her jacket. Then she wiped her eyes on her sleeve and climbed onto the table.

"Thank you for letting me and Muffy stay in the fortress. And thank you for searching Taboo for Nicholas." Looking at the sea of sad faces, she didn't have the heart to call Nick her servant. It just didn't feel right, somehow. It would be like slapping someone who had just saved you from being run over by a bus. She sniffled loudly. "I'll never forget you."

One of the Giants stood up and cleared his throat. "Farewell, little Princess. We will miss you. Come back sometime."

"And bring the yellow furry one," said another fellow.

"Farewell," echoed all the Giants. "We won't forget you."

"Just make sure you have girls in the National Mountain Patrol when I come back," said Penelope, at which the Giants laughed so hard the entire fortress shook as if it were about to collapse.

A short time later, a large white creature appeared through the brand new fortress gates. Outside, it paused for a second, its raptor-like head cocked as if it were listening for a sound only its ears could detect, and then it moved silently away from the fortress toward a little-traveled trail that led westward. In its white fur coat, the giant

Carovorare, whose name was Kurr, was almost invisible against the snow-covered ground. The only things that gave its presence away were brief, bright glints as moonlight stuck the sharp spines pressed tightly against the creature's sides.

Following in Kurr's wake, his backpack stuffed with supplies for the long journey, strode Otavite, breathing deeply of the chilly mountain air and wondering about the dangers that lurked ahead, waiting for them on the long, winding path as surely as nocturnal hunters awaited night. On his massive head, the bird, Eegar, remained as still as death. Beside the Giant, running to keep pace with his long strides, came Penelope, one arm pressed against her chest cushioning Muffy who squirmed like an eel to be set free. In seconds, they had melted into the landscape and were gone. In the huge watchtower at the base of the Bronks, Otavite's companions watched until he disappeared into the night. Then, they turned away, wondering if they'd ever see the young Giant again.

"Wait up!" cried Penelope, breathlessly. They hadn't been on the trail for more than fifteen minutes but she was already exhausted from running flat out.

Otavite stopped abruptly. He had been so engrossed in his own thoughts that he had completely forgotten the child. "I'm sorry," he said, picking her up and placing her on his shoulder.

"Wow!" breathed Penelope. From her lofty perch, the moonlit landscape was breathtaking. She was amazed that she could see for miles in the middle of the night.

"There is nothing like it," agreed Otavite, happily.

They travelled for a long time in silence. Wrapped in a warm, fleecy cloak that covered her from her head to her toes (a parting gift from the Giants), Penelope didn't mind the freezing wind. Beneath the cloak, she unzipped her jacket and Muffy poked her head out and sniffed the air excitedly, her long yellow ears flapping in the girl's face, striking her cheeks like slaps. Penelope hugged her dog, too preoccupied by the prospect of overtaking Nick's captors to even think about curling up on the Giant's broad shoulder and trying to sleep.

The thought that Nicholas might have escaped from Malcolm and the Ogres and was wandering lost in the vast mountains flitted across her mind, but she dismissed it. No, the Ogres had taken him. Besides, there was only one way into the Bronks and that was through the fissure. They had searched Taboo thoroughly and hadn't found a trace of the boy. If he had escaped, surely the Carovorari would have picked up his scent or detected his movements by now. No, she thought. *It's the Ogres, and I'm going to rescue him.*

Penelope hadn't realized she had fallen asleep until the Giant suddenly stubbed his booted toes on a rock half-buried under the snow and came to an abrupt stop. She sat up with a start, surprised that it was morning already. Looking back, she saw the red-tipped Bronks, still visible in the distance, but they had covered a lot of ground during the night. When Otavite set her on the snow-covered trail, Penelope peered about for Kurr, but she couldn't spot the Carovorare. Relieved, she opened her jacket and released Muffy. The Giant chuckled as the poodle sped through the snow like a bullet, barking shrilly as it explored new territory, and chased its puffball tail.

Unsheathing his long knife, Otavite cut dead twigs from the squat bushy trees and placed them in a mound for a fire. Then the companions sculpted crude seats in the snow, settled down by the huge fire, and consumed a hearty breakfast, washed down with steaming hot mugs of coffee sweetened with creamy white syrup that tasted like vanilla ice cream. The Giant was in good spirits after the brisk trek along the mountain trail and chatted amicably about his family.

"What's your sister's name?" asked Penelope, trying to imagine what it would be like to go through life as a Giant, unaware that Otavite was wondering how people her size managed to stay alive.

"Beryl," he answered, suddenly feeling homesick. But then he proceeded to tell her the names of his entire family, which Penelope found so confusing, she promptly forgot.

"How do you communicate with the Carovorari?" she asked.

"Hmm!" Otavite thought for a minute. "It's hard to explain," he said. "We think our thoughts."

"You mean telepathy?"

"We call it . . ." And the Giant said another long word that Penelope added to her *forget* list.

They chatted until the last drops of coffee disappeared and then Otavite tried unsuccessfully to rouse Eegar and coax the stubborn bird from his hair. They were back on the trail within an hour, Muffy as snug as a bug inside Penelope's jacket under the warm cloak. Penelope found herself thinking about Eegar. She knew that Otavite was worried to death over the bird's behaviour and the fact that the creature hadn't eaten anything for days. She hated the vicious giantpecker, but what if the bird wasn't pretending after all? What if it really was dead? Cautiously, she peered at the Giant's head, trying to spot Eegar through the thick russet hairs.

Then, she saw bright red feathers. Leaning closer, her nose practically touching the Giant's head, she stared at the motionless bird. Its eyes were open wide and had a glazed appearance. It certainly looked dead. She focused on the bird's breast looking for a faint pulse that would tell her if its heart were still beating. But she saw nothing, not even the faintest flutter. *It's dead!* she realized with a shock, whipping her head back. *It's been dead the whole time.* Poor Otavite! Should she tell him now, or wait until he had grown more accustomed to the bird's lack of response? She hesitated for only a second, then, using her thumb and index finger like a pair of tweezers, she gently plucked Eegar from the Giant's head and flung the dead bird into the deep snow by the side of the trail.

CHAPTER TWENTY-ONE

ATTACK
FROM THE SKIES

r. Little scowled and snapped his fingers at the two Ogres. "Sitruc! And you, Yekim! Come with me!" He spat out the names as if he were clearing his throat of an insect. "SNAP TO IT!" he screamed, swatting the unfortunate Yekim with the switch he carried to replace the classroom pointer he had once used to threaten Miranda and the other students at Hopewell Elementary School in Ottawa.

Whistling in fear, Sitruc and Yekim twisted sideways and dropped the heavy stone blocks from their backs. Then they straightened, exchanged frightened glances, and hurried after the former teacher.

As he strode toward the stone guardhouse, Mr. Little bristled like an angry swan, muttering incoherently, mimicking the Wizard's voice. "Check the boy, Little! Make sure he's alive, Little! We don't want anything to happen to the boy, do we, Little? Or we might have to arrange a *Little* accident?" Stubby's face still burned with rage at the sight of Indolent cackling uncontrollably at his tasteless *Little* joke.

The guardhouse was basically a large self-contained room constructed of stone blocks similar to those being used on the new

Castle of Indolence. It formed a square addition to the Castle's foundation. Inside, on the wall opposite the entrance stood a sturdy, barred door. Behind the door, stone steps led down to Indolent's dungeon. The only way into and out of the dungeon was through the guardhouse and past the massive wooden table where a half-dozen large, blank-faced Trolls sat on duty around the clock.

Little stomped up the wide steps and burst into the guardhouse, surprising the Trolls who hastily tried to hide a board game they had been playing, or trying to play, by shoving it under the table. Small, translucent red and yellow stones scattered about the floor. Stubby almost laughed at the Trolls' clumsy attempt to hide the stones by stomping on them. But, he was still too incensed over the way Indolent had treated him to waste laughter on these stupid, bumbling creatures. Ignoring them, he snapped his fingers and pointed to the barred door on the opposite wall.

"Eh, Boss." One of the guards lumbered to his feet, shuffled over to the door, grasped the thick iron latch, and lifted it out of its fastening. The door opened inward with a loud clang. Delivering three stinging swats to the Troll's bare legs, Stubby passed through the doorway and thumped angrily down the steps. Heads bowed to avoid eye contact with the guards, Yekim and Sitruc snatched flaming torches from brackets on the stone wall and followed closely on Mr. Little's heels.

At the end of a narrow, smelly corridor, Stubby stopped before a solid stone door mounted on strong iron hinges and secured by three huge bolts that slid into hollowed out cases in the wall, and a long iron bar that dropped into a metal slot.

"Open it," he commanded, his temper cooled slightly by the terrified expressions on the idiotic Ogres' faces. *They're afraid I'm going to lock them away,* he thought, forcing a giggle back down his throat. For a second, he toyed with the idea, but then he grabbed the torch from Yekim and held it in front of him as he pushed on the heavy door that opened into Nicholas's pitch-black, windowless cell.

"Oh, Nicholas! Eiznek, you little worm . . . " sang Little, peering into the circle of light cast by the torch.

The singing stopped abruptly when Stubby noticed the large stone block on the floor near the outer wall. What was that doing there? Something was very wrong! He rushed into the cell, his Ogre shadows less than a heartbeat behind, sweeping his arm about to throw light into the shadowed corners. Then he saw the large, square hole in the wall above the stone block and felt his body go numb. The torch fell from his hand, hitting the floor and sputtering out, filling the cell with black smoke. The cell was empty. The devious boy and the filthy Eiznek had escaped through the wall.

The former teacher opened his mouth to alert the Troll guards, but before he could utter a word, he heard the familiar grinding sound of stone on stone. The hair on his head stiffened. The door was closing. Finally, he remembered to scream, but it was too late. He heard a series of dull *clangs* as the bolts shot home and the heavy bar dropped into its slot.

Ogres have keener hearing than ex-teachers. Yekim's and Sitruc's sharp ears picked up the sound of the heavy door just as it began to close. Whistling shrilly, Sitruc tightened his grip on the torch and leaped toward the opening. Yekim got there first and barged into the corridor. His companion sucked in his breath and just managed to squeeze through the narrowing slit before the door closed and the solid bar came down.

Nicholas nudged his fellow prisoner excitedly. He couldn't believe his plan was working. As he had sat slumped on the stone block watching the light from the outer corridor spill into the cell as the heavy door inched open, he realized that the door opened into the room, and an idea took hold of his brain. He didn't have time to think about whether it was a good idea or not. It was an idea, and it was all he had.

"Quickly!" he whispered, grabbing his inmate's arm and dragging him into the corner behind the door. Hardly daring to breathe, he waited, hoping that somehow things would work in his favour for a change. Then, he recognized Stubby's taunting voice calling their names, and he kept his eyes glued to the former teacher, as he and two Ogres rushed into the cell.

Now! thought Nicholas, jabbing his elbow into his companion's rib. The prisoners edged around the door and slipped like silent shadows into the corridor. Working frantically, they gripped the iron bar, braced themselves, and pulled the heavy barrier shut.

"Ahhh!" yelled Nicholas, turning and finding himself face to face with Stubby's petrified Ogres.

"Sssst!" whistled the Ogres, returning his stare, their yellow eyes as round as marbles.

"Aiiii!" shrieked Eiznek, suddenly getting a look at Nicholas for the first time.

Nicholas recovered first. "Shut up!" he hissed, turning to the Ogre jailors and cocking his head at the cell door. "Listen! I know that little creep. He's going to be very upset when he discovers that he's in there, but you're out here." He held up his hand to silence the sudden whistling. "If you shout, the guards will come, and we . . ." he indicated his companion. "We'll probably just end up back in the cell. But you're going to be in real trouble for running away and deserting Stubby. Do you understand?"

The Ogres took a second to recover from their fright, then their heads nodded vigorously. "Good," sighed Nicholas. "Now, we have to work together if we want to get out of here with our skins intact. And remember, once we get outside there's no turning back. Don't pay any attention to anything. If someone calls, don't look back. Just keep walking until we can make a run for it."

He looked from one Ogre to the other. "Well, what's it going to be, the four of us locked up in that black cell eating live rats for the rest of our lives, or do we try to get out of here?" He felt his skin crawl as a light came on in the Ogres' eyes when he mentioned the live rats and, for a second, he almost panicked, thinking they were going to choose the dark cell and a diet of rodents over the chance to escape. But, when they nodded again and whistled excitedly, he felt weak with relief.

At the sound of footsteps mounting the dungeon steps, the Trolls looked toward the door, their lumpy, white faces wearing guilty expressions as if they'd been caught in the act of wolfing down Indolent's bugs. Mumbling "Eh, Boss," they hastily crawled from under the table where they had been gathering up the pieces of their board game that hadn't been crushed to powder when they had stomped on them.

Slapping his switch against his leg, Stubby stormed past without so much as a quick glance their way. Behind came Little's two toadies supporting the wretched human boy between them. One of the Trolls grinned wickedly, and ran his black tongue over his fat lips when he noticed Nicholas looking at him. The other Trolls laughed harshly and pounded the table with their fists, smashing the last of the little red and yellow stones.

Nicholas felt sweat running down his neck and back. *What was I thinking?* he asked in his mind. *I must be crazy. We'll never pull this off.* He quickly shifted his eyes from the horrible, leering guard to the door waiting just ahead. *Only a few more steps,* he thought. *Please, don't let them catch us.* At this moment, those few steps seemed as if they were a thousand miles away. He glanced at his little Ogre cellmate doing a pretty good imitation of Stubby as he strode toward the exit, ignoring the Trolls as if they were invisible.

The Ogres had folded their arms and whistled furiously when the boy insisted they go back into the cell and subdue the teacher while he and Eiznek stripped him of his hooded robe. But Nicholas knew it was the only chance they had of getting past the guards. Luckily, when Eiznek slipped the robe over his head, it fit him to a tee. *Oh, oh!* Nicholas suddenly noticed the Ogre's bare, clawed feet showing between the hem of the robe and the floor. They were so blatantly obvious the Trolls had to know that the figure in the robe wasn't their Boss. *Don't stop, Eiznek!* he whispered, afraid that even if the Trolls missed the bare feet, they'd see his heart banging against his chest, signalling them that he was in the act of escaping.

And then, suddenly, they were outside, breathing in the foul air of Indolent's valley as if it were as pure and fresh as a mountain breeze. Nicholas grabbed the railing to steady his trembling legs and looked about. It was night, but he noticed the long line of Ogres emerging from the large, black quarry and shook his head. *Poor things!* he thought sadly, wondering why they didn't unite and fight the Trolls, or run away, or something. He gazed up at the night sky.

Neither stars nor moon were visible beyond the black cloud that hung like solid smoke just above the partly constructed castle. He still couldn't believe they'd actually pulled it off—marched straight past the Trolls as bold as brass. He wanted to shout and laugh, but he knew they weren't out of danger yet. They had to keep going, put some distance between them and the guards inside the guardhouse and the whip-wielding Trolls outside.

He took a step and almost pitched forward onto his face. He was weaker than he had thought. "I should have eaten the rats!" he muttered. He had only taken a few steps when Sitruc and Yekim released his arms, opened their mouths, and began whistling loudly. Then they were gone, racing toward the line of Ogres and the Troll guards, waving their arms and gesticulating frantically at the prisoners.

"TRAITORS!" yelled Nicholas, forgetting his weakness as he leaped down the wide steps and ran blindly toward the darkness away from the Guards. "I HOPE YOU CHOKE ON A RAT BONE." Glancing quickly over his shoulder, he saw Eiznek—his companion of many dark days, a forlorn figure standing as still as a statue, staring after him. "COME ON," he shouted, motioning for the Ogre to follow.

Eiznek didn't wait to be asked twice. His eyes lit up like yellow gemstones and he sped after the boy, a wide grin making his ugly face almost beautiful.

"I hope you know where we're going, because I sure don't," said Nicholas when his friend came alongside.

In answer, Eiznek took the lead, loping easily toward the blacker shape of a hill, silhouetted against the dark horizon. Nicholas kept his eyes focused on the creature's back and followed closely, fighting down waves of dizziness that threatened to topple him. But, somehow, he found within a well of hidden strength that enabled him to keep going. That they were heading for one of the hills troubled him though. He had noticed the hills, manned with guards, when he and his Ogre captors came through the narrow defile into Indolent's valley. Except for a few stunted bushes, there was no cover, no place to hide. If they didn't get off the hills before daylight, they'd be as exposed as a baboon's backside.

CHAPTER TWENTY-TWO

HEAD FOR THE HILLS

"Look!" cried Penelope, jabbing her elbow into Otavite's head and pointing toward one of the low, rolling hills in the distance. "Over there! In the grass! Something's moving!"

Otavite stopped abruptly, almost jolting Penelope from her perch on his broad shoulder. He raised one mighty arm to shield his eyes from the glare of the afternoon sun, and followed the direction the Princess indicated, peering at the far hillside. He counted ten large creatures moving swiftly down the hill, and he recognized them immediately by their white, bloated shapes. "Trolls!" he spat in disgust. "They're moving awfully fast. Must be tracking something."

He reached up to lift Penelope from his shoulder, but the girl realized his intent and clung to his fleecy vest like a leech stuck on a swimmer's leg. "No," she cried. "I refuse to be left behind. It might be Nicholas. I'm coming with you."

The Giant sighed. First Eegar, now the Princess. Why was she being so difficult when all he wanted was to return her to her home in one piece? Was he too soft? None of the other giantpeckers behaved like Eegar. In fact, he rarely caught a glimpse of them on his friends' heads. They seemed content to stay in one place. Now, the Elf girl was acting just like the bird. "It's for your own good," he said finally. "You'll be safer here while Kurr and I find out what the Trolls are hunting."

"No! I told you I'm not staying here." Penelope dug her fingers deeper into his vest.

Otavite sighed again. "Suit yourself. But if you get killed, it will be your own fault," he warned. "Kurr will be nearby, so keep the Muffy dog out of sight."

He raised his hand to his mouth and uttered a strange, deep, bellowing sound. A few seconds later, an answering bellow came from far off to their left. Penelope looked about, but she couldn't see the elusive Carovorare. Then, Otavite set out, moving so swiftly Penelope had to tighten her grip on his vest to keep from flying off onto the hard ground.

They had left the mountains and the snow behind hours ago, and had been following the same trail as it wound among low, rolling foothills. Penelope had discarded her heavy, woolen cloak as the frosty mountain air thawed and the sun shone brightly down on the travellers, warming their faces. Out of the corner of her eye, she thought she saw sudden movement and turned her head quickly. But all she could make out were sparkles as the sun danced on something huge and white tearing through the short trees fringing the earthen trail.

Ahead, the Trolls were clearly visible now. Their numbers had quadrupled as more creatures appeared from around the sides of the hill and advanced toward their descending comrades. Whatever they were hunting was trapped between the three bands. "Please hurry," Penelope pleaded, knowing that Otavite was moving as swiftly as the wind.

But suddenly the Giant slowed and came to a complete stop. "We must hide ourselves and approach unseen," he said, summoning the magic camouflage. He waited for the tingling sensation that always travelled up his arms when he evoked Eegar's special gift. Nothing happened. He remained motionless and tried again. Still nothing. Something was wrong. "I don't understand," he said. "The magic has never failed me before."

"What on earth are you doing?" asked Penelope, wondering if her new friend were losing his mind.

"Eegar's magic," explained Otavite, his voice quiet. "As long as the giantpecker lives on my head, I can use his magic to hide us, to make us blend with the landscape. He is gone, Penelope."

"What are you talking about?" Penelope cried, a sick feeling growing inside her.

Otavite took a deep breath. "In my country, birds like Eegar make their homes on our heads. We welcome them, because they let us share their gift of camouflage. Eegar is like a chameleon, only a bird chameleon. When I don't want to be seen, I use his gift." He shook his head sadly. "I do not know why he flew away."

Oh, oh! Penelope was glad the Giant couldn't see her face because it had suddenly gone as white as the snow back at the fortress. How was she going to tell him that there was no more Eegar—that she had pitched the dead bird away? *I've got to tell him,* she thought, wishing with all her heart that she had left the stupid dead bird in his head. She wondered what Otavite would do when he found out what she'd done. *The worst he can do is kill me,* she thought. *Oh well! I might as well do it now and get it over with.*

"Otavite . . .?" she gulped.

"Yes, Princess."

"Stop calling me that. I told you my name is Penelope."

"I know, Princess, but I do not feel right calling you by your given name."

"You're not making this very easy," she sighed, tears sticking to her eyelashes. "I have to tell you something. You're not going to like it . . ."

"Not now!" said the Giant, abruptly breaking into a run. "There! The Trolls are closing in on something. They haven't spotted it yet. Wait! There are two creatures . . . small like you. Can you see them? Do you know them?"

Penelope squinted, straining to see the trapped creatures against the glare of the sun. "Oh Otavite, it's Nicholas . . . and . . . I can't believe it . . . but it looks like . . . Yikes! It's one of those horrible Ogres."

Crouching in the tall grass halfway down the hill, Nicholas clapped his trembling companion on the back. It was all over. There were Trolls combing the hill above and more Trolls climbing the hill on either side. "I'm sorry, Eiznek," he said. "I don't know how we're going to wriggle out of this one. There's nowhere left to run."

Eiznek nodded, whistling sadly. Nicholas's heart ached for his companion. He sensed the other's fear and he felt responsible. "It's my fault," he said, forcing himself to meet the Ogre's gaze. "I got you into this. You probably would have been better off staying in the cell."

"Sssst!" The Ogre shook his head vehemently. "Sssst!"

But Nicholas didn't feel any better. He was responsible, because he had urged the creature to come with him. He was the one who had said, *'I'll get us out of here. I won't let anything happen to you. Trust me.'* His words sounded glib as they echoed in his mind. Talk really is cheap, he thought, feeling as guilty as if he had stabbed Eiznek in the back. "Look what trusting me got you." he said softly, dropping his eyes and turning away. And what about Miranda? How was he going to get to her before Malcolm found her . . . with that egg?

But then he was grabbing the Ogre's arm so tightly the other winced in pain. "I just thought of something," he said, his eyes bright with excitement. "Remember how we got past the guards?" When his companion nodded, he continued. "None of this lot was there, so they don't know what happened in the dungeon. And I don't think those two Ogres had time to tell them that we locked Stubby in the cell. So why don't we do the same thing again? Do something to get their attention, then grab my arm and pretend you captured me. What do you think?"

For a second Eiznek stared blankly at the boy as if he didn't understand, but Nicholas figured, or hoped, that he was digesting the plan. He held his breath, unable to read the other's expression. But then, the Ogre broke out in a wide grin, nodding and whistling happily.

"All right!" agreed Nicholas, also grinning and slapping the Ogre's hand in a totally lame attempt to give the other a high five. The Ogre looked from his palm to the boy curiously.

"Never mind," said Nicholas. "It would take too long to explain. Now, listen! We might be able to sneak away as long as they think you're the Boss. Hopefully they won't tie me up. But you'll have to be strong and brave. Show them you want the credit for capturing me. Don't let them take me from your control. And don't let them see your face. Act like Stubby."

The Ogre nodded and, before Nicholas could blink, grabbed him by the arm and stood, waving wildly. Forty Trolls whipped their lumpy heads in the direction of the disguised Ogre and the escaped prisoner. Eiznek shook his charge roughly and started up the hill toward the advancing guards.

And then, a loud bellowing roar thundered over the hill, bending the long grass almost flat, and almost knocking Nicholas and Eiznek off their feet. A huge, nightmare monster plowed up the hill, leaving a wide path of trampled grass in its wake. Kurr's sharp bristles stood out like the quills of a giant porcupine, but everyone on the hill could see that this creature was not a porcupine. Nicholas forgot that he was supposed to be the prisoner. He grabbed Eiznek's arm and started running. He didn't care if he ran straight into the Trolls; his only thought was to put as much distance as he could between him and the charging terror. The Trolls screamed and scattered in every direction, knocking one another out of the way in their mad scramble to escape.

Penelope gasped as Kurr smashed into a band of Trolls, lips curled back as his sharp teeth snapped at the enemy. It was a horrible sight. The giant Carovorare looked like a monster machine gone berserk. Its great spiked tail struck again and again. The giant spikes on its sides stabbed deep into the Trolls, impaling the creatures whose futile struggles only drove the spines deeper into their bodies. Kurr's sharp claws sliced the enemy apart before they could scream out. In less than a minute over a dozen Trolls lay dead, bodies shredded like giant Michelin men run over by a lawnmower.

"Put me down!" cried Penelope, fighting to keep the bile down her throat. But Otavite ignored her, or else he was so focused on the battle ahead that the little Elven princess simple ceased to exist for him. Penelope buried her face in the Giant's vest and sobbed uncontrollably, arms squeezing Muffy so tightly the dog whined and squirmed in alarm.

Realizing they couldn't outrun the giant creature, the Trolls came together and turned to fight, moving out to surround the Carovorare.

"Die, big ugly stupid," they chanted, exchanging enraged glances before lunging at the creature simultaneously from all directions, whips cracking and thick, curved swords slashing.

"Go away!" shouted Otavite, waving his arm toward the hilltop. "We will not harm you if you go now."

At the unexpected sound of the Giant's voice, Penelope risked a quick peek to see if the Trolls would obey him. But they laughed and half of them turned and came at him, pressing closer and closer. Penelope saw that Otavite was doing his best to brush the Trolls aside with his great arms without killing them, but they were starting to pose a serious threat to the Giant, charging at him, long whips lashing the air, cracking with sounds like air-filled paper bags bursting just as they struck flesh. The giant's arms were coated with a mass of bleeding cuts, but he didn't seem to notice. Still, he tried to reason with the crazed guards.

"Stop now! You cannot fight Kurr. Turn and go back the way you came and you will live to see the dawn. We only want the servant, Nicholas."

Penelope noticed that the Carovorare didn't share Otavite's qualms about killing Trolls. That's because it's just an animal, she thought. Acting purely by instinct. "But Otavite is human, and his very humanness could get him killed by creatures that don't value human or any other life. Not even their own," she whispered, watching in disgust as they grabbed their comrades and tried to offer them to the beast to protect themselves.

And then one of the Trolls feinted and thrust at Otavite with his sword, cutting deep into the Giant's leg. Before the creature could pull the weapon free, Otavite roared in pain and anger, and lashed out with his long knife, slicing through three Trolls in one smooth sweep. The creatures' knees buckled and they toppled over like trees in a landslide. Penelope tried to duck behind the Giant's head to avoid being splattered by gobs of milky green scuz that squirted from the Trolls' wounds, but she wasn't fast enough. The stinking matter rained on her head and shoulders, coating her with sticky ichor that smelled worse than three-day-old road kill.

"Yuck!" she screamed, scraping the horrible guck out of her hair and flicking it off her fingers. "BAD DOG!" She smacked Muffy on her snout when she noticed the dog liked the taste of the Trolls' insides and was busily licking a blob on the neck of her jacket. Out of the corner of her eye, she saw more Trolls appear, surging over the brow and around the sides of the hill. They looked like huge white maggots swarming over a body. In a matter of minutes, Otavite would be overwhelmed.

"Let's go!" she cried. "More are coming. Let's get out of here."
She felt that his injuries were her fault.

Otavite filled his great lungs with air. The Princess was right. He could hear the shouts of many Trolls coming to join their comrades. He swung his long knife in a great sweeping arc from right to left, and back, cutting down six or seven creatures. Then he backed away quickly and followed the girl's directions to the way the nasty little Ogre had taken her servant. They easily outdistanced the Trolls who chased after them, bellowing like wild boars, before turning back to the enemy beast with the wicked spiked tail.

"NII-IIK?" Penelope shouted. "NICHOLAS?" She almost giggled when the giant opened his big mouth and roared.

"NICH-O-LAS?" It reminded her of an ad on TV about a man standing on an Alp in Switzerland and shouting out the name of some cough drop.

"There he is!" Penelope itched to jump off the Giant's shoulder and run toward Nicholas, but she knew she'd get there faster if she remained where she was. It just seemed slower because she was totally immobile.

Nicholas heard his name echoing across the hillside as if it were coming through a loudspeaker. He wheeled about, blinking in disbelief at the source of the loud voice. Before he could react, the hugest human creature he had ever seen reached down and grabbed Eiznek, who had been cowering behind him. Only then did Nicholas move. He charged the Giant's leg, kicking, punching, and yelling until he thought his lungs would explode.

"NO! Let him go, you creep!"

Penelope was dumbfounded. Had Nicholas finally lost his mind? Why should he give a hoot about what happened to the nasty little toad? Aha! she thought. He's identifying with his captors, like a lot of kidnap victims. It's the Stockholm syndrome. Poor Nicholas. She called her friend's name.

Nicholas froze. He recognized that voice. *Penelope! But . . . how?*
He slowly raised his head, not even daring to guess how Penelope's
voice just happened to be coming from this huge creature.

"Nick! Up here. Otavite won't hurt you. We've come to rescue you."

"Penelope?" Nicholas stared at the small girl perched on the Giant's
shoulder as if she owned him. "What are you doing up there?"

"It's a long story," said Penelope.

"Tell your friend to let Eiznek go. He's not like the others. He
helped me escape."

Otavite gently set the little Ogre on the ground and turned his
head toward Penelope. "Princess, is this your lost servant?"

Nicholas looked confused. "Princess? Servant? What's going on?"

Penelope turned as red as Eegar's feathers. "Umm . . . er . . .
That's another long story."

"I suggest we get going," said Otavite, turning and striding up
the hill.

"Where?" asked Nicholas, running to keep up with the Giant.

"I am accompanying the Princess to the land of the Elves,"
said Otavite.

Penelope put her finger to her lips, cautioning Nicholas to be
quiet. "I'll explain later," she mouthed the words.

"We've got to find Miranda," said Nicholas. "I found out what
they're planning to do with the last egg. Malcolm is saving it for her.
We've got to find her first and warn her."

"Oh my God!" cried Penelope, suddenly shivering as the image
of a red-eyed snake bursting from the body of its human host
suddenly filled her mind. She had seen such a serpent once before.
In Bethany. At King Elester's Crowning. She couldn't bear to think
that something so horrible could happen to Miranda—that one of
the Demon's serpents would kill her friend and live inside her body.
"Oh, Otavite. Please hurry."

They quickly left the surviving Trolls behind. Penelope looked about for Kurr, but there was no sign of the great white beast. When they stopped to rest in a secluded spot between two hills, Otavite said that he must sleep. Penelope couldn't believe that he'd been walking, non-stop, for almost two days. While the Giant tended his wounds and curled up in the tall grass, Penelope let Muffy out of her jacket and she and Nicholas huddled together and whispered long into the night. When she glanced at the Ogre, he grinned shyly and twisted his large splayed fingers nervously.

"How did you meet up with . . . what's its name?"

"His name is Eiznek," said Nicholas, protectively.

Nicholas went first, telling her how the Ogres had finally taken him to Indolent's new Castle. He told her everything that happened, and how the wicked Wizard had thrown him in the dungeon. "That's where I found Eiznek. He was locked up too."

"We've got to tell King Elester and the Druid about Indolent," said Penelope.

"Yes," agreed Nicholas. "And about that cavern place, and Malcolm. Something's going on and I don't understand it. When I was at Castle Cockroach, I felt like I was in a dream. Something was different, but I can't figure it out. It was a feeling that everybody was waiting for something or someone." He fell silent, shaking his head. Then he looked at Eiznek. "I wish my friend could speak English, I think he knows what's going on."

Eiznek whistled his agreement.

"I know some of it," said Penelope. "But I think Otavite knows a lot more than he's saying. He talked about a pool and kept saying that if Malcolm had you, he'd feed you to the pool. Then he asked me about the King of the Dead." She looked at Nicholas and shrugged. "I didn't know what he was talking about."

"Let's ask him," said Nicholas.

"Ask me what?" said Otavite, rubbing his eyes.

"About the pool and the King of the Dead," said Nicholas.

So Otavite told them everything that had happened inside the Bronks. His companions' eyes grew bigger and bigger when he described the Sarcophagus and the body that the Elf and the Ogres removed and slid into the still pool.

Nicholas looked at Penelope. "The Elf. It has to be Mathus."

"You're right. I forgot all about Mathus. It's because he was so, you know, passive."

"Not passive anymore," said Otavite. "He's gone. One of my colleagues kicked him into the pool. I saw him sink with my own eyes."

The companions fell silent. They knew that some terrible plan was being hatched, but there were too many missing pieces to the puzzle and their brains were dead from trying to figure it out. One by one they drifted off to sleep, but giant skeletons and hissing serpents invaded their dreams and caused them to cry out in the darkness.

CHAPTER TWENTY-THREE

FLIGHT TO THE DARK LANDS

espair washed over Miranda like a heavy, black wave, threatening to pull her under and drag her down to the bottom of the ocean. It was early morning and they had been in the air for a day and a night. The winged Hunters had flown without stopping, the sound of their wings rolling like thunder across the sky. Ahead, she saw a black smudge on the far horizon. She didn't have to get any closer to it. She knew it as surely as she recognized the Peace Tower back home in Ottawa. The swirling, screaming Cataclysm guarded the Demon's lands as effectively as if it were a solid wall. But it wasn't a wall. It was a storm of the essence of all those creatures who had looked to Hate for the power they craved, and found her waiting.

Miranda had mixed emotions about Hate's half-dead followers. They terrified her to death, but she also felt sorry for them. She remembered Naim saying once that they had known what they were doing when they willingly chose Evil. But, she wasn't so sure. If they had known that Hate would rip out their minds and destroy what they had been, leaving nothing but empty shells, would they have gone to her? If they had known that they would cease to exist, would they have gone? The questions troubled her. She desperately wanted to understand why the Thugs and Werecurs had turned to the Demon. Perhaps, she thought, it was the same hunger that drove Calad-Chold to forge his terrible swords.

She wasn't really surprised to learn that the Dark Lands was their final destination. She had been so intent on trying to work out why the Demon wanted her alive that she just hadn't given much thought to where they were going. Now, the knowledge chilled her to the bone. What was waiting for her within the twisting, curling blackness? Was it the Demon? What if Hate *had* escaped from the Place with No Name undetected by the Elves? What if . . .? "Don't go there!" she whispered silently.

She thought about her friends. Where were they now? Were Nick and Penelope safe? Had they found each other and made their way back home? Or had they ended up here, somewhere in this world? What if the King of the Dead had found them? And, what about Bell? The last she'd seen of her best friend was a small, dark shape running away as if Miranda were her worst enemy. *Oh Bell, I'm sorry*, she thought. *Please be OK.* She wondered if she'd ever see any of them again. She imagined that they were thinking of her as her thoughts went out to them, and she clung to that notion with all of her heart.

Suddenly, a screech ripped through the air, scraping along Miranda's jagged nerves like a dull knife cutting through glass. She felt a ripple of some deep emotion run through the Hunter, setting the sharp claws encircling her chest trembling. Was it fear? Were the Hunters afraid of something? She twisted her head about, her eyes scoping the sky for the source of the creatures' fear or rage. But she saw nothing amiss. Then, the Werecurs reacted as one, dipping their heads and dropping like monstrous black flies toward the distant ground. The fleshy wings furled about Miranda, cutting off her vision and smothering her half to death.

It's Naim! she thought, knowing even as the thought flew into her mind that the creatures weren't reacting to the Druid. They were at least a thousand feet in the air, and miles beyond the reach of the man's powers. Unable to see, she squeezed her eyes shut and listened to the rapid pounding of her heart, counting the beats to keep from screaming.

High in the sky, southeast of the White Mountains, the great double-headed Eagle, Charlemagne, glided on the hot air currents. Where the sun touched his gold-tipped wings, he appeared as a burst of flame—a living fireball. His sharp, amber-coloured eyes were fixed on the black host below, winging swiftly toward the Dark Lands. Curious, he banked toward it.

For many days now, he had been sailing the skies, scouring the land for Naim the Druid, because he was deeply troubled by what was happening throughout the land. When he had first spotted the blackened, wasted earth, he thought it was a river, fouled and polluted beyond salvation, winding across the valley toward the northeast. He dropped for a closer look, but he hadn't landed. The stench and the feeling of evil warned him away. He saw that it wasn't a river. It was a track, and something huge had made it. So he had soared higher and higher until he saw all across the land vast swatches of black and smoking trails all leading into or out of the Dark Lands. What was this new evil the Demon had unleashed?

Turbulence slammed into him, buffeting him with invisible fists, and knocked him spinning and somersaulting through the sudden disturbance. He straightened and skimmed the edges of the rough wind, and then tensed as the sky turned dark and a gigantic shadow passed over him.

Ten thousand feet above the Werecurs where the air nipped at his flesh with teeth of ice, an enormous Black Dragon circled lazily in the morning sky. He twisted his head to the side and spat into the wind, clearing the last of a throatful of bones from his cavernous mouth. The one thing he couldn't stomach about Ogres was their bones. Their small bones were just too much trouble. "Give me Trolls any day," he muttered. "Same number of bones but bigger, easier to eject."

Hunting had been good during the night, but the deep rumble coming from his stomach told the monstrous Dragon that he was still hungry. He rolled onto his back and coasted on the air currents, savouring the tastes of the various creatures he had devoured over the past six hours, not counting the band of Ogres, that while filling, tasted like soot. First there was that long serpent thing. *Not bad. A bit ripe, though.* Still, he'd keep his eyes peeled for another. Next, he swooped down upon a dozen Trolls, surprising them. He got two of them before the others made it into the forest. Trolls weren't an exotic meal, but you could always count on them tasting the same, sort of like cottage cheese.

The huge flying predator drooled as he recalled the night's most delectable dish—a herd of cattle. The Dragon loved cattle. They were rare though and, whenever he happened upon a herd, his eyes were bigger than his stomach, and he tended to overeat. How many had he scarfed down last night? A dozen? Two dozen? He couldn't remember, but he figured it had to be more than ten. Funny, but unlike Troll and Ogre bones, cow bones were actually quite scrumptious, especially when you ate the whole cow in a couple of bites. All those tantalizing tastes at once!

His keen eyes had detected the movement of other living creatures during the night, rabbits and smaller prey that failed to excite his taste buds. But he had also seen something else, and it still puzzled him. Landing in a dense forest amidst a violent storm of trees and boulders whipped up by the power of his great wings and lashing tail, he had sensed the presence of something dark and menacing. Normally, *menacing* had little meaning for Dragons, because nothing menaced them, ever. But, the unnaturally heavy silence of the trees and forest denizens told the Dragon that something evil had entered the woods unbidden. He felt as if the entire world were holding its breath, waiting in fear for the end to come.

He hadn't discovered the source of the evil, but his wide nostrils had picked up a sweet, mouldy odour, and he saw with his own eyes the smouldering earth where the being had passed. It was the smell of the creature that puzzled him. His nose told him that it came from something that had been dead for centuries. But, the scorched, smoking earth spoke of recent passage. The Dragon shivered. A blast of flames spewed from his mouth, taking the chill out of the surrounding air, but doing little to melt the ice that settled in his heart.

Rolling back into a flying position, the Dragon stretched his mighty wings and descended in wide slow spirals, scanning the earth below for anything alien, anything that didn't belong. He spotted the glowing Eagle and, for a moment, thought about blasting its feathers to kingdom come, but his eyes were drawn to a large black cloud scudding swiftly across the sky like a shadow, obliterating the surface of the earth. The Dragon almost turned toward the White Mountains then, but something about the cloud held his gaze. The wide spirals tightened and he dropped for a closer look.

The Dragon's piercing, flame-coloured eyes locked on the blackness. *If that's a cloud, I'll eat my tail.* Steam whistled from his giant nostrils when he recognized the creatures. *Hate's Hunters!* For a second, he thought he had solved the riddle of the forest. But then, he snorted at the very idea. No! It wasn't the stinking Werecurs that had petrified the forest. The winged ones were neither cunning nor intelligent. They couldn't think. They couldn't reason. They couldn't feel happy or sad. The Demon had seen to that, stripping them of their humanity and remaking them into mindless aberrations, subservient to her will. They might frighten Elves and Dwarves but they didn't frighten Dragons, and they certainly didn't smoulder like the presence in the forest.

What were the Hunters doing beyond the borders of the Dark Lands? The last time he had encountered the winged ones, he and a great host of Dragons had driven them back into the darkness. That was over a year ago, and he hadn't spied them since. Something was afoot. "It is not my concern." He breathed the words through a stream of flames and plummeted toward the black cloud.

The Werecurs screeched and streaked toward the shelter of the trees, biting and slashing frenziedly at the slower members of their grotesque flock. Miranda felt as if she were riding a giant roller coaster in a dark, airless place. She could hardly breathe. Furled in the creature's foul wings, the reek of death and decay enveloped her, making her gag again and again. Suddenly, she felt the creature lurch as if something huge had slammed into it. The next thing she knew, the hunter's body went limp, its wings peeled away, and Miranda was free-falling through the air, hurtling head-over-heels toward the rapidly advancing trees.

Typhon, chief of the Black Dragons and guardian of the hoard, roared fire as he collided with the Werecur. His sharp foreclaws slashed once, but that was enough. The creature was finished. Even before its lifeless form began to fall, the Dragon had forgotten about it and had already marked another foe. But a movement below, to his right, caught his eye and he swung his gigantic head about. Something besides dead Werecurs was falling through the air. He plunged down and down, his long forelimbs stretched to scoop up the small silver pouch that had slipped through the Thug's clawed hands.

Delighted with the treasure, Typhon chased the Hunters toward the Dark Lands and then banked steeply and wheeled toward the White Mountains and home.

CHAPTER TWENTY-FOUR

THE COUNCIL OF BETHANY

"Pardon, Sire. Are you saying that we can not lift a finger to stop this Dead King?"

Elester had just finished advising the Council that Calad-Chold had been called back from the dead and was amassing his fell legions in the Dark Lands. "Their deadly sight is fixed on Bethany," he had ended. "And they coming. They are coming as surely as winter comes to the high mountains."

He turned to the speaker. Airlie was the most senior Elf in the kingdom, and Chief Advisor of the Erudicia. "There is one thing," he said. "But our chances of finding it in time are practically non-existent." The young King of the Elves gripped his father's green wisdom stone tightly in his hand as he looked at the grim expressions on the faces of the men and women seated about the long table. "Calad-Chold forged a knife for himself. The Druid believes that this Twisted Blade is the only weapon that can be used against him."

"Where is this blade?" It was Airlie again. Her emerald green eyes were sharp and intelligent.

Elester shook his head wearily. "I do not know. It could be anywhere."

"I tell you, it's here!" At the sound of the raspy voice, all eyes shifted to the gruff Dwarf seated near the foot of the table.

"Nonsense!" answered Airlie. "I beg your pardon, Dwarf friend, but if the Dead King's knife were hidden anywhere on this Island I, for one, would know of it. We are Elves, Sir. Our magic would have detected it the moment it entered our lands."

"Hrumph!" snorted Gregor. "Didn't detect Demon's eggs!"

A moment of embarassed silence followed Gregor's outburst.

"You are right," admitted Elester, finally. "Even Elves grow complacent. We forgot to use our seeking powers. Perhaps we hoped that the Battle of Dundurum signaled an end to the Demon's terror. But since then, not a single night has gone by when I have not used my powers to search for evil on this Island. The knife is evil. It is not here."

It was not a hard and fast rule but, like his father before him, the young Elven King made decisions affecting the security of Ellesmere Island after soliciting the advice of the Council of Bethany. Members of the Council included the Erudicia, twelve of the wisest men and women in the Kingdom, chosen by the Elven people. Heads of the various arms of the military, and any person or being with knowledge to share were also entitled, and even encouraged, to attend and participate in special meetings of the Council.

From her position in one of the three chairs at the foot of the table, Arabella sat as straight as a poker, trying to make herself appear bigger. She also examined the others in the room and had noticed the blood drain from the faces of the Erudicia as the King gave his report. Their flesh looked as bleached as the white hooded tunics they wore as a symbol of their office, as if they had aged a hundred years before her eyes. She felt sorry for them because all of their combined wisdom was useless against the horror that was coming.

It's the end of the world! she thought. And, for a moment, she could think of nothing else. Arabella believed it so completely she almost choked on despair. Then she clenched her fists and fought her thoughts, driving them into the dark places in her mind where she refused to go.

Her eyes travelled along the table. King Gregor scowled and muttered rudely as he impatiently scraped his boots on the floor and banged the polished wooden surface with his elbows. Arabella couldn't help grinning, but she covered her mouth with her hand and quickly looked away before he noticed.

The Dwarf King was a man of action. He hated sitting about when he could be out tracking down the enemy. Arabella sighed. *But this time it's different*, she thought. How could you track and fight an enemy that was already dead—an enemy that couldn't be stopped? Still, she understood his impatience, because she also longed to be doing something. All this sitting around and waiting was driving her crazy.

Looking toward the head of the table, she noticed Andrew Furth busily taking notes. As if he felt her eyes on him, the young aide looked up and winked, his grin like a brief flash of light in the somber room. Arabella threw him a quick smile and returned to her study of the others. Of the thirty or forty people present, she knew only three. The realization depressed her, pushing down on her shoulders until she felt she was shrinking—melting into the fabric of the chair. She sighed, wondering what on earth she was doing here. What was her role in the war that was coming to this land with the might of a tsunami? What did she know about war? *I'd probably take one look at Calad-Chold and run away like a mouse from a hawk.*

It rankled more than anything to come face to face with the fact that she was only eleven years old. She had always seen herself as tough and smart—a leader, although some of her friends called her *control freak* to her face. She devoured books, and knew about lots of things. Her marks in school were excellent. Yet, in this room, among the smartest people in the world, and soldiers with hard faces and cold, icy green eyes, she felt small and stupid—utterly powerless. There wasn't one single thing she could do to help save the Elves and their world from the evil King and his deadly army. The realization that she was as insignificant as a droplet of water in a heavy rainfall made her itch with frustration.

Arabella sighed again. *I want to go home!* The thought came to her out of the blue. And, suddenly, she wished that she could blink and find herself back in Ottawa, safe at home, watching a movie, or hanging out with her friends. Even one of her endless arguments with her mother would be better than waiting for the dead to come and take her. But then she remembered the rift that had opened along the Rideau River near her house, and the creatures Miranda said were lurking in the darkness at the bottom of the wide chasm. She realized that even if she were back home, she would not find safety there. When Calad-Chold gave the order, the dead would pour out of the crack in the earth, flooding Ottawa like a swollen river, and killing everyone in their path. It was too horrible to contemplate. The girl's mind raced as it frantically searched for a way to escape the killing horde, but it was trapped, like a wild bird beating its wings against the bars of its cage.

"We're going to die!" Arabella hadn't realized she had spoken aloud until the heavy silence made her sit up with a start. Every head in the room was turned toward her. Her face burned, and tears welled up in her eyes. "I'm sorry," she said, her voice a tiny squeak. "It's just that everybody keeps talking about dead things that can't be stopped, and I'm scared. I'm so scared I hurt here." She crossed her fists over her chest and pressed tightly against her breastbone. "I can't stand it anymore," she continued, looking from one unsmiling face to another. "So, please, just tell me. Are we just going to sit around here and let it happen?"

For a second, no one spoke. Then Elester's soft chuckle broke the silence. "Come here, child."

Arabella slid off her chair and walked slowly toward the head of the long table, aware that everyone was staring at her. She didn't care. There was nothing mean or nasty about the stares. The adults were worried about her, because she was just a little kid. When she reached the King, she stopped. Elester gently placed his hands on her shoulders.

"You are right to be afraid, Arabella," he said. "But you are not alone. Look!" He indicated the men and woman in the room. "Look in their eyes. Do you not see that we are all frightened?"

Arabella obeyed. She looked at the people around the table and others in chairs against the walls. This time, she didn't see a bunch of adults. She saw human beings like herself, only older. And, as she gazed into their eyes, she saw that Elester was right. *They're scared out of their minds too!* Somehow, the sight of a room full of terrified adults didn't comfort her.

"As long as there is a second's worth of time remaining, there is hope," Elester said. "This is not the first time evil has threatened to wipe us from the face of the earth. And it will not be the last."

"But, Sir, are we going to die?" Fear still clawed at the girl's heart.

"I will not lie to you, child," said Elester, the strain of the past days making him look old. "Against this enemy, we may very well die."

Arabella broke down then, sobbing and sniffling uncontrollably. "I-I'm s-so s-scared. I-I d-don't w-want t-to b-be a c-coward."

No one knew what to do to comfort the despairing girl. Elester took a long breath. "Arabella." He spoke softly, but his voice was strong and steady, and filled with such resolve that, for a moment, the dark mood in the council chamber lightened, and hope flared in Arabella's heart. She raised her head and met the clear, green eyes of the only person in the entire world she could trust to keep her alive.

"Arabella, you are not of Elven blood, but you have the heart of one of my bravest warriors. If you were not afraid, I would pity you. But, to know what Evil is, and to fear it, is the beginning of wisdom. And you, child, are wise beyond your years."

Then, to Arabella's astonishment, he praised her to the others. "This human girl journeyed with our kin, Miranda, from another world to warn us of danger despite the fact that she fears with every fibre of her being the evil that has been summoned and will soon be loosed against us. Her presence here today must be a reminder to the Elven nation never to stop fearing evil." He paused and smiled at Arabella. "But we have to be strong and not let fear do Evil's work."

Arabella nodded. She wasn't sure she understood every word King Elester has just spoken, but she knew what he meant. If she allowed her fear to paralyze her, she might as well just give up, or lie down and die, because she was already lost. She started to return to her own seat, but the King placed his hand on her arm, stopping her. He tilted his head toward the empty place beside him. "Stay," he said. "In case I have further need of your wisdom." Then he turned and addressed the others.

"I leave for Vark tonight," he said, holding up his hand to still the sudden murmurs of protest. "This mission would not be necessary if the Druid were here. But our plans to track the Twisted Blade from the Vark/Rhan War to its present location failed when the Demon's Hunters snatched the child, Miranda. Our friend, Naim, could not abandon her. He has gone after her. Without the benefit of the Druid's counsel, I must go and look upon this iron coffin, and satisfy myself that the Dead King walks."

Arabella sat up with a start, her eyes shining with excitement. *Finally!* she thought. *We're doing something.* She glanced at King Gregor and fought to stifle the giggle that tried to escape when she saw the Dwarf's face crack into a wide toothy grin. He, too, was glad to be doing something.

"Think, Sire," cautioned Coran, the grizzled Commander of the Elven Guard. "You are our King. Your place is here. You do not know what dangers may be waiting on the road to the Red Mountains. I would gladly undertake the journey in your place."

"Coran is right," said Math, a soft-spoken Elder who had been a close friend and confidant of the late King Ruthar. Arabella would have been surprised to learn that the frail, kind-looking man once commanded the entire Elven military. "To risk your own life on a mission that does nothing to help us fight the Dead King and his armies is foolhardy."

Elester listened patiently as other voices joined the Elder's in protest over his plans. Then he shook his head wearily. "You are right," he said quietly. "And wrong. As a soldier, I slept on the hard ground with the men and woman under my command. I have never asked another to do something that I would not do. As your King, do you not think that I have a duty to know all there is to know about the evil we face before I ask others to die defending against that evil?"

"But, what if . . .?"

Elester raised his hand to silence the Elder. "It is not on a mere whim that I have made this decision. We will make our first stand off the Island. Troops are assembling as we speak. If the Dead Army cannot be defeated, I will order our soldiers to the ships. My journey will be short and quick. Airlie will tend the Kingdom in my absence with the help of her colleagues in the Erudicia. Math will command the bulk of the army that will remain here to defend our homeland, and handle security matters. In the morning our people will evacuate the cities. They will assemble at Basil. And if all fails, we will take to the water and sail our people West."

"Where's Basil?" asked Arabella, forgetting that it was rude to interrupt a king. But Elester didn't seem to mind.

"Basil is our walled fortress in the northern mountains. It is a vast place that can easily accommodate the entire Elven nation. You will see it for yourself, Arabella, since you will be travelling with Airlie."

"What?" Arabella was on her feet before the word was out of her mouth. "What do you mean, I'll be travelling with Airlie?"

"You will be safer in the mountains," said Elester.

That's not fair! screamed Arabella silently. And it wasn't fair. One minute they acted as if she were really important and the next minute they treated her like a little kid. Well, they didn't own her. She wasn't even from their world. She was free, and could go where, and do whatever, she wanted. *No way am I staying behind,* she vowed, smiling innocently at Andrew Furth who was looking at her suspiciously.

After the meeting, Arabella wandered aimlessly through the city, but she noticed nothing. Her mind was racing trying to figure out how to follow Elester and the others. It was dusk when she found herself at the southern end of the city near the harbour.

"I can not find the child anywhere. But, Sire, I was watching her closely when you said that she was to remain here, and I could read in her face that she is up to something."

Elester took Noble's reins and led the gray stallion out of the stable. "She is confused and frightened," he said. "Imagine what she must be feeling . . . alone . . . without her friends. Let her be, Andrew. She is intelligent and will work things out in her own way." He clapped his aide on the shoulder. "She will see the wisdom in staying here."

Andrew shrugged. "I am afraid I do not share your certainty, Sire."

Elester slipped his foot into the stirrup and swung himself into the saddle. Then he wheeled Noble about until he was facing the men who were accompanying him to the land of the Giants. There was Gregor, King of the Dwarves, as stiff as if he were sitting on a saddle of sharp spikes instead of fine, seasoned leather. Accompanying him were two Dwarf soldiers, the flag of the Dwarves and the King's standard furled on long poles. Andrew Furth was there, unable to hide his amusement at the Dwarf King's discomfort. Faron, Captain of the King's Riders, and ten of his best

Riders, made up the last members of the Company.

"Let us go," said the King. "Our ship is waiting." Then he led them toward the harbour. The horses' hooves made no sound on the grassy streets and pathways as the Company moved like shadows through the sleeping city. No one noticed the small ship glide out of the harbour like a silent, black wraith, and follow in the wake of ten massive troop carriers.

CHAPTER TWENTY-FIVE

JUST IN TIME
FOR DINNER

he old man would have tripped over the small form lying on the snow, if his Wolfhound hadn't growled menacingly. The man's eyesight had been failing for so many years he couldn't remember when the problem started. But he refused to wear glasses, insisting that it was just a temporary thing and, one day soon, his vision would return to what it had been when he was a lad of twenty.

"What's that, boy? What have you found, eh?" He moved toward the blurred shape of the dog, his slow steps exaggerated as if he were stepping over large exposed roots. "That's a good boy," he said, patting the Wolfhound's head. Aged bones creaked as the old man knelt on the ground, heedless of the snow and the sharp pine needles that bit his frail knees. "Well, well, Seeker. It's a human. A human girl." He pressed a wrinkled finger against the child's neck, seeking a pulse. "She's alive, boy! Barely!"

The old man gently gathered the frozen girl in his arms, struggled to his feet, and tottered through the blizzard toward the little house barely visible in the clearing at the edge of the woods. The large Wolfhound led the way, dashing ahead and back, announcing their arrival with a series of sharp barks.

Miranda was falling. Below, under the thick canopy of boughs, concealed among the tall pine trees, something waited. She didn't know what it was, but she knew what it wanted. It wanted to kill her. So, she had to be careful, and cunning. She mustn't let it find her. Her body crashed through the trees, snapping off branches that clawed at the bare flesh on her arms and face. She grabbed at the limbs in a futile attempt to slow her fall. The needles pricked her hands and fingers, and stuck there, embedded like splinters. The last thing she remembered before slamming into the ground was pain shooting through her body, and later, much later, the sound of a large dog barking. She wondered what Nicholas's dog was doing here.

She opened her eyes and blinked. "Where am I?" she asked aloud, kicking the bedclothes to the foot of the bed and struggling to sit up. "Ouch!" She ached all over, as if a car had plowed into her. Her head felt as if it were split wide open. She tried to reach up to hold her head together, and realized that one arm, her left, was bound tightly against her ribs. *Broken?* she wondered. Squinting in the gray light coming from a small paned glass window, she peered about, her brain registering the details of the room. It was almost bare, except for the single bed, a small night table, and a large standing mirror in a corner near an ancient wooden wardrobe.

She looked down and saw that she was still wearing her old clothes. Her lips formed a frown as she noticed how tattered and dirty they were after her brush with the Werecurs and her fall through the trees. She eased her body off the bed and made her slow way toward the wardrobe, stopping to gape at her image in the long mirror. "Yuck!" she cried, moving closer to examine the network of scratches on her face and arms. "You're ugly, but I still like you," she whispered. As she removed the sling on her arm, she suddenly tensed. She felt as if . . . as if she had been here before, in this very room, before this mirror, staring at cuts and scrapes from some other time. No! She chased the feeling away and opened the cupboard door. Then she froze, staring in disbelief at the contents of the old wardrobe.

"It's impossible!" she whispered, her uninjured arm reaching for a pair of baggy flannel trousers hanging from a wooden peg on the back of the wardrobe door. For a second, she was sure that she was finally losing her mind. She knew these trousers. She had worn them. Then she saw the red wooly tights and long yellow robe that she had left for Nicholas. A flicker of a smile crossed her face as she remembered how she had dissolved into laughter when Nicholas came out of this room wearing the stupid wooly tights and goofy robe. His face had turned as red as the tights.

Miranda shook her head. No matter what she was seeing, these weren't the same garments. They couldn't be. The idea was ridiculous. She and Nicholas had run away in those clothes and had tossed them in a fire, somewhere on the way to Dunmorrow. That's why they couldn't be the same. Besides, the trousers she had worn had holes in both knees when she finally discarded them. Almost fearfully, she lifted the legs and searched along the length of the fabric. *Whew! No holes!* She was just about to drop the legs, when she noticed the fine, almost invisible stitching around the knees. Her face was deathly pale and her hand was trembling when she finally turned away from the wardrobe.

She had watched the clothes burn, poking them with a stick, until they were ashes. How had they ended up back in this cupboard . . . in the Augurs' house?

The realization that she was back in the insane world of the Augurs, filled her with dread. For a minute, she couldn't think clearly, couldn't move.

"I've got to get out of here," she muttered finally, shuffling cautiously toward the door. Pressing her ear against the space between the door and the frame, she listened intently, but she heard nothing. She reached for the doorknob, snatching her hand back as if she had touched a hot burner when the glass knob turned under her hand. Someone was on the other side of the door. Miranda backed away, trying to put as much distance as possible between her and whatever was coming through the slowly opening door.

The door creaked as it inched open. Then, a round, red-cheeked face poked through the opening. "Aha! Welcome to the land of the living," said the old man, beaming happily. "We thought you were a goner."

Miranda forced herself to smile, but her spirits fell as flat as a flounder as she stared into the amber-coloured eyes of the jolly old man.

"Well! Well! You've awakened just in time for dinner." His eyes twinkled merrily. "Come along. The old girl's been cooking all day. Mustn't keep her waiting." He looked at Miranda's tattered clothes, as if noticing them for the first time. "We always dress for dinner in this house," he said. "When you're ready, join us." Then his head vanished and the door closed with a *click.*

Miranda opened her mouth to protest, but promptly shut it. She didn't want to wear those creepy trousers again, but she wasn't about to argue with the unpredictable old man. *I'm not wearing those clothes.* But, what choice did she have? None, she decided, angrily pulling the trousers off the peg. For a second she stared at the baggy garment, and then quickly stepped into the trousers, and pulled them on over her own ragged jeans. She did the same with a large sweatshirt. Checking in the mirror, she was satisfied that no one could tell she was wearing two sets of clothes. Nodding at her image, she took a deep breath and moved toward the door.

The old man was slumped in a rocking chair by a crackling fire, his chin resting on his chest, soft snores coming from his open mouth. It was such a normal, comforting scene it made Miranda's flesh tingle. The old man's head jerked up at the sound of the door closing.

"Morda, love of my life," he cried, jumping excitedly to his feet. "Our guest is here and looking hungry enough to eat us out of house and home."

Miranda's eyes darted about the cozy room. Near the wall opposite the fireplace, a long, narrow refectory table was set for dinner. Miranda peered at a small silver animal, a badger she thought, holding a metal plate between its paws. To her surprise, her name was engraved on the plate. Just like last time, she thought. Only it was some kind of large bird then, not a badger.

Glancing toward the fireplace, she noticed a large dog curled up on a mat in front of the hearth, its head resting on its forepaws, its yellow eyes following her every move. The dog lifted its head, and Miranda started as the colour of its eyes changed from yellow to green. *That dog wasn't here last time,* she thought.

"You dear, precious child! You had us so worried." The woman who appeared in the darkened doorway from another part of the house was as beautiful as her voice. Miranda couldn't tear her eyes away from her. Morda's face was a perfect oval, framing a pair of amber-coloured eyes. Her chin-length hair that she wore tucked behind her ears, was pale blonde, almost white. She entered the room, wiping her hands on a spotless apron, and took Miranda's hand. "Welcome to our humble home!"

This time the woman's lovely, gentle voice didn't warm Miranda's heart. It froze her to the bone, and she found that she was shivering uncontrollably. *The minute she recognizes me, it's all over,* she thought.

"Look! The poor thing is freezing to death. Get her a wrap, old man."

Miranda wished that things could be different—that the old couple were exactly what they appeared to be, gentle, kindly souls. She remembered how she had longed to have grandparents just like them. *Yeah! Right!* she thought. *Just what I need—demented, homicidal grandparents.*

Last summer, when she followed the Druid through the Kingsmere Portal, she, Nicholas, and the cantankerous Dwarf, Emmet, exited into a raging blizzard. Ignoring the Dwarf's warning, Naim had led the group to the tiny yellow cottage, seeking warmth and shelter from the storm. But, the crazy couple had driven them from the table and from the house before they had a chance to taste Morda's fare. Miranda shuddered as she recalled that other visit. Now, here she was, back inside the cozy little cottage about to share another meal with the strange old man and woman whose sweet gentle faces and angelic manners hid a pair of deranged minds.

"My dear," cooed the old woman, releasing Miranda's hand and draping the wrap about her shoulders. "I can't believe the change in you. Fit as a fiddle." She indicated the chair to her left with a tilt of her head. "Sit there, child." Then she turned and disappeared through the dark doorway.

Miranda gulped and obediently sat down at the table.

Don't touch anything! Don't ask questions! she cautioned herself, remembering the Druid's warning from her last visit. *And, whatever you do, don't ask about the future or anything that will make them angry.* That's what happened last time. She had blurted out a question without thinking. Well, this time she intended to make sure that didn't happen. *I'll just smile politely and say really nice things,* she said to herself.

Miranda felt like she was trapped in a recurring nightmare and couldn't make herself wake up. *Maybe I can change things,* she thought. *If she asks me to help set out the food, I'll look sad and show her my injured arm.* But, she soon realized that, without being seriously rude, she didn't have much choice in the matter.

"Here, child," said Morda, appearing in the doorway and holding out a steaming bowl. "Put it on the table. That's a good girl." Then, noticing Miranda glance down at her sprained arm, she added. "It's not heavy, dear. You can manage quite nicely with one hand."

Miranda's mind raced, trying to think of a way to stop the dinner from happening. What if she dropped the bowl? Would that end the dinner? Or would it turn the old couple into maniacal monsters? Forcing her lips into a sweet smile, she took the bowl from the old woman and placed it on the table.

"Come and take the others," called Morda from the kitchen.

As before, the old woman met her in the doorway. Miranda tried to peer past her into the room, but she couldn't see anything. She had a wild thought that there wasn't any room there at all—just nothing. But, if that were true, where was the food coming from? *I've got to get out of here,* she repeated to herself.

Miranda measured the distance between her chair and the front door. If she made a dash for it now, she was sure she could make it. But, as if he had read her mind and knew what she intended, the old man slipped into a chair at the foot of the table between her and the door. Then, Morda entered the room bearing a large platter containing a gigantic roasted fowl. All thoughts of escape flew out of Miranda's head like a flock of migrating birds as the most wonderful aroma tickled her nose and made her mouth water. She hadn't eaten since the night the Demon's Hunters attacked the camp and snatched her away. How long ago was that? She didn't know. But she knew she was starving, and if she didn't eat something soon, she'd attack the roast fowl with her fingers.

Morda placed the platter on the table in front of her and looked from Miranda to the old man, beaming happily. "Isn't it lovely?"

"Yum!" agreed Miranda. "It smells delicious."

"Well, aren't you sweet. Thank you, dear." She shook her head in mock exasperation, looking along the length of the table. "Now, what on earth happened to my carving knife?" She looked at Miranda and smiled like the Mona Lisa. "Did you take it, dear?"

Miranda shook her head frantically. "No," she answered. "It wasn't here when I brought in the vegetables." Her hands felt clammy and her face paled. She remembered Morda's butcher knife. In a fit of rage, the old woman had almost skewered her hand to the table when she stabbed at the girl with the wicked knife last summer.

"Oh, please," she whispered. "Don't let her find it."

For a second, complete silence settled over the room. *Oh! Oh!* Miranda tried to look innocent, but she felt her face burning and she knew she looked as guilty as if she *had* taken the knife. Then, to her relief, Morda's soft laugh broke the silence, the sound tinkling like bells in the warm room. "Of course you didn't," she said, patting Miranda's hand. "I remember now. I left it on a wooden block in the kitchen." She disappeared into the kitchen. All the light seemed to end at the doorway.

Miranda used her napkin to wipe her damp forehead and clammy palms. She was as tense as a bow string and terrified of doing or saying something that would set the old woman off. "Please, just let me get out of here alive," she whispered.

"The old girl's getting forgetful," sighed the old man. "What she needs is a drop of wine with dinner. It's good for the memory."

Oh no! cried Miranda silently, aware that things were quickly going from bad to worse. *Not wine!* Now she remembered. She wasn't the one who had upset the old couple last time. It was Naim! He was adamant, even rude, about the wine. *We will not have wine!* he had said, his voice as cold as a winter wind. That's when Morda went berserk.

The girl sighed, watching the old man shuffle to a small cupboard in the corner next to the fireplace. Miranda glanced at the door. *Run! Now!* But, at that moment, Seeker rose from the mat by the fire and padded across the room. The huge Wolfhound paused behind Miranda's chair, his nostrils catching the scent of fear emanating from the little stranger. Then he moved away, dropping onto the floor in front of the door, effectively cutting off any chance of escape.

Miranda almost screamed out her frustration. The sound of glass bottles crashing against one another as the old man rooted in the bottom of the cupboard grated on her nerves. Finally he gave a triumphant cry and waved a bottle over his head. "Nothing hits the spot like a drop of Pomegranate wine," he announced, shuffling back to his chair.

The old man wrestled with the cork, finally holding the bottle between his knees and pulling on the corkscrew with all of his strength. When the cork popped free, he lost his balance and would have toppled over backwards if Miranda hadn't grabbed his arm. He moved to the head of the table and filled Morda's glass. When he came to Miranda, she put her hand over her glass. "No thank you! I don't drink wine," she said, politely.

"Nonsense!" said the old man.

Miranda decided not to argue. She removed her hand and watched him fill her glass. *I just won't drink it,* she said to herself.

"Oh, goody!" cried the old woman, appearing from the kitchen with a long knife in one hand and a whetstone in the other. "I do love wine. Don't you, dear?" She looked at Miranda, her eyes as bright and shining as a young girl's.

Miranda nodded, her eyes riveted on the knife. *I'm not giving her a chance to stab me this time,* she thought.

Morda began sharpening the long carving knife, sliding the sharp edge of the blade along the whetstone with smooth, fluid movements. Miranda was hypnotized by the motion of the blade moving along the stone. Abruptly, Morda pushed the whetstone aside, stuck a fork in the side of the fowl, and began carving slices of white meat from the breast.

"Now tell us about yourself, child. Where do you come from and what are you doing in our neck of the woods?"

Be careful what you say! Miranda took a breath. "I'm from a place called Ottawa. It's the Capital of Canada." As soon as the words left her mouth she knew she had made a mistake. *She's going to remember me now,* she thought, waiting for the light to click on in the old woman's brain. She almost fell off her chair with relief when the woman reacted as if she'd never heard of Ottawa, or Canada.

The old woman paused while she took a long sip of wine. Then she chuckled. "If you say so, dear." She looked at her husband. "Isn't she sweet?"

Miranda hated adults who talked about children as if they weren't there. "But it's true," she cried, instantly regretting her outburst.

"Of course it's true," soothed the old woman, patting Miranda's hand. "Now, drink your wine, child. It'll make you calm."

"I am," lied Miranda.

"No!" snapped the old woman. "You haven't taken one sip."

Miranda fidgeted desperately. She could sense Morda becoming more agitated by the second. "Please," she tried. "I am grateful for everything you did for me. I don't mean to be rude, it's just that I'm only eleven and I don't drink wine."

"You won't grow if you don't drink every last drop."

"And I thought she was such a nice, sweet girl," said the old man, shaking his head sadly.

Miranda had to still her trembling hand. Blinking to keep from crying, she involuntarily reached for the tiny, silver place card. She had expected the polished metal to feel cold against her skin, but it was warm, almost hot. It was the most adorable little badger she had ever seen. She picked it up.

"Ouch!" The silver badger dropped onto the table with a *thunk*. Miranda stared at her finger, where blood was seeping from two small puncture marks in the soft flesh. "It bit me!" she cried, turning to the old woman and holding out her hand. "Look! That thing bit me!"

"JUST SHUT UP!" screamed Morda, swiping her arm across the table and knocking the steaming bowls of vegetables onto the floor. Then she pushed herself to her feet and rested her hands on the table. She glared at Miranda, her eyes narrowed in anger. "WE SAVED YOUR LIFE AND THIS IS HOW YOU REPAY OUR HOSPITALITY—WITH LIES AND DECEIT!"

"Don't be too hard on the child, pet. She's from Canada and children there obviously don't know any better."

Miranda couldn't take it anymore. "That's the meanest thing I've ever heard," she cried, pushing back her chair and standing up. "And it's not true. You're the liar, not me."

Morda grabbed the carving knife and drove it into the huge fowl again and again, until the meat was pulp. "GET HER OUT OF MY SIGHT!" she shrieked, spittle flying from her lips onto the roasted bird. The veins in her neck protruded like worms as she raised the knife again.

Miranda followed the up and down motion of the old woman's arm, her eyes stuck to the long, sharp blade. *I'm not going to get out of here alive*, she thought, her face the colour of cold ashes. *But I'm going to try.* She backed away from the table, staggering as if she had drunk a whole bottle of wine.

From his spot by the door, Seeker opened his eyes and growled until the girl moved back to the table. The old woman slammed the knife down, and attacked one of the legs of the bird, wrenched it free, and threw it at Miranda, who ducked seconds before the missile whizzed past where her face had been. When she stood up again, she saw the old woman wrestling with the other leg. Tearing it loose, she hurled it at the old man.

"Easy old girl. You know I prefer white meat."

"SHUT UP! YOU DESPICABLE OLD FART!" Morda grabbed the carving knife again and waved it threateningly at the old man.

"THREATEN ME, WILL YOU?" shrieked the old man, jumping to his feet and grabbing the wine bottle by its neck. "WE'LL SEE WHO WEARS THE PANTS IN THIS HOUSE." He smashed the bottom of the bottle against the table and advanced on the old woman, his eyes bulging out of his head and his face contorted with rage.

Miranda was in shock. Things were getting out of hand so rapidly she couldn't think clearly. *They're going to kill each other*, she thought, inching toward the table. *Quick! Think of something!*

Up went Morda's arm. The light from the fireplace made the sharp edge of the blade glint wickedly.

Trembling from a combination of fear and hope, Miranda slipped into her chair and slid her hand along the table toward the old woman. She knew that what she was about to do was dangerous, perhaps fatal. Naim's warning rang in her ears as if he were in the room beside her. *Whatever you do, do not ask questions about the future!* But she had to do something to take the old couple's minds off killing each other.

"Are you really an Augur?" she asked. "Can you really tell the future?"

Down came the knife, faster than Miranda's eye could follow. She snatched her hand back, feeling air from the force of the blow ruffle the fine, pale hairs on the back of her hand. The sharp knife plunged into the table, slicing through the loose flesh between Miranda's middle and index fingers. Her eyes stung as her flesh tore away. Then she jumped up and shoved the old woman back and away from the carving knife. Morda shrieked and lunged through the blackness into the kitchen or whatever was behind the opening.

She glanced at the old man and was relieved to see that he was staring at the broken bottle as if he didn't know how it had ended up in his hand. Muttering incoherently, he shuffled to the rocking chair by the fire and sank into the cushioned seat. Within seconds the sound of snoring drifted through the room.

Miranda gripped the handle of the long carving knife and, summoning strength from a hidden reserve within, she pulled the blade from the wooden table. Then, thinking she might need to keep the carving knife for a weapon, she snatched the serving fork from beside the platter and raced for the door.

That's when Seeker, the Wolfhound, growled, teeth bared, from deep in his throat, hackles rising along his spine. Pointing the carving knife at the huge dog, Miranda charged at him. "GO!" she shouted. Startled by the stranger's aggressive, alpha-like behaviour, the dog yelped, tucked its tail between its legs, and slinked away from the door.

Miranda grabbed the door handle just as Morda appeared in the black opening. The sight of the old woman's sly smile sent shivers down her back. She pushed the door open and flew outside, hardly pausing as she turned and slammed her uninjured shoulder against the door and wedged the serving fork into the space between the door and the frame. Then she ran into the snowstorm that raged continuously about the little yellow cottage, and disappeared from sight.

At the edge of the forest, Calad-Chold wrenched back on the reins and his horse slid to a stop, rearing and striking. The trail of the Twisted Blade suddenly went as cold as winter in the far north. The Dead King roared into the storm that raged about the clearing. He shook the reins, urging the huge horse of bones forward. But the horse balked and shied nervously. The King dismounted, the sound of brittle bone rubbing against bone was absorbed into the roar of the wind. Hunching his shoulders and lowering his head, Calad-Chold tried to push through the driving snow, but something seemed to be holding him back—a force that he could not identify.

The King of the Dead swung his bony frame into the saddle and wheeled the great warhorse about into the storm, back to the Dark Lands.

CHAPTER TWENTY-SIX

THE SILVER POUCH

vatar flew like the wind. Hunched forward along the horse's strong neck like a black-winged bird, Naim, the Druid, drifted in a dark haze of despair—despair such as he had never known. As they sped in pursuit of the Demon's Hunters, they skirted vast stretches of scorched and smoking lands where great hordes of the dead had passed as silent and unfeeling as a plague, making their purposeful way to the Dark Lands where Calad-Chold awaited them. Avatar had refused to cross the defiled ground and so they had travelled many miles out of their way. Naim was overwhelmed by the sheer immensity of the destruction. He was afraid the poor earth would never recover from the shock. But he was even more afraid of the dead. *There are so many of them,* he thought. *How can we withstand so many?*

The Druid also blamed himself for Miranda's abduction. If he had been watching out for her as he once promised her mother, she would be here now, perched behind him, gripping his cloak, and plying him with a thousand questions he couldn't begin to answer. He had known from the beginning that the Hunters were after the girl. Yet, he had allowed himself to get so caught up in fighting the wicked creatures that he had neglected to protect the child. Now, because of him, the search for the Twisted Blade had failed before it had barely begun. And, without the blade, they were lost.

With all of his powers, the Druid still hadn't figured out how to be in two places at the same time. He had made the only decision possible—abandon the quest and go after Miranda. He ran his hand along Avatar's neck, and felt the slick sweat coat his hand. The horse had been galloping flat out for several hours. And while he might seem tireless, he was a creature of flesh and bone. It was time to stop and rest.

"Easy, old friend," said the Druid, sitting erect and easing back on the reins, slowing Avatar into a quick trot, and then a walk. Naim dropped the reins, letting the horse have his head. Avatar walked until his sides were no longer heaving and his heart rate had slowed. Then the big horse stopped, and snorted loudly. Naim slid to the ground, his aging joints as stiff and brittle as dry twigs after the long hours spent in the saddle. Picking his way over a rock-strewn trail, the old man led Avatar toward an ancient crumbling fortress. In the pale, pre-dawn light, it resembled a giant sleeping bear. Naim briefly wondered about its history. He guessed that it had not heard the harsh sounds of soldiers' voices for over a thousand years. "There is something sad about ruins," he said softly, thinking that if he survived the coming holocaust, he would learn more about this lonely, desolate place.

Near the outer wall, the Druid removed Avatar's tack and rubbed him down with a soft cloth, talking softly to the horse as he worked. The stallion's ears twitched as if answering to the old man's chatter. While Naim busied himself with feeding and watering Avatar, he tried to come up with a plan to snatch Miranda from the clutches of the Demon's creatures without getting them both killed in the process. He turned toward the northeast and squinted into the distance. Ahead, where earth and sky met, even in the gray light, he could make out the black blot in the lower sky. The cataclysm, a violent storm of the empty shells of naïve creatures who had gone looking for Hate, and to their everlasting torment, had found her, raged about the Dark Lands like a living wall.

"It will be full light soon," he said. "I must get a few hours rest." He settled on the hard ground, wrapped his cloak about him to ward off the chill and, within minutes, dropped into a troubled sleep.

Avatar's scream was filled with rage and hatred. It brought the Druid awake with a start. Squinting in the bright sunlight, he pushed his cloak back and off his shoulders, grabbed the wooden staff as he leaped to his feet and dropped into a crouch. He looked about for the source of the stallion's fear. But he saw nothing. Gripping the staff tightly, he summoned his inner sight and sent it out in a wide sweeping circle. Again, nothing! But there was something out there and Avatar sensed it. The horse was still stamping and screaming, and Naim trusted his horse's finely-honed sense of danger.

The Druid dashed toward the animal, his eyes scanning the shadows of the ruins. "What is it?" he asked, gently stroking Avatar's neck. Then the horse reared, and Naim looked up and saw the creatures dropping on them from the sky like giant, black flies.

In a flash, Naim pointed the staff skyward, summoning the white fire of the Druids. But, just as he was about to unleash the flaming fury, something in the sky beyond the Hunters caught his eye. Then he realized that the Hunters were totally unaware of him and Avatar. They weren't launching an attack. They were fleeing for their lives. And the creature they were fleeing from was a gigantic Black Dragon.

But where had they come from? he wondered, counting a dozen of the creatures. Surely the Hunters he had been pursuing had already reached the Dark Lands. Had this lot strayed from the flock? He had never heard of Hunters breaking up into small units. They always hunted as one.

Quickly, he ran along the outer wall until he came to a wide gap in the crumbling stonework. He had to find a safe place to wait out the impending battle between the Dragon and the Werecurs or risk being dashed to pieces. Satisfied that Avatar could fit easily through the opening, he turned and whistled softly. The great horse broke into a spirited trot and followed his master through the wide gap into an old stable. The old man was glad to see that the roof was still in place. He could only pray that it wouldn't collapse on them.

They had just made it through the door when the ground buckled beneath their feet. Huge chunks of stone slammed into the structure, shaking the walls and dislodging crumbling mortar that rained on him like a gritty dusting of dandruff. Pulling a handkerchief from a pocket inside his cloak, the Druid pressed it against his nose and mouth. Then, he moved toward the door and peered into the chaos outside the shelter.

It was clear that the Demon's Hunters were losing the battle. The monstrous Dragon lashed his powerful tail, whacking several creatures senseless, propelling them through the air to land in broken heaps hundreds of feet away. Without pausing, the mighty tail descended upon another doomed creature, swatting it into a black and yellow blob that looked like a magnified squashed fly. At the same time, a quick burst of flame erupted from the great beast's open mouth, toasting two Werecurs whose shrill screams ended abruptly. Naim shook his head in wonder at the awesome might of the monster Dragon, and stepped through the stable door.

"Why are you hunting in my lands, Druid?" spat the Dragon, reaching for the last surviving Werecur and pinning it to the ground with its sharp claws.

"Greetings to you, too, Typhon," said Naim, sarcastically. He looked at the Werecur trapped beneath the Dragon's enormous clawed limb and almost felt sorry for the creature.

"Answer my question or get out of here before I run out of

patience," said the Dragon, opening its cavernous mouth and snapping the squirming Werecur's head off. "What are you doing here?"

Naim's stomach lurched and he quickly turned away from the grisly sight. "Like you, I hunt the Hunters." *But I don't eat them,* he said to himself. Suddenly, his sharp eyes caught a flash of light reflected off something in the Dragon's claws. He turned quickly, his heart jumping as he saw the silver chain entwined about one of the creature's claws.

"Are you still here?" rumbled the Dragon. "I distinctly remember telling you to GET OUT!"

"I will not leave until I know how you came by the silver pouch."

"What business is it of yours?" snapped the Dragon, thumping his tail on the ground for emphasis, and spitting out a mouthful of bones.

When the Druid spoke, his voice was as hard as flint. "That pouch hung about the neck of an Elven child taken by the Hunters two nights ago."

"That may be true," said the Dragon, ripping the Werecur's arm clear of its socket and chomping vigourously. "But, it's mine now." The enormous creature turned his back on the Druid, whipping his deadly tail back and forth less than an inch from the man's face.

"IT—IS—*NOT*—YOURS!"

The Dragon tensed, massive muscles rippling the scales along his great length. He realized he had just made an error in judgment. Normally, Dragons were immune to magic, as long as they faced the wielder. But, by turning his back on the Druid, he had rendered himself vulnerable. Too late, he whipped his head about, just in time to see the Druid strike the ground hard with his magic staff and give it a sharp twist. Without warning, Typhon, proud Dragon Chief, found himself rising into the air.

"DRUID!" He roared, hot steam exploding from his wide nostrils.

A snort of laughter shook Naim's shoulders. He twisted the staff again. The Dragon began to spin, slowly at first, and then faster and faster until he was a blur. When Naim saw a small shiny object shoot out of the spinning mass, he lifted the staff off the ground and quickly retrieved Miranda's silver pouch. He was relieved to feel the six oval shapes of the Bloodstones through the fine mesh. He dropped it into a pocket and walked toward the stable. He didn't even look back when Typhon hit the ground with the sound and force of a twenty-storey building imploding.

Avatar was waiting just outside the old stone stable, his ears flat against his head. "Perhaps our journey does not take us to the Dark Lands after all," said the Druid, easing himself into the saddle. He caught the reins and urged the horse back to where he had left the Dragon in a heap of tangled limbs.

"You went too far this time, Druid," complained Typhon, untangling himself and spitting out the last word as if it were an inedible Hunter bone that had stuck in his throat.

Naim pulled Avatar to a stop a short distance from the irate Dragon. "Typhon, I do not have time for your games. I must know where you found the girl's pouch."

The Dragon fixed the Druid with a glassy stare. "If the trifling affairs of children have become so important to you in your dotage, I will tell you."

"As usual, Dragon, you do not know what is happening in your own backyard."

Typhon snorted contemptuously, rolling his enormous eyes skyward. "And, as usual, you are about to tell me." He pushed himself up and peered down at the old man seated on his red horse. What he saw was a minuscule figure, little more than a toy. For a second, the great Dragon wondered why he put up with this man's harrassment. One bite, that's all it would take to rid the world of this festering thorn of a man for good.

Naim returned the Dragon's stare, unwaveringly. "Yes," he said. "I am going to tell you. Why? Because a terrible Evil has been awakened and it is coming to wipe out every living being in this world."

"Please," sighed the Dragon with mock weariness. "Don't include my kind in your little drama. We came to your aid in the past, involving ourselves in your petty little wars of attrition. This time the answer is *NO!*"

"Have I asked for your help?" said Naim softly.

The Dragon thought for a moment before laughing. "Not yet. But it's coming, Druid. I can read you like a book."

"You are a bigger fool that I thought," snapped the Druid, tugging on Avatar's reins. "I did not come here seeking you, or help from your clique. This is not a war of attrition where the Demon's half-dead creatures wear us down. Against this Evil, we can only flee. What we face this time is not even a war because nothing, not even the Black Dragons, can withstand an enemy that cannot be stopped."

"HA! My kin have yet to face such an enemy."

"Until now," said Naim. "But, when the King of the Dead leads his army from the Dark Lands, the Age of Dragons will pass. Your species will vanish." The Dragon opened his mouth to protest, but the Druid continued. "If any are lucky enough to survive, they will dwindle in size until the once mighty Black Dragons are little more than chameleons."

Well, he thought. *I've certainly got his attention now.* "I will show you this Evil," he said. "But to do so, I must touch you with the staff."

Typhon turned about and inched closer to the man. "No tricks, Druid. Or you will join the spirits of your ancestors."

"No tricks," said Naim, knowing that Typhon's was no idle promise. One quick rap from his deadly claws and it would be all over for the Druid. The great Dragon would not turn his back and leave himself open to the magic a second time. He reached out with the wooden staff and gently made contact with the Dragon's forelimb. Then he sent all that he knew about Calad-Chold into the staff.

Typhon's giant body went as rigid as a steel bar as images flowed from the Druid's mind through the staff and into his brain. His eyes opened wider and wider until Naim was afraid they'd pop out of his head. The Black Dragon saw a massive army of dead creatures sweep from the Dark Lands like a giant blazing broom. And where they passed, nothing remained but smoke and ruin. Mighty forests that had withstood the changing world for thousands of years vanished in the blink of an eye. Rivers boiled, regurgitating fleshless fish and other creatures until nothing remained. He saw mountains blackened and cities turned to ashes. The black scales along the Dragon's spine tingled at the sight of the living, falling before the menace. And then, to his horror, he saw the newly dead rise up and follow Calad-Chold, swelling his army until the entire world was a writhing, sweeping storm that could not be stopped. When the images ended, he could not find the words to describe what he had seen.

"I do not believe you," he whispered finally, but his voice made a lie of his words.

The Druid did not answer. There was no need. Typhon knew that what he had been shown was true.

"There is only one thing that will stop the King of the Dead," he said. "I was searching for this talisman when the Hunters snatched the child. I abandoned my search to rescue the girl. If I can find her, there may be time to continue the search and recover this thing before it is too late." He sighed heavily. "I must find the girl, Typhon."

"I saw no girl, Druid, but I saw the Hunters and one of the black assassins. I caught the silver trinket as it dropped toward the ground. If this girl was with them, perhaps she, too, fell. I came upon them several hours flight behind you."

Naim wheeled Avatar about. "Thank you. Now fly like the wind and do what you must to hide your fellows from the eyes of the dead." Then he spoke softly to Avatar and the great horse lunged forward.

CHAPTER TWENTY-SEVEN

BACK TO THE CASTLE

'm going back," said Nicholas. "Indolent took my sword and I'm not leaving without it."

"In your dreams," cried Penelope, squeezing Muffy until the miserable poodle yelped in pain. "Otavite, don't listen to him. Ever since he got that stupid sword, it's all he thinks about. We're not going back." She opened her arms and the little dog leaped to the ground and was swallowed up in the tall grass, creating a twisting, rippling path as she raced here and there across the hillside, barking excitedly.

"Did I ask you to come with me?" challenged the boy. "Did I?"

The Ogre, Eiznek, grabbed his arm and whistled excitedly.

"See, even Eiznek thinks you're crazy to go back."

"That's not what he said," snapped Nicholas. "For your information, he said if I go back, he's coming with me."

"That's not true," said Otavite. "The little Ogre is afraid of what will happen to you if you return to the Wizard's Castle alone, and he is afraid of what will happen to him if he accompanies you."

"Right!" snapped Nicholas. "And I suppose you gleaned all that from one little whistle?"

"Yes," replied Otavite. "Did I forget to mention that most Giants

are able to communicate with Ogres?"

Nicholas and Penelope exchanged looks that clearly said they didn't believe the Giant. Nicholas turned to Eiznek. "Is that true?"

Eiznek nodded vigorously, putting an end to the entire question of whether Giants and Ogres understood each other.

"All right, forget about the sword," said Nicholas. "There's another reason we have to go back."

"I knew it!" cried Penelope. "So now it's *we.*"

"Tell us why we must go back," said Otavite.

"This should be good," muttered Penelope under her breath.

Nicholas ignored the girl. "It's Indolent," he said. "He's up to something, and I think it's important that we find out how he's involved with this King of the Dead."

"You're such a liar!" Penelope laughed harshly.

"No! Listen!" pleaded Nicholas. "I was there. You weren't. Remember when we saw Malcolm in the mountain cavern?"

Penelope nodded, reluctantly.

"The Dwarf-snake," said Otavite softly.

"I told you it was one of the Demon's serpents using Malcolm the Dwarf's body," said Penelope.

"Yes," said Otavite. "If I had not seen it with my own eyes, I would not have believed it. I saw the flesh fall away from the Dwarf and this snake creature was there. It grew into a huge, hissing serpent. I will never forget what it did to so many of my friends." He bowed his head sadly.

"I'm sorry about your friends," said Nicholas. "That's why we have to find out what's going on with Indolent." Seeing that everyone was staring at him intently, he continued. "So far, here's what we know. An earthquake created a deep crevice in the ground along the Rideau River in Ottawa. Penelope and I fell into this crevice and, somehow, ended up inside a mountain in Vark."

"But," interrupted the Giant, looking at Penelope suspiciously, "that's not what you told me, Princess." He either didn't hear Nicholas's rude snort or he ignored it. "You said that while on a secret mission for your cousin, King Elester, a band of Ogres attacked you and your servant and took you to the Bronks."

"OK!" laughed Nicholas. "Enough with this servant/Princess story." He frowned at his friend. "Tell him, Penelope."

"No!" cried Penelope, her face burning. "I told you . . ."

"Shut up! If you hadn't lied in the first place, you wouldn't be in this mess." He turned to Otavite. "First, Penelope isn't a Princess, except in her dreams. Second, I'm not her servant. We're not Elves and we're not from this world. We come from a country called Canada."

"What do you mean you come from another world?" asked the flabbergasted Giant.

"It's a long story," said Nicholas. "A long time ago, our worlds used to be one, but the Elves split the world into two. It had something to do with magic. Anyway, Penelope and I live in the new world." As Otavite and Eiznek listened spellbound, Nicholas proceeded to tell them everything from the very beginning, starting with their first adventure in the old world to find the Serpent's Egg. When he finished, there was a moment of stunned silence before three pairs of eyes fixed on Penelope.

"I'm sorry I lied," sniffed the wretched girl. "I didn't think you'd believe me if I told you I came from another world. So I made up a story that you would believe."

"You should have told the truth," said Otavite.

"I guess," said Penelope. "But remember, I had never seen Giants before and I didn't know if you were friendly or not." She wiped her eyes with her hands. "Please don't be angry."

"I am not angry," said Otavite. "Because Giants don't lie, I guess I just don't understand. Perhaps if I were in your little boots, I would have lied too. But I can't help wondering what else you lied about."

"Nothing!" cried Penelope, turning red. "Honest!"

"Excuse me," said Nicholas. "Can we please get back to Indolent?" When the others looked at him, he continued. "As I was saying, Penelope and I ended up inside a Mountain in Vark. But, before we got there, Malcolm and the others attacked the fortress, broke into the cavern, and opened the seals on this coffin, right?"

"Yes," answered Otavite. "They removed the body from the coffin and slid it into a deep pool." His voice broke when he told how Malcolm had fed his friends to the still, oily waters. "And then a gigantic creature calling himself the King of the Dead rose out of the pool and Malcolm told him to call the dead, and go kill the Elves and Dwarves." He thought for a second. "There was someone else he wanted dead. A girl, I think." He patted Penelope's shoulder. "Perhaps it was you, Princess. I mean Penelope."

"Think," said Nicholas. "Did he say a name?"

"No," answered the Giant. "He said *'there's a wicked human girl. Find her and snatch a small silver pouch from her cold, dead body and bring it to me.'*" He looked at the others apologetically. "I'm afraid that's all he said."

Nicholas and Penelope stared at each other. "Miranda!" they cried, simultaneously.

The Giant shrugged. "The Dwarf-snake didn't say the girl's name."

"It's our friend, Miranda," explained Nicholas.

"Well, that settles it. We don't have a choice now," said Penelope. "We've got to get to Bethany and back to Ottawa to warn Miranda. If we're not too late."

"I still say we find out what Indolent is up to."

"Maybe he's not up to anything. Have you thought of that?"

"He's involved," said Nicholas. "I'd wager my sword on it. When the Ogres captured us, you ran away . . ."

Penelope turned away to avoid meeting the Giant's reproachful glare. OK, so she hadn't had to battle a hundred Ogres. Of course she'd run away. Was she stupid?

"But," continued Nicholas. "I was dragged before Malcolm, who told the Ogres to take me away and keep me alive until they had Miranda. Well, you know where the Ogres took me. The new Castle Cockroach."

Otavite looked confused. "Don't mind Nick," said Penelope. "He and the Wizard are old friends."

"Yeah! Right!" snapped Nicholas. "Listen, Otavite. I know Indolent. I've tasted his nasty magic once or twice. I've spent a few nights in the dump he used to called his Castle." He told the Giant about his previous encounters with the wicked Wizard. "He always thought that he was smarter than the Demon—that he could pretend to work with her and then snatch power for himself. But he belongs to her now. I saw the gold skull in his arm." Suddenly he turned to Penelope and grabbed her arm as if he'd just remembered something important. "Guess who else I saw there?"

Penelope shrugged. Otavite and Eiznek followed suit.

"Stubby!" said Nicholas triumphantly, giving a brief history of the wretched former teacher for the benefit of the Giant and Ogre. "He's wearing Hate's mark, too."

Penelope's mouth dropped in shock. "How did he escape from Ellesmere?"

"Who cares? What matters is he's free and working for Indolent."

For a second, the companions looked from one to the other in silence. Then Eiznek emitted several soft whistles. Nicholas and Penelope looked from the little Ogre to the Giant, questioningly.

"Eiznek says the Wizard's place is crawling with Trolls and hundreds of bad Ogres," interpreted Otavite.

"It's true," said Nicholas, flashing Eiznek an appreciative smile. "I almost forgot. There's this huge quarry, and the Trolls are using enslaved Ogres to build Indolent's new Castle." He stopped and looked at the Giant. "So you see how everything's connected? That's why we've got to go back. We've got to find out what Indolent's up to."

"And I say we make tracks for Bethany and the Portal," said Penelope.

"I vote on going back," said Nicholas. "What about you, Eiznek?" When the Ogre nodded, the boy turned to Otavite.

"Nicholas is right," said the Giant. "We must go back."

"It doesn't make sense," cried Penelope. "Can't you see what he's doing? He's baited the trap and now he's reeling you in. HE WANTS HIS SWORD."

"Shut up, Princess," taunted Nicholas. Then he appealed to the Giant, saying meaningfully. "*I* won't lie to you, Otavite. Yes, I want my sword. But if that were all I wanted, I wouldn't put the rest of you in danger. I'd go myself."

"I will return with you," said Otavite.

"Go then!" said Penelope angrily. "Get killed. I'm staying here. MUFFERS!" She walked away from the others, watching for ripples in the tall grass.

"We can't leave Penelope behind," said Otavite.

"Why not?" said Nicholas. "She'll just whine the whole way."

"She is very brave, Nicholas."

"You don't know her."

"I will not leave her," said Otavite, stubbornly.

Nicholas sighed. They'd never get to the Castle at this rate. Maybe he should go back alone. He walked over to Penelope. "Look! I know you're mad because I tore down your story in front of Otavite. I didn't do it to hurt you. I'm just tired of lies. If we're going to ask people to trust us, we have to start with the truth."

"I'm not mad at that," said Penelope. "I was going to tell him anyway. I was just waiting for the right time."

"Penelope, there's never a right time. I'm sorry, but Otavite won't leave you behind. If you really don't want to come with me, I'll understand. I'll go by myself."

"No," said Penelope. "I'll come. It's just that you're so arrogant.

You think you're always right. Well, you can be wrong too, you know." She called out to her dog again, suddenly feeling uneasy. She tried to recall the last time she had heard the poodle bark.

"MUFFY!"

They scoured the hillside, calling Muffy's name over and over again and listening for her shrill barks, but their calls went unanswered and the dog was nowhere to be found. Muffy had disappeared without a trace.

Penelope was devastated. "Something's happened to her."

Her companions tried to comfort her, but the fact remained that Muffy *was* missing and nothing they said could change that. When Otavite suggested that they should think about setting out for the Castle, Penelope started crying again.

"Muffy will find us," said Nicholas. "Dogs are good trackers." Still he wondered what had happened to the poodle.

As soon as the three smaller companions were settled on his shoulders, Otavite set out, favouring his right leg that still smarted from the spear wound inflicted by one of the Trolls. Despite the limp, Nicholas was amazed at the Giant's speed. "He's got to be going thirty miles an hour," he said, doing the math calculations in his head. At that rate, the boy figured it would take about an hour to reach the Castle of Indolence.

And he was right. They had been travelling just under an hour when they saw the black cloud hanging over the Wizard's valley like a solid roof of smog.

"I don't like this place," said Otavite, watching lightning fork from the blackness.

"Take my word for it," said Nicholas. "The Wizard Indolent is not a nice person."

"I do not care about your Wizard," answered Otavite. "I will tear this place apart until I find the Dwarf-snake. Then I will make him pay for murdering my comrades and the guard, Ve." His voice

was so icy, Nicholas felt a chill run down his spine.

Because Eiznek knew the area, they elected him their guide. The Ogre's chest swelled with pride at his companions' gesture of trust. They followed him over grassy hills, across desolate flatlands, and up unto a spur between two of the hills forming part of a ring that hemmed in and sheltered the Wizard's Castle. From there, they could see the entire valley spread out below. And what they saw filled them with despair.

Black smoke belched from a gaping quarry and spiralled funnel-like into the air, feeding the black cloud. The entire valley had been stripped bare. All of the trees had been chopped down, the grass burned, and the earth pitted and ruined.

"Everything he touches, he spoils," said Nicholas.

The Giant studied the valley for a long time. He noticed where guards were stationed. He noticed the huge cradles holding enormous logs. He noticed the Trolls cracking their long whips at the exposed backs and legs of Ogre slaves. Then he made a rough count of the Trolls, knowing that there had to be more in barracks somewhere. He looked for stores of food and supplies and weapons. When he was satisfied that he had memorized the important details, he turned to the others. "We will wait for darkness."

"What's the plan?" asked Nicholas.

"It's a simple plan," answered the Giant. "I plan to destroy this place." Then he turned and strode back down the hill.

Mr. Little muttered to himself as he made the rounds of the Castle of Indolence. He didn't mind the responsibility. In fact he enjoyed it. It made him feel important. The duty also gave him time to think, and right now he needed to think. When Indolent had finally realized that his assistant was missing, Stubby had already spent hours and hours locked in the windowless dungeon beneath the Castle. The scuttling of rats' claws on the stone and the sound of their dry, scaly tails swishing on the floor had almost driven him out of his mind. He had screamed and screamed until his throat was raw. Then he had pounded on the cell door and scratched the stone walls until his fists were scraped and blistered and his fingernails worn down to the cuticles.

"Oops!" was all Indolent had offered by way of an apology.

Stubby had been as appalled as if a Troll had spat on him. How could the Wizard have forgotten about him? What if he hadn't been missed? He'd still be rotting in that filthy, airless cell, that's what. Did he mean so little to Indolent? It was insulting to be treated like an Ogre after all that he had done for the Wizard.

"Ungrateful swine!" he snarled, lashing his legs with his switch. "Well, excuse me! But, *Oops!* just doesn't cut it."

It was just after midnight when he paused and rested his arms on a parapet high on the Castle's west side and watched a bright flash of lightning explode out of the foul air overhead and streak toward the ground like a bright, white snake. The man giggled as Ogres and Trolls shrieked and scuttled for safety. He was happy to see that one or two Ogres didn't get out of the way in time. *Serves them right!* he thought. He hated Ogres. Filthy, rat-eating animals.

Still wearing a remnant of the malicious smile, Stubby turned away from the parapet and walked purposefully toward the tower door. He passed an Ogre guard and swatted him with the switch before moving through the arched doorway and following a narrow corridor to a flight of stone steps that led down to ground level. The former teacher descended the stairs, entered the main courtyard, and crossed the open space. Half a dozen Ogre guards snapped to attention at his approach, but returned to whatever they had been doing when they recognized who it was.

Stubby frowned when out of sight. "You're too soft," he scolded himself. "You should march back there and show them who's the Boss." He almost caved in to the urge to retrace his steps and beat the insolent guards until he wiped the smirks off their faces and fixed their bad attitudes. But he had a lot of ground to cover before he

completed his rounds. Vowing to deal with the insubordination before the next watch, he passed a back stairway leading down from the huge food storerooms. Distracted by a sudden tingling sensation in his left forearm, he didn't notice the three figures hiding in the shadows on the stairwell just above his head.

Stubby massaged the pulsing image of the skull that Malcolm, the Dwarf, had pocketed into the soft flesh on his inner forearm using thin shavings of gold.

"The Lady is lonely," explained the Dwarf. "She longs for someone to talk with—to keep her company in the endless darkness." The little man's heart beat rapidly and he hurried along the passage until he came to a stone door. Ignoring the guard, he passed through the doorway onto a small balcony.

"What is it, Lady?" he asked softly, glancing furtively about to make sure he was alone.

Stubby loved the Lady who spoke to him through the golden skull. He felt sorry for her because she was imprisoned in a terrible blackness, imprisoned by the very same Elves that had kept him trapped inside a tree stump for almost a year. He hated them and he would do anything to hurt them if it would free his Lady. He smiled slyly. She believed in him, appreciated him. Even wanted to help him achieve greatness. *You have earned it*, she had whispered to him. And she was right. He had earned it. He remembered all the years he had spent trying to impart wisdom into the empty heads of half-witted brats. He remembered all the stupid, senseless rules, rules that belittled him and robbed him of power. But, most of all, he remembered the snotty way Indolent had treated him.

Well, he'd show him! He'd show everybody!

The Demon had been subtle in winning the former teacher and making him her own. She had used flattery, encouraging the little man to feed his own inflated ego with notions of greatness. She had used sympathy, listening patiently to his whining voice, letting him chain himself to her with his own words. Now, even if she were to appear before him in her true, monstrous form and reveal to him her real nature, it wouldn't make any difference. He belonged to her. It had been so easy, it made her laugh so hard she almost choked on her thick, protruding tongue.

CHAPTER TWENTY-EIGHT

THE MARCH
OF THE DEAD

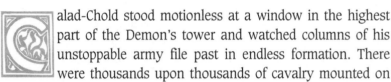alad-Chold stood motionless at a window in the highest part of the Demon's tower and watched columns of his unstoppable army file past in endless formation. There were thousands upon thousands of cavalry mounted on fleshless horses, uncountable units of indefatigable infantry from all the battles ever fought since the dawn of man. There were legions of enormous fanged and clawed things that had not walked the earth for millions of years, and wave upon wave of fell soldiers in rotting plaids, gripping guns fitted with bayonets.

In their wake came ancient warriors in battered, rusting armor, broken lances clutched in skeletal fingers. And still they came. Soldiers from recent wars in dented helmets and tattered camouflage with empty canteens slung about their bony necks, Sten guns clutched tightly in dead hands. Behind them came Hellhags slinking on four limbs, gray bones glistening like silver in the darkness, and black-cloaked Thugs, red eyes burning with hatred against old enemies that had cut them down in the great battle when the Demon was first defeated and driven into The Place with No Name.

There were no cumbersome food trains or supplies of weapons

and other implements of war. The Dead had no need for such things.

For days, the Black Army had flowed past the tower, its numbers too vast to calculate. It was an endless, smoking river of Death. And still it came.

"Ahhh!" breathed the King of the Dead in satisfaction. It was time. He turned from the window and strode to the far end of the tower where he had summoned his commanders for a council of war.

"It is time," he repeated, his hooded head moving from one featureless face to another.

"Ahhh!" breathed the commanders, like a grisly echo, rising to their feet and moving toward the tower stairs.

Outside, Calad-Chold tilted his head back and called his favourite warhorse. In answer, lightning exploded and thunder crashed about him as Khalkedon erupted out of the sudden, violent storm, ebony bones glistening like oil, eye sockets ablaze. Sparks flew from the horse's hooves as they struck the cobbled ground and, from the creature's open mouth came an unearthly whinny, like the sound of a scream echoing in a cavernous hall.

The Dead King caught the horse's stringy reins and hoisted himself into the rotting saddle. He stood up in the stirrups and raised his gauntleted fist. The mighty army paused and a hush fell over the Dark Lands as if the world had suddenly come to an end and all life had been extinguished.

"WE RIDE!" bellowed the King of the Dead, his voice rumbling like thunder, shaking the smoking earth beneath his army's burning feet. Then he beckoned to his First Officer, spun Khalkedon about, spurred the lifeless horse into a slow gallop, and rode to the head of the seething sea of destruction.

In the quiet hour just before dawn, Calad-Chold left the Dark Lands, passing in a swirl of blackness between the two massive Dar sentinels that stood petrified at the entrance to the Demon's Kingdom—tragic monuments to Otavite's cousins—a race of Giants

that had dared to defy the Demon and was wiped from the face of the earth. Behind the Dead King, as silent as the tombs and barrows that had contained them, came his terrible army—a raging, unstoppable cancer.

Far from there, Naim reined Avatar to a stop, reeling in the saddle as if an invisible fist had struck him again and again. Gasping for air, he slid to the ground, keeping one hand on the pommel to steady himself. He turned toward the northeast, his blue-black eyes fixed on the darkness that was growing thicker even as the first streaks of light appeared in the eastern sky. "So, it has begun," he whispered harshly.

For a moment, he wondered how the others were faring. Were they, too, gazing at the darkness in despair? Or were they sleeping fitfully, dreaming about the coming horror, unaware that their nightmares had already turned real? The old Druid pressed his head against Avatar's side, afraid to turn his thoughts to Miranda. Was she still alive? Without the Bloodstones, would the Demon's Monsters keep her alive? *No!* He hated his own certainty. As long as the Bloodstones existed, Miranda was a threat. But if the child were eliminated, the Stones would be powerless—six pretty little pebbles. Nothing more.

Naim sighed and gently ran his hand along Avatar's side. He looked up at the lightening sky and felt a strange sensation creep over him. It was going to be a beautiful day. His eyes swept the surrounding countryside. Off to his left stood a ridge of tall trees that marked the end of the grasslands and the edge of a forest. The smell of clean, green grass and cool pine lingered on the gentle morning breeze and, far beyond the forest, the Mountains of the Moon glimmered like mounds of polished silver. He almost laughed out loud at the tragic irony of the perfect, peaceful scene spread out before him and the unspeakable terror that was spilling out of the Dark Lands.

It should not be a beautiful day. The sun should not rise on such a day as this. The sky should not be such an achingly clear blue. The tops of the trees shouldn't be swaying in the breeze; they should be frozen stiff with fear. The sweet, green grass should be shrinking into its roots. He knew he was being irrational, but he wanted to shout at Nature—to warn her that something was coming—to warn her that She, too, would fall before the might of Calad-Chold.

The trees would burst into flames. The grass would shrivel and die. A pall of black smoke would hide the blue sky and blot out the sun. No! It should not be a beautiful day. Naim tilted his head and listened. There is something missing, he thought, realizing that the only thing marring the perfect rural scene was the complete and utter silence. There were no sounds of birds, or squirrels, or the scolding chatter of chipmunks. It was as if no creatures inhabited this place. But Naim knew that was untrue. The forest was home to many different species of animals, birds, reptiles, and insects. *They have gone, before the storm reaches them*, he said to himself. *Or they are hiding, their voices stilled by fear.*

Suddenly the Druid felt a slight tremor run along Avatar's smooth flesh. He snatched the wooden staff from its bindings along the horse's side and spun about, his back pushing against the animal. His eyes measured the distance between him and the forest, lingering on the ridge of trees. Now he, too, sensed an alien presence. *Over there!* he thought, his eyes trying to penetrate the shadows that marked the edge of the thick forest. Quickly, he remounted.

"Be wary, old friend," he said softly, urging Avatar toward the trees and whatever was lurking there, waiting as still as death. "Whatever it is, it is not afraid of an old Druid and his horse."

The red roan needed no urging. His keen nostrils had pinpointed the location of the creature by its malodorous scent. The smell enraged him. He also sensed the Druid's trepidation and that

247

emotion fuelled his rage. He would fight to the death to protect the man he loved with every beat of his great heart. The courageous stallion was alive today because Naim had saved him from drowning in a quagmire on the rugged Isles of Sand, a string of seven floating islands in the Last Ocean. The horse and the man had been inseparable since then. Neighing fiercely, Avatar reared up on his hind legs. Then he flew across the mist-enshrouded grasslands like a streak of red lightning.

At the edge of the forest, the Druid reined the big horse to a stop. "Wait here," he said, sliding to the ground and grabbing his long wooden staff. He gave the horse a soft pat on his neck and stepped under the limbs of a giant evergreen and into the still forest. The air here was musty with the smell of decomposing leaves and other vegetation. Naim breathed through his mouth and cautiously moved farther into the trees.

The silence was as thick as smoke and as deep as a grave. Naim felt as if he had stumbled into another dimension where animal and human life had not yet evolved. He listened for the drone of insects, but he heard nothing except his soft breathing. The absence of sound in a forest was as unnatural as silent children in a playground. His anxiety grew until he felt he couldn't stand it anymore.

That's when the huge creature dropped from above, knocking the old man face down on the forest floor. The staff flew out of Naim's hand and landed in a patch of wild ferns growing on the bank of a small stream. Desperately, Naim tried to twist onto his back, but the creature had him pinned to the ground. He felt a gush of warmth on his arm and knew that his assailant had used a sharp knife or claws to pierce his flesh and draw blood. He knew he had to do something, and do it fast. Otherwise he'd be dead before he could escape. Clenching his teeth, he pushed his body up and back. Then, without pausing, he flexed his knees and sprang to his feet like a coiled wire, flinging his attacker away. Swiftly, he leaped to the right, where he had seen the staff land in the long ferns, and wheeled around to face his enemy.

Naim's heart skipped a beat when he saw the Thug. He should have known. The reek of death coming from the creature should have warned him.

The Demon's assassin raised his head and hissed with pleasure at the sight of blood trailing from the fingers of the Druid's left hand. His surprise attack had damaged the evil man and weakened him. Now, he'd finish him off.

The Thug had been tracking the little Elf girl when he had spied the Druid in the clearing. He couldn't believe his luck when the stupid man actually steered his horse toward the trees. Quickly, he had dug his claws into the bark of an ancient tree and climbed until his huge body was concealed among the thick boughs high above the ground. The unsuspecting human had been so intent on watching for him to pop out from behind one of the massive trunks that he hadn't thought to glance skyward. The creature's shoulders shook as he hissed again and again, hideous sounds that reverberated off the trees like crazed laughter.

Naim backed slowly toward the stream and his wooden staff, his deep blue eyes locked on the Thug's hood where a pair of red eyes burned in the blackness. He cleared his mind of everything that would distract him from the battle that he feared would end in death for one of them. He felt his heel strike something hard. The staff! Could he grab it before the creature reached him? He took another step back, and then another, to place himself behind the staff.

The Thug stood motionless, his red eyes boring into the old man. The senile fool should have run when he had the chance! Now it was too late! He hissed again and lunged for the Druid. The swiftness of the charge caught Naim by surprise. Before he could blink, the creature was on him, lashing out with claws that sliced through his cloak like scissors and cut into his upper body and across his shoulder.

But Naim was surprisingly strong and agile. Ignoring the searing pain, he bent double and slammed into the creature's middle, at the same time grabbing one of its arms. The sickening sound of bone snapping drowned out the Thug's sharp inhalation as he pitched over the Druid's back and landed in a heap on the ground. Naim wasted no time. He dived for the staff, snatching it up, and spinning about as the Thug shot to his feet and came at him again.

White fire burst from the tip of the staff and blasted into the assassin, burning into its hideous, black flesh. But, instead of slowing the creature, the magic flame seemed to feed its rage. The Thug hissed with laughter, oblivious to the weeping wound in its side. Then it dodged and snaked as it tore toward the Druid, its broken arm flapping wildly at its side.

Naim raised the staff. "STOP!" he shouted.

The black creature hesitated, startled by the unexpected sound of the man's voice.

"YOU CANNOT FIGHT ME!"

The Druid's words rang in the Thug's head. He staggered back as if something had bashed his head in.

"GO, NOW! WHILE YOU CAN!" Naim's voice was strong and filled with confidence.

The Thug shook his head to rid it of the arrogant voice. He knew this Druid. He had almost killed him once before—would have killed him if the flying Dragon hadn't meddled in the Demon's business and snatched the weakling away. A shudder sent ripples through the creature's black cloak as he relived the terrible moment when he stood before Hate and confessed how he had failed to dispatch the evil Druid and the little Elf girl. Without a word, the Demon had raised her sharp, iron stake and driven it deep into his black heart. She struck again and again until his body was ruined and broken, and the red fire in his eyes had dimmed to a pale spark. When she was satisfied that he had been punished sufficiently, she spread her huge, black cloak and rose into the sky like an obscene vulture. *Fail me again and you will die!*

She had left his battered, maimed carcass in the bloody grass outside Dundurum. But she had let him live, sending one of her serpents to heal the deep stab wounds. He was as good as new now, except for pain that was as constant as the course of the stars across the sky. He didn't mind the pain anymore. In fact, it made him stronger, made the rage more intense.

The Thug glared at the Druid through narrowed red eyes, then he hurtled toward him, closing the distance between them in three strides, clawed hand extended in front of him. He reached Naim and slashed at him but, at the last moment, the man dropped into a crouch and rolled to one side. Then Naim was up again, oblivious to the blood-soaked earth where he had rolled. He turned in time to see the Thug kick up earth as his clawed feet skidded to a stop.

The creature wheeled about and came at him again.

Naim aimed the staff, sending a stream of fire pounding into the Thug. The assassin's hissing scream shattered the silence, like the sudden, raucous cry of a giant bird. The force of the flames lifted the huge creature off his feet, hurtled him backwards where he crashed into a tree and dropped to the ground, his black cloak smoking like green wood on a campfire.

"YOU CANNOT WIN THIS BATTLE!" Naim shouted, watching the Thug leap up as effortlessly as if he had merely tripped and fallen. Naim couldn't believe the creature was still able to stand, let alone fight. Where its cloak had burned away, he saw that the fire had blasted clean through the assassin's flesh, leaving white bones exposed.

But the Thug was no longer capable of heeding the Druid's warning. His tortured mind was a twisted, writhing mass of hatred and the only voice that he could hear was the voice of Hate, his Mistress, screaming in his head, repeating two words over and over.

Die! Druid! Hissing and spitting, the Thug sprang. This time, Naim was not fast enough. The Thug smashed into him and they crashed to the ground, rolling down the bank and into the shallow brook. Naim was on his feet first, the blood from his wounds dying the clear water crimson. He splashed through the brook and scrambled up the far bank, the sound of his pursuer loud in his ears. Reaching level ground, he raised the staff and pivoted about. Then, he drove the staff into the Thug's chest and pushed with all of his strength, knocking the creature over and back down the bank.

The Thug was back on his feet in a flash, ripping out great chunks of earth and grass as he tore up the bank to get at the evil Druid. Naim shook his head wearily. He felt weak and his eyes were losing focus. The gashes on his chest, arm, and shoulder were deep. He was losing too much blood. He had to put an end to the fight and take care of his wounds before he was rendered helpless. He pointed the staff at the Thug. "It is wrong to kill," he whispered, recalling Elester's words to Arabella. "It is wrong to kill," he repeated, his eyes locked on the creature that had once been human but was now a thing of pure evil, a rabid, insensate killer, a shadow of the Demon Hate. Should he pity it? Should he spare it?

Naim struck the ground with the end of his staff and raised it toward the sky. Where his hand gripped the pale wood a white spark ignited and abruptly burst into a flame that grew until it seemed to engulf both man and staff. An eerie roaring sound filled the air as the flame grew in size and brilliance. As he turned his head away and squeezed his eyes shut, Naim thought the roar was like the sound of a giant furnace. The brilliance of the flame sliced into the blackness beneath the Thug's hood, draining the red Demon fire from the creature's eyes and absorbing it into its whiteness. It washed over the creature like molten iron, melting the thin slivers of gold pocketed under the skin on the Thug's forearm. Then the flame flared once in a blinding display and was gone.

Silence settled over the forest once more. Naim swayed unsteadily, leaning on the staff for support. For a long time, he stared at the inert creature sprawled in a blackened heap half in and half out of the water. Then, he turned his back and walked slowly, painfully, back to where he had left Avatar, one arm pressed tightly against his body. Where he passed, he left a trail of blood on the forest floor.

As he made his slow, laboured way among the trees, he wondered if he had done the right thing by sparing the Thug. What sort of creature was it now that he had doused the red fire of Hate in its eyes? Who would command it now that he had destroyed the Demon's hideous tattoo on its arm? Could he dare hope that some good might come from his actions—that the creature might have a chance?

"I am not that wise," he whispered. "I do not know."

Ahead, he saw Avatar waiting motionless in the shadows at the edge of the forest. The stallion's ears perked up and he whickered softly when he spotted the man coming slowly toward him. Despite the spasms of pain that wracked his body, Naim smiled weakly, amazed that such a noble creature should choose to stick by him through thick and thin.

Suddenly, the horse struck the ground with a forehoof. He reared up on his hind limbs, his eyes rolling in rage. Screaming, he lunged toward the Druid. Naim saw the change come over the powerful stallion and, for a second, he froze, stunned, as the horse streaked straight at him. What happened to drive Avatar into a frenzy? Was the animal possessed? Is this what Miranda saw in the stable in Bethany? Naim raised his arms in a vain attempt to protect his head from the horse's powerful hooves but, just when he thought that his old friend was about to trample the life out of him, Avatar veered to the side and shot past, toppling him onto the hard ground beside a large tree. Naim struggled to rise, but his injuries made him slow and clumsy. He crawled forward and peered around the tree, his heart racing like water over a mighty falls.

Avatar dodged and twisted to avoid the raking claws. Then he reared into the air, smashing the Thug with his powerful forelegs. The thing the Druid had spared slashed at the horse again and again with its uninjured arm in a frenzied, unrelenting attack. But Avatar was rested and, despite the Thug's massive size, stronger in purpose. He knew about evil over the course of long years spent with the Druid. He knew about it because it reeked of death. Together he and the man had fought Hellhags, Werecurs, Thugs, and other creatures the Demon had sent to destroy them, and they all smelled the same—like rotting flesh.

He would not turn his back on this crazed, spitting, half-dead being that had followed the Druid's bloody trail, its inhuman heart set on murder. Lashing out, he landed a staggering blow directly on the gaping wound in the Thug's chest. The creature screamed and stumbled to his knees. Avatar was not burdened by human concerns. Right and wrong were abstracts in his mind. All he knew was that if he did not down this enemy, it would kill him and the man. He must not let that happen. Before the Thug could regain his feet, Avatar's powerful hooves rose and came down on the black-cloaked creature again and again until the hissing was silenced and the thing was still.

CHAPTER TWENTY-NINE

THE CASTLE
OF INDOLENCE

he army of Giants attacked just after midnight. Peering out through an embrasure in a partly constructed battlement high up on the Castle wall, Penelope and Nicholas gasped and stared, awestruck, as the humongous figures poured down the hills and swarmed over the ruined valley. The Ogre Eiznek whistled excitedly. They had been mounting a flight of stairs when they heard footsteps in the passageway below. Quickly, they had pressed back into the shadows on the landing and huddled there, not daring to breathe until the shadowy figure appeared and passed along the corridor. Then they ran lightly up the stairs and followed a narrow passage to the battlement.

Now, as she watched the Giants spill down the hillsides, Penelope gasped. "Where did they come from?"

"Be quiet," hissed Nicholas, blinking rapidly to make sure he wasn't seeing things that weren't there. "Wow!" he breathed. Then he caught sight of one of the white beasts bounding down the hill like a giant white rubber ball. "What on earth *is* that?"

"You don't want to know," said Penelope.

"Seriously," pressed Nicholas. "What it is?"

"It's one of the Giant guards," said Penelope. "Some kind of animal." She enjoyed the look of wonder that crossed the boy's face as she described the ferocious beast.

"Tell me I'm not dreaming," whispered Nicholas. "I thought Manticores were mythological creatures."

"It's not a Manticore," snapped Penelope, happy to discover that even the great Nicholas could be wrong. "It's a Carovorare. I just told you it's got a raptor's head, not a man's."

"I forgot about the head," said Nicholas. "But the rest of it sounds like a Manticore or, I suppose it could be a Rapticore." Then, hiding his grin, he turned away from the embrasure and hurried toward the doorway that led out of the battlement.

"Where do you think you're going?" demanded Penelope. "Otavite told us to wait here."

"Wait here if you want," said Nicholas. "I'm going to get a closer look at that creature."

"Smart!" said Penelope. "And get yourself killed. Are you crazy?"

Eiznek grabbed Nicholas's arm and shook it furiously.

"I'm not going to get killed," said Nicholas, prying the Ogre's fingers off his arm, and grinning conspiratorially. "Anyway, I didn't hear Otavite make you the leader. Listen! I'm the one who was locked up in Indolent's basement. Remember? So, if Otavite thinks I'm going to wait around up here while he and his Giant buddies have all the fun, he's in for a surprise. I intend to make sure Weasel the Wizard and Stubby rat-face don't take off." He stopped and turned back. "And, I want my sword."

"I knew it! All right!" sighed Penelope. "Wait up. I'm coming too."

Realizing that he was about to be left behind, Eiznek uttered a shrill whistle and raced after his new friends. Nicholas urged the Ogre to lead the way through the narrow corridors to the stairs that led down to the courtyard.

"Are you sure he or it or whatever can be trusted?" asked Penelope, staring fascinated at the little Ogre as it leaped onto the wall and scuttled crab-like down the corridor.

"Yes," answered Nicholas without hesitation. "I'd trust him with my life." He suddenly laughed. "When I first met him, he was standing on my chest and I thought he was a cannibal. I really freaked. But he wasn't trying to take a bite out of my stomach or anything. He was just trying to keep me alive by feeding me."

"That's so sweet," said Penelope, glad that the little fellow had turned out to be a friend. "What do Ogres eat?"

"Rats," said Nicholas, doubling over with laughter at the look of disgust that appeared on his friend's face. He waited a few seconds and then said, "Dead rats," for effect.

"That's so gross," gagged Penelope, sticking her finger down her throat.

"Actually," continued Nicholas, trying to keep a straight face. "You should try them. They're not bad. You sort of get a craving for them after awhile." He peered intently at a spot on the floor against the wall. "Speaking of rats . . ."

Penelope shrieked and grabbed his arm, looking about for something to leap onto. Nicholas laughed so hard, he had to stop and hold his sides.

"You're disgusting," snapped Penelope, rubbing her arms furiously to smooth away the goose bumps on her flesh.

She glared at Nicholas. Then she ran to catch up with Eiznek. She didn't want to hear another word about Nicholas's prison diet. The boy's mischievous laughter followed her, bouncing like ping-pong balls off the walls of the narrow corridor. At a junction in the passageway, Eiznek dropped from the wall and waved at the others to keep their voices down. He couldn't understand how his friend could laugh at a time like this. As far as he was concerned there was nothing funny about being in a situation where they could be captured and killed at any second.

"Yeah," said Penelope, over her shoulder. "Shut up, Nick."

"Come back, Penelope! Look, I caught one for you."

Eiznek looked at the girl questioningly. Penelope shrugged and tapped her head. "Bottom of the gene pool," she said, breaking into a grin as the Ogre scratched his head and blinked his yellow eyes in confusion. She patted the little fellow on the shoulder. "Never mind," she said. "You'd have to be from my world to understand."

Chaos reigned outside the Castle walls. Thunder clapped with ear-shattering explosions. Lightning snaked across the blackness and zapped the ground, sizzling and snapping. Like giant steamrollers, massive logs thundered across the valley, flattening everything in their paths. Huge blocks of stone sailed through the air like rockets, smashing into the Castle walls and shooting shards of rock through the air like darts. The screams of Trolls mingled with the Ogres' shrill whistles.

"Watch out!" yelled Nicholas, pushing Penelope aside and ducking for cover as a massive rock crashed into the wall over his head and thudded to the ground creating a crater the size of an airplane tire.

"I want to go back!" screamed Penelope, scrambling to her feet and staring in horror at the hole in the ground where she had been standing a second before the huge rock struck.

"No!" Nicholas grabbed the girl's arm and dragged her away from the wall. "The Castle's going to collapse. We're dead if we go back." Frantically, he looked about for Eiznek, finally spotting the Ogre huddled in a ball back by the tower doorway, his entire body trembling uncontrollably as if he had suddenly contracted an advanced form of Parkinson's disease.

"Eiznek!" Nicholas dropped Penelope's arm and raced over to the terrified creature. Kneeling beside him, he wrapped his arms about his companion and held him until the tremors stopped. He could feel the creature's heart beating wildly. "I won't leave you," he whispered, his heart breaking for the little fellow. "But we've got to get out of here before the wall comes down on our heads." He took Eiznek's hand. "Let's go."

The Ogre blinked and whistled softly. The he let the boy help him up and he followed like a shadow as Nicholas grabbed Penelope and made a wild dash in the direction of Indolent's tumble-down shelter.

"Please, please let us get out of here alive!" pleaded Nicholas, leading his companions across the treacherous battlefield. His heart leaped into his throat when a large Troll toppled across their path, almost crushing them to death. Unable to slow their momentum, the panicked threesome scrambled over the kicking, screaming creature, landing on the other side in the midst of a band of Ogre slaves pouring out of the quarry and stampeding toward the hills, their ugly faces green with terror.

"We're going to die," wailed Penelope, clinging to Nicholas's arm like a leech, unaware that she was pinching him so hard her nails were cutting into his skin.

But Nicholas barely noticed. He was desperately trying to peer through the crush of advancing Ogres for a clearing or a place to hide until the fear-crazed mob passed. Suddenly, a mammoth creature plunged toward them. Nicholas and the others froze, oblivious to the maddened Ogres jostling, bruising, and scratching them. "We're dead!" said Nicholas, terrified out of his mind and fascinated as the same time. "I wish I had a camera."

"Forget the camera," hissed Penelope, jabbing her elbow into the boy's bruised ribs. "Move!"

Nicholas gulped and plowed through the Ogres. He tried to keep his head down, but his eyes kept darting back to the great white Carovorare. The beast mesmerized him. He couldn't get enough of it. "It's incredible!" he breathed. "Like watching an erupting volcano."

What finally took his mind off the creature was a deafening rumble that abruptly filled the air and shook the ground. Nicholas spun about in a circle, dreading what he might see. Eiznek nudged him and pointed toward a massive pile of logs tumbling toward them as the Giants tore apart the cradle that had contained them.

"Oh, no!" groaned Nicholas, eyes riveted on the monster logs thundering closer and closer, pulverizing stone blocks and squashing Ogres and Trolls as flat as pancakes.

"DO SOMETHING!" screamed Penelope.

"What do you want me to do?" snapped Nicholas, his heart thumping louder than the bouncing logs. He wiped his sweaty palms on the legs of his jeans. What could he do? There was no way they were going to get out of their path before the first of the logs reached them. There was nowhere to hide, and nothing short of a miracle could save them.

The miracle was huge and powerful. Otavite scooped the miniature figures up in his cupped hands, jumped over the first giant log, and bounded out of the way less than a heartbeat before the mountain of logs roared past with the might of a thousand avalanches rolled into one.

Penelope buried her face against the Giant's wrist and burst into tears.

"Nicholas! What are we going to do? I think the Princess is crying."

"She's not a Princess and she's always crying," said Nicholas. "You'll see. She'll be okay in a minute. Now let's go find my sword."

Otavite set the youngsters and the Ogre on the ground. "If you stay away from the Castle, you should be safe. But I must leave you now. We still haven't found the Dwarf-snake."

"I hope you find him," said Nicholas. "But be really careful, Otavite. He doesn't look it, but he's very powerful. He's got the Demon's magic."

Otavite nodded. He knew enough about the Dwarf-snake to know that Penelope's friend was speaking the truth. Over the course of his service as a soldier, the young Giant had fought many enemies, mostly Ogres and Trolls, but he had never come face to face with a being that was truly evil inside and out until he had seen the Malcolm creature in the cavern within the Bronx. The image of the serpent slithering out of the Dwarf's body made the coarse red hairs on his neck stick straight out as if they had been starched. He must find this fiendish viper and stop it from killing anyone else.

Nicholas, Penelope, and Eiznek watched until Otavite melted into a large mass of Giants busily tearing down the battlements and walls of the Castle. They noticed that most of the Ogre slaves had fled by now. There were a few Trolls trying to defend the remaining part of the Castle. They hurled spears and threw stones at the Giants, but the huge soldiers swatted the missiles aside as if they were flies. A great number of Trolls lay scattered about the grounds outside the Castle, and the children turned away, sickened by the sight of so many dead creatures. Finally, Nicholas began moving, and the others followed him toward the crude shelter where he had last seen his sword.

"What are we going to do if the Wizard's there, or Malcolm?" asked Penelope, who had finally stopped crying.

"I don't know," replied Nicholas. "I'll probably punch his lights out."

"Ha!" scoffed Penelope. "You and what army?"

"If you think I'm afraid of Indolent, you're wrong."

"Give it a rest," said Penelope. "Everybody's afraid of Indolent."

"Speak for yourself," snapped the boy. "I'm too angry to be scared."

"Yeah! Right!"

They reached the shelter and burst through the opening, surprised that it was still standing after the Giants had stormed through the valley. On the makeshift desk in the middle of the shack, a small lamp burned with a dim light. The companions saw at once that the place was deserted. Nicholas strode across the earthen floor, eyes squinting at the ground. "Did I mention that Indolent has a collection of new pets?" he asked, turning to Penelope.

Half expecting to see the floor crawling with rats, Penelope climbed onto a stool. "What sort of pets?" she asked, peering at the floor.

"Spiders," answered Nicholas. "Tarantulas, to be precise."

At mention of the word, *tarantulas*, Eiznek's eyes grew as large as Loonies, Canada's dollar coins. He tried to leap up beside Penelope, but she pushed him away and snapped at him. "Go find your own stool."

Penelope's flesh crawled. "Aren't tarantulas those big, black, hairy spiders?"

Nicholas nodded. "Tarantulas, or tarantulae if you like, belong to the family Theraphosidae. In southern parts of Europe they're called Lycosa tarentula, and people used to think . . ."

"Shut up!" screamed Penelope. "I hate it when you do that."

"What?" asked Nicholas, innocently. "I thought you'd want to know something about the giant, hairy thing crawling up your back."

"Yikes! Get it off me!" Penelope hopped up and down on the stool trying to jolt the non-existent tarantula off her back, her fingers brushing frantically at her hair and clothing.

Seeing how upset she was, Nicholas suddenly felt bad about teasing her. "Sorry!" he said. "I was just kidding. There's nothing on your back."

Penelope flew off the stool and knocked the boy onto his back on the ground. "I HATE YOU!" she screamed, her fists pounding his upraised arms. "YOU THINK YOU'RE BEING FUNNY, BUT YOU'RE MEAN. I'M SICK OF YOUR STUPID TEASING."

"Hey!" shouted Nicholas, trying to grab her wrists. "Okay! Okay! I won't tease you anymore. Just get off me."

Penelope punched him again. Then she jumped up, turned her back, and walked toward the doorway.

"I've had enough, OK?" Her voice sounded sad and weary.

"I almost got killed tonight, not once, but about ten times. I don't need you making me any more scared than I already am."

"I'm sorry," said Nicholas, getting up and brushing the dirt off his clothes. "I wasn't thinking. And Penelope, I wasn't doing it to be mean. I was just trying to make us laugh. Haven't you noticed, we hardly ever laugh anymore?"

Penelope turned and looked at him, her anger gone as quickly as it had appeared. "It's OK." Then she burst out laughing. "Do you know how funny you look?"

"What?"

"I can't believe you'd bother brushing dirt off your clothes. Look at them. They were filthy before I knocked you down."

Nicholas looked at the front of his tattered T-shirt and grubby jeans and grinned sheepishly. "You're right." After a while, he told his companions what the Wizard had done to the tarantulas with his sharp surgical scalpel.

"That's sick!" cried Penelope, feeling as if she were going to throw up.

"It's sick and cruel," said Nicholas, kneeling in the dirt and rummaging among the heaps of junk at the rear of the shelter. "I'd like to let them loose in his bed some night." Suddenly he stood and gave a triumphant shout. "My sword! Look!" he held up the sword, waving it at his shadow on the wall.

"Good," said Penelope, hopping off the stool. "Let's get out of here. This place gives me the creeps."

Back outside, they kept a safe distance from the Giants and watched the Castle of Indolence come down block by block. The huge soldiers hefted the massive stone blocks above their heads and tossed them into the quarry as if they were scraps of Styrofoam.

"It's sort of surreal," observed Penelope after a while. "Like watching children playing with building blocks."

"Except Giants aren't children, and each of those stone blocks weighs over four hundred pounds," added Nicholas.

"You're such a know-it-all," laughed Penelope.

"Look!" cried Nicholas, pointing toward the last standing tower. "Someone's up there."

"I don't see anyone."

"Remember when we were hiding on the stairs and someone passed down the hallway?"

"So?"

"It wasn't Indolent, but it might have been Stubby. And, if so, he's still up there. Come on! Let's go check it out."

"Have you lost your mind?" cried Penelope. "Otavite said we'd be safe as long as we stayed here. The Giants aren't going to be thinking of us when they start ripping that tower apart." She folded her arms and plopped down onto a flat-topped boulder. "For once I'm not doing what you want. I'm not going near that tower, and you know you shouldn't either."

"Stay here, then," said Nicholas. "I'll be back as soon as I find out who's up there." He turned to the Ogre. "Are you staying here or coming with me?"

Eiznek folded his arms and sat down on the stone next to Penelope.

Nicholas sighed. Deep down he knew his friend was right, but he ignored her and the voice in his head that whispered, *Don't go there!* He wanted to show the Giants that he wasn't just a helpless kid, always needing adults to look after him. He was determined not to let whoever was still lurking on the battlement get away, so he turned and, keeping to the side of the battlefield, darted from cover to cover, zigzagging toward the Castle.

Penelope and Eiznek kept their eyes glued on Nicholas's back until the night gobbled him up. Then they looked about at their surroundings, their eyes lingering on shadows that suddenly coalesced into giant, black spiders. Without a word, they exchanged frightened glances and shot off the rock as if it were a red-hot iron.

"Nick! Wait for us!" cried Penelope, dashing after the boy as if hundreds of giant tarantulas were crawling toward her. Eiznek's high-pitched whistles told her that the little Ogre was less than spitting distance behind.

Nicholas wisely kept his mouth shut when he saw his companions, but he quickly turned aside to hide the smug grin that spread across his face.

They never reached the tower. Before they had taken a dozen steps, the last remaining part of the Castle of Indolence collapsed in a cloud of dust, accompanied by a resounding roar. Nicholas and Penelope squeezed their eyes shut and covered their mouths and noses with their shirts while they waited for the dust to settle. Eiznek didn't seem to mind the choking dust. He stared at the devastated Castle in disbelief. Then he whistled and shook Nicholas until the boy opened his eyes.

"Penelope, you've got to see this," said Nicholas, whistling softly.

What Penelope saw when she opened her eyes was Otavite lumbering toward her, something wiggly dangling from his hand. "He's got the Wizard," she said, triumphantly.

But it wasn't Indolent. Otavite stopped before the youngsters and dropped the captive on the ground at their feet.

"Well, well! If it isn't little Stubby," gloated Nicholas, pointing his sword at the man's chest. "Where's your Boss and the Dwarf, Malcolm?"

"Shut your filthy mouth," spat the former teacher. Then he spotted Penelope. That she might be involved with wicked Miranda and her barfy little friends was too much for him. "Penelope? What are you doing here with this . . . this . . . evil boy?"

Penelope looked at him sadly and shook her head. "No, Mr. Little. You're the one who's evil. Don't you know what you've done? Don't you know about the Demon? Don't you know that Indolent belongs to her?"

"I thought you were smarter than that," sneered Stubby. "I thought you'd understand. But you're just like all the others—stupid and weak." Then he giggled hysterically, rolling over and over in the dirt.

"What are you going to do with him?" asked Penelope, looking up at Otavite.

"Let him go," answered the Giant. "He was not in the cavern. He has done nothing to harm us."

"No!" cried Nicholas, lifting the sleeve on Stubby's robe. "Look! It's the Demon's mark. He's one of them, and he knows where the others are. We've got to bring him to Bethany."

As soon as Nicholas mentioned the Elven capital, Stubby's body went as rigid as a poker and his eyes rolled back into his head until only the whites were visible. "Nooo! Nooo!" he shrieked. "Don't take me back." And then he curled into a fetal position and burst into another giggling fit. "We'll see about that!" he giggled. "We'll just see about that!"

The four companions stared flabbergasted at the figure on the ground.

"He's finally gone over the edge," said Nicholas, pricking Stubby's forearm with the tip of his sword.

"What are you doing?" asked Otavite.

"I'm going to make sure that he can't communicate with Hate. I'm going to remove the skull tattoo."

"Eeeuw!" cried Penelope, turning away as Nicholas set to work on the former teacher's arm.

CHAPTER THIRTY

ARABELLA
TO THE RESCUE

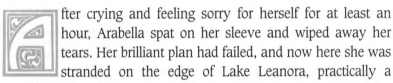fter crying and feeling sorry for herself for at least an hour, Arabella spat on her sleeve and wiped away her tears. Her brilliant plan had failed, and now here she was stranded on the edge of Lake Leanora, practically a prisoner. She went over the plan in her mind. Sneaking aboard the *ES Peridot* and stowing away in the hold where the horses would be stabled during the overnight trip had been as easy as pie.

She hadn't meant to fall asleep, but the next thing she knew, Noble and the other horses were being led off the ship. Frantically, she grabbed a heavy sack and debarked in the midst of several young Elven grooms, also laden down with saddles and gear belonging to the Riders who were accompanying the King to the Red Mountains. Arabella's plan had been to hide until the ship weighed anchor and sailed back to Bethany. Then she'd come out of hiding and they'd have no choice but to take her along.

But, everything went wrong. To her surprise, the Elven ship did not leave the small dock. How could she have known that the Captain had orders to wait for the King's party to return? How could she have anticipated that one of the grooms would rat on her?

Shortly, she had found herself standing before Andrew Furth, head unbowed, brown eyes flashing angrily.

"What on earth were you thinking?" Andrew had asked, looking as if he'd like to lock her up in the brig and throw away the key.

"I wanted to help," she had said. "It's not fair. My friends are missing and you expected me to do nothing. Well, you were wrong."

The young Elf had shaken his head. He felt sorry for the child, but he had his orders. "You cannot come with us." Then he had walked over and spoken with the ship's Captain—about her.

"They're not going to leave me behind," she had vowed.

But they did, without so much as a backward glance. "As if I'm not alive," she had whispered fiercely, watching the small company until it disappeared in the distance. Then she ran to her cabin and cried until she had no more tears left.

The Captain and his crew tried to keep the child busy. They treated her as if she were a member of the crew and assigned tasks that would, hopefully, take her mind off the King's journey to Vark. Arabella did what she was told, but all the while, her mind was scheming and plotting to follow Elester and the others.

The next evening, as she leaned over the railing on the ship's bow, she saw movement on a faraway hillside that puzzled her. Quickly, she ran to her cabin, grabbed her backpack and the food and water that she had snitched from the galley earlier. Then she ran down the gangplank and headed toward the hill to get a closer look. The distance was farther than she had thought, but she kept going, glancing back now and then to keep the ship in sight. Some of the crew saw the girl walking toward the far hill, but they weren't unduly concerned. After all, how far could she travel on two legs?

At first, Arabella couldn't believe her eyes. Then she was running, shouting "Marigold!" at the top of her lungs.

Hearing her name, the small gray mare lifted her head toward the figure running through the long grass. Whickering softly, the horse

ARABELLA TO THE RESCUE

trotted to greet the familiar human. Arabella was overjoyed to know that the animal was alive. She wrapped her arms about the mare's neck and kissed her soft face. "Oh, Marigold! I thought I'd never see you again." Avoiding Marigold's excited nuzzling of her face, neck, and hair, Arabella removed the horse's tack and used one of her shirts to brush the animal down, checking for chafing and other injuries while she worked. Next, she lifted each leg and examined the hooves to make sure the horse hadn't lost a shoe. Then she caught the reins and led the horse a dozen paces while she watched for signs of lameness.

She re-saddled the mare, caught the reins, and walked to the top of the hill, casting furtive glances back toward the tiny ship tied up at the dock and the huge troop carriers anchored just offshore in the calm water. Then, she climbed into the saddle and disappeared over the brow of the hill, out of sight of the harbour and any sharp, Elven eyes.

The way I see it, we've got two choices," she said to the horse. "We can go back to the ship and wait around for the others to return, or we can go after them. What do you say?"

As if she were replying to the child's questions, Marigold lifted her head and whinnied. "I agree," said Arabella, laughing happily. "Let's go."

Back on the ship, the first mate also glimpsed movement on the hillside. He raised his binoculars to his eyes and identified the gray horse as Elven. Then he focused on the child just as she glanced furtively toward the ship and disappeared over the top of the hill.

"Arabella!" he swore softly, dropping the binoculars and making his way toward the Captain's quarters to report the girl's absence. Within minutes, a dozen Riders set out in pursuit.

"What's that?" asked Arabella, reining the mare to a stop and staring at the black smoke rising into the overcast sky. They had travelled throughout the night, but with a lot of pit stops. Arabella thought they were still moving east, but the morning sky was

269

covered by black clouds and it had begun to rain, so she had no idea if she were steering the horse in the right direction or not. So far there had been no sign of Elester and the rest of his company.

"We're not lost," she said brightly, dismounting and walking to work the stiffness out of her legs. She led Marigold up a small grassy knoll and looked across the valley to locate the fire. What she saw wasn't a fire, but a swirling black mass, like a swarm of locusts, cutting across the land, and she was afraid.

Suddenly, a shrill chittering sound coming from the long, wet grass startled Marigold. The mare tensed.

"It's OK," said Arabella, keeping her voice calm and steady as she gently stroked the frightened animal and stepped cautiously through the grass.

A round head popped out of the grass, followed by another and another until the girl and the horse were completely surrounded. Arabella drew in a sharp breath and held it. She recognized the nasty, little, roly-poly creatures. She didn't know how it happened, but somehow she had strayed far to the north, onto Simurgh land.

"Wobbles!" hissed Arabella, using the name Miranda had coined for the creatures.

All about her, cutting off any chance of escape, were hundreds of Simurghs, cold, pink eyes locked on her, sharp, filed teeth visible in their grinning mouths. She noticed that they clutched heavy, spiked clubs in their chubby hands. "What am I going to do?" she whispered to herself, remembering all too clearly the last time she had encountered the cruel-hearted creatures.

"ARREST THE DEARS!" yelled a particularly round Simurgh, wobbling forward and waving his club at the girl and horse.

"Don't even think about it!" snapped Arabella, more angry than scared at this point. "This isn't your land and I haven't broken any of your stupid laws."

"HA!" shouted the obvious leader, looking meaningfully at his companions. "The Dear thinks she's smarter than we."

"AHA!" shouted the rest of the Wobbles. "That's against the law."

"What law?" sneered Arabella.

"Read the charge, Crumb," ordered the leader.

The one called Crumb was only too happy to oblige. He cleared his throat and spat something disgusting into the grass. "The charge is making comparisons, Edict 412(a)," he recited, triumphantly.

Arabella realized it was pointless to argue. Instead, she pointed toward the black, swirling mass in the distance. "See that?" she shouted. "The King of the Dead is coming and you're going to die if you don't get out of here."

The creatures' heads spun toward the blackness, paused for an instant, and then continued spinning in the same direction until they were facing Arabella again. *How do they do that?* she wondered, as the Simurghs erupted into laughter, chittering uncontrollably and falling down and rolling about in the grass.

"I'm serious," said Arabella. "I'm trying to help you."

"Listen to it," laughed the leader, pounding the ground in front of him with his club. "DON'T LIE TO ME, DEAR!"

"LIAR! LIAR! CUT OUT HER TONGUE!" chanted the disgusting creatures, aping their leader by beating the ground with *their* clubs.

Arabella sighed. If she could leap onto Marigold, she might be able to break through the circle of Simurghs. They weren't very tall, and, if she remembered correctly, they were terrified of horses. She took several slow steps backwards until she was standing beside the mare. *Now!* she thought, raising her leg to slip her foot into the stirrup.

"GRAB HER! SHE'S TRYING TO ESCAPE!" screeched the Simurghs, pressing closer.

Marigold reared up on her hind legs, scattering the creatures in all directions, but also knocking Arabella over in the process. Thankful that her foot hadn't been caught in the stirrup when the horse reared, Arabella jumped to her feet and dived for the mare's reins. She was too late. Marigold kicked out with her hind legs, knocking the roundness out of an unfortunate Wobble that had dared come too close to the frightened animal. The creature sailed through the air for about a dozen feet before smashing into the ground and remaining motionless. Marigold whinnied fiercely and bolted through the knot of Simurghs, and then she was gone.

Arabella screamed as the Wobbles grabbed her and wound a rough length of rope about her torso, pinning her arms to her sides. But it was a scream of helplessness. "Please listen to me!" she pleaded. "You've got to get away!"

The leader spat on the ground at her feet. "SHUT UP, DEAR!" Then, he turned toward the black cloud. "Cousin Bliss, and you, Cousin Crumb, guard the prisoner. The rest of you come with me." Then he wobbled down the hill toward the approaching darkness.

"Come back!" cried Arabella, tears of frustration spilling from her eyes. She twisted her arms under the rough bindings until angry welts formed on her skin. "You can't fight them!" She turned to her guards. "They're all going to die . . . all of them."

"LIAR! LIAR!" screamed the guards in unison, nudging her roughly with the end of their clubs and toppling her over. Laughing hysterically, they grabbed her by the hair and dragged her to her feet. Then, Crumb touched the white patch just over her right eye. Twining his fingers to get a firm grim, he yanked a handful of the white hairs out of her head.

Arabella's eyes stung, but she gritted her teeth and suffered the pain in silence. She felt rain mingling with the blood oozing from her head. *You deserve to die!* she thought.

Bliss jabbed the club against her ribs, prodding her forward through the wet grass. "MOVE!" he ordered. "KAP! KAP!"

Arabella moved as quickly as she could with her arms bound against her sides. "I detest Wobbles," she muttered, feeling the loathing for the creatures building inside her like a fire. "Mean, putrid creatures. I don't care if they all die."

What am I saying? Arabella was horrified by the words that had slipped so easily from her mouth. Did she really want the Wobbles to die? Did she seriously believe they deserved to die because they had hurt her? Should people die for hurting others? *Not that Wobbles are people, exactly,* she thought. *No! Just because I hate them and think they're nasty and vicious and disgusting doesn't mean they shouldn't be allowed to live. But it doesn't mean I have to like them either.*

She stopped and stared at the swirling blackness moving ever closer to the huge band of Simurghs. "Well," she whispered, "You're going to die, every last one of you, unless someone comes up with a brilliant idea and fast."

Instead of whacking her with their clubs, or knocking her down, or pulling her hair out until she was completely bald, the two guards also stared across the valley, chittering and cheering their comrades on to battle.

"You stupid, stupid Wobbles," said Arabella, swallowing the bitter taste in her mouth. She watched the blackness smash into the front line of Simurghs, consuming them and belching their twisted, deflated dead bodies back into the seething ranks of the army where they clutched their clubs and rose up to follow Calad-Chold, smoke rising from the blackened earth beneath their feet.

Still the Simurghs advanced, more incensed than ever at the loss of so many of their comrades. But they didn't stand a chance. The blackness devoured them.

"RUN!" screamed Arabella, crying freely now. But she might as well have been screaming at the Moon for all the good it did. The Wobbles were too far away and even if they had been within earshot, they were past caring. Within seconds, most of them were dead. Finally, the few that remained turned to flee, but they were too late. The Dead reached out from the blackness and took them.

A loud cry of anguish exploded from Arabella's throat. She slumped down onto her knees in the grass, unable to turn her face to the terrible thing she had witnessed. Then she heard a strange whimpering sound and looked up. The two Simurgh guards were wobbling down the hill toward the dead army. Arabella scrambled awkwardly to her feet. "Stop!" she yelled. "Are you crazy?" But they ignored her. *Think of something!* she screamed silently. *Make them so mad they'll turn around and chase you.*

"HA, HA, HA!" she shouted, hating herself, but knowing she had only one chance to enrage them. "ALL YOUR STUPID FRIENDS ARE DEAD. HA, HA, HA! STUPID, STUPID WOBBLES!"

The guards wobbled to a stop, their heads swivelling around to face the wicked human girl.

"YOU CALL THAT SMART? I CALL IT STUPID. DEARS!"

The guards swung their round shapes about and started back up the hill, shouting in their shrill voices.

"WE'LL TEACH YOU TO INSULT US, DEAR!"

"LIAR! LIAR! WE'RE GOING TO TEAR YOUR TONGUE OUT!"

"WE'RE GOING TO CUT OFF YOUR EARS!"

"THEN WE'RE GOING TO SKIN YOU! DEAR!"

Arabella laughed at them, and then she turned and ran. Even bound, she thought she could probably outrun the creatures, especially with a head start. But, when she paused and looked about, there was no sign of her pursuers. For a second the girl hesitated, unsure whether to keep running or go back and find out why the Wobbles had given up the chase. What if it's a trap? She sighed and retraced her steps, keeping her eyes peeled for any sudden stirring of the long blades of grass. When she reached the top of the hill and peered down the far slope, she felt sick. She had failed.

The Simurghs, fingers stuck in their ears to mute the girl's voice, bounced down the hill, screaming curses and threats at the seething blackness that seemed to cover the earth as far as the eye could see.

Arabella almost laughed at the two ridiculous, toy-like figures wobbling purposefully toward the insuperable army of Calad-Chold.

In a thunder of hooves, a dozen gray Elven horses thundered over the brow of the hill behind Arabella. She whirled about, fighting down the impulse to clap and cheer at the sight of the Elves. Her eyes lit up as she noticed Marigold trotting along behind the larger horses.

"Please! Oh please save the Wobbles," she cried, oblivious to the curious glances the Elves exchanged as they mouthed the word *Wobbles?* "There!" She pointed down the hill. "They're going to fight Calad-Chold."

Without a word, the Riders spurred their horses after the Simurghs. One leaped to the ground, pulled a long knife from a sheath secured about his lower leg, and sliced through Arabella's bonds as if the thick rope were made of air.

Arabella rubbed her arms gently to take away the numbness. Then she ran toward Marigold and climbed into the saddle. "I knew you'd come back," she said.

"Go!" ordered the Rider. "To the ship."

For once, Arabella didn't argue. She wheeled Marigold about and took off like a bullet, not daring to glance over her shoulder until she reached the safety of the King's ship. The sight of the massive troop carriers anchored in the deeper waters just offshore did nothing to quell the despair in her heart. As the Riders galloped past, she noticed that the two Simurghs weren't with them. Always, always, she had felt safer with the Elves than with anyone else on earth. But, Calad-Chold was coming! She'd just seen his Black Army destroy an entire race in the snap of a finger. And now the same thing was going to happen to the Elves. She and they would all die, just like the Simurghs. Inside, her grief grew like a tumour. She should have been able to do something to save the miserable Wobbles from such a terrible end.

CHAPTER THIRTY-ONE
CALAD-CHOLD

he King of the Dead raised his fist and reined Khalkedon to a halt. Behind, his vast army went as still as a graveyard at midnight. The King's First Officer turned to his superior, eye sockets burning with a yellow flame beneath his worm-eaten hood, long white-boned teeth gleaming from his gumless, black mouth.

A moment, sighed Calad-Chold, without speaking. He tilted his crowned head to one side and listened intently. Seconds passed, and then minutes. But still the King remained motionless, following a path in his mind that none but he could take. *The Blade . . . I feel its presence like a living, beating heart.* Then his head turned until he was facing his First Officer. *The Talisman that I went to recover eluded me. I came back without it. It is a knife . . . my own blade . . . forged in Hell. I must have it. In the wrong hands, it will destroy us.*

I will get this knife and bring it back to you, volunteered the First Officer.

No, said the King of the Dead. *You are a good man and I trust you.* His chuckle was a deep rattle in his throat. *I trust you*, he repeated, *because you must obey.*

The First Officer nodded slowly. What the other said was true. He had been called back from the dead and he must obey his King, just as Calad-Chold must obey the one who had brought him back.

"What is the meaning of thiss? Why have we sstopped?" Both heads spun about at the sound of the sibilant voice.

Silence, snake! commanded the King of the Dead, his hand reaching for the sword at his side.

The Dwarf-serpent hissed and spat at the dead creature. "She iss not pleassed. She ssaid sstrike the Elvess now! She ssummoned you. You musst obey!"

Calad-Chold threw back his head and laughed. The terrible sound tore apart everything that had not been burned to ashes by the deadly army. It spared Hate's servants and their living Troll and Ogre slaves from death, but it ripped into the serpent, inflicting unbearable pain, and drove it screaming and hissing back into the midst of the silent, unmoving mass of dead beings.

Tell your Mistress to be patient, snake, laughed the King. *I will obey. I will destroy the Elves for her . . . after I dispose of another small matter.* He maneuvered Khalkedon alongside his First Officer and rested his hand on his subordinate's shoulder. *Ride with me,* he said.

Calad-Chold faced his mighty army and ordered it to stand ready to march on his command. Then he pointed ahead to the grass waving on the hillside. A shudder rippled through his black cloak. *There are living beings coming to challenge us. Take them!* He dug his spurs into Khalkedon's wet, black bones and turned the horse away from the invincible horde, back in the direction of the homey little cottage where the trail of the Twisted Blade had gone as cold as death. At his side, wrapped in a swirl of black smoke, rode the King's First Officer, his skeletal hand resting lightly on the hilt of his long sword.

"Stop!" cried Miranda, flapping her arms against her sides to keep blood circulating through her frozen body. "You're back where you started." She had been stomping furiously through the snow trying to find her way out of the storm and away from the Augurs as quickly as possible. But something was terribly wrong. She found that she just kept retracing her steps over and over again. Now, here she was back at the edge of the clearing where the soft yellow light above the Augur's front door twinkled like a welcoming beacon in the storm that raged outside. "Some welcome," she laughed. "Wait till I tell Nick about this."

When Miranda flew out of the Augurs' house, she had no idea where she was going, or how she intended to get there. Only one thought filled her mind—put as much distance as she could between her and the Augurs. But, as she plowed through the snow, making a beeline for the trees at the edge of the clearing, she suddenly stopped. "Where are you going?" she whispered, afraid that if she spoke too loudly the old couple would find her. For a second, she wondered about the Augurs. Who were they? Where had they come from? Did they act out the same crazed dinner scene every day of their lives? Or did they only really exist when strangers found their way to the front door of the little cottage?

"Forget the Augurs," she muttered. "Think of a way to get out of here."

When she and Nicholas had followed Naim here, it had taken them only a few minutes to reach the cottage. When they had been forced to flee from the enraged couple, they had encountered no problems. *Not like now*, she thought, judging that she'd been walking for over an hour. Discouraged, she wished that she had paid more attention to her surroundings the last time she was here. If she had, maybe she'd be able to identify one or two landmarks that would show her the way out.

Using her arm, she brushed snow from a large rock and sat,

wracking her brain for a clue to the path they had taken last year. "Think!" she commanded her brain.

OK! said her brain. *What was the first thing you saw when you got here?*

She replayed the images in her mind. "Nothing," she answered. "Everything was black."

Come on, urged her brain. *You must have noticed something.*

"You'd think," agreed Miranda. "But, except for the snow storm, there was nothing to notice."

You're hopeless. You'd make a terrible witness.

Miranda nodded. She slumped forward on the rock and rested her elbows on her knees. A little voice in her head told her to keep moving or she'd freeze to death. But, as she stared at the long knife still clutched tightly in her hand, she felt the last drop of energy drain from her body. Slowly, she turned the knife over, shivering as an image of Morda stabbing the giant bird flashed through her mind. She looked at her hand where the knife had sliced through the soft flesh between her fingers. The freezing air had stemmed the bleeding, and her hand was so numb from the cold that she couldn't feel anything.

Absentmindedly, she sliced at the snow, telling herself she was just taking a little rest. "I'm so tired," she said softly. She opened her fingers and let the knife drop into the snow. "As if I need a knife," she laughed. "As if I'd be able to use it." Miranda wrapped her arms about her body. She stayed like that for a long time. She thought of her friends. Where were they? What were they doing? Were they thinking about her? She missed them so much her heart ached. But, after a while her head fell forward onto her chest and her eyes closed.

A loud voice jarred on Miranda's raw nerves like a fork scraping on a plate. Her eyes twitched open and, for a second, she had no idea where she was. What was she doing outside in a blizzard wearing these goofy clothes? And how did she get here? Then it all came flooding back . . . the Augurs . . . finding the clothes she had burned as good as new . . . the old man pouring wine . . . Morda raising the carving knife . . . the knife plunging into the table . . . and then herself running . . .

What had awakened her? A voice—a loud voice! Suddenly afraid, Miranda looked down at the spot where she had dropped the carving knife in the snow. Her eyes widened in stunned disbelief. The deep snow about her feet had melted and formed a pool of steaming water. Miranda blinked. The carving knife was gone. But, through the steam, lying on the ground at the bottom of the pool of water, she saw a rippling, wavering image—an alien, winding piece of metal.

She had found the Twisted Blade!

"That's impossible," she said. "It's a trick. It's the water making Morda's knife look like the Twisted Blade."

Hardly daring to breathe, she cautiously tested the water with her index finger. "Ouch!" she cried, abruptly snatching her finger back. The melted snow was boiling hot. She stuck her finger in her mouth and slid off the rock, using her boots to smooth away the snow and drain the pool. She was just reaching for the knife when she froze.

Had the Druid said something important about the Twisted Blade? Something about the finder being the wielder? Or was she imagining a conversation that never happened? Miranda sighed. The odds against her finding Calad-Chold's knife had to be more than a billion to one. But, to her astonishment, she had beaten the odds. The knife on the ground at her feet was the Twisted Blade. She knew it, but she was afraid to touch it. If she picked it up, would that make her the wielder—the only one who could use it against the King of the Dead?

She sat down on the rock and stared at the knife. "I can't touch it," she said, wondering how the Twisted Blade had managed to disguise itself as a carving knife. Or did the Augurs have something to do with it? "Oh Naim, I wish you were here. There are so many things I don't understand."

At that moment, two hideous fiends, mounted on grotesque skeleton horses, broke through the trees and leaped to the ground, melting the snow about their feet.

Miranda's heart stopped. *RUN! RUN!* screamed her inner voice. She wanted to run. She wanted to turn and run faster than she had ever run before. But her limbs wouldn't obey. She was like a puppet whose manipulating strings had all been severed. She couldn't move, couldn't speak, couldn't lift a finger to save herself. All she could do was watch, scared to death, as the creatures came for her, their grisly arms outstretched toward the blade lying on the steaming ground at her feet.

"Do not look around," said a voice from behind. "Move back slowly. Do not stop."

Naim!

Miranda's eyes filled with tears that blurred the terrible creatures into vague, writhing shapes. She blinked and took a small step backwards.

"Good," said the Druid. "Do not panic. Keep moving back."

Don't panic! Don't panic!

Then, she panicked. Without thinking, she grabbed the steaming Twisted Blade, oblivious to the searing pain that spread from her hand up her arm to her shoulder, and spun about, running blindly toward the black-cloaked figure waiting motionless near a large, snow-covered boulder. She didn't dare look back because she knew if she saw how close her pursuers were she'd never make it. She kept her eyes pinned on the Druid.

Faster! She screamed to herself, focusing all of her strength into her pounding legs, forcing them to move faster than thought. Ahead, Naim reached out for her and Miranda saw the shiny silver pouch resting in the palm of his hand. Abruptly, the pouch slipped through his long fingers and the Druid disappeared into thin air. Summoning the last of her strength, Miranda threw herself forward into the spot where Naim had been standing a second ago. At the last second, she scooped up the Bloodstones, almost angrily. Then, she vanished in a burst of white light.

Calad-Chold stopped abruptly and screamed his rage into the wind. The sound smashed into the trees, blasting them into splinters. It melted the snow into a raging torrent that surged through the forest like a millrace. It smashed into the ground, hurling chunks of earth into the air and grinding rocks into gravel. When the scream died away, all that remained of the area for miles about was a large boulder, and the small, yellow cottage with the soft light shining warmly over the front door. Everything else was a wasteland.

In the hands of a child, the knife cannot harm us, said the First Officer, moving toward his horse.

Wrong! answered the King of the Dead, stopping the other with a hand on his arm. *In that child's hand the Twisted Blade is my bane—a sickle of Death.*

CHAPTER THIRTY-TWO

NEW AND OLD FRIENDS

he valley was a cesspool. Elester's blood simmered as his eyes travelled across the despoiled, deserted landscape. "So this is where Indolent has been hiding," he said, barely able to contain his anger at the terrible outrage done to this once beautiful place.

It was early morning when Elester and the others had noticed the black cloud blanketing a ring of hills directly ahead. "Looks like a storm building," said Andrew Furth, staring into the distance.

"It is not a storm," answered the King of the Elves. "Notice how it hangs over the hills like a giant bird of prey, impervious to the winds?"

"What is it?" asked Andrew, suddenly anxious to be gone from there.

"I have seen the Wizard Indolent work his evil on the lands before," answered Elester, his mouth a hard, thin line. "It looked like that."

Now, as he peered into the valley, a feeling of sadness swept over him. He knew beyond certainty that Indolent was responsible for the gaping, stinking quarry where bodies of Ogre slaves lay where they had fallen, and for the dead trees scattered about the floor of the valley like giant matchsticks. The Wizard was a destroyer—a killer of Nature. Where he went, he polluted the soil so that nothing could grow for a hundred years. He poisoned the air and fouled the waters. Elester's sadness overwhelmed him. His aide's voice in his ear snapped him back to the present.

"Some people believe there's a Heaven after life on earth," said Andrew. "But, I wonder what makes them think that after they die they'll go from this world to a perfect world where they can do this all over again."

"Hrumph!" snorted the King of the Dwarves. "Deluded fools! Don't realize the test's *here*. Must make *here* better before doors open *there*." He waved his beefy arm skyward in a vague arc. Then he swung it toward the valley. "No Heaven for the Wizard."

Elester and his aide exchanged quick glances almost as if they shared a deep secret. Then Elester smiled and clapped Gregor on the shoulder. "No," he agreed. "There is no Heaven for Indolent. But, something besides the Wizard was here, and recently. Some great force found this place and destroyed him and his new Castle, or drove him away."

"Or took him captive," said Andrew.

"Whatever it was," growled Gregor, "was big."

"Where are they now?" questioned Elester. "Surely if it or they were big, we would have seen something."

"I think it is still here," said Andrew, his voice a mere whisper. "And I think it has spotted us." The aide touched his King and pointed at a hill on the opposite side of the valley directly across from where they lay in the grass.

Elester saw the solitary figure standing motionless on the brow of the hill. "A Giant!" he murmured.

"A *big* Giant," corrected Gregor.

"Is there any other kind?" said Andrew, his eyes riveted on the huge form.

Then he turned to Elester, his face lined with worry. "How are relations between our nation and the Giants, Sire?"

"We are allied with Vark," said the King. "But this lone Giant could be a renegade." He grinned. "Or there is a bigger surprise waiting just beyond the hill."

"Nothing for it but to identify ourselves," said Gregor. "Show our standards."

Elester nodded and spoke to his aide. "Do it."

Andrew inched backwards until he was out of sight of the huge figure standing as still as a stone pillar on the brow of the hill across the valley. He was back shortly with Gregor's soldiers and two Riders in tow. They worked openly now, unfurling the two nations' flags and anchoring them by driving the ends of the long poles into the earth. Then they unfurled the standards of their Kings and stood them alongside the flags.

"What are you looking at?" asked Nicholas, coming up to stand beside the Giant.

"There," answered the Giant, pointing toward the top of the hill directly opposite.

"What is it?"

"I don't know. I saw something move."

The Giant and the boy stared across the valley. Suddenly, a dazzling flash of golden light burst from the hillside that they had been staring at.

"Get down!" Otavite threw himself flat on the ground, momentarily blinded by the bright flash.

"It's OK!" cried Nicholas, excitedly. He leaped to his feet and called Penelope. "Come on! Hurry! It's the Elves!"

Otavite sat up. He realized that the dazzling golden flash was a reflection from something gold on a green and white background. He supposed it could be the Golden Crown that dominated the Elven flag. But what was the other one? "Dwarves!", he said, staring at the silver, arched structure against a blue background. He'd seen it before in the cavern in Taboo. He noticed, too, that Nicholas was halfway down the hill. For just a second, he wondered if this were a trap, an illusion created by the wicked Malcolm-snake to snare them.

"Is it true?" cried Penelope, her face flushed after running up the hill. "Is it really the Elves?"

"Those are the Kings' standards," said Otavite. "Elves and Dwarves."

"You mean Elester and King Gregor are here?" stammered Penelope, hardly daring to hope it was true.

Otavite nodded, amused at the child's excitement. "Come," he said. "I have only seen one Elf in my life, and I have never forgotten. Come! We must find out why they are heading toward Vark, and what else they know."

The parties met in the valley. As they watched Elester and Gregor ride toward them, accompanied by the company of Riders and Dwarf soldiers, their long standards streaming in the breeze, Nicholas and Penelope suddenly felt an unfamiliar feeling sweep over them as if their old friends had become strangers. Neither youngster had ever been shy. They had known Elester when he was a Prince and had been present at his Crowning in Bethany the previous summer. And they had known King Gregor, too. They had spent time in Dundurum, the old Dwarf kingdom and in Dunmorrow in the Mountains of the Moon.

"Do you think they'll remember us?" asked Nicholas.

"I hope so," said Penelope.

"I don't know what to say," confessed Nicholas.

"I know," said Penelope. "I feel the same."

"I guess I never really thought it was real," mused the boy. "But now, seeing Elester and King Gregor on their horses and the flags, it's like they're bigger and different somehow. I think if I were a girl I'd start to cry."

Penelope jabbed her elbow into his ribs hard. "That is the most obnoxious thing I've ever heard. I can't believe you said that. As if boys never cry."

"I didn't mean it like that," said Nicholas hastily. "What I meant was that seeing them makes me emotional. I feel like crying, but I can't. But if I were a girl, I could. Girls cry easier than boys. That's all. It doesn't mean we don't feel the same."

"Shut up before you make it worse," groaned Penelope. "What are we going to say? Do we call him Your Majesty, or what?"

But they needn't have worried. Elester leaped from his horse and his grim Elven face broke into a wide smile that warmed their hearts and made them feel as if they were the only people in the entire world.

"King Elester," said Nicholas, stepping forward to clasp Elester's outstretched hand.

"You must call me Sire," grinned the King, eyeing the Elven short sword at the boy's belt. "The other Riders seem to favour that title."

"Yes, Sire!" said Nicholas, beaming proudly. Then he caught Eiznek's arm and dragged the little fellow forward. "This is Eiznek. He helped me escape from Indolent's dungeon."

Elester looked at the Ogre in surprise. "Then you are a friend, indeed," he said, grinning in response to the smile that lit up the other's face. He clapped Nicholas on the shoulder. "Now, lad, if you survive King Gregor's welcome, report to Captain Faron. He is your commander. And take Eiznek with you."

"Yes, Sire!" repeated Nicholas, looking about for his new Captain, only to come face to face with the Dwarf King, who caught him in a bear hug and almost squeezed the life out of him. After enduring a couple of hearty whacks on his back Nicholas went to look for Captain Faron.

"And Penelope," said Elester, embracing the girl and looking about curiously. "Where is your little white dog? The Elfhound?"

Penelope hated the tears that sprang to her eyes as easily as if what Nicholas had said were true. "I don't know," she cried. "She's lost."

Elester patted her shoulder. Then he beckoned his aide to his side. "This is Andrew, whom you already know," he said. "Tell him about your dog and he will send a party to search these hills."

"Sire," said Otavite, stepping forward and dropping to one knee before the King of the Elves. Penelope stifled a giggle at the sight of the kneeling Giant towering above Elester.

"Stand," said Elester gently. "I would know what happened in this valley, and where you found the boy and girl. I would know about the one they call Calad-Chold. But let us leave this Evil place and meet beyond the hills."

Otavite turned and pointed at a hill behind him. "Sire, the Vark army is camped just over there. We travel simply, but we would be honoured to welcome Your Majesties to our humble campsite and share what we have with you and your men."

They gathered about a great fire and talked until the wee hours of the morning. Otavite went first. The golden hairs on Elester's neck stiffened as he listened to the Giant's chilling report. The young soldier related the horrific events chronologically, leaving nothing out. The others listened in silence until he reached the part where the hidden door slid open and the black-cloaked Druid appeared through the opening like death itself.

Then, unable to restrain himself any longer, Gregor kicked a log, sending giant sparks shooting into the air. "Not a Druid!" he snorted.

"But it was, Sire," insisted Otavite. "It was just like I always imagined."

"I tell you it wasn't a Druid," stormed Gregor.

"Describe this creature," pressed Elester.

Otavite's flesh turned as green as a large olive when he described the creature. "It came up to here," he said, standing and slapping a spot near his belt.

"Nine feet," said Nicholas, ignoring the dirty look Penelope aimed at him.

"And it had long claws," said Otavite, looking about for something to show the length of the creature's nails. "Long like your sword, Nicholas."

"Otavite," said King Elester. "The creature you saw inside Taboo was not a Druid. It was a Thug—a cold, heartless killer."

"Belongs to the Demon," said Gregor. "Kills for Hate."

Otavite wasn't prepared to give up a lifelong conviction that Druids were evil just because the King of the Elves and the King of the Dwarves said differently. "Druids eat children, suck out their brains," he said. "If you look into their eyes you will die."

Nicholas and Penelope burst out laughing.

"Oh, Otavite!" laughed Penelope. "Don't tell me you still believe in the Bogyman!"

"That's rich," scoffed Nicholas. "I remember when you didn't believe in monsters, or Trolls, or Ogres, or Dragons, or Elves. Shall I go on?"

"Shut up," snapped Penelope, throwing a clod of dirt at Nicholas.

"No," said Elester quietly. "Druids are not the creatures of your nightmares. They are committed to fighting Evil. That is what they do. I hope that you will meet my oldest friend. He is a Druid, and he has worn himself out in the endless fight."

Otavite and the other Giants nearby stared at the King speechlessly. The frightening stories they had been told since they were children had just been laughed at. How could so many people be wrong? How could the entire population of a nation be wrong? Surely it wasn't possible. After the shock wore off, he gave the rest of his report to a rapt audience.

"Naim was right!" exclaimed King Elester. "Not that I ever doubted. But I had to hear these things for myself."

"Demon's work," agreed Gregor. "Kill the Elves, destroy prison."

"That is what the chief said and that is why he sent the army to stand with the Elves."

"But, what about your own country?" asked Nicholas.

"Out people have already been evacuated to the Isles of Sand," said Otavite. "Can the dead cross water?"

"I do not know," said the King of the Elves. "But it appears we will find out soon enough."

Nicholas went next. His story corroborated what Miranda had already told them about the earthquake in Ottawa that swallowed him and his entire house. What Elester found fascinating was how Nicholas and Penelope had fallen from their world into the cavern in the Bronks. Then Nicholas told about his capture by the Ogres and meeting Eiznek in the dungeon.

"Tell him about Stubby," prompted Penelope.

"Oh yes," said Nicholas. "Guess who I found with Indolent: Stubby. And I cut out the Demon's skull tattoo from his arm. We captured him. And you should have seen Otavite and the rest of the Giants tear this place apart. This Calad-Chold better start running."

"Giants can't fight dead," snapped Gregor irritably.

"You haven't seen these guys in action," said Nicholas.

"My old friend is right, Nicholas. Nothing can stand against the King of the Dead. He cannot be killed because he is already dead."

"I still say you can lop off their legs. They may not die but they won't be able to move very fast."

Then Elester, with a lot of rude interruptions from King Gregor, told about Miranda and Arabella coming to Bethany to try to find their friends. He spoke of the voices Miranda had heard coming out of the rift, and he confirmed that he had heard them, too.

"That's why we were coming to Bethany," said Nicholas. "I've got to warn Miranda that the fifth Demon egg is meant for her.

Malcolm wants to kill her and have the serpent animate her body to see if they can control the Bloodstones."

"Miranda has been taken by the Demon's hunters," said Elester quietly, staring into the fire as if he were seeing into a place far away. "The Druid searches for her even now."

"What are we waiting for?" cried Nicholas, jumping up and facing the others. "We've got to find her."

"Sit down, Nicholas," said Elester. "As soon as it is light, you will see a darkness growing just north of where our ships lay at anchor. Calad-Chold has called the dead and they have answered. Now he marches across the lands, making his slow, inevitable way to Ellesmere Island. There is nothing we can do for Miranda now."

They broke camp at first light. Otavite, with Penelope perched on his shoulder, strode ahead, effortlessly keeping pace with the Elven horses. Behind came the small company of Riders and Gregor's Guards. Eiznek rode behind Nicholas, his ugly face beaming with excitement. The mighty Giant army followed, spread out across the land like a vast surging wave. But they were a mere puddle compared with the Black Army halted about ten miles north and covering the earth as far north and east as the eye could see.

Fierce battle cries reached their ears long before they sighted the harbour. "The ships are under attack!" shouted an Elven scout, halting on the crest of a hill and waiting for the others. Elester rode up beside him and reined Noble to a halt. Below, thousands upon thousands of Trolls and Ogres poured from the northern hillside like molasses and swarmed over the flatlands. The sky over the harbour was dark with the Demon's winged hunters. The air was charged with the creatures' shrill screeching as they swooped down on the Elven and Dwarf soldiers with outstretched claws.

But it was the vast, silent ocean of blackness to the north that made Elester's blood run as cold as a glacier. As he stared at the unmoving mass of Calad-Chold's army of death, despair welled up inside him. *It is the end of everything!* he thought. *We will be blown away like dry leaves in the wind.* The King shook his head. *Do not give up before the battle begins*, he thought.

"What's it waiting for?" barked Gregor, whose eyes were also focused on the Dead King's army. "Why hasn't it attacked?"

"That is the burning question," answered Elester. "What is it waiting for?" Then he drew his long sword and urged Nobel into a gallop. "We may not be able to fight the dead," he cried. "But I see living Trolls and Ogres down there."

CHAPTER THIRTY-THREE
THE TWISTED BLADE

"aim! Naim! Where are you?" Miranda ran blindly through the blackness, screaming the Druid's name over and over until her throat was raw and her voice raspy. She knew immediately where she was. Somehow, she had blundered into the portal near the Augur's house. Now, she couldn't find her way out. Fear spread through her body like fire, consuming her and eating away at her sanity. There was no sound except her own ragged breathing. There were no boundaries, no signposts, nothing to guide her. There was only black—so complete it seemed to absorb her into its very core, until she felt that she was melting, becoming one with the nothingness. She tried to keep her mind from going down the road that led to the terrible truth. But she knew she was lost in the portal.

She remembered describing travel through the Bethany portal as instantaneous—like lifting her foot in Ottawa and putting it down on the Moon. But the portal under Parliament Hill wasn't at all like that. Travelling from Ottawa to Bethany was just like falling through the sky. Scary, yes! But nothing that compared to this portal. Entering this portal was like walking into a void, an absolute emptiness. It made her think of the Place with No Name and, for just a brief moment, she felt a pang of pity for the Demon. What would it be like to live in this black nothing for the rest of her life? How long before her mind and heart turned as black as the inside of Hate's hood? She didn't know, but she guessed it wouldn't take very long at all.

"Naim!" She thought of turning back but was afraid that the skeleton creatures would still be outside waiting for her. No! She couldn't go back. That left her only one choice: keep going. "And don't you dare start crying," she said to herself.

"It's no use," she said after she had been running for what seemed like hours. "I'm never going to find my way out." And then she squinted and peered ahead. *What's that?* she wondered. It was like an infinitesimal flicker of yellow light, bobbing in the distance. She moved quickly forward and after a long time, the light grew and she saw a short, stocky figure ahead. In its hand it held a lantern that bobbed with the figure's swinging gait. The light cast shadows on rocky walls and Miranda was surprised to discover she was in a tunnel somewhere.

"Excuse me!" she yelled.

The unexpected voice startled the squat figure. It jumped and spun about, holding up the lantern to get a look at the intruder. "Who are you? What do you want?" The voice was gruff and cold as a winter wind.

Oh no! thought Miranda, her heart sinking. "I don't have time for this. Emmet?" she said, moving quickly toward the Dwarf. "You've got to help me get back to Bethany fast." The realization that she was back home in Ottawa, in the tunnels under Parliament Hill, astounded Miranda. How was it possible? If anything, she should be in Kingsmere. She could have sworn that Naim said the portal near the Augurs exited at Kingsmere.

The Dwarf took a step toward the girl, stopping abruptly when he spotted a long, twisted dagger in her raised hand. "Here, now, girl! No need to get violent. Put that down."

Miranda hadn't realized that she was still gripping the Twisted Blade. Sheepishly, she lowered her arm. "Sorry," she said. "I have to get this knife to Bethany to stop the King of the Dead. I took a carving knife from the Augurs and it turned into this blade. Then these horrible skeleton creatures came after me to get it. I ran away and somehow ended up in a black hole. And here I am."

"Where's the boy?" asked Emmet, peering past her into the darkness.

"I don't know," snapped Miranda. "Please, Emmet. Help me before it's too late."

"Come, then!" said Emmet, turning and leading the way down the tunnel.

A sound from the darkness behind made the Dwarf and girl leap practically out of their skins. Miranda gasped and spun about.

WHO'S THERE?" bellowed the Dwarf.

"It's Naim!" cried Miranda, ignoring Emmet's warning shout, and running toward the tall black shape coming slowly toward her in the dark tunnel. "Oh, Naim! I thought . . ."

Miranda faltered. Something was wrong with her eyes. Naim seemed to expand into two figures. She froze, already knowing the terrible thing she had done. There were two figures. For a second, sheer terror paralyzed her and something seemed to tighten about her throat blocking her breathing passage. "Emmet," she whispered finally, her voice weak and as thin as air. "Run!"

What had she done? What horror had she led into her world?

"No!" hissed the Dwarf. "You go. I'll hold them off."

"You can't!" cried Miranda. "They're dead. You can't stop them."

Together they turned and ran, the sound of creaking bones echoing in the long, dark tunnel followed like cold air on their necks.

"Got to douse the light," muttered Emmet, plunging them into darkness. "When we reach the end of this passage. You go left. Keep to the side against the wall. There's a stairs at the third fork off the main tunnel. At the top, reach up. There's a ledge. At the near end you'll feel a latch. Press it and then push against the right wall. It'll get you out of the tunnels. I'll go left and make a commotion. Lead them astray." Then he gripped her arm. "Go! Good luck, girl." His voice was gruff but filled with a strange emotion.

"Thanks, Emmet."

Miranda turned left. She could barely see, but she *could* see. The Dwarves must have rigged lighting along the main tunnel since she had last been here. The passageway stretched before her like a giant, gaping mouth. She took Emmet's advice, keeping to the side where the pale light couldn't penetrate the deep shadows, and ran until she flew past a flight of narrow stone stairs that she almost missed. Skidding to a stop, she glanced back along the tunnel but she detected no movement. Silently, she thanked Emmet for leading the horrible skeletons away from her. Then, she took a deep breath, filling her lungs with the stale, musty smelling air, and ran lightly up the steps.

Her fingers fumbled along the ledge feeling for the latch. "Come on," she whispered. "It's got to be here." She ran her fingers over the ledge again but she couldn't find the latch. Desperately, she put her shoulder against the rough wall and pushed with all of her strength. Nothing happened.

Wrong stairs! The words screamed in her head. She flew down the steps and continued along the passage, her eyes scanning the shadows for another exit. *I've gone too far!* she thought, a feeling of panic building like a storm inside her. She turned around and started retracing her steps. "Please, please," she whispered. "Help me!" Ahead, she heard the harsh sounds of shouting and high-pitched screams. "You can't fight them!" she whispered, her eyes filling with tears at the sound of Dwarves dying.

And then, as if someone heard her plea for help, the darkness seemed to lift slightly and she saw a set of stairs on the other side of the main tunnel. Quickly, she dashed across the limestone floor to the shadows against the opposite wall. At the same instant, something dark appeared in the passageway ahead.

"It's them!" She knew they couldn't possibly see her in the shadows, but she wasn't thinking rationally. She felt naked and vulnerable as if their eyes were burning into her, seeing right through her. She took the stairs two at a time, knowing that if this weren't the right exit, she'd never get away. Time had just run out.

"Yes!" she cheered softly as her fingers pressed the small latch and she heard a soft *click*. She put her weight against the wall and pushed, feeling it give as it slowly creaked open. When she figured the opening was wide enough, she squeezed through and pushed the door shut. Then she took a second to get her bearings, blinking in surprise to find herself in the Library of Parliament. "That's odd," she said. "How on Earth did I end up here?"

"Where can I run?" she wondered aloud, eyes travelling about the dimly lit library and noting that the damage the Demon had wreaked on this breathtakingly beautiful building was slowly being repaired. *Thanks to the Dwarves,* she thought, *it is almost as good as new.*

Go home! whispered a tiny voice in her mind. "Home," she said, suddenly seeing her mother working on her computer in her little office. "I'm going home," she said, almost as if she were in a dream. Then she ran toward the new wood and stained glass doors that opened into the Hall of Honours.

She moved swiftly along the Hall of Honours to Confederation Hall, the magnificent rotunda, with its vaulted marble ceiling and ornate gables and pillars. Next to the Library, the Peace Tower and the Great Hall were Miranda's favourite places on Parliament Hill. She loved the rich neo-Gothic architecture and took pride in showing others how the story of a nation was told in the stone.

Like the Dwarves, she thought, remembering the black walls of Dundurum that had told the history of the Dwarves in pictures painstakingly carved into the stone.

It was as quiet as a tomb in the Great Hall. The *slap slap* of her boots on the marble floor sounded loud and discordant in the silent building. She reached the front door and pushed. Nothing happened. She tried again. The doors were locked. She looked about wildly. There was nowhere left to run. Then Miranda's heart stopped as the black-cloaked skeletal forms of Calad-Chold and his First Officer entered the Great Hall from the Hall of Honours, the stench of death drifting ahead of them, swords gleaming like polished glass in their fingers of bone.

CHAPTER THIRTY-FOUR

WAR WITH
THE LIVING

The roar that erupted from the mouths of Otavite and ten thousand Giants shook the ground, drowning out the harsh sounds of battle, the screams of dying men and beasts, and the screeches of enraged Werecurs. For the briefest second, Nicholas saw everyone freeze, as though the humans and other creatures on the battlefield had switched to a state of suspended animation. He blinked and the image was gone.

Eiznek's initial excitement quickly palled as Nicholas followed Captain Faron, guiding his horse into the thick of the battle. The Ogre squeezed his round eyes shut, dug his claws into his friend's ribs, and hung on for dear life.

"Cut it out!" barked Nicholas, wincing as the creature's sharp nails pierced his flesh. "What do you think you're doing?"

Eiznek whistled apologetically and removed his claws from the boy's sides. Instead, to Nicholas's dismay, he wrapped his long, gangly arms tightly about his waist. The boy felt as if he were being crushed to death by a large serpent, but he knew the Ogre was even more frightened than he was, so he remained silent.

Nicholas's horse was a swift gray named Boreas, after the North Wind. He reminded the boy of the gray winged horse on Elester's standard. Nicholas wondered about his own family. Had the Halls carried standards into battle long ago? He wondered if they had a family crest and what it looked like. He wouldn't mind having Elester's standard with the gray horse arcing through the sky on a trail of fire, its great wings outstretched, its eyes as green as emeralds. Did creatures like that really exist?

His thoughts scattered like Indolent's tarantulas as several large Trolls broke through a line of Dwarf soldiers directly ahead, cutting him off from Captain Faron and the other Riders. Until now, Nicholas hadn't really felt threatened, despite the fierce fighting going on about him. But the sight of the huge Trolls petrified him. He had only one thought. *Run!* But Boreas had a different thought—one that left no room for flight. The Elven horse had been aptly named. In battle he was as cold as the North Wind and as violent. Instead of turning aside, he lunged at the Trolls, his powerful body sweeping them aside as if they were stuffed with old rags. In a heartbeat, he left them behind and rejoined the Riders.

"NICK!"

A small gray mare dodged and twisted, eluding club-wielding Ogres and spear-hurling Trolls as it flew toward him. Nicholas's mouth dropped open when he recognized the girl pressed forward against the horse's neck. "BELL!" he shouted, waving excitedly.

The friends met in a swirl of dust as the horses wheeled in a wild circle. "Where's Miranda?" shouted the boy.

Arabella shook her head. Then she noticed the Ogre clinging to Nicholas as if it were a growth on the boy's back. Her eyes widened and she looked back at her friend questioningly.

"A friend," said Nicholas, looking up in time to see the Demon's Hunter swooping toward them. He pulled his sword free, rose up in the stirrups, and swiped at the creature, hacking off one of its bloodstained talons.

Arabella stared in horror at the severed claw, wriggling spasmodically on the dusty ground. Then she leaped from Marigold, ran toward an unmoving Troll body and pried a long knife from its stiff, pudgy fingers.

"Look out!"

Nicholas's warning stopped her dead. Holding the knife away from her body, she dropped, rolling to the side, just as another Werecur raked its claws over the ground where she had been standing. The creature tilted its head back and screeched. Then it flapped its fleshy wings to steady itself and streaked toward the girl. Arabella took one look at the monstrous, reeking thing, dropped the Troll's knife, and ran screaming toward Marigold.

"Hurry!" shouted Nicholas. "Let's get out of here!"

The Druid paused near the invisible entrance to the Portal, muttering angrily. He was furious with himself. He had finally, against all odds, found Miranda. Alive! She had been so near he could have reached out and touched her. Then she was gone—swallowed up in the Kingsmere Portal. And, he, of all people, should have known the location of the Portal. He had travelled through the thing—had exited here, in this very spot.

"Anger is not helpful," he said. "I should be with Elester when the Black Army comes, but I will not allow those creatures to hurt the child."

He saw Miranda vanish in a burst of light, but not before he noticed her small hand gripping the Twisted Blade of Calad-Chold. "So that is what lured the King and his minion away from the Dark Lands and occupies their thoughts," he said. "They are afraid of the child who wields the knife."

When the two black-cloaked skeletons saw Miranda disappear,

the Druid had thought they would turn away, believing that the blade had been transported with the girl to a place where it could do no harm. But he had been wrong. The smouldering creatures had hesitated for only a second before they, too, stepped forward and were gone.

The old man sighed. Then he straightened his back and gently tapped the earth with the long, wooden staff, as if he were knocking lightly at the door of a sleeping child's room. He closed his eyes and evoked an image of the Druid's Close nestled within a circle of massive white stone tablets. He placed himself in the image, seated at the round, oak table in a richly panelled library. The other four Druids occupied the remaining seats. Then, Naim formed words in his mind and his image spoke those words to his fellow Druids. When he said all that he had to say, he opened his eyes, took a deep breath, and melted into the Portal.

For a moment, Otavite thought that Eegar had returned, and his heart raced with happiness. But then he realized that it was Penelope tapping on his head.

"Look!" cried the girl, pointing to a large blue bubble drifting lazily toward the battlefield. "Quick! We've got to do something! That's Wizard-fire!"

Otavite stared at the strange bubble. He had never met a Wizard, but the bubble looked so pretty against the overcast sky, he couldn't understand what the child was getting so worked up about. Until he saw the bubble burst in an explosion of blue fire.

Screams and cries rose from the battlefield as fire rained down upon the allied warriors, and ranks of enemy Trolls, Ogres, and Werecurs indiscriminately. Penelope and Otavite watched horrified as blue rain ignited the white fur of a Carovorare Guard. Penelope screamed and buried her face in the collar of the Giant's fleecy vest, unable to look upon the flaming creature as it thrashed about wildly.

But its dying screams echoed in her mind for a long, long time.

Otavite roared in rage, and charged toward the northwestern edge of the battlefield where another large bubble shot from a cluster of rocks and hovered momentarily in the air until the breeze caught it and carried it toward the raging battle. With no thought for his own safety, or Penelope's for that matter, the Giant soldier waded through a bunch of Ogres, stomping on them as if they were grapes under his massive feet. He mowed through a tight knot of Trolls, flinging them into the air like blades of grass.

Suddenly, out of a banging big flash of white fire came four, tall, black-cloaked figures. Otavite jerked to a stop, stupefied by the dazzling flame and the sinister creatures. What new menace had the Wizard unleashed?

"I've got a very bad feeling about this," he said under his breath.

Penelope felt heat on her tightly closed eyelids. Fearing that Otavite was on fire, her eyes popped open. "Yikes!" she cried, catching sight of the backs of four cloaked and hooded figures just ahead. "Thugs! Run, Otavite! Get us out of here!"

At the sound of the frightened voice, one of the figures turned and regarded the Giant with the small child cowering on his shoulder. Otavite knew instinctively that his great size meant nothing to this creature. He took a step backwards. The figure lifted its arm and pointed toward the battle raging behind the Giant. "Go back!" it said. "You are not needed here." Then, the creature turned and, together with its three companions, strode purposefully toward the cluster of rocks where Indolent the Wizard giggled hysterically as he released another fireball. Nearby, two tiny creatures looked up from the large foot they were devouring and, for a moment, watched their master through adoring red eyes.

"NOW!" shouted Elester, holding his breath in suspense as a hail of arrows streaked through the air, homing in on the Wizard's blue bubble as it shot skyward. If these arrows could pierce the ball and burst it before the wind took it and carried it over the battlefield, the Wizard would get a nasty shock—a dose of his own magic. The King's suspense was short-lived. Before the arrows penetrated the fireball, the wood ignited and disintegrated into ashes. Elester turned away to hide his disappointment from the troops. He had hoped that even if the arrows burned, the filed metal points would separate and strike the fireball.

Indolent had to be stopped. The allied forces had enough on their hands fighting Trolls and Ogres, not to mention the threat from the skies in the form of the winged Hunters, without having to contend with burning rain. "He must be stopped," repeated Elester, his eyes cold and resolute. "And I *will* stop him."

But, as he stepped through the protective ring of Riders, one of the Demon's Hunters dropped from above, knocking him sprawling face down on the ground. But not before the monster's curved talons had lacerated his shoulders and upper back. More Werecurs followed, landing awkwardly between the young King and the Riders, cutting him off from his protectors.

Slay the King of the Elves! screamed the Demon in their twisted minds. *Kill the feeble human!*

Elester was back on his feet instantly, his hand gripping the hilt of his long sword. Blood flowed down his back, staining his dark shirt black. He heard the Riders shouting as they lunged at the Werecurs in an attempt to draw the creatures away from their King. *They knew to go after me. They singled me out,* he reasoned, stunned by the Monsters' devious scheme. *They mean to destroy me to sow fear and chaos among the Elves.*

"You will not leave this place alive," he swore, his eyes locked on the creature's red eyes.

The Werecur flapped its wings and hopped up and down on its bowed legs, screeching and snarling until saliva bubbled about its long blunt muzzle. Then it crouched and sprang at Elester. The King waited motionless until the rabid creature was too committed to the attack to change its course, then he leaped aside in a burst of speed. The Werecur tore past, its talons digging into the earth as it slowed and pivoted about to come at him again. But Elester was ready. He feinted to the left as he dropped into a crouch and rushed at the creature, thrusting his sword at the monster's stomach. The Hunter was moving too fast to stop. It ran smack into the sharp Elven blade, impaling itself and dying even before the sound of its scream of mingled surprise and dismay faded away.

The Wizard Indolent almost died of heart failure when he noticed the four black-robed Druids. "Get out!" he spluttered, waving his switch threateningly.

The Druids laughed. "No!" said the one who had warned Otavite away. "We are not leaving without you. Indolent, the time has come when you must answer for the things you have done."

"Pay day!" Indolent giggled. "Oh, pul-eese! Spare me your holier-than-thou speech. I am not one of your prissy Pledges. Haven't you heard? I don't want to be a Druid any more. I am Indolent the Wizard, and my power comes from a greater source than yours. Now leave, you drivelling old fools in your silly black robes, before you test my patience too far."

"You have no power," said the Head Druid, noticing an Ogre huddled on the ground, its arms wrapped about a small wooden box, and nearby two small creatures fighting over something that looked suspiciously like a large foot.

"Ha!" cackled the Wizard, pulling a dirty handkerchief from a pocket in his robe and wiping sweat from his forehead. "Don't say I didn't warn you." Then he rubbed the skull on his forearm and waved the switch at the Druids.

Nothing happened. He waved it again. Still nothing happened. He shook the switch and slapped it against a rock. Then he waved it again.

"We have destroyed your power," repeated the Head Druid, taking the box from the Ogre, who gladly gave it up before slinking past the Wizard and loping away as fast as his gangly legs could take him. The Druid opened the box and stared at the jewel-encrusted tarantulas. "Tsk! Tsk!" he said, shaking his hooded head sadly. "Yes, you have a lot to answer for."

Indolent screamed, clawing at his black and yellow hair in rage. He spat at the Head Druid. "Give that back! It's mine!"

"I do not think so," replied the Head Druid. He closed the box and turned to his companions. "You can do nothing about the dead, but you must stay and help our friends fight the living enemy." Then he nodded to his companions and moved toward the Wizard. "The world needs a rest from you," he said, thumping his wooden staff on the hard ground. Then he, Indolent, and the box of tarantulas vanished in a burst of white light.

Momentarily stunned by the blinding light, Penelope and Otavite blinked and stared at the cluster of rocks aware that something had happened here that they didn't understand. But they understood one thing: The Wizard Indolent was gone. And, that meant no more fireballs. The Giant moved back to give the three black-cloaked figures that emerged from among the rocks plenty of room.

"They have staffs like Druids," whispered Penelope in his ear. "I think they are Druids."

Otavite shivered and quickly dropped his eyes from the black hoods. "Don't look in their eyes, Penelope."

"Do they look like the creature you saw in Taboo?"

Otavite thought for a second. "No," he said. "That creature was much taller and it had red eyes."

"See?" snapped Penelope. "We told you it wasn't a Druid."

Suddenly a small red bird staggered drunkenly out from the rocks followed by a little yellow dog in a similar dazed state.

"Muffy!" cried Penelope, sliding down the Giant's arm and

landing on the ground with a bump. "Muffy!"

"Eegar?" said Otavite, afraid to believe his eyes.

Penelope ran to Muffy and caught the dog in a crushing embrace. Tears of happiness streamed down her face. "Oh! My poor little Muffs!" she sobbed, planting a dozen kisses on the ratty poodle's face and thin rubbery lips. "Eeuw!" she cried, wrinkling her nose. "You smell like dirty feet!"

"Is it really you, Eegar?" asked Otavite, gently picking up the bird and placing it on his head.

In reply, Eegar pecked viciously at the Giant's scalp, uprooting several coarse hairs and plumping up others before settling down contentedly. Otavite sighed and grinned sheepishly at several of his Giant comrades who had come to check out the strange bursts of light. "Eegar's back!" he said.

"What's he been up to?" asked one of the Giants, laughing. "He smells like your feet."

"THE DEAD! LOOK! THE DEAD ARE COMING!"

The cry went up all over the battlefield. The fighting stopped abruptly and a hush fell over the soldiers as all heads turned toward the Northeast.

"We're going to die!" wailed Penelope, shoving Muffy down the front of her jacket and leaping into Otavite's hand.

"Head for the Lake!" shouted Otavite. Then he explained for Penelope's benefit. "We can't fight the Black Army, but maybe the water will protect us."

Not likely! said Penelope silently. *You obviously haven't met Dilemma.*

Gregor and the Dwarf army turned their bruised and bloody faces toward the far hills where the front lines of the Black Army had been visible for several days. In fact, the troops had become so used to the motionless mass that they had stopped fretting about it, and almost regarded it as part of the landscape—a dark, inanimate forest. Gregor gasped at the enormity of the blackness spilling down the hills like despair come alive. "RUN!" he bellowed. "TO THE SHIPS!"

"Whisst! Whisst!" whistled the Ogres, as the Dwarves sheathed their weapons and fled toward the tenuous safety of the harbour. But their shrill, excited whistles suddenly switched to confused, questioning wheezes. The Ogres looked about bewildered as if they had suddenly awakened in the last place they wanted to be. Indolent was gone. Without a leader, the Ogres ran aimlessly about the battlefield, whistling mournfully, heedless or unaware of the danger raging toward them like a wall of fire.

Elsewhere on the battlefield, the Trolls suddenly went berserk. They turned their spears and clubs on each other, fighting with insane fury. Gregor shook his head at the change that had come over the enemy. "First Ogres, now Trolls," he muttered. "Something's up."

The Dwarf King's heart pumped wildly when he spotted the massive black flock of Werecurs winging swiftly toward the ships from across the Lake. "I'm getting too old for this," he groaned, wondering briefly when or if he would ever again enjoy the comfort of his own bed.

"DRAGONS!" came a shout from among the soldiers leading the Dwarf retreat.

It was an awesome sight, one Nicholas would never forget. Thousands upon thousands of great Black Dragons plummeted from the sky, blasting the Werecurs into eternity, and gliding low over the battlefield, the tips of their massive wings skimming the slick, bloody ground.

"Wow!" breathed the boy, diving for cover.

"Yea!" cheered Arabella, noticing that across the entire battlefield not a single soul was left standing. All had flattened themselves into the earth at the approach of the Dragons. All, that is, except the

Trolls, who had worked themselves into such a frenzy they didn't know the Dragons had arrived until it was too late. Those the Dragons flattened.

Typhon, Chief of the Black Dragons of the White Mountains, glared at the Black Army pouring over the hills and swarming across the flats toward Lake Leanora. "THIS IS MAGIC!" he roared, the words erupting from his throat in a blast of fire. "WE HAVE NOTHING TO FEAR FROM THE DEAD!"

The Dragons flew straight at the advancing army. The steam issuing from thousands of nostrils formed giant clouds that rose into the sky and rained a fine mist upon the battle-weary soldiers. Just when it appeared that a collision between the great flock of Dragons and the Black Army was inevitable, the Dragons opened their mouths and let loose their fire. Then they soared skyward to bank and make another pass.

Where it struck, the Dragon-fire blew the Dead into smithereens. But, as he soared higher and higher, Typhon gulped at the sheer size of Calad-Chold's forces. There was no end to the massive blackness. He and his Dragon kin might be able to slow it down, to buy the Dwarves and Elves time to reach their ships and sail away. But they could not fight this army forever. Even Dragons needed food and rest to kindle their fire.

Below, the mighty Dragon spied three black-robed figures standing between the Black Army and the battlefield. He snorted. They looked like ants on the shore waving miniature twigs at the giant black tidal wave roaring toward them.

"Druids!" He snorted contemptuously and dropped from the sky.

CHAPTER THIRTY-FIVE

THE SEVERING

he King of the Dead saw the girl and laughed softly. The sound smashed into Miranda, lifted her off her feet, and flung her through the main doors and out through the arched entrance where she landed in a crumpled heap at the bottom of the Peace Tower steps. Dazed, she scrambled to her feet and staggered back as Calad-Chold appeared like the grim reaper in the archway, his silent companion a dark shadow at his heels.

You took something that belongs to me. I want it back.

She almost blacked out as the voice exploded in her head. She acted without thinking. Gripping the knife and raising her arm as if she intended to strike out, she took a step forward. "You are dead," she said. "Go back to your dark coffin where you belong."

The dead King's ghastly chuckle knocked Miranda backwards. She fought to keep from slamming onto the concrete walkway.

Give me the knife and I will spare you. Calad-Chold looked about as if he only just realized that he was in an alien world. *Put the blade in my hand and I will spare this place.*

He's lying! Don't listen to him!

But Miranda wasn't strong enough to resist. She was so tired she could barely stand without support. How easy it would be to give him what he wanted—to hand over the knife and put an end to the nightmare. Her hand automatically reached for the silver pouch dangling from the chain about her neck. *Please tell me what to do?* she pleaded silently. But the Bloodstones were as cold as the Dead King's heart and as still.

Give me the blade!

"I don't think so," said Miranda, her dull green eyes fixed on the blackness under the Dead King's crown.

Enough! roared Calad-Chold, raising his sword in one hand and reaching for the girl with the other.

Stop him! Use the knife! Miranda knew what she had to do, but she hesitated.

What are you waiting for? Use the knife!

Still she hesitated, part of her recoiling at the very thought of plunging the knife into another being. She believed that she would accept death for herself if, by dying, her mother, and her friends, and all of Ottawa would be spared. But she could not take a life, not to save herself, not even to save millions of lives. She just couldn't do it because, if she did, if she dared take that step, she'd be lost. Something would happen inside her, something evil, and it would grow and grow until she was as vile and twisted as the Demon.

A long cry of anguish came from her throat. "I can't!" she cried, her shoulders convulsing as she broke into gasping sobs. "I can't!"

The First Officer stepped forward as if he were the other's shadow come alive. Slowly, menacingly, he advanced on the forlorn child, his long skeletal arm outstretched. Miranda screamed in terror. The Twisted Blade slipped from her fingers as if it had a mind of its own, and clattered on the sidewalk. She turned to run, but her limbs seemed to be stuck to the ground. Her hand tightened about the Bloodstones like a vice.

Bones creaked as the First Officer bent and grasped the Twisted Blade.

Ahhhh! breathed Calad-Chold. And, nearby, in the rift along the Rideau River, millions upon millions of dead creatures clawed their way to the surface. At the same time, far away in the old world, the Black Army surged toward the battlefield where the allied warriors were locked in mortal combat with the Demon's living forces.

Miranda stood frozen in horror, unable to look away from the twin yellow flames within the First Officer's hood. The creature raised the knife and lunged at the girl. Miranda's eyes grew wide for a second before she squeezed them shut and tried to dull her senses to lessen the pain when the knife pierced her body.

When nothing happened, she forced her eyes open, surprised to find the First Officer leaning toward her, staring at her. He was so close she could almost count the long golden hairs that had escaped from inside his hood and straggled in front of the blackness where no face was visible. No, she thought. It's the Bloodstones. He wants the Bloodstones!

Slowly the skeleton reached for the girl's neck, stopping less than a hair's-breadth from the small, silver pouch. A low groan escaped from the darkness of his hood and, briefly, his eye sockets shone like the brightest stars in the night sky. His hand gently traced the outline of Miranda's face, carefully avoiding contact with her skin. Then, with a deep, sad sigh, the First Officer straightened, turned away, and before Miranda knew what had happened, he drove the Twisted Blade deep into Calad-Chold's chest.

The King of the Dead roared and the world about Miranda went mad. A violent, swirling funnel of wind swept down from the sky and tore into the concrete sidewalk, sucking up slabs of cement and chunks of steps. Clawing at his chest, the King of the Dead vanished into the twisting, spinning cloud along with his First Officer. It was all over in a second. Silence reigned over Parliament Hill once more. Except for the ruined sidewalk and steps, there was nothing to show that, while Ottawa slept, a battle to determine the fate of Miranda's world had raged outside the Peace Tower.

Miranda stood rooted to a spot only a few feet away from the ruined sidewalk, her mind struggling to come to grips with her astonishing discovery. She replayed the images of the First Officer over and over in her mind. The long, golden hair . . . the way he recognized the Bloodstones . . . and then his recognition of her.

"Miranda!"

The girl turned her tear-streaked face to the man framing the arched entrance to the Peace Tower. "Oh, Naim!" she whispered. "My father was here. He saved us!"

The Druid's heart ached for the child. He rushed to her side and took her in his arms, holding her trembling body while she cried her eyes out. "It is over, child," he said softly, his face stinging as his own tears seeped into the deep wounds the Thug's claws had gouged in his flesh.

"Come," he said, when Miranda's tears had finally stopped and the trembling had left her body. "It is time to go home." He needed to talk with the child, but that would have to wait. Right now, she should be with her mother.

Miranda nodded. Sniffling loudly, she reached for Naim's hand and turned to lead the way. Then, she heard his wooden staff clatter to the ground and an angry hissing sound erupted from the spot where he had been standing. She spun about, raising her arms protectively and shrinking back from the monstrous serpent that was coiled about the Druid, squeezing him to death.

"Naim!" But she could see that the man was powerless. And, in a few seconds he'd be dead unless she did something. But what could she do? How could she save Naim from Malcolm?

Use us! Use us!

Stunned, Miranda felt the Bloodstones pulsing against her neck. Slowly, she reached for the silver pouch. *They're working!* And then, as if a light clicked on in her head, she knew why the Stones had failed her before. They could not respond to her because when she had sought their help they were no longer hers. They had belonged to her father. She didn't think to question it, she knew with all of her heart that she was right. Her father had been here tonight. He had saved her life. Now that he was gone, the Bloodstones came back to her.

Hate's serpent hissed again, its red eyes sizzling with rage. "Evil child! Destroyer! You will watch the Druid die for what you did. Before this night is over, you will beg me to kill you." His death grip on the Druid tightened.

Miranda barely heard the creature. All she cared about was saving Naim. She gathered the six oval stones in the palm of her hand and let herself melt into and become one with them. The Snake blinked as the girl abruptly disappeared. He had been warned that the magic of the Bloodstones was more potent than anything in the Demon's vast arsenal of power, but he hadn't really believed that the wretched girl knew how to use it effectively. He was so wrong.

Hurtling through the Bloodstones was the most frightening thing that had ever happened to Miranda—a hundred times more terrible than facing the King of the Dead, a thousand times scarier than dropping through the portal to Bethany and almost being eaten by the monstrous Dilemma, a million times worse than dinner with the demented Augurs.

She felt that she had been absorbed into a vast network of minds. All of her senses were heightened and, for a flickering moment, she knew all things—past, present, and those yet to come. She travelled faster than thought through all time. She saw everything that ever was or ever would be.

Then the Bloodstones unleashed their awesome magic on Malcolm, the sadistic Dwarf-snake, the real Destroyer. They used the creature's own senses to plant an insatiable hunger in its mind and heart—a hunger that burned greater than the hunger of Calad-Chold, the King it had brought back from the Dead. They fed it power beyond the Demon's pathetic magic, and when Malcolm smelled it and felt it and tasted it he wanted more. He wanted and wanted until his being became a great wanting pit that nothing could satisfy.

Hate's creation recoiled in pain, releasing its hold on the Druid. The old man slumped exhausted to the ground, but his hand reached for the long wooden staff. He inched away from the writhing, twisting, hissing monster that had already begun to devour its own body to appease the terrible hunger. Naim put his weight on the staff and rose slowly to his feet. He stared as the frenzied creature gorged on its flesh and then he pointed the staff at the thing and burned it to ashes.

"Is it over?" asked Miranda, suddenly appearing at his side.

Naim laid his hand on her shoulder. "Yes," he answered. "It is over."

"I don't think so," said Miranda, pointing at a small, round, black object that rolled out of the ashes like a marble. Then she marched over to it, raised her foot, and brought it down hard, crushing the last of the Demon's eggs.

"*Now* it's over," she said.

EPILOGUE

he Druids didn't know who or what had caused it to happen, but they knew the exact moment the Twisted Blade severed the summons that bound the King of the Dead to the Demon. The unassailable Black Army faltered, seething and gurgling like a vast sink clogged by a single leaf. As one, the Druids turned their staffs to the blackness, holding the agitated mass together as its core disintegrated into a whirling tempest—the mother of the infant storm that reached down from the sky and snatched Calad-Chold. It built, feeding on the ranks of dead, drawing the Black Army into its burning eye. It built and built until it threatened to consume hills, and valleys, and Lake Leanora. Still the massive army of dead poured into it like dust disappearing into a vacuum cleaner.

Abruptly, the Druids lowered their staffs and planted them firmly in the ground. Almost instantly, the polished wooden rods began to bend and flex like pale snakes. The Druids tightened their grips as the living wood shook violently and thin streams of white smoke curled from the tips of the staves. The smoke drifted together, forming a cloud that spiralled toward the dark tempest, spinning and growling like a living thing. Chunks of the darkness split from the mass and disappeared into the swirling white smoke. In seconds, the entire darkness was gone. The army of Calad-Chold had been swallowed by the Druid magic and sent to resting places deep in the earth. Then, the Druids, too, were gone.

They met on the shore of Lake Leanora to bid Otavite and King Gregor farewell. They were a sorry sight in their dirty, torn clothing. Nicholas counted fourteen nicks and scratches on his bare flesh, including a nasty puncture on the back of his hand where an ogre had bitten him. Eiznek clenched his fists and whistled angrily when Nicholas showed him the mark. Arabella's brown arms were scratched, and bruises made her skin appear darker in patches. But, by far her worst injury was the scab forming over the round bald spot where Crumb the Wobble had yanked her white hair out by the roots. Penelope, who hadn't suffered any physical injuries, turned away and gnawed on several fingernails and tore a few holes in her clothes. But then she noticed the blood-soaked bandages through the tears in Elester's shirt and she felt ashamed. *Anyway*, she thought. *I don't have to have injuries to prove anything.*

The King of the Dwarves kicked at the sand impatiently. The war was over and he was anxious to begin the long march to Dunmorrow and assess the damage Calad-Chold had done to the lands between here and there. He had refused Elester's offer of a horse, muttering something about Dwarves and horses not being a good mix. The Elf chuckled, thinking of the poor horses, and agreed that Gregor had a point.

"Keep an eye out for the Druid," said Elester, clasping Gregor's hand warmly. "And Miranda."

Gregor nodded solemnly. Elester's cloudy green eyes told him the young King was in considerable pain.

"They found the Blade. Had to." He looked back over the battlefield with tired eyes. "Just in time."

"Yes," said Elester. "One of them found the Twisted Blade. I only hope that they found each other." He, too, turned and surveyed the deserted field where the Elves and their allies had stood against Evil one more time. "It looks so peaceful. As if nothing at all happened here. Look! Even the dead are gone."

"Gone to the Black Army," snorted Gregor. "At rest now." Then he sighed heavily and turned away, signalling to his Commanders to move out. "Freedom's not free," he said over his shoulder.

"Goodbye!" sniffed Penelope, blotting her tears on Muffy's yellow fur. "I'm sorry about the reward. I'll miss you."

Otavite smiled. "Having new friends is all the reward I need. Someday I would like to meet your Druid. I'd also like to know where Eegar was the whole time I thought he was on my head."

Penelope gulped, and smiled weakly.

"Goodbye, Princess! I'll miss you, too." He winked at her. "And I think Eegar will miss your d-o-g." Eegar pecked his ear as if to say, *Not!*

"So long, Otavite," said Nicholas, shaking one of the Giant's fingers. "It was a pleasure meeting you. I'd like to visit Vark someday."

"Then come," said Otavite. "You and Arabella and Penelope, and all of your friends are welcome. And bring the Druid."

"Goodbye, Otavite! Goodbye!" The children waved and shouted until the Giants were far away. Then they turned and walked in silence toward the ship that would take them to the Elven capital, a single question burning in their minds. Was Miranda still alive?

"What about him?" asked Arabella, noticing the Ogre hanging back, looking as if his best friend had just died in his arms.

Nicholas leaned over the railing and waved. "You're holding up the ship, Eiznek! Come on!"

"BAD DOG!" shouted Penelope, suddenly realizing that Muffy had escaped from her clutches and was backing toward the ship, her teeth buried in a large object. "DROP THAT!"

"What's she got?" asked Nicholas, squinting at the bristling, yellow poodle.

"I don't know," said Arabella. "It sort of looks like a big foot."

There wasn't a dry eye in Miranda's house when she finished telling her mother and Naim how her father had saved the world from the King of the Dead. Dr. D'arte sniffled and dabbed at her eyes with a tissue. The Druid coughed harshly. And Miranda let her tears fall where they would.

"At last I know the truth," said Dr. D'arte. "All those years of not knowing whether he was alive or dead . . ."

"Yes," said Naim. "There is sadness in knowing, but there is also comfort and closure."

Miranda looked at the Druid. "Why was my father in Calad-Chold's army? " she asked.

Naim reached for the girl's hand and clasped it tightly. "The Elves burn their dead. But, your father died away from his homeland. His body was not burned."

"Oh," whispered Miranda, wishing that things had been different.

The Druid stayed with Miranda and her mother for three days. On the first night, they talked about everything that had happened, asking and answering each other's questions until dawn.

"I still don't understand about the Bloodstones," said Dr. D'arte. "Why they reverted to Garrett. It's not as though he were really alive."

"I have no answer," said Naim. "But you are Elven. You will admit that Elves are different."

"Yes," said Miranda's mother, thoughtfully. "But I don't know how we're different. Perhaps I will only know the answer after I leave this life."

As daylight crept into the morning sky, Miranda walked with Naim through the garden. She showed him where the ground had split open and swallowed Nicholas's house. She stared through the gaps in the white picket fence at the Halls' new home, almost finished, and her heart constricted. Where was Nicholas? Would she ever see him and Penelope again? Was Arabella safe?

"Will we ever know who spooked Avatar in the stable in Bethany?" Miranda asked as they strolled back toward the terrace. "I'd really like to know if it were Indolent."

Naim rested his arm on her shoulder. "I was wrong about Indolent," he said. "But I believe I know what Avatar sensed or saw."

"What?"

"I believe it was the Bloodstones. You mentioned that you sought their help but they did not respond. That was the first time they failed to work for you."

"That's right!" cried Miranda. "But I still don't understand."

"I think that is when your father was called from the dead," answered Naim. "I think that Avatar sensed a change in the Stones that showed him the real owner in place of you."

Later, in bed unable to sleep, she listened to the soft creaking of the swinging wicker sofa outside, and knew that sleep had not come to Naim either.

On the second evening, old Mrs. Smedley saw six short, stout creatures dressed in odd costumes stomp up to the D'arte's front door and disappear inside. She raised her binoculars, trying to peer through the thick hedge onto her neighbour's terrace. That same evening, Nicholas's parents slipped through the fence that separated their property from Miranda's and listened in shocked disbelief while the girl they'd known since the day she was born told them what she and their son and others, including some of those present, had been up to in a strange world they had stumbled into under the Parliament Buildings.

When Miranda got to the part where the Demon threw her tantrum in Confederation Hall, hissing down the vaulted ceiling and then tearing up the Hall of Honours and blasting the Library of

Parliament apart, Mrs. Hall glanced nervously at her husband, terrified that the girl's story would drive him back under the bed—for good this time. But she needn't have worried. Mr. Hall nodded slowly, as if everything suddenly made sense. He and the Dwarves moved off to a corner and talked excitedly about architecture and stonework. He even offered them huge salaries if they'd stay and work with him. But the Dwarves politely declined.

Late on the third day, Naim announced that it was time for him to return to his own world. He removed his long, black cloak from a peg on the wall near the front door, wrapped it about his shoulders, took his staff, and disappeared into the night. Miranda stood in the darkened doorway and watched him go, afraid that she would never see him again. Long after he had gone, she lay in bed awake, face pressed into her pillow to muffle the sound of crying.

The next day, Arabella and Penelope, with Muffy on a pink leash at her side, appeared on her doorstep, their sad faces streaked with tears. When Miranda opened the door, they jumped about a foot off the ground, turning as green as if a ghost were standing before them. They had come to tell Dr. D'arte that Miranda had been taken by the Demon's Hunters, and she and the Druid were still missing.

Miranda ushered them outside, but not before Muffy peed on the brand-new carpet in her mother's office. The girls perched cross-legged on the swinging sofa and chatted excitedly, sharing their adventures. Shrieks of horror and shouts of laughter filled the afternoon air. Miranda cried and laughed at the same time when she heard that Nicholas was alive and had been invited to stay in Bethany and train with the Riders until September.

"He's got a new friend," said Penelope. Then she shouted at Muffy who was happily digging up Dr. D'arte's rose bushes. "BAD DOG!"

"An Ogre," said Arabella. "And Nick's bringing him back to Ottawa."

"He's so insufferable, now that he's a Rider," said Arabella.

"Intolerable!" cried Penelope.

"That's what I said," said Arabella.

"No, you said *insufferable*. I said *intolerable*."

"Shut up. They mean the same thing."

Miranda laughed and flung her arms about her friends' shoulders. "Some things never change," she said.

They talked throughout the afternoon and long after the sun had set. Arabella told them about the Wobbles rushing off to fight Calad-Chold's army and how she had tried to save Bliss and Crumb after all of the others had been destroyed. "It was horrible," she said. "The stupid things wouldn't come back. They were laughing and calling the Black Army the most obnoxious things. Anyway, I thought they had been destroyed too, but when we got to Bethany, there they were. Charlemagne the Eagle had rescued them. So the Wobbles aren't extinct after all."

"I hate those slimy creatures," said Penelope. "They're disgusting."

"And ugly," said Arabella.

"And really stupid," laughed Miranda.

As the long, lazy afternoon wore away, Penelope and Arabella told her about the Druids coming to take Indolent away to answer for all the bad things he had done, including what he had done to the tarantulas. They described how the Druid magic had destroyed the Black Army and how the Giants had torn down the new Castle of Indolence. They told her about Taboo, and Otavite, and Eegar, and the fabulous Carovorari.

"And Stubby's a tree stump again," they said.

As the sun went down in a blaze of orange and crimson, Miranda told them how the Augurs carving knife had turned into the Twisted Blade, and how Calad-Chold had followed her through the Portal into Ottawa. She told them how she had used the Bloodstones to destroy the Evil Malcolm. Then, in a brief moment of silence while they caught their breaths and drank iced tea, Miranda told them about her father.

The last days of summer flew by, and the girls were busy shopping for clothing and supplies for the new school year. September was usually an exciting time for Miranda, but Dr. D'arte noticed that this year she didn't seem to care whether she had new clothes or not. The child was abstracted. Nothing seemed to interest her. *She's pining for Naim*, thought the doctor sadly, wishing she possessed a magic remedy that would snap Miranda back from wherever she had gone.

One night, towards the end of August, Miranda came to her room and hugged her fiercely. "Do you want to talk?" she had asked, but the girl shook her head and went back upstairs to her own room. A few days later, over barbecued shrimp on the terrace, she caught Miranda staring at her with tears in her eyes. "Please, Mir. Won't you tell me what's the matter?"

But, Miranda just smiled sadly. "It's not important."

On the last night of August, Miranda slung her backpack over her shoulder and left the house she had shared with her mother for eleven years. Outside, she paused for a moment as if she were unsure of what to do next. Then she took a last, long look at her home and sprinted to the corner, turning right on Beechwood Avenue in the direction of Parliament Hill. Back home, on her mother's pillow rested a long, tear-stained letter.

Miranda had worked on the letter for two nights, sitting at her computer while her mother slept, agonizing over every word. *Goodbye Mom!* How could something as simple as saying goodbye be so difficult? How could she tell her mother that no matter how much she loved her, she didn't belong here anymore? How could she make her understand how much it hurt to be torn between two places? In the letter she said it felt as if her heart had been cut in half. Finally, she had simply blurted out everything and put it all on paper. At the end, she wrote *Goodbye Mom. I love you!*

The streets were deserted at this hour, but Miranda kept to the shadows because she was alone and frightened and tonight she felt safer away from the glare of streetlights. It was tough going. Not a minute passed without her mind screaming at her to turn back. She almost gave in, wanting more than anything to turn around and go back home. But she knew that if she did she might feel better for a night or two, but after that, the aching would begin again and it would grow until she couldn't stand it. Then, she'd write another letter and try to leave and it would go on and on until she went out of her mind.

Miranda wished that she had had the courage to tell her mother face to face that she was leaving and why. She had tried, but when she saw the fear in her mother's face as she asked what was wrong, she knew she'd never be able to leave. She slipped through the gates and entered Parliament Hill, running lightly past the East Block and jogging right toward the Centre Block. Ahead, the Peace Tower reached toward the stars, the hands of the massive four-sided clock fixing the time at two-thirty in the morning. She looked up and saw the giant Maple Leaf flag of Canada fluttering gently in the breeze. *This is a good country*, she thought. *I'm going to miss it.*

And I'm going to miss my friends. Just before leaving the house, she had sent e-mails to Arabella and Penelope. *Until we meet again. I'll miss you.* She didn't e-mail Nicholas. She'd be seeing him soon enough.

Ahead, a figure detached itself from the shadows near the arched entrance and waited motionless for the girl to approach. Miranda stopped, thinking about her father and the King of the Dead who had followed her to this spot only a few weeks ago. What if they had come back? Or, what if it was Malcolm, the Demon's Evil snake? No! No! They were gone!

"Miranda!"

Miranda sighed. So, her mother had guessed after all. "Hi, Mom!"

she said, a part of her glad that she could now go back home. "I guess you found my letter."

"No," answered her mother, taking her daughter's hand and squeezing it firmly. "I've been here waiting for you to make a run for it for the past few nights. You were wrong not to tell me how you felt."

Miranda nodded. "I know. I wanted to. I even tried, but I knew if I saw how much I was hurting you, I'd never be able to do it."

"Come on," said her mother. "We can talk about it when we get home."

Miranda nodded again. "OK, but I'm not saying I won't do this again." She tugged on her mother's arm. "Well, aren't you coming?"

"Not that home," answered her mother. "I meant our real home."

Miranda was flabbergasted. "Are you serious? You're coming with me?"

"Of course," snapped Dr. D'arte in her no nonsense voice. "If you think I'm letting you go off on another wild adventure by yourself, you're wrong, young lady."

"You sound more like Naim every day," laughed Miranda.

They stood in the darkness under the Library of Parliament staring at the stars over Bethany. Behind, six dwarves huddled in silence. They were all that remained of the dozen stoneworkers King Gregor had sent to Canada to restore the Parliament Buildings. The others, including Malcolm, had died at the hands of Hate, the Demon.

Presently, they heard the flutter of wings and they hurried away from the opening as a great double-headed Eagle swooped through the portal and landed on the stone floor. One head bowed to Miranda, the other to her mother.

"Charlemagne!" cried Miranda. "What are you . . .? How did . . .?"

"The Druid sent me," answered Charlemagne. "Come! The Elves are waiting."

Miranda looked at her mother. "You knew! You and Naim! You did this!"

Her mother smiled. "Yes," she said. "Naim thinks it's time for you to go and study at the Druid's Close. I agree."

"You might have told *me*!" said Miranda.

As the huge, powerful Eagle glided in a long, slow spiral toward the tiny island below, Miranda turned back to her Mother. "By the way, how was your date?"

Dr. D'arte laughed. "It wasn't a date, it was a disaster," she said. "He just kept telling me how much I reminded him of his dear, departed mother, and asking me if I enjoyed sweetbread for dinner as much as he did."

Miranda giggled. "What's sweetbread?"

"A pancreas or thymus gland."

"Yuck!" cried Miranda, dissolving in laughter. "I have one more question, OK? This one's been bugging me for about a year."

"So ask!"

"Now, can you finally tell me where you went to hide the night Naim came to Ottawa to find me?"

It was her mother's turn to laugh. "Why not? It doesn't matter now. Disneyland."

Miranda stared at her mother in shock. "What!!!" she cried. "You mean while I was being chased by the Demon, you went to Disneyland?"

"Yes, dear," said her mother, mischievously, "It was awful— the hardest thing I've ever done."

Celtic Ogham Alphabet

Use the following alphabet to decipher the message or warning found on page 8.

A = ✛		N = ⊤⊤⊤	
B = ⊤		O = ✛	
C = ⊥⊥⊥		P = #	
D = ⊥⊥		Q = ⊥⊥⊥⊥	
E = ✚		R = ⫽⫽⫽	
F = ⊤⊤		S = ⊤⊤⊤	
G = ≠		T = ⊥⊥⊥	
H = ⊥		U = ✚	
I = ✚		V =	
J =		W =	
K =		X =	
L = ⊤⊤		Y = ⫽⫽⫽ *	
M = ✛		Z = ⫽⫽⫽	

*Author's creation

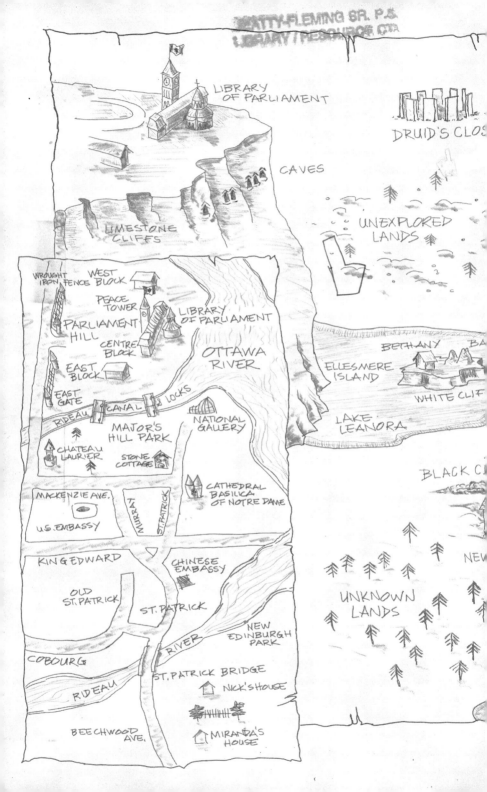